This one is for you, Herb Rea.

For being the best father Mac could ask for, a surrogate parent to me, and just the forever source of good humor, good advice, and unfettered support.

May you tread lightly across the Veil, and smile upon our earthly endeavors.

J. LEIGH
WITH MAC J. REA

WAY WALKERS:
NEGATING DESTINY

Way Walkers: Negating Destiny
The Tazu Saga™: Book 4
Red Adept Publishing, LLC
104 Bugenfield Court
Garner, NC 27529
https://RedAdeptPublishing.com/
Copyright © 2021 by J. Leigh. All rights reserved.
COVER ART BY Streetlight Graphics[1]

---

1. http://StreetlightGraphics.com

The Red Adept Publishing App

Read free short fiction, get our authors' favorite recipes, enjoy author interviews, read cool listicles, and more!
You'll be kept informed of special sales, new releases, and upcoming new books and notified of contests and giveaways.

1

2

3

---

1. https://bit.ly/RAPAppPage

2. https://apps.apple.com/us/app/red-adept-publishing/id1537765717

Prologue: Dreams

For the Prophet.

The thought was calming to Yala, allowing her to swallow her rage again beneath a polite mask. The Presence-that-was-not-Yala rested calmly under this Red fog, patient. The tiny ice mage shivered in her unfamiliar blankets in the unfamiliar room. Yala's body was impervious to the cold, but the intoxicating brew of anger and fear in her blood made her mental defenses brittle. She tried to remember the words of her fellow Balori and the comfort of resting together in the Prophet's presence. Yala had felt safe there even though their home had been destroyed, even though they had tried to kill the Prophet. When Yala thought of safety, she thought of the strongest members of her new family: the Prophet, of course; Umummanna, the shield-maid; Ku'un, the ever-fierce *debesh*; wise, far-seeing Or'sen; Nan, who had been through so much; and even quiet Zu'rui, who bore his brand so bravely. The Balori were not a true family, but they had only each other.

...and the Prophet, Yala reminded herself. *He knows the Way.*

Yala could have rested with this thought, in the comfort of this faith, but that would not do. The Presence-that-was-not-Yala whispered to Yala in the parts of the mind that do not understand words.

Yala remembered the Prophet breaking bread at the end of the kitchen table. The Presence-that-was-not-Yala remembered the broken table in the rubble of her home.

The child remembered the warmth of a crowded sofa. The voice within the child remembered the sofa had been reduced to dust.

Yala remembered feeling the way the laughter of her friends could shake the room. The Presence-that-was-not-Yala remembered how Nan now shook the whole bed in her night terrors, completely silent in her dreams even when her mouth was open to scream.

Yala remembered the sneer of jewel-robed Walkers walking past the crowd of Balori penitents outside the Temple, the way their noses wrinkled as if they had accidently walked past an open sewer in their polished armor and shiny silks. Yala remembered the way Or'sen would rest a gentle hand on her shoulder in those moments, singing all the louder.

The Presence-that-was-not-Yala paused and, just that once, let the feeling of safety linger. Yala never had a brother, or at least one she knew about. She liked to think that if she had a brother, he would be like Or'sen. Whenever Nan couldn't sleep or Ku'un stopped eating again, Or'sen was the one who gave them hope. "This will change. They will see," he would say, the light of true Sight in his eyes brighter than a smithy's coals. "I've seen it. You will too, soon."

Yala was comforted by prophecy. The Presence-that-was-not-Yala fed the tiny ember of this comfort diligently. In time, Yala slept, and the Presence-that-was-not-Yala lingered on the borders of this dream state, watching, waiting... considering.

Somewhere in her dreams, the child was sculpting ice again, conjuring a mountain of snow, and riding an avalanche into the heart of a city. In the malleable landscape of her dream, the three citadels rose no higher than her knees, and the mountain could be raised over and over again. What started as a dream of power and rage softened. Yala giggled as she rode the icy blocks like a horse, dashing down the side of the mountain over a toy-sized city with careless glee.

The Presence-that-was-not-Yala had been waiting for that moment. What Yala dreamed of—what the Moot feared—might or might not yet come to pass. An avalanche first touched off in a child's dreams could yet take form above the citadels. Or perhaps not. With so many Precognitive Talents in this city, the tides of time and prophecy were far more complicated than usual. Long had been the debate over the best course of action—whether to stall the little ice mage and hide the true plot in the shadow of a false prophecy or to ensure its actuality and take over this little prophecy as a distraction.

Yala snuggled deeper into her blankets, mind pillowed in powdery white vengeance. Yet Yala was not the only one who dreamed. Her friend Or'sen was not the only Talent with the Sight. The Presence-that-was-not-Yala was counting on that. So many possibilities were still hanging in the balance. Too many decisive moments would come between this and that, between this quiet night and the future that may or may not yet be. The Presence-that-was-not-Yala was able to see both paths, even now, as Yala dreamed.

Instructor

Chapter 1

I'm regretting this.

Intimidated, Jathen swallowed hard as he measured the round training room inside one of the Rosinic complexes adjacent to the Temple Citadel. Erin Manna had "commandeered" the space from High Walker Jiāojīn, who had sputtered and trembled in fury when Galduran told her an Original would be using it to train Jathen but had turned the key over nonetheless. Lady Erin Manna hadn't even flinched as she merely took it, her face a mask of Clan neutrality.

Still, Walker Jiāojīn's displeasure wasn't why Jathen's stomach was doing flip-flops and D'ilinde was buzzing in his chest. The magically crafted room meant to train Rosinics looked as if Spirit had gotten drunk one day and thrown up a dozen different terrains at once. A flat disk of white marble about a dragon's length in diameter sat centrally, but the rest of the space had textures: sand, soil, glass, or spikes. Large, bubbly-looking *things* Jathen could only assume were squishy covered a portion of floor off to his right, while in the ground straight ahead, past the disk of marble, lay a black void to nowhere. The ceiling and walls weren't much more comforting, the latter bedecked in warped mirrors showing Jathen a thousand times over in grotesque, golden-scaled deformity but not reflecting Erin at all, while the former had been glamoured to appear on fire. Bright cracking flames ran all along the beams, and while Jathen felt no heat, it reminded him disconcertingly of the day he ran into the charm shop, trying to save Hatori and Jephue.

He bit his lip, deeply uncertain.

"I thought I had earned trust, Jathen," his tutor observed. Standing in the center of the marble, she looked regal, clad in a salmon-pink-and-yellow dress with tight sleeves. Her upswept hair resembled a crown, complete with a golden thunderbird hairpin perched on top, as if guarding a regal nest.

Jathen pointed up. "Bad memories." Steeling himself, he vacated the doorway and picked his way across the sandy portion of the floor to meet her.

"I am aware. The glamour is such that the illusion is different for everyone." Her golden eyes flicked upward. "Our worst fears are made manifest on the ceiling."

Jathen resisted the urge to ask what she saw above. "So how are we to start?"

"Rosinics and, indeed, any mage, will claim there are different types of energy to draw from. Earth, air, fire, water... and still others will argue for emotional energy or Spirit energy as well. Ignore them." She pointed at him. "There is only one *true* type of energy, and you, True Negater, are proof of it, because you negate *all* of it. Everything is Spirit. All energy *is* Spirit energy. All that is physical doesn't exist, yet at the same time, it has always existed and will always exist."

She lowered her hand. "Some mages will also tell you they absorb one energy type better than another. This is because of perception. For whatever reason, their subconscious recognizes and understands the *illusion* of that type better. It is the same philosophy behind how every mage casts differently. Some need words, a verbal declaration to solidify their thoughts into action. Some require hand gestures or elaborate rituals to garner the proper effect. And others..." A flash of lightning struck the floor, making Jathen jump nearly a full length across the room and clear off the center disk. "Need no outward tell. They simply do."

"And what am I?" As he dusted from his legs the sand he'd kicked up upon landing, he eyed the black mark still smoking on the marble. "Half the time, I have no idea I've even done anything."

"Do you know why your sword cane penetrated the ward around the Artifact half that night on the summit?"

"How did you...?"

One quick glance from those golden eyes stanched Jathen's voice as he realized that asking the nearly nine-thousand-year-old Clanswoman how she knew something without being told was... a rather stupid inquiry.

Especially when I let her into my head, no matter how briefly. Though she promised to only see what I wanted her to. Still. "Hatori had told me about how steel can penetrate weaker wards, and I took a chance."

"So, you think your renegade Gray used a *weaker* ward that night?"

Jathen opened his mouth, only to shut it again, unsure.

"Come." She led him off the marble and around a glass spike protruding from the ground.

Nestled between another two spikes, a pedestal stood nearly at the edge of the mirrored wall. One of those purple vegetables she liked so much sat atop it.

Erin Manna handed him a simple steel dagger. "Hit it."

"Very well," Jathen muttered, uncertain as he grasped the handle. A touch out of practice, he still took his stance then a single slow breath before letting it fly. The throw looked to be on mark until, a hair's width away, the blade hit an invisible force and sparked, deflecting to one side. The dagger hit the glass floor with a clatter, and the purple vegetable didn't so much as shiver on its roost.

"*That* was a weak ward," she said, walking around behind him. "The dagger in your coat pocket—you've worn it for some time?"

Jathen patted his chest and confirmed one was there. He'd nearly forgotten about it. "Yes. I bought it in Kinawa."

"Throw it."

Pulling it from his coat, Jathen furrowed his brow. "It's just a common dagger, same as the one you just—"

"I am aware of its composition, young Tazu. Throw it at the target, please."

Shrugging once, he repeated the process, and his dagger planted itself deep into the purple vegetable.

He turned to her, startled. "How?"

"You asked me what type of mage you are. You, young Tazu, simply *do*, without tells, by instinct." She continued to stroll around him while explaining. "The same way metals in the presence of a magnet will often themselves become magnetized, items in a True Negater's possession will, too, begin to retain a certain amount of vibrational negation."

"So Hatori's sword cane broke Mikkal's ward not because it was made of steel but because I'd been carrying it around for a few weeks by then."

"Precisely." She stopped to face him. "Just how you are unable to negate *every* spell or charm you interact with, not every item in your possession will gain this advantage. You can rely on most steel to pick it up, however. As it is naturally less likely to be affected by traditional magic, it is thus more likely to become affected by negation."

"How *do* I know what I will or will not negate entirely, though?" He touched his wrist, where he'd once worn the lovely master-charm watch cuff his mother had commissioned Hatori to make him. It'd been a ward in its own right and had saved his life several times before Skaniss had destroyed it.

"Unfortunately, as you grow in power, all spells that have prolonged, intimate contact with you will degrade. The strength of the charm or spell will determine its longevity, which is why you don't instantaneously negate everything you touch—though obviously, charms will be longer-lasting than, say, a brief attack spell." She also pointed at his wrist. "Did you not think it odd an item created to protect you, which deflected so much, could be so easily trampled into the dirt?"

Jathen shivered again at her insight. "I thought my thoughts were closed to telepathy because I'm a Negater—and you promised to keep your time in my head limited to my vision."

Those overly red lips twitched in a slight smirk. "And I told you that I had. I also implied the chattering of your Guides, however, is something many a strong medium will still be privy to, so long as the Guides deem the information helpful to you. Though 'helpful' to a Guide is very subjective. Emotional impressions that flow from you are readable as well, though admittedly, you are making progress on that end. And as said before, you can also choose to allow someone to hear you telepathically, even if it is only a subconscious desire. Perhaps keep all that in mind, and you'll be less disquieted or surprised in the future."

Squinting at her light admonishments, Jathen nodded, thinking of Seren. However, he didn't bring up the sparks because Erin Manna giggling at him wasn't a pleasant thought. "I will. Though I'd prefer to learn to control it."

"And so I shall teach you. Though not in today's lesson." Nodding, she seemed pleased with him, though Jathen had to admit that was tough to tell for certain. A new dagger appeared in her hand, or perhaps it was the one that had clattered away earlier. "Let us see if you can learn to extend your natural aura of negation onto a fresh dagger and accelerate the process."

Jathen spent the next half an hour being lectured on how to visualize his "negation aura" expanding out over the new dagger... then the next two hours trying to do it. After what felt like the hundredth time watching the dagger deflect from the purple vegetable and clatter on the floor, he found himself wringing his hands through his hair and stomping halfway across the room to kick at the sand. "I can't rectify the difference between my 'negation aura' and the ward visualizations," he griped. "It's just not coalescing in my head."

"It shall take time," Lady Erin said to his frustrations. "What I offer you here are merely structures, forms, and methods to take with you and practice once we part ways. If you keep to these, you will in time be able to project that aura out and away from yourself for a measurable distance and thus negate spells not directly aimed at yourself."

"So I'd be able to extend it over another person?" Regulating his breathing, Jathen smoothed out his mussed hair, though he imagined it would need to be rebraided. "To protect them?"

"That is one method of use. There are others for you to discover." She turned her golden eyes toward a random curvature of the amorphous-looking glass floor, where she took in an elaborate clock suddenly ticking away there. "A break is called for. Come—we'll take some tea."

Intrigued, Jathen followed her back around the largest glass spike to the marble disk, where a table and two chairs had been set up. Covering the striped tablecloth were a Clan-style tea set complete with a piping-hot pot and more of those tiny cakes Annakki seemed to enjoy. Grateful for the rest, Jathen didn't bother to ponder where it'd all come from but settled into the plush seat, content to sip and chew away his weariness under a mountain of subtly sweet Clan desserts.

"Do you know how long," he asked after they'd been nibbling in silence for a while, "before we 'part ways,' as you put it?"

"Short term, I'll be departing for home this afternoon and returning in a few days. But for the long term, no." She sipped her tea, the saucer barely moving. "Too many factors to predict. The range, though, is limited to a few weeks to a few years, though most scenarios playing out at this moment lean toward several months' duration, specifically into spring."

"Ah." Jathen nodded and swallowed his tea as if he fully understood, but the nuances of precognition were still lost on him despite his being beset with the "bastard Ability" himself.

"Come," Lady Erin stated, rising from her chair after draining her second cup. "We start again."

Jathen sighed, wondering again what he'd managed to get himself into.

"YOU'VE BEEN TAUGHT," Annakki commented to Izzy, her tourmaline eyes tracking the fauni's footwork.

Kneeling beside the Clanswoman in the solarium, Jathen found it strange to see the poised lady in a gi—a short robe-and-pants set used for hand-to-hand training—her long dark hair braided so tight that not a single strand lay out of place. A few minutes into his first lesson, he'd already found her to be most efficient, with a firm but gentle mien—not unlike Hkym, who'd taught him knife throwing.

"Rudimentary Rheanic defense," Izzy replied, stepping back away from Spinnek.

The pair had been demonstrating Spinnek's newly learned kata, and Annakki had suggested Izzy herself act as the dummy for the fighting form instead of Orne. She'd hesitated at first but eventually obliged.

"There was a Rheanic Temple in the Solkies, where I trained to use Orne," Izzy went on. "Fauni fighting styles are based in Rheanic as well, in all honesty."

Annakki nodded, and the lesson continued, Spinnek gleefully "attacking" with a series of punches. None of them landed, as Izzy continued stepping back with the footwork Annakki had just praised.

"You know, I learned a little bit before, in the Furōrin-Iki," Jathen told her, rubbing his upper arms for warmth. Though Izzy and Spinnek might've been counteracting the frigid early-morning air, Jathen was shivering heavily under his robe. "Setsu taught me pressure points."

"Then we can build on that foundation."

Jathen snorted, recalling his many moments of being flipped over Ass'shiri's shoulder. "I didn't say I was any good."

"Kubeshian attacks are different from Rheanic, Jathen," Izzy replied, stopping her stint with Spinnek. "Setsu is Tesgree. His style is meant for his combat, not yours."

"*I'm* still not sure what my combat is, let alone my style," Jathen mumbled.

"Not die," Spinnek supplied.

Annakki actually smiled. "Do not think of it as learning combat, Jathen. Think of it as training agility, speed, skills needed to improve what you already do well—knife throwing, dodging." She cocked her head, eyes falling upon the sword cane Jathen had tucked into his belt. "And, I think, that as well—blocking maneuvers. Practicality." She sprang up, standing more quickly than Jathen could blink. "Come. I'm going to teach you a new kata."

"You mean different from the one you taught Spinnek?"

"Yes. Entirely new, just for you."

Jathen raised a dubious eyebrow, but after exchanging glances with Izzy, he refrained from questioning Annakki. If a daughter of

Rhean said she could make up an entirely new kata specifically for him, who was he to argue?

He spent the better part of an hour learning the new stances, while Izzy and Spinnek continued to practice on the other side of the little space they'd cleared by shoving the table and some of the potted plants aside. Annakki insisted he learn footwork first, then they would add the arm motions later. While he felt silly, he had to admit that made it easier to retain.

"Fine progress for a first lesson," Annakki said at the end. "Practice when you have some time, and I'll see you again tomorrow morning."

"Not tomorrow," Jathen replied. "Galduran and Lady Manna set me up with the other Ways—I'm meeting Master Enillydd for strategy and tactics. But I can do the day after, as long as you're all right with me skipping the next day for me to meet with Master Volatile. Though you can have me again the next morning."

"That will do." She smiled slightly. "I see your taskmasters are already keeping you busy."

"Very. In fact..." He turned toward Izzy. "Don't we have to be off? Some lecture Seren wanted me to sit in on?"

"Yes." Izzy wiped her forehead with a towel while Spinnek did cartwheels behind her. "I checked the schedule Headmaster Ophisa sent over, and there's a Second Tier lecture on the nature of the Ways I thought might do Spinnek some good at the same time."

"Spinnek go school?" The boy stopped twirling, brown eyes eager.

"Yes, but we've enough time to clean up first," Izzy said. "And you need to wear *shoes* in the university."

Spinnek let out an overdramatic exasperated sigh but relented after the group had changed clothes. But he complained about it. "Not like," he whined the entire walk over, stopping as they passed University Park. He rubbed the toe of one shiny black leather boot on the back of his other calf. "Feet... muffled. No feel ground energy."

"You'll be thankful for that when you get into the school proper," Izzy said knowingly. "Magic-crafted structure with built-in wards—your feet will vibrate off if you keep them bare on the floor for too long."

"Have you been barefoot in the university before?" Jathen asked her while Spinnek decided to walk backward between the pair, purposefully scuffing up his soles.

Izzy was quiet for a moment before shaking her head. "In the Solkies, where I trained, we had a similar building that had that effect. I can only imagine the result would be amplified in one of the citadels."

Jathen squinted, certain Izzy had just lied somewhat. The part about the Solkies rang true, but he felt a sense of withholding from her as well. He pursed his lips, debating whether he wanted a confrontation when she'd already admitted she didn't wish to tell him Orne's secrets just yet.

Suddenly, a loud *crack* filled the air, derailing Jathen's deliberation. Panic rose as a deep rumbling echoed across the mountains, and his head spun in the direction of the sound. Raw terror took hold as he watched a wave of snow cascading down the Sentinel to the west. Slithering like a waterfall, the snow ended in a distant *puff* far outside the walls, probably meeting the Drayu's Mouth, a river a few leagues from the city, if that.

"It's a controlled avalanche," Izzy assured him, placing a steadying hand on his elbow and pointing with the other. "See?"

Jathen watched with bated breath as another crack sounded and an arc of magic flew into the mountain face. It collided with a blooming flower of white snow and cracking, fiery energy, then another waterfall of powdery snow drifted down. His exhaled breath came in sync with the falling snow.

"That ruddy well gave me a heart attack," he said.

"They do similar in the Solkies." Izzy squeezed his elbow once then returned her arm inside her cloak. "If it's any consolation, this probably means Na'vosh is being mindful of your vision."

Giving her a noncommittal hum, Jathen glanced across that western mountain, trying to summon his vision from memory. *It's not the same. Too far away. And the snow... It wasn't powdery. There was ice, a great sheet of it...* He glanced about, hoping to get an idea of what direction the wintery death had come from, but too many buildings were blocking the view. *Well, at least I know I wasn't on this road.*

"Strange man," Spinnek announced, calling Jathen's squinting gaze from the city.

Turning around, Izzy and Jathen both stiffened, but he alone sucked in a sharp breath.

A'ron De'contes grinned, waving a nonchalant hand at the trio. "Jathen, what a pleasant surprise," he practically cooed, bright-red eyes darting with interest across Izzy and resting with an unmistakably hungry glint on Spinnek.

"Neither pleasant nor, I'm sure, a surprise for you, De'contes," Jathen shot back.

Izzy scowled, putting a hand on Spinnek's shoulder. Jathen followed suit, doing his best to turn the Exemplary Talent away from the head of the Balori.

"We'll just be on our way, thank you," Jathen said.

"Oh, don't be so crass," the Clansman proclaimed, falling into step with the group even as they continued walking away. As Spinnek eyed him curiously, he smiled, showcasing his Clan teeth. "After all, you never did get back to me about my offer—and now I've heard a rumor you've gone and found yourself a teacher. Now I'm truly at a loss, since I still *really* want to know why you came back for me that day."

"Well, that's just terribly unfortunate for you, since I'm no longer in need of your... services," Jathen retorted.

Since he'd seen his death in red-and-black robes, the Balori were no longer an option beyond Jathen not needing De'contes to learn to be a Negater. Also, the vote was approaching soon, on whether the Ways would let the Balori in as an accepted Way, leaving Jathen with few illusions as to why De'contes was pestering him.

"You'll have to learn, as I have, that some mysteries are often never answered," Jathen said. "Good day."

De'contes sighed long, following them through the street crowd and feigning sadness despite Jathen's rebuffs. "Well, I suppose if that's how you feel about it, one can't go impeding your free will. Though one cannot truly go impeding mine, were I to press the Chancellor a bit harder about finding my wayward assassin. A lot of circumstantial evidence is just lying about, of course, but then again, such things really only have to be just enough to get a few Tar'citadel telepaths involved..."

Jathen thumbed down hard the desire to threaten to kill the Red Mage. *Annakki is right—he is ruthless.* Gathering his thoughts, Jathen managed to reply somewhat stiffly, "That's your prerogative, De'contes, so by all means, do so. After all, hypocrisy is something most High Walkers are accustomed to dealing with when it comes to you, having claimed sanctuary after murdering thousands, after all. One can't allow an *attempted* murder to go unpunished while so many *actual* murders won't be as long as you're still living. Perhaps I can even discuss it over my lessons, since I have become rather friendly with a number of High Walkers as of late: Galduran, Volaille, Plajă, Zhìliáo—not to mention I work with Master Enillydd, who has Kriger's ear and his voting rights while he's in the Middle Lands. Spirit, that's pretty much all of the liberal Ways right there. How interesting. We'd have such a lovely time discussing Temple politics and how certain votes need to be unanimous to pass."

De'contes pursed his lips in a mildly sheepish expression, while across the top of Spinnek's head, Izzy looked downright impressed, to the point of repressing a giggle-snort.

"Well, I am glad to know your tutoring is proceeding under so many accomplished Talents," De'contes returned. "Though I admit I'm surprised there is no expert on Negaters among those mentioned. Could it be you've decided to forego this aspect of your training after all?"

Jathen sniffed and tried to sound stern when he said, "No."

"So someone else *is* training you?"

"Lady train," Spinnek replied, his voice coming out slightly shaky despite his clear desire to be helpful. "Scary."

"A 'scary Lady,' you say? My Red, I wonder who on the continent that could be," De'contes replied with no small amount of relish. He seemed filled with a desire to learn that fact more than anything else. Those red eyes suddenly narrowed on Spinnek, sparking with an even deeper interest. "You, sir, are masking your aura." De'contes took a step past Jathen toward the boy, who squeaked slightly and squirmed around behind Izzy. "Your friend is quite a bit more pow-erful than he lets on, Jathen. If I could—"

"Enough!" Jathen put a forearm up against the Red Mage's chest and shoved angrily.

Even though it felt as futile as pressing against a steel-plated wall, the action made D'ilinde buzz angrily, and A'ron De'contes turned a shade paler. Jathen felt something else as well, a surge, a sense of tendrils pulling at his arm, little licking fingers that churned Jathen's stomach. A flash filled his vision as well, brief but clear, of A'ron covered in blood and... sobbing. Gasping at what was apparently a shared vision, De'contes stepped back of his own accord, much to Ja-then's relief.

Quaking from what he'd seen and still angry, Jathen snapped, "You leave Spinnek alone, do you hear me?"

As he rubbed his chest, De'contes's expression said he'd lost all interest in Spinnek, his garnet eyes wide and slightly manic as they stared at Jathen. Body rigid and exuding a deadly seriousness, he took an authoritative step back into Jathen's space, though he kept a certain distance. With a mixture of deep concern and genuine fear, he whispered, "Never, *ever* tell *anyone* what you just did to me, Jathen. Do you understand? Red-mad followers *will kill you* for it."

"I... What?" Jathen blinked repeatedly, torn between being terrified, angry, and downright confused.

"Loosen red from black," Spinnek whispered.

Then Jathen understood in a burst of horrifying revelation.

I started to negate the part of him that's a Red Mage. He exchanged a terrified glance with Izzy, who looked equally alarmed by this turn of events. "Is that... Is that even possible?"

De'contes broke in before Izzy could take a breath to reply. "Do *not* speak of it," he hissed, placing a finger over his lips. "For all my bravado and word-weaving, I genuinely do not mean you harm, Jathen. But this is a thing you'll find yourself dead from by the mere implication. Speak of it to *no one*—not even your tutor."

Fear bled back into anger as Jathen narrowed his eyes at the Red Mage. "What I share or do not share with *Erin Manna* is my business, De'contes." Picking up the pace once more, he physically pressed Izzy and Spinnek forward to a fervent speed. "Though your advice is duly noted."

De'contes let himself fall behind. "Erin is in the city?" The way he asked sent a chill down Jathen's spine.

Turning, Jathen caught a glimpse of absolute vulnerability upon De'contes's face, though the cause might have been a remnant of what Jathen had just done. He swallowed, and Jathen caught a glimmer of sadness and longing waft from the Clansman.

"Sorry to have troubled you," he murmured, just loud enough to be heard.

Spinning back around, Jathen continued to shuffle Izzy and Spinnek farther down the street, not slowing until they rounded a corner.

"Strange man," Spinnek said once they slowed back to a sane pace.

"To say the very least," Izzy replied then turned to Jathen. "You actually handled that rather well. Though I admit my heart jumped into my throat when you tried to shove him."

"Yes. Wish I'd rethought that." Rubbing his forearm, he winced. *This is going to bruise something fierce. Not certain if it will amuse or horrify Annakki when she learns how it happened. And now, I need to somehow find a way to mention negating Red Mages to Erin Manna—no easy feat in and of itself.* He swallowed, trying to sound more confident than he felt. "Though I knew he wouldn't retaliate. It's either against his code or against the code of a persona he's trying to maintain. He'd not break that with his vote coming up."

"One has to wonder upon his true motivations for that encounter, though." Izzy adjusted her hood, it having become askew during their hasty departure. "Because we know, with such a man, they cannot be what he presented."

"Or they were what was presented because he knows everyone thinks that way when it comes to him." Jathen shook out his hand, trying to alleviate the pain. "And Spirit knows, he did seem genuinely unnerved by my shove, not to mention Lady Erin's name."

Spinnek shivered. "Scary Lady."

The three of them continued onward in silence until they reached the university, where Spinnek became a bug-eyed gawker. Jathen couldn't blame him, as he still found his breath catching in his throat no matter how many times he saw the crystalline details of the grand foyer. The fifteen-year-old even squeaked when the elevator they'd shuffled him into began to rise, then he pressed his face against the glass window.

"What floor is your and Seren's lecture on?" Izzy asked as the elevator stopped. Nonchalantly, she grabbed the collar of Spinnek's shirt, pulling him out despite his sputtering protests about the pretty view.

Jathen suppressed a smile while fishing the schedule out of his pocket. "It's up on Third Tier, so... one hundred five. Lecture Hall Ten Fifty-eight." He squinted at where the paper had become slightly smudged. "You two are up here, Lecture Hall Five Fifty-nine." He escorted them down the hall, weaving among students between the ages of perhaps sixteen to twenty, though some appeared more Spinnek's age, perhaps even a few years younger. The Exemplary Talent continued to drink them all in with wide eyes, sounding impressed and murmuring in that guttural language of his.

"Back to Dodbyen speech?" Jathen asked him playfully.

"Think better in it," Spinnek admitted. "Lots of auras here. Hard to sorting."

"You'll do fine," Jathen reassured his friend, patting him on the shoulder once they reached their destined door.

Acolyte Way Walkers were already filing in and taking up spots across the five levels of seats.

"Our lecture will probably run longer than yours," Jathen told Izzy. "When you're done, just head up to Third Tier to wait, and I'll—" His mouth fell open. What he was seeing was unbelievable.

Down the hall, A'ron De'contes exited the elevator, glancing about.

"Damn him—he's *back*," Jathen hissed. Pressing Izzy and Spinnek forward, he followed them into the lecture hall just before the doors closed.

"You're going to miss meeting Seren," Izzy whispered.

"I know—I know," Jathen replied, shuffling them into some seats. "But I am *not* going back out there alone, and you are *not* leaving Spinnek alone in here."

The boy snorted as he planted himself in a seat between them. "Alone most life. Why care now?"

"Don't argue. Just sit and listen," he snapped.

Spinnek slipped lower into his chair, pouting.

Where are you? Seren's concerned voice suddenly filled his mind.

Jathen sighed long as a human Way Walker sporting silver-and-violet-trimmed robes walked to the front of the room. He reminded Jathen slightly of Galduran but looked quite a bit older, with bits of silver and gray in his auburn hair. *Though he's probably younger by a few millennia at least. High Mages and Clansman—you can never tell their ages.*

What?

Jathen flinched, remembering Seren. *Sorry. Stuck down in Lecture Hall Five Fifty-nine. De'contes already cornered us outside and was trying again, so I slipped in with Izzy and Spinnek. I'm sorry, but I'm not going to get up there for yours so long as he's stalking me.*

Ugh. Very well, I'm coming down to you. I can check for overbearing evil Red Mages lurking in hallways.

Jathen had to bite his lips to keep the laughter in. *Thank you.*

"So let us pick up," the Walker began, cutting off any response Jathen could have conjured, "from where we left off yesterday, with Illionan's question." He cleared his throat after nodding in the direction of a student, a young Lu'shun-looking version of a Tazu with blue hair, turquoise-colored scales, and the telltale bright-blue eyes. "What, exactly, *is* Spirit? Well, Spirit is all things, and all things are Spirit. But 'all things' is a very difficult concept to grasp while in cardinal form. So we break Spirit down into different facets so we may better understand that-which-is-all and our place or path within the makeup of the universe of Spirit. First, we have consciousness. Spirit is all things: it is a rock, it is a bird, it is energy, it is light, it is people, it is love, it is *everything*. Spirit is conscious, but we recognize in both the physical plane and the spiritual plane that there are higher and lower consciousnesses within Spirit."

Jathen bit back a deeper sigh. Such lectures were reminiscent of Old Basimess's sermons back in Kidwellith—reminders and reiterations of basic Way Walker doctrines. *I hope Spinnek gains something from this.* Looking about the room, he noted most students were closer to the age of his younger Exemplary friend than of Seren or him. *Because I'm likely to fall asleep.*

You would have enjoyed the lecture I wanted you at, Seren shot at him as she slipped in, closing the door gently behind herself.

I'm sorry, but I really didn't want a scene in the middle of the citadel. Is he still out there? Jathen asked as she settled into the empty seat next to him.

Yes. He told me to tell you he wished to speak to you. She slipped her book satchel off her shoulder and put it under her chair. *I told him you were not inclined and if he insisted on stalking you, we'd bring it up with Chancellor Dàshī.*

Good. Well done.

Her lovely blue eyes held his with a penitent stare. *I actually felt bad. He looked... downtrodden. What did he want?*

Again, Jathen was cut short as the Walker asked the class, "An example of a higher consciousness, please?"

A hesitant hand went up, and he nodded at the student, who then offered, "One of the Children?"

"Both correct and yet not quite correct," he replied. "The Children are absolutely mortal beings of higher consciousness, but they are also what we consider *focused* aspects of Spirit given form within beings of higher consciousness. So yes, they would fall under what's considered higher, but they actually would go *beyond* the typical higher-consciousness form when Ascended. Can someone give me an example of a 'normal' higher consciousness of Spirit?"

Someone behind them called out, "A person, any Ishim?"

"Yes. Another?"

"Angel Guide?"

"Yes. Can we see the pattern?"

The girl Illionan concluded, "Higher consciousness is anything that is a part of Spirit that's capable of conscious thought—things that can think."

"Close." The Walker smiled. "Can a dog think? Can a dragon?"

"Yes, somewhat," replied Illionan, though she looked puzzled. "So we include animals as well?"

"You were half right. Higher consciousness actually includes all things that can have emotional *and* rational responses. For example, who has ever felt the difference between a living tree that was thriving and one that was dying? The dying one would actually have an emotional signature of pain, of sadness. A thriving one *feels* happy. This is an example of lower consciousness—anything we can sense an emotional response from only, no matter how subtle. Air, earth, water, fire—all energy forms can carry emotional responses of the greater Spirit but *no* rational thoughts. Also remember higher consciousness can manipulate and control lower consciousness. If you send positive energy to a plant, it will grow faster, or charge a stone with a negative emotion, and you can create a cursed object of it. It is still a part of the conscious Spirit, but it has *no free will*. If it can make a choice, even as simple as I walk left or right, it is part of higher consciousness."

The Walker took a breath then a sip of water from a glass on a small table beside him on the raised platform from which he was lecturing.

"Not understand," Spinnek actually whispered politely to Jathen. "Some animals no choose. Some animal just *do*. No thinking about do."

"Instincts, yes," Jathen said softly, a smile playing at his lips. "I was thinking the same thing, Spinnek. How can something be a higher consciousness if it doesn't actually have a thought process to weigh the choices? I think his terms are far too broad."

"Animals can choose to ignore their instincts, you two. It's just harder," Seren whispered. "Now, shush. If I'm stuck in here with you three, I want to listen."

Refreshed, the Walker started up again. "Now, going back to the Children and higher consciousness. As said, the Children are beings of mortal ink, of higher consciousness. But they are different, a recognized *focused* aspect of Spirit. So what does that mean? Well, most agree that while Spirit is *not* a specific being, it is everything and all of us. It is also recognized that there is a pool of energy or consciousness that makes up the 'core' of Spirit—sort of a brain within the consciousness whole that is Spirit. Think of yourself within Spirit as a body part, say, the hand. If you're the hand, then Spirit would be the brain, and so would the Children be the different parts of the brain that control different sections of the body."

"Similar to how the left side of the brain controls the right side of the body," Seren called out.

"Exactly," the Walker said in praise. "And how one part of the brain controls memory, one part vision, one part breathing, one part creativity, and so on."

A human boy clad in Desmoulein green extrapolated, "So as each part of the brain controls each part of the body, each person has a different Child they shall feel most comfortable under?"

The Walker replied, "Very good! Exactly! Twelve Children, embodying twelve different parts of Spirit consciousness. Now, each of the twelve are also further broken down into similar aspect combinations. These Aspects are recognized as singular conscious souls that incarnate as well, but we still clump them with their primaries because their differences often are very subtle."

Spinnek surprised Jathen by raising his hand and asking, "Why separate then?"

"Because they are individual souls that incarnate," the Walker explained, looking pleased to have engaged the Exemplary Talent in the room. "Essentially, they are the twin flames of each Child. For example"—he nodded with deference at Izzy—"let us examine the most obviously diverse pair: Turin and his Aspect. Turin is death, the end of life, the termination of the mortal cycle. This is a deconstructive energy, but his Aspect is life. Creation and the beginning of the mortal cycle are a constructive energy. As a whole, they are life and death, the cycle. Now, not all the Children's pairings are this obviously balanced, nor are they necessarily *male* and *female*, as the true state of all Ishim is without gender. Only in the mortal body do we even consider the concept. But they do tend to fall along binary energy couplings wherein they complement each other highly. Again, we have both sides of the spectrum, as well as all facets between, to accommodate all the diversity of Spirit."

Brow furrowed, Spinnek surprised Jathen again by calling out, "But how Red fit?" Struggling, he squirmed in his seat, trying to get the right words out. "Say Red turn from Spirit. How, then, it part Spirit? Does make destruction... ah, *needed* evil?" He shrugged, holding up his hands. "If true, why fight Red?"

Scanning the room, Jathen wondered for a moment if everyone else was scrutinizing Spinnek as deeply as he and the Walker were.

Finally, the man replied, "Valid questions. We remember, when it comes to the Red, that there is a difference between deconstruction or destruction and *disruption*. Destruction does not exist. Energy cannot be created nor destroyed, only redirected—therefore, we refer to the concept more often as deconstructive. This is a natural aspect of Spirit and, before the Red went mad, His domain. However, the Red now preaches *disruption*, the negative de-evolution of the soul—selfishness, indulgence, the preoccupation with the mortal world and carnal gain. These things lead away from the evolution of the soul. They *disrupt* the learning process. To strive only to gain, only to win and indulge, only to satisfy oneself—this is *not* the natural cycle of evolution. 'Bad things' happen in our lives not only because of the Red. We require conflict and resolution in order to evolve."

Jathen found himself squirming in his chair slightly. That sounded alarmingly close to what De'contes had been preaching at him the other night.

The Walker continued, "But the Red says, 'Do not learn from your suffering, do not grow because of it, but instead use it to cause more suffering—inflict more upon others so that you may feel better, so you may gain.' This is a false gratification and a false sense of evolution."

"So Balori right," Spinnek stated matter-of-factly, which set off a great deal of heated murmuring throughout the room.

"Spinnek," Izzy admonished in a harsh whisper as Jathen and Seren exchanged concerned glances. "You can*not* say things like that."

The boy huffed, crossing his arms and defiantly sitting back in his chair. Meanwhile, the Way Walker motioned gently for silence, bringing the class back to order.

"Recall what Way holds first in this room, students," he said firmly. "*Truth*. Ulic himself told us that truth in it of itself is relative. Often, what we believe to be true is true. This does not necessarily dictate in stone what is *right* and what is *wrong*. For that, refer to the five laws and know in your hearts for yourselves, but only yourselves. In the end, it is *your* evolution to Spirit you are responsible for and no one else's. If you are not comfortable with a particular Way or path of thinking, then it is not for *you*." He held up a warning finger. "But that does not, necessarily, make it *wrong* for others to follow it."

"So much easier said than done," Jathen murmured, wondering if De'contes was still lurking in the hall. *Not certain I'm going to sit much longer through this.*

"Come on. If he's still there, we can easily get him removed," Seren whispered.

"Yes. Go," Spinnek begged. "Not like this talk. Too... *narrow*."

Taking in more concerned glares from students while the Walker prattled on about some of the nuances of the Five Laws, Izzy shrugged, defeated. "We'd benefit from some lunch."

Slipping out with his group, Jathen spared a brief glimpse at the mildly relieved expression in the Walker's dark-blue eyes, making him feel slightly better for the choice. *Last thing we need is another brood of rumors circulating about Spinnek being the incarnation of the Red or some nonsense. Though if he thinks this Walker was being narrow-minded, he's going to be in for a rude shock if he ever gets to the Tazu Nation.*

"Thank Spirit, no De'contes," Jathen said once in the hall. "I truly didn't want any more of him."

"Well, we can't slip into my intended lecture at this point," Seren said with a sigh. "So we might as well head for the dining floor."

At the mention of food, Spinnek immediately perked up and happily skipped after Jathen and Seren, with Izzy following along like an indigo shadow.

"So how are classes?" Jathen asked Seren as they stepped into the elevator. "Keeping you busy?"

She shrugged, fingers toying with the strap of her book satchel. "It's a light load this semester."

Jathen smirked, thinking about their last meeting. "Leaving room for your favorite pastime, research?"

"Hardly. Just because I'm good at it doesn't mean it's a favorite." She leaned against the inside of the elevator while Spinnek pressed his face against the window again, eyes wide as they descended. "Sorry. I'm just irritated we missed that lecture. It was an open forum about Erin Manna's grand prophecy, and I really wanted to hear it, as well as to get your take."

"Her what?"

Seren rolled her eyes while Izzy chuckled. "Ugh, you are so obtuse still."

"Erin Manna's grand prophecy is arguably the single most influential piece of prophecy ever penned. Even small portions have shaped nations over the millennia," Izzy said. "I'm surprised that you, a precognitive, haven't even heard it mentioned, Jathen."

He shrugged, mimicking Seren's earlier ambivalence. "It's not as if someone made an effort to train my precognition back home."

"That I do believe," Seren said.

Izzy pursed her lips but added nothing.

"So tell me about it, then," Jathen retorted.

Seren shot him a low-lidded glare but then began, "Erin Manna locked herself in a room in Clana-Ca'sta sometime right after the Great Fall and wrote this *massive* tome of prophecies—something like twenty-seven scrolls, each six heads long—all written in verse, all with dozens of variations of how certain events could play out. It was a channeled writing, coming directly from Spirit, so complex and detailed even *she* doesn't know the interpretations of most of it. There's an entire semester precognition class dedicated to it in Third Tier—I spent half of yesterday discussing tidbits with the teacher. Sorely annoyed I hadn't known of it beforehand. I'd have signed up for it. Hence my other reason I wanted to sit in on the standalone lecture today." She sighed, straightening away from the wall as the elevator came to a halt. "As it is, I might still transfer in."

"The Lady Manna does take dinner with us at Annakki's townhouse in a few days," Izzy said as they exited the elevator. "Perhaps you can pose your questions directly to Erin Manna herself?"

Seren shook her head. "Aside from my not wanting to be nearly so presumptuous, others have inquired before, and as I said, it was a channeled writing—she wasn't aware of half of what she wrote. And to top it off, a good portion of the scrolls have been lost over the years. Still, it's a fascinating piece."

Presented with the fullness of the dining floor, Spinnek froze in abject awe at the entrance to the massive room, lined with dozens of counters featuring a multitude of cuisines from the varying cultures across the continent. Large round tables and chairs filled the center of the slate floors, and while not particularly crowded, the space was fuller and louder than Jathen had seen before, when classes weren't in session.

The Exemplary Talent turned to Jathen, nearly reverent. "Spinnek... pick?"

"Much as you want, egg," Jathen assured him, handing him the slip of paper that'd arrived with the lecture schedule. "Ophisa gave us student passes, so everything is free. Eat to your heart's content."

Clasping the paper in his hands, Spinnek choked a little sob before squealing with joy and bolting off toward the nearest counter.

"I think Spinnek might have just found his true religion," Jathen declared. "Way of *food*."

"Culinary arts fall dually under Desmoulein and Bree," Seren said with a smirk. "Anyways, I'm going to get my normal Tazu Nation fare."

"I'll supervise Spinnek—make sure he doesn't climb over the counters into the kitchens," Izzy offered with a somewhat knowing gaze. "We'll meet in the middle at a table."

Jathen repressed an urge to blush but then nodded before hurrying off to catch up to Seren. "So," he murmured to her once they'd stepped into their chosen food line, "I don't suppose there was anything about the Balori divination in Erin Manna's grand prophecy, was there?"

"Ah, so you *do* know how my mind works." Giving him a playful wink over her shoulder, Seren seemed slightly too pleased about that as she pulled a paper out of her bag.

The truth was *she* knew how *his* mind worked. The *why* of the day he saved a possible monster still haunted Jathen even as he waited in line with his nose full of the glorious smell of charred meats. A'ron's earlier desperation didn't ease his burdens, either: *"I suffer, Jathen."*

And it's not as if I can just bluntly ask Erin Manna about him or about negating Red Mages—not with how she reacted to just the man's name that first day. He worried at his bottom lip, wondering whether she was aware of Ra'vien's hand in saving De'contes—and if so, whether Erin knew *why* the Aspect did so.

And if not, should I tell her? And if so, can I ask her? She might just tell me again that my knowing might make things worse... which, in and of itself, I'd honestly rather not *know, considering how I still have this strange feeling I should* know. *Ugh. I always longed to be a Talent, but Spirit, has my life gotten more complicated. No wonder so many fall to the Red's Taint—being a Talent alone is enough to drive someone mad, even with training.*

Seren scanned her paper while they moved a step forward in line. "Most standard interpretations claim that three of the original scrolls specifically detail the Middle Lands and the rise and fall of the Red. They, of course, were *stolen* by Red Mages during the Red Tide. The originals have never been recovered, but bits and pieces of them have been smuggled out by Way Walkers and defecting Annarites for years—as well as innumerable propaganda pieces written by Red followers."

Jathen nodded, unsurprised. "So what exists on record is a highly suspect mess."

"Oh yes. But that's what makes it interesting."

They paused the conversation for a few moments while putting in their orders then receiving trays with plates full of piping-hot drake meat served with pecan-and-pepper brown rice.

When they finally settled at an empty table, she showed him the paper she'd taken out. "This is the most modern fragment and interpretation. 'Author of new magic shall fall—a sacrifice to the

Red—shall be born anew the Prophet, to return the Red-mad to the world.'"

Jathen leaned closer, examining the paper while chewing on his skewered meat. A little dry and slightly overpeppered, it wasn't quite the delectable fare he would find at home or in the embassy, but it was still a respite from Annakki's Clan food, which he'd begun to find slightly bland.

"That's what the Balori girl in the street said to me," he said.

"I told you it's the most modern. The interesting part is the interpretation. 'Author of new magic shall fall.' Most currently believe this was Marin Manna. He'd been researching new ways to fight Red Mages when he died."

A'ron's reaction to Erin certainly puts more credence to that claim. From what I've seen, if he's faking being Marin reborn, it's an act worthy of history books. Then again, so was his betrayal of the last Avatar and Aspect of Rhean. If he could lie bold-faced to them, he can probably confound me easily. Jathen closed his eyes, recalling the image of a blood-soaked De'contes crying his eyes out. *But Raleigh said he was Marin. That might lend some credence to the claim, if an old-soul student of Galduran would hold such an opinion. Though Erin certainly hates him enough to think the man wasn't her husband in a past life.* Jathen swallowed another mouthful of food. "Didn't Hatori once tell me that he was supposed to have had his heart eaten out by the Red?"

"That's one of the legends. Anyways, that's where the 'sacrifice to the Red' part comes in."

"And since A'ron De'contes claims to be Marin Manna reincarnated, that's how he's supposedly the Prophet to lead the Red back to the Ways." Handing the paper back, Jathen frowned, and not just because he was unsettled by De'contes claiming to be the reincarnation of his tutor's dead husband. "No wonder he's suspect. If any Red follower had heard this prophecy beforehand, it'd be easy to make claims of being Marin in order to sway the masses to follow him."

"Exactly."

Izzy and Spinnek rejoined them, Spinnek carrying a tray laden with more food than he could possibly consume in a single sitting.

Jathen cocked an eyebrow at the cornucopia. "Did he get a plate from every vendor?"

"Half." Izzy placed a moderate bowl of soup and a slice of crunchy Tazu Nation bread on the table then sat. "I made him stop after Nor'wah."

"You are going to get a stomachache, Mr. Spider," Seren warned.

He ignored her, crouching, not sitting, on his chair and proceeding to shovel a cheesy rice dish from Casfeild into his mouth without the use of utensils.

Seren choked back a laugh. "Not to mention sticky fingers."

While Izzy tried to get Spinnek to utilize a fork or at least a napkin, Seren shuffled more papers, bringing some rather large, tightly rolled scrolls out of her bag. "Speaking of prophecies and the resulting conjecture, I have something for you." She unfurled the papers between them, taking up a significant section in the center of the table.

Jathen immediately recognized it as a topographic map of the area surrounding Tar'citadel by the ringed contour lines showing the ridges and peaks of the Three Sentinels, the most prominent mountains to the north, east, and west of the city. A deep gorge cut by the broad Cathiny River separated the northern mountain from the extremely elevated plateau Tar'citadel was built on. The city's outline was traced between the forks of the high alpine river, Drayu's Mouth, held like a faceted jewel in a dragon's mouth. Sharp demarcation lines indicated both the cliffs to the north of the city on the south bank of the Cathiny River and the sharp rise of the gorge walls surrounding the Red's Whirlpools and buttressing the base of the northern mountain.

Arching an eyebrow at the familiar map, Jathen asked, "Why are you showing me something I stared at in my atlas for years on end?"

Seren glared briefly at him then pointed at the mountain to the west of the city on the far side of the Drayu's Mouth—the one on which he'd seen the high-altitude explosions earlier in the day. Jathen noted the extreme width of the river separating Tar'citadel from the Middle Lands. Its massive waterfall, Dragon's Teeth, was responsible for the deadly whirlpools in the Cathiny River that made naval passage to the base of Tar'citadel's plateau nigh impossible. *And the river makes it unlikely for avalanches to reach the city from the west.*

Seren's finger, tracing across the contours of the western Sentinel, reclaimed his gaze. "This map shows the glacial fields, permanent snowfields, and avalanche-abatement procedures. You can see on Mt. Mourning the blast zones where they start controlled avalanches."

Jathen huffed, recalling his earlier panic. "I saw them throw their ruddy magic rockets at that side. Probably took a few years off my heart. But it's the wrong Sentinel." With the tip of his tongue wetting his lips, he peered across the lines, seeking recognizable peaks. "There. The vision showed the avalanche coming down off the eastern mountain, over the..." Jathen leaned over the table to look more closely at the tiny print. "Really? They call those ridge peaks the Reverent Steps?"

Spinnek made a little gurgling snicker, probably an attempt to laugh with a full mouth. He swallowed then asked, "No climb on them?"

"A Tazu atlas would call that ridge the Throat Spine," Izzy explained coolly. "There are multiple names for most of the geography around Tar'citadel, due to the sheer number of visitors from other countries and the colossal length of its history."

Jathen nodded. Na'vosh had used different names for the mountains as well.

Izzy traced her dark finger across the map, following the ridge, while Seren looked on in intellectual approval. "Though I do believe there *are* actual steps carved into the Reverent Steps, on account of the Observatory's presence up there, as well as all these watchtowers marked here."

"Anyway, steps or no," Jathen proclaimed, running his own finger across the map, "almost this whole side of the eastern Sentinel was engulfed. I remember because the ice floes split in two around that spine—or the steps or whatever anyone wants to call it—of the mountain."

Arching an eyebrow, Izzy murmured, "Perhaps we should have made that clearer to Na'vosh?"

Nose scrunched up, Seren shook her head. "But what you're de-scribing, Jathen, really is not possible. Do you see how Mt. Reverence has two blue glacier fields marked on either side of the Steps? They end at the Dragon Tongue River because of this."

She traced a claw along the southeastern bank of the much small-er tributary river that shot off from Drayu's Mouth. Meandering northeast and separating Tar'citadel's high plateau from the steep flanks of the mountain in question, it was the source of the second waterfall into the Cathiny River in that area. The Dragon Tongue's southeastern bank was bounded by a doubled bold line, punctuated by unusually small topography markers.

"That is an ice levee," she explained.

Jathen cocked his head, realizing that what he'd thought were unfamiliar topography symbols were actually hydrological engineer-ing markers. "What is an ice levee? Does that have anything to do with the hydroelectric generators at the top of the Cathiny Falls?"

"So much for hours spent staring at your atlas," Seren said with an eyeroll. "This whole structure acts as a retaining dam for the snow outflow fields of Mt. Reverence's glaciers, but it has hundreds of melting stations, where snow and ice are taken into the levee gates to be melted and given a controlled entrance into the Dragon Tongue River." She grinned as that certain gleam appeared in her eyes, as if catching the scent again of a newly discovered fact she found particularly fascinating during her last library hunt. "Did you know that before Tar'citadel was built, Dragon Tongue was a seasonal river only? It and the Cathiny Falls would get completely dammed with ice. *Something* had to be done. Otherwise, your precious hydroelectric dam would not be working year-round."

"Na'vosh mentioned melting stations as well, though for some reason I thought there were fewer of them." Rubbing his eyes to avoid another glare from her, Jathen begged, "Is there a point to this?"

"Yes! The point is that there can*not* be an avalanche on that side. And I researched the ruddy hell out of this because I want you to be able to sleep at night, you complete slaga's ass!" Huffing, she stabbed more fervently at the map. "Look, these glaciers are directly on solid bedrock. There are large systems, both magical and mundane, in place to ensure that Mt. Reverence and Mt. Mourning pose no danger to Tar'citadel."

Biting the inside of his cheek lightly, Jathen squirmed a little in his chair as the memory of his vision played out once more. *It all begins at the fall.* "There has to be a way to make it fail, though. I *saw* it. Are there schematics for the melting stations? Seren, please, I saw tower-size chunks of ice coming for us. Who can I talk to so they check the ice levee for sabotage? Or the wards? Or any of it?"

"Jathen." Seren moaned, putting her head onto the pillow of her arms crossed atop the table, her plate of food pushed aside. "I am trying to reassure you," she said, muffled by her arms. Then she straightened to glare at him some more. "There are guards! Watchtowers! There is even a new young Ice Mage who has been recruited this year to assist the magi-glaciologists with reshaping some of Mt. Mourning's powder fields. Do you know how *rare* that is?"

"Mt. Mourning? What? No, the other one." He looked at the map, silently cursing Spirit for everyone calling the peaks anything other than the Three Sentinels. "Mt. Reverence. Copperwatch. Whatever you want to call the ruddy east mountain with the ice levee. Have they had the Ice Mage check *that* one?"

"I *just said* that those glaciers are on stable bedrock. They are monitored because of the power station. They are fine." She groaned, rubbing her eyes for emphasis. "I'm not discounting your vision, but it may be the far future or a future with such an infinitesimal chance of happening you have already negated it. Or it may be the far past! I didn't check the history section of the library for first-age records of avalanches."

"It was precognitive," Jathen insisted. "The whole thing was. I felt it."

"Perhaps you *should* consider bringing this up with the Lady Manna," Izzy suggested softly.

Giving her a noncommittal grunt, Jathen bit into his cooling skewer of meat. Chewing silently on his food, Jathen let his mind spin out scenarios while Seren and Izzy struck up a conversation about crevasses and cornices.

Erin Manna had hinted about the extent of her long-flung visions, and she's said she won't tell people things unless it helps the situation, so it's not too much of a stretch to believe this might be similar for me. Then there's also the possibility she might have foreseen De'contes's plans to murder Rhean and Ra'vien, as well as Yvette Ashton, thusly getting Annakki and then later Hatori banished. She may have let it happen all to bring about the rise of the Balori and the return of the Red to the Ways—which seems monumentally far-fetched in addition to disturbing. But if it's true, there's a possibility that even with her having seen my vision firsthand from my own head, she might not do *anything to prevent it. After all, she also mentioned knowing about Mikkal's betrayal, but so far as I can tell, she's made no mention of it to the Grays or any other authority in the Clan Lands. But she might have only a few pieces of the puzzle*—he scanned the map once more, frowning at the line of the ice levee along the Dragon's Tongue—*as I am all too aware it can be like with prophecy.*

"Which is what I have been saying," Seren replied to his thoughts. "Though admittedly, you probably should bring up Mikkal in detail with her at some point, if only to determine if she's making plans with your visions in mind or not."

Izzy narrowed her eyes at the pair, clearly noticing the supposedly impossible telepathy going on. Jathen ignored her. If she wasn't going to tell him what the sparks meant, he wasn't going to address any other concerns.

"Maybe," he said. "Though I think the other parts of all that are something we very much *shouldn't* bring up to the Lady Manna, Seren."

"Oh, Spirit, no," she replied, mildly appalled. "It's all just conjecture anyways. You and I are probably not the first people to consider it." She smoothed her hair behind her ear then rolled up the map to replace it in her bag. Then, picking up her last skewer, she asked, "So... learn to do anything interesting with the negation yet?"

Deeply relieved to be on a slightly less disturbing—if not frustrating—topic, Jathen replied, "I'm still struggling to expand my negation aura over fresh daggers to send them through minor wards." *Well, it's worked once now, at least.* "And I tried to make a little negation bubble yesterday." He didn't mention his scheduled trainer had been knocked across the room so hard by the negated wind energy that he'd broken his arm, while Jathen had been too physically drained to get up and help for a good ten minutes.

She swallowed. "That's actually very impressive, Jathen."

"I keep telling him that," Izzy added.

"Well, it doesn't feel it," he griped, doing his best to hide the disastrous memory behind his mental wards. "My little bubble just negates, which means the energy can divert into a whirlwind or fire burst or stone spikes or a *ruddy downpour*, which causes more havoc than help. And Lady Manna isn't exactly... generous with praise. Not that I've done much *to* praise, mind."

"Well, have you at least asked her about D'ilinde? Your visions of Ra'vien and Yvette dismantling it and sending it away?" Seren asked. "She might have some insight on what happened to it... and how it got sent to *me*, of all people."

As Izzy coughed twice on her soup, Jathen shifted a bit in his chair. "We've not discussed it."

"Jathen!" Seren admonished him while handing Izzy a napkin. "She's Erin Manna. She probably knows ninety percent of the secrets on the continent."

"And you've not been in a room with her yet. And I've only had a whopping *two* lessons with her so far. The rest has been arranged sparring partners. Trust me, she's *not* a woman to ask whatever I wish of her."

Seren arched an eye ridge. "You're scared of her."

"I'd not say *scared*..." Indeed, he wasn't—not the way Annakki was, at least. "I honestly don't think she'd hurt me, but I'm not a hundred percent certain she'd also not let me get horribly maimed if she believed it'd teach me a lesson of some sort. And I don't think she'd necessarily bat an eye if I died. I doubt she'd consider it more distressing than losing a pet. A *beloved* pet—and I'm sure she'd be distraught for a bit—but ultimately, I'm a footnote in her long history and very much aware of it."

Finishing off the meat, Seren dabbed her lips with a napkin. "I think you're being dramatic. Basic common sense or propriety might keep you from bringing up De'contes, but these other things are in direct relation to your training, both as a Negater and on how to use the Artifact and where it came from. That's too important to leave in mystery over some imagined terror of a Clanswoman—a powerful

Clanswoman, mind—but, Jathen, you *aren't* Clan. You aren't as be-holden to her whims as they would be."

"No," Spinnek declared with a dire certainty that gave Jathen chills. "*Scary* aura."

Seren squirmed slightly, and Jathen snorted when he noticed goose bumps on the softer underside of her half-blood arms.

"See?" he insisted. "She's intimidating, Seren. In some respects, I'd rather have a chat with Kyanith."

"Prince Jathen!"

Turning, Jathen arched an eyebrow at the sight of Teal trotting up, weaving toward them among tables and chairs. The Dodbyen-born Tazu looked at home clothed in the crisp Monortith guard uniform of purple and gold, but his dark-scaled face was stiff with restrained worry. He stopped short at their table, panting. "Sorry... interrupt, but there's a matter that requires your particular input." Composing himself, he waved away the roll Spinnek was brandishing at him and bowed slightly. "That is, if it does not inconvenience you."

"Seems like the inconvenience is more on your side, running from the embassy to Annakki's and then here just to find me," Jathen replied. "The least I can do is hear whatever it is that requires my in-put."

"It's Rhyo, Highness."

Jathen stiffened in his chair, his heart suddenly pounding. "Is he all right?"

"Yes. At least, for now. He's recovered enough that they are re-leasing him, actually. Practically this very moment."

A long relieved sigh seeped from Jathen's lungs. As much as he was plagued by Rhyo's actions, another death from Dodbyen wouldn't have been comforting at all. "And Marcasith still doesn't think he should be housed with the rest of the refugees, I take it."

"I'm afraid it's a bit more dire than that." Teal rubbed the back of his neck. "Daughters of Desmoulein want to find him housing with the Anganites, but Marcasith is rumbling about the incident with you and, well, them taking out their annoyances on Rhyo instead. Trust all around is a mess. At this rate, he's going to end up on the streets—and when I left the embassy, there were a few choice Tazu already talking about doing him harm either on the way from the hospital or out near the embassy gate, should he head that way."

Seren shot Jathen a concerned look before frowning at Teal. "What do you mean, harm? Isn't my mother willing to accommodate his safety? Even after the incident in Dodbyen, he's still considered a Tazu Nation citizen in Tar'citadel."

"Of course, um, Lady, but she can't set guards on him every second of the day." Teal hopped from foot to foot again. "Honestly, I didn't see who was making the threats." He tapped his temple, indicating telepathy. "I only overheard them. But they were set on going to try to confront him when he tried to leave the hospital. And if that didn't work, they would 'find another way to be rid of him.'"

Jathen gritted his teeth. "Why didn't you tell Marc?"

"I did. And he said he'd sort something, but without knowing *exactly* who the problem is going to be"—Teal smiled knowingly at Jathen—"I was hoping you'd have a solution we didn't consider. As you tend to do."

Jathen laughed ironically. "And I think you already considered the solution but came here to see if I'd be all right with it." He sighed then nodded. "I'll ask Annakki if he can stay with us. I imagine, if nothing else, he'll be a sobering influence on Spinnek." He grinned at the boy, who glared back at Jathen while chewing slowly and dramatically on the roll Teal had refused.

Relief softened the line of Teal's shoulders. "Thank you." He bit his lower lip. "Are you able to come now, to help? I don't think the ambassador or Marcasith would like it if there was a scene."

"I see you've been in the world long enough to grasp the joys of politics already," Seren retorted, standing. "I need to get back to class, but he's right, Jathen—Mother will have a fit, *especially* if it happens near the embassy."

"That'd be a legitimate reaction if Tazu start squabbling to the point of gaining tar'ka-besh attention." Izzy stood also, dabbing her lips with her napkin then leaving it on the table. "We'd best go see if we can intercept Rhyo before he tries to leave the hospital. I'm sure Annakki will be accommodating once we explain the timing of the situation."

"Agreed." Cleaning his own hands off, Jathen gained his feet as well. "Come, Spinnek. We have to go help Rhyo."

The boy groaned, clearly hating to leave his buffet, but he acquiesced after stuffing his pockets with a variety of snacks. The boy nibbled along the edges of a Nor'wah meat pie as they entered the elevator, and Jathen shook his head. He bade Seren farewell as she got on another heading upward.

After the doors closed, Jathen turned to Teal. "May I ask why you've gone out of your way to help Rhyo, Teal? When so many others from Dodbyen would condemn him as a traitor?"

While Izzy arched an interested eyebrow at the question, the Tazu stepped from foot to foot, uncertainty flowing from him. "I've known Rhyo our whole lives, so perhaps it's out of a desire for comfort, to keep at least one more face out of so many lost. Yet I suppose it's for the same reason you care, that Marc cares—he meant well. He meant to do right by everyone, even our enemies, because he didn't see an enemy, he saw people—misguided people, but ones he thought he could help. And he was wrong. No one with a heart that good deserves to be forever condemned for a single mistake."

"No, I don't suppose we do," Jathen murmured. He closed his eyes, where his own past still lingered, haunting. *I'll forever regret making you go get Ishane instead of heading for Nosalia's, Ass'shiri. Might be the greatest regret of my life.*

Spirit, pray I never make any larger ones.

Outside, they had a direct view of the Tazu Embassy with its dome of gold and great iron gates. With no sign of Rhyo or an embittered crowd, they continued past it to the Temple Hospital. Once there, however, they discovered Rhyo was nowhere to be found.

"What do you *mean* he left after you read him Marcasith's note to wait here?" Jathen asked the Daughter of Desmoulein.

The Ki'ra was the same one he'd met when he first came to see the survivors, and her ears flattened against her head as she shook it. "I can't *force* the boy to stay, not after he's been discharged." She huffed, those ears twitching worriedly. "He did say he was thinking about walking by the embassy anyways, though—"

"*What?*" Jathen practically squawked. He immediately winced, realizing the Walker didn't deserve the brunt of his concern for Rhyo. "Sorry, thank you." Turning away, he headed back down the hall toward the exit, his friends all close on his heels.

"We must have passed him on the way—or he took a different route," Izzy said. "Hopefully, this city's unknown streets will delay him enough for us to intervene."

"But *why* would he go to the embassy?" Rereading Marcasith's warning note, Teal crinkled his brow ridge. "When he knows someone means to hurt him?"

"He *wants* them to." Jathen closed his eyes, understanding all too well. "It's what he thinks he deserves."

"They could kill him!"

"Suicide by mob justice," Izzy murmured. She fiddled with the top clasp of Orne's bag, turning hard brown eyes toward Jathen. "Such a thing will do no one any good—even if the guards stop it, Rhyo will most likely be turned out into the streets, and the others will seek more vengeance upon him at a later date."

"Right, we need to stop him." Jathen quickened his pace to a near run down the hall.

"I can stop?" Spinnek asked, skipping along between Jathen and Izzy.

"Ah, no, Spinnek," Jathen replied as images went through his head of what the Exemplary Talent might do to "stop" things. Practically diving through the exit door, he flinched in the bright afternoon sun glaring off the buildings and patches of snow. "When we get there, I'll handle this."

"You need to move faster than we can, though." Izzy beckoned Teal forward. "Give Jathen a ride. Spinnek and I shall follow."

"No, you need Teal to circle and search in case he's lost." An idea sparked in Jathen's mind, and D'ilinde hummed, excited by the prospect. "Spinnek, can you hit me with an energy bolt of some sort?"

Intrigued, Spinnek cocked his head.

Izzy's mouth fell open. "You want him to do *what*?"

"Give me an energy push so D'ilinde can teleport me over there," Jathen replied. "I'd tell you to do it, but you're not an energy manipulator."

"Jathen—"

"There's no time to argue," he snapped before turning back to Spinnek. "You think you can do it? Not too strong—I don't have to go far." He sputtered a laugh. "Then again, I don't think I *can* go far."

Spinnek shrugged then put a hand on Jathen's shoulder. "No bolt, just give."

Jathen felt a wave of power flow into him.

"Quicker. Better."

Ruddy hell, that boy is Talented. Jathen snuffed the rest of the thought and focused on directing D'ilinde as the world around him blurred. *To the Tazu Embassy. And don't drop me on anyone or anything weird!* The Grand Artifact seemed to huff indignantly just before he landed on the steps of the Embassy. On either side of him, two guards jumped, startled by his sudden arrival.

"What the ruddy—" Scmit blinked twice then ran one gray-scaled hand through her white hair while the other loosened the death grip she had on her long spear. "Jathen! Damn. I thought you didn't teleport without something blowing up."

"I've been working on subtlety." Jathen had no time to revel in his teleportation triumph as he straightened his shirt while scanning the area. "Have you seen Rhyo?"

"The traitorous little shit?" Her blue eyes flinched hard when Jathen glared sideways at her. "Ah, no." When the other guard—a deep-purple-scaled Tazu Jathen didn't know—gave her a sharp glower, she added, "My prince."

"Did any Dodbyen Tazu leave here recently?"

"Leave?" She exchanged glances with the other Tazu guard before admitting, "Actually, yes. Five Tazu and half-bloods, along with a few humans. They hung about up here for a bit then headed off that way in a hurry." She pointed a claw toward the center of the International Market. "Not but a few moments ago, honestly."

"Ruddy hell." Slipping between them and down the embassy steps, Jathen ordered them, "Go now. Get Marcasith and the ambassador out here and find me immediately. I'll be pursuing them."

"Right!" Scmit said, followed by a "Yes, your Highness" from the other guard.

The International Market was a massive district unto itself, centered exactly between the three citadels and oppressively crowded. Hundreds of people navigated the narrow streets in the late lunch hour, making purchases at the innumerable vendors or patronizing the various restaurants. Jathen wove and ducked as best he could while silently berating himself for not getting a better description of the group of Tazu from Scmit before gallivanting off after them. *Ruddy hell, I'd kill to be a better empathic right now.* Powerful empathic Talents could focus on a single person and detect their energy in a crowd or across vast distances. *Instead, I'm going in circles while*

Rhyo is probably getting beaten to death. Jathen clenched his fists, regretting not bidding Spinnek to follow him. The Exemplary Talent could easily have led him to Rhyo. *Stupid, not thinking things through.*

Passing a side street, Jathen felt D'ilinde buzz in his chest, urgent. Backtracking, he looked down the alley, only to catch a glimpse of a group of Tazu and humans turning down a corner farther down. A feral grin splitting his lips, Jathen darted forward to follow. *Might be stupid, but at least I've got luck living in my chest.*

Just hope I'm not too late.

His feet pounded against the cobblestones, and when Jathen finally caught up, he was too breathless to call a halt to the onslaught taking place. The group of five pure-blooded and half-blood Tazu and six humans had formed a semicircle around Rhyo, who was cowering with his back pressed against the splotchy whitewash of an unmaintained building. Calling insults and curses, the miniature mob flung refuse and rocks, one of which slammed hard next to the cowering Tazu's head, sending small chips of gravel against his shoulders.

Gritting his teeth against the rising rage, Jathen pressed forward through the little mob. Utilizing some of his Annakki-taught footwork, he didn't spare those in his way some sore toes or elbowed ribs. They protested his passage with angry calls but then stilled their voices when he turned around upon reaching Rhyo and they saw their prince. Scanning them, he recognized each and every face from Dodbyen, though he lamented not knowing their names. Still, he pitched his chin up and raised his hands high while putting as much empathic authority as he could muster into his voice. "Enough!"

As a unit, the crowd lowered their projectiles, and Jathen heaved a small internal sigh of relief, though the emotions coming from the group were still tilting on the verge of murderous. Jathen lowered his hands, not certain what to do next.

A large Tazu with pale-blue scales and silver-blue eyes, whom Jathen recognized as a relative of the fallen Spinelith, stepped forward. His claws danced across the large rock he still held. "Savior, you need to step aside and let justice be done."

Savior? Jathen brushed aside the odd moniker and crossed his arms, immovable. "I know things were different in Dodbyen, but this isn't there. What you are doing here—this is *not* justice. It's a twisted kind of self-satisfaction all of you need to give up on and walk away from."

"Walk away? And let the *traitor* walk away after what he's done? He should *pay*!" With an angry roar, he hurled his rock onto the cobbles, where it smashed into gravel. "We'd all have made it if not for him. He's the reason the sanbarna attacked! He's the reason our kin *died*!" The emotion blasting Jathen in the face was more sorrow than rage as the Tazu's fingers curled and uncurled.

"No." Jathen felt tired as he stared into the silver-blue eyes manic with pain. "We could have warned the sanbarna, just at a different time, in a different way. We *should* have. The failing belongs not just to Rhyo—it also belongs to Marc and me. We thought too narrowly. Fewer people on both sides would have died if we'd *listened* to Rhyo."

"But... but he disobeyed you and Marcasith!"

"And you aren't disobeying Jathen and me now?" Above them, Marcasith circled once in tyrn form before landing beside Jathen with a *thud*. Putting his wedge-shaped head between Jathen and the other Tazu, he practically growled, "Back off, Hauyne, unless you're fixing to dance with *me*."

Hauyne exchanged a few wary glances with his fellow disgruntled Tazu and humans and then did take a step back, though he still replied, "You can't just turn him loose, Marc. It's not enough after what he did! It's not fair he's not got to pay for the lives that were taken!"

Noting the circling form of Ambassador Chertith, Jathen sighed, stepping up in front of Marc just as Seren's mother landed on the opposite side of him and shifted to Tazu form. Before she could speak, Jathen addressed the crowd as a whole. "And when will it end? Will you feel better if you choke the life out of him? What punishment should we then level upon you for murdering a fellow Tazu?" As the crowd squirmed, Jathen focused on Hauyne, whom he assumed was the mastermind. "Look at him." Jathen put an arm out in Rhyo's direction, where the Tazu cowered with sad eyes. "Do you honestly think he isn't suffering enough? You think he doesn't carry every single one of those deaths on his conscience? *Look at him!*"

Hauyne's silver-blue eyes darted toward Rhyo, taking in what Jathen saw—a shaking youth whose own eyes were pressed tightly shut as streams of tears flowed from the corners. Hauyne swallowed hard, eyes darting back to Jathen.

"It's enough," Jathen said softly. "You don't get to decide his fate. It falls to me, Marcasith, and Bengal, and we have ruled on it. Now, get back to the embassy and mourn your dead as they should be mourned—with quiet reverence, not violence."

With some huffing and puffing but no further words, the group dispersed, most looking mollified, if not downright shamefaced. A few still had expressions of distaste, but they held their tongues and left with the rest, leaving Jathen, Marcasith, and the ambassador with Rhyo.

Jathen crouched beside the thin Tazu, where he was still cowering against the wall. "You all right?"

Rhyo raised his eyes to Jathen, the smoky-quartz color of his irises seeming foggy against the backdrop of bloodshot whites as he whispered, "I'm not certain how deserving I am of your mercy."

Jathen's shoulders slumped as he tried to conjure something to say. "I don't think it's about deserving or undeserving. My friends didn't deserve to die, but they did because I made the wrong choices... even though they *seemed* to be the correct ones at the time. I don't feel I deserved to live when they didn't. But I did. And so I'm here, and you're here, and I suppose we'll just have to do the best we can with what we have."

"And try to be worthy of it," Rhyo murmured. A tiny light of hope shimmered in his eyes as he nodded, making Jathen sigh in relief.

Standing above them, Ambassador Chertith cleared her throat. Her lips pursed just slightly, a glimmer of what might be respect fluxing around her. "That was... impressive, Prince Jathen," she said softly.

Jathen gazed at her without bothering to hide the exhaustion in his soul. "That was what needed to be done—nothing more." Not sparing her another glance, he put an arm around Rhyo, helped him to stand, and led him back to Annakki's.

Chapter 2

"You."

Purposefully ignoring Jathen's sputter of surprise, Raleigh sat cross-legged on a chair placed at the center of the disk in the Rosinic's training room. Clad in tight indigo-blue pants, with another orange Kubeshian tunic over a bold pink Beleskie shirt with billowy sleeves and under a sleeveless silver over-robe with gold trim, she also sported black-rimmed glasses perched at the very tip of her nose. She turned a page in the book she was holding, a thick thing with a deep-violet cover and the scrolling title, *Spanning Transdimensional Consciousness: A Theory on the Omnipotence of Spirit Energy*, written in gold on its spine.

"The ruddy hell are you doing here?" Jathen demanded.

Over the weeks since the incident with Rhyo, he'd become accustomed to using the space with either Erin Manna herself or one of the sparring partners she'd arranged. The sessions had been much the same, with mages of varying levels of skill and elemental usage tossing energy at him in the hopes of getting his negation bubble to work. The progress had been literally hit or miss, with Jathen several times getting himself teleported back up to Galduran's office via D'ilinde and often having to wait for the High Mage to arrive and give him the necessary energy to be teleported back. Raleigh's sudden appearance didn't improve Jathen's mood.

When she continued to ignore him, flipping another page, Jathen huffed and stomped a foot. "Fine—if you won't get out, it won't be my fault if you get hit with a stray energy bolt."

She turned another page. "I just want to finish this chapter."

"Ugh. Seren's right. You are unhinged." Jathen stabbed Hatori's sword cane into the sand portion of the floor next to the marble disk, his standard out-of-the-way place for it. "Read your damn chapter somewhere else and stop plaguing me."

"That would be counterproductive."

"Counterproductive?"

"Yes, much like repeating words already said."

Jathen crossed his arms, as much to show his vexation as to resist the urge to toss one of his daggers at her. "Do I literally need to fetch a *High Mage* to drag you out of here?"

"I doubt Galduran would do that."

"Whyever not?"

"Because, you twittering little young soul"—snapping her book shut, she glared at him with her mismatched eyes—"*I'm* your ruddy sparring partner for the day."

Caught off guard, Jathen raised his eyebrows. "You? The one who swore to all the Twelve that you wanted nothing to do with me or any Negater as long as I wasn't the Aspect for Rosin? The one who insisted I'd be better off with A'ron De'contes? Who treats Galduran like a disliked uncle? You expect me to believe *Erin Manna* somehow managed to get you to agree to work with me?"

"Yes, well..." After removing her glasses, she folded them and tucked one of the earpieces into the top of her shirt so that they hung down over the collar. "Erin had a lot more to offer than you did."

"What out of the ruddy Pit could she give you that I couldn't have?" He unfolded his arms and held them out incredulously. "Hell, you didn't even *ask* me what I could have given you!"

"Because I knew *you* couldn't give it," Raleigh retorted.

Eyeing her little curve of a smile, made more dramatic by the brilliant-blue lipstick she was sporting, Jathen suddenly understood. "Lady Manna promised to tell you where the ruddy Aspect of Rosin is in exchange for helping me train?" He barked a disbelieving laugh. "You *are* insane! How do you even know an Aspect is alive right now to find and train?"

"Pfft." Releasing her grip on her book, she huffed, and it disappeared before hitting the ground. "Young souls and your assumptions. Everything is so... *linear* with you."

Peering at her, Jathen asked, "You're the reincarnation of Sharhara, aren't you? The High Mage that Galduran told me ascended out a few hundred years ago or something."

She arched an eyebrow. "Interesting theory you have there."

"Makes sense," Jathen said with a shrug. "You work with him but don't seem to *really* defer to him, and he said you were an aspiring High Mage. You keep insulting 'young souls' and seem obsessed with topping your last lifetime's achievements by training Rosin's Aspect." He snorted. "Also, you wouldn't care if Erin Manna told you there wouldn't be an Aspect of Rosin for a dozen or so generations—if it's your intention to eventually reclaim your High Mage status from the previous lifetime." Snickering at his own genius, he added, "*And* that'd explain why you'd refer to De'contes as Marin Manna."

"Well, since you just figured it all out so neatly"—those strange eyes of hers rolled as she stood—"can we get on with this now? I do have other, more *diverting* things I'd rather be attending to."

"Well, if you aren't inclined to give me your *full* attention and experience, I could just tell Lady Manna—"

She put a hand up, literal sparks flying from it. "Do not try to blackmail me, young soul. You do *not* have the experience for it."

Jathen narrowed his eyes. "Just want to be certain you're dedicated to this."

"I don't have to be dedicated for you to learn from me, young Negater. I'm *that* damn good."

"I'll believe it when I see it." He smirked. "At least I've upgraded to a 'young Negater' from a 'young soul.'"

"Cute."

The very marble disk he stood upon tipped forward and slid him down onto his rump. Jathen cried out, panicking and trying to throw up his negation bubble. It half worked, surging slightly then popping with an audible burst and a little explosion of earth-energy dust that covered him like soot from the burned-out sector of Dodbyen.

"Ruddy hell!" He sputtered, wiping dust from his eyes. "I wasn't ready!"

"Clearly." Raleigh chuckled in pity, standing unaffected on the tilted marble even as it slowly returned to level. "A bit of advice—you will *never* be 'ready.' Ever. You know that already from the circumstances life has dealt you. Lose the whining. It's a crutch you fall back on from your sad little moot days, and I'm *not* one to put up with it."

Jathen shot her a vicious glare, and she met him with an even gaze, those blue lips pursed only slightly. *Bet there's some "kiss of death" analogy in that shade.* He gritted his teeth then nodded. *She's a brat, but she's right.* Standing, he tried to brush off more dirt. "So I suppose the day will entail you surprising me over and over again while I try to raise a bubble?"

"No. You do that on your own time with your... *amateur* mages." Fire blossomed at the ends of her fingertips. "Today is a crash course in Negater tactics and skills. You, sir, are going to start *doing* things with your extra energy instead of letting it revert."

Suddenly, Jathen was less miffed about being dirty. "Excellent!" He bit his lip, eyeing the fire slowly growing around her hand. "Um, how?"

"You've already done it a few times—to heal, to increase speed, and probably a few I missed. Technically, you can do anything a normal mage can do with energy. You just need to be whacked in the face with it first."

"Ah..." Jathen held his hands up as she raised her own. "Can I have a minute bit more direction than that?"

"Ugh." Lowering her hands with a groan, she shook her head. "Grab the energy and *think* of a use. Simple."

"Physically or mental—" Jathen yelped as she threw the fireball at him. Darting away, he actually dodged the thing, proof that Annakki's training had taken at least some hold.

"Physically *and* mentally," she clarified, another fire-flower sparking to life in her palm. She threw it with a feral grin.

Hitting him, the fire burned as Jathen tried to "grab" it, and surprisingly, he felt he had a certain hold upon the energy for a moment but failed to direct it. Interestingly, it didn't divert to earth again but rather water, forming a puddle that had him skidding across the glasslike section of artificial terrain. *She can convert more than one element easily—and store it for later.* Not an impossible feat, it was, however, rather rare and spoke volumes more of her skill than all her actual verbal declarations.

The next hour had Jathen grabbing and dodging while Raleigh spouted either insults or the odd bit of technical help at him, punctuated by groans of disgust when he didn't instantly apply the knowledge.

"Remember, you must not be arrogant, must not be fooled. Not all magic can be negated, so you must be vigilant." Energy swirled, bubbling about Raleigh, and a lightning strike hit Jathen full in the chest. It hummed and crackled through him, and he tried to catch it but failed against its immensity. Wind energy exploded, knocking him about the soft bubbly rubber portion of the floor. Raleigh spoke over the commotion, ignoring his failure. "Creation of lightning from nothing can always be negated. However, as a Storm Mage, Erin Manna's skill comes also from being able to manipulate the very particles of a cloud, of stirring the positive and negative electrons to do her bidding. You can't negate what a mage has bent in nature."

"So if I'm outside, don't piss her off," Jathen grumbled, sore, as he sat up. "Got it."

"She's not the only Talent who can dissuade you. Empathics cannot force emotions onto you, but some can fan emotions already in play. A telepath cannot affect your mind, but they can affect the minds of those around you, turning friends into foes. Mediums can speak to your spirit guides. Other nontraditional Talents can cause havoc. An ice mage will freeze the world around you, causing hypothermia or creating ice-laden ground."

"I'll remember that when I deal with an ice mage."

Looming over him as he still sat upon the ground, Raleigh thrust a hip out and crossed her arms. "You're mocking me."

"I'm mocking myself. Apart from the fact I've heard most of this already—it's all very good advice for someone who has managed to use his ruddy Ability for something—all I can seem to do with large spells is get smacked around. I can't focus enough to do more than yell at D'ilinde not to get creative with extra energy or *maybe* pop up a little negation bubble, which then knocks me around some more." He sighed long, feeling drained down to his core. "And all you are doing is reminding me of it while tossing me about for an hour, so yes, I'm frustrated and mocking myself for it."

She snorted. "Were you or were you not told by Erin Manna and High Walker Volaille of the benefits of training your mind to give the negated energy use?"

"What do you think I've been *trying* all this time?" He smacked the rubbery floor with the palm of one hand. "I just can't *think* that fast."

Above him, Raleigh cocked her head, her longer dark hair falling across the shaved rainbow side and into her lighter eye. "Sounds like what you need is to adjust your perceived responses." She fiddled delicately with an amulet hanging from a choker that had probably been jostled free from under her collar, as Jathen hadn't noticed it before. A stunning piece, it was an exquisitely bright labradorite stone glimmering in greens and oranges, with a deep-blue inclusion stripe that made the whole thing look like a dragon's eye, further supplemented by a silver setting layered to look like scales. "All right. Get up, and we'll fix this."

After tucking his legs under himself, he rolled to his feet. "Are we going to negate time now? Or somehow slow it down?"

She snorted, her tone ebbing back to irritated. "There is no way to slow time without controlling gravity or magnetic forces." She walked back over to the marble floor as Jathen followed. "Neither of which can be manipulated by any kind of Talent—same as creating organic matter."

"Mages magically throw things around all the time, and I've personally seen the Pearl's stasis bubbles and another mage craft wings and fly around on them. How are Talents *not* affecting gravity or organics?"

She huffed, rolling her eyes as she rounded on him. "Wings are an energy illusion. They can *look* organic, but trust me—they are *not* new, living organic material. And as far as supplementation, turning skin to stone or whatnot, it's very limited, and you can only do it to yourself—just ask Zhìliáo about how difficult it is to heal a body, and it usually *wants* to do that. Now, lifting objects telekinetically or holding them in place with stasis bubbles does stem from affecting energy within a unified field of matter—technically, all things are both connected and not connected. But the force itself of gravity is not affected during this alteration."

"How—"

"Think of it as if being in water. You can cause a current that moves an object far from you, but you cannot stop it from sinking on its own if you are not holding it. Talents work against the natural forces to make things move—they do not control the force itself."

"So then how am I going to gain time?"

"By holding your breath."

"I do hope you're being figurative."

"Somewhat." Twirling a finger, she explained, "This next volley, instead of trying to give the negated energy a form or purpose, I want you to focus on holding it. Hold your breath to start, as a trigger your mind can easily trace. Let's see if we can delay the redirected burst."

Jathen arched an eyebrow. "And D'ilinde?"

She snorted. "If the two of you haven't struck a deal regarding who gets first use of any additional energy, that is not my fault, Jathen."

He sighed begrudgingly as the Grand Artifact hummed a giggle. "All right. But if I teleport off somewhere, please, for the love of Spirit, find me *quickly*."

Narrowing her eyes, Raleigh zapped him with a small ball of lightning to the chest.

Jathen hissed—such attacks still stung—then inhaled as deeply as he could and held the breath. *Not for you!* he yelled mentally at D'ilinde, only to receive the emotional equivalent of an indignant huff. Amazingly, though, it worked. He felt very strange, tingling and shivering as if holding a storm within the seal of his lips. *Then again, in a way, I am.*

"Give it a use before I die of old age," Raleigh said, twirling one of her many rings.

Jathen panicked, his thoughts scattered, and the energy ruptured free, popping around him in little bursts like fireworks. "Well, at least it wasn't a whirlwind," he said once the colorful display subsided. "Or D'ilinde making off with me somewhere."

"Very true. You did alter the energy from its original state into a third option." Those penetrative mismatched eyes turned condescending again. "You need more focus, though."

"I'm trying. It's just... there're *so many* things I can do with redirecting energy. It's hard to decide on one and then hope I have enough energy to do it *or* what I want done doesn't give D'ilinde leftover energy to play with *or* the energy just turns back into what it had been and knocks me around."

"Meditation will help you to control your thoughts and better sense the levels of energy. The skill will come when you actually do that and stop being a silly young soul."

"I don't think I can just 'stop' being a 'silly young soul' without, you know, actually *living* more lives."

"Exactly." Crossing her arms again, she sported a smug little smile, but then she actually softened. "Really, though, you've made decent progress in a very short span. There's a reason Talents—especially energy manipulators—begin their training at twelve. It can take a lifetime or, in my case, several, before you can create with a thought."

Jathen resisted the urge to grin widely, as the praise warmed him more than he would've liked to admit. "What about using a tell? Lady Manna said some Talents use words or gestures to make their spells happen. Can't I do the same?"

"In case you've forgotten what you've been whining about all session, the transfer is too fast—a symptom of a Negater. You could try it, but it would probably just keep pissing you off." When Jathen snorted, she arched an eyebrow. "Exactly. Come, let's fit another try in. I do have other places to be today."

Over five more passes, Jathen managed to create firework bursts for three of them, as well as a massive headache. Still, he pushed himself, unable to shake a deep foreboding in his bones that he was going to need to use his Ability sooner than later. *I might finally be on the right path, but there was so much more to my vision than my deaths.*

"All right. We're done," Raleigh said, glancing at a timepiece fetched from her pocket. "Practice when you can and with your other partners. Erin will pick up on it when you see her again."

"Wait, that's it?" Jathen straightened up from where he'd been lying flat on the marble disk, panting. "You're not helping me again?"

"Not for *one* piece of information, no." Slipping her watch back into her pocket, she slicked her hair behind her ear with the other before plucking her glasses from her shirt and fixing them once more upon her face. "Besides, it's not as if what you've learned today isn't going to be a cornerstone for your training that will keep you busy for months on end as you try to perfect it or anything."

"All right, yes, you have a point." Jathen smirked at her. "It's just... you *are* good at this, you know."

"*That* was never in contention." Hand on her hip, she measured him for a moment. "For what it's worth, young soul, good luck."

Memories from his vision of the world cracking and breaking made his stomach tighten. "Let me guess. I'm going to need it?"

She laughed. "Luck lives in your chest for the moment. If *you* need it, what does that say about the state of the world for the rest of us?" With that baffling and mildly unnerving statement, Raleigh disappeared.

JATHEN BIT BACK A LOUD curse when a scalding bit of oil jumped up from the pan to singe his finger. "Why are we doing this instead of negation training?" he asked before sticking the marred finger into his mouth. He sucked once, which relieved some of the pain, but a blister started rising against his tongue.

"To multitask," the Lady Manna answered, chopping herbs across from him at Annakki's kitchen table while observing his pain at the stove. Pointing with her knife at the strange purple-skinned chicken cutlets lying on another cutting board, she reminded him, "You need to bread those before your oil gets too hot."

"Right, right, the breasts," Jathen muttered.

She'd been teaching him little tasks and tricks for the past month and a half, but this was the first time she'd insisted on making him truly *cook* while discussing the events of his days since she'd last been in the city. He'd managed the skinning and breaking down of the chicken without losing fingers to the knife but had gotten complete-ly lost on grinding the spices. The order in which he had to put things onto the heated pans proved problematic as well, especially when he tried to explain his lesson with Raleigh to her at the same time. Af-ter dredging the breasts first in beaten eggs then flour, he put them in the pan, where they sizzled loudly. Lady Erin cleared her throat, and he turned with a start to find her holding out a cutting board full of herbs. He groaned, taking it from her, and liberally sprinkled the green morsels onto the chicken.

"You must be able to focus on a task and execute it exactly, all while your attention is being demanded elsewhere," she continued over the rising sounds of sizzling and his irritated mutterings. "This is needed in both life and combat, to sort the many stimuli coming at you from your Abilities and to learn to judge the immediacy of physical and spiritual tasks set before you. There is no better way to learn this than in a kitchen. There is science and magic here, in both following recipes and intuition, planning out your steps and making snap decisions." She paused a moment. "Also, your butter pan is on fire."

Jathen jumped, frantic to grab the thing off the stove and transfer it to the sink.

"You ignored a sense—and an obvious one—smell. You cannot do that and succeed."

Jathen put the heels of his palms into his eyes, trying to quell the headache brewing behind them. That coated his eyelids in a thin layer of butter, making them feel weighted when opened, though that may have been fatigue. "I'm exhausted. You've been running me utterly ragged since this whole training began. How am I supposed to juggle all of this? I almost feel as stressed as in Dodbyen!"

"Were you under some impression that returning to the Tazu Nation and claiming your throne would somehow become *easier* than the events in Dodbyen? Or avoiding your vision? Or that any other task you might find yourself entangled in as a True Negater would come in a more simplistic package? Everything you have been through, Jathen Monortith, and all I put you through now is to make certain you are strong. Life, for those with Ability, never gets easier. You just get to the point where you are strong enough that it seems so."

Jathen groaned, staring at the smoking pan in the sink. It smelled of burnt garlic, butter, and herbs, caustic to his nose. "Well, right now, it seems I've ruined dinner. Or at least the sauce portion."

"Don't be silly. I highly doubt anyone of Annakki's status would leave the particulars of the supper hour to the off-chance of your culinary skill proving decent," someone said in a familiar voice.

Turning, Jathen genuinely brightened at the sight of Seren on the steps.

The pretty half-blood grinned, holding up a cloth-covered basket. "Luckily, I come bearing gluant pastries from the café. Spinnek has already stolen three, and I gave one to Izzy and Annakki each. That leaves seven to split between us." She bowed deeply to the Clanswoman, slightly tentative. "You are, of course, welcome to them as well, Lady Manna."

"Bribery to release my student early from his training?" she asked in her terse tone.

"I wouldn't dream of it." Seren tried to sound nonchalant, though Jathen could practically see waves of nervousness spewing from her. "Pastries can wait until his suffering is over for the night."

Jathen found he did not fully trust the way Erin Manna was gazing at Seren—not hostile but perhaps calculating. *Or maybe I'm just getting too used to sensing what people feel and not liking when they block it. Spirit knows Annakki still taxes me in this.*

"Very well. You may have him," Erin Manna stated, which downright shocked Jathen. "Then he resumes with Master Enillydd tomorrow morning."

"Tomorrow?" Jathen asked. Typically, when she visited, she trotted him out to their Rosinic room for more work after dinner. "No more training tonight?"

"You are always training with me," she replied, stepping past him to salvage what he'd destroyed. "You just don't recognize the extent of it."

Once they were well out of the kitchen, Seren mentally said, *All right, the three of you were correct—she* is *rather intense, even for Clan.*

Were you honestly expecting anything less from an Original?

"No." She handed over a pastry. "Annakki said only one, by the way. You'll spoil your dinner."

"As you saw, I already spoiled dinner." Jathen sighed but took it anyway, the flaky crust hot against his fingers and making his sore one throb. "Though I'm starting to feel as if I have four extra mothers: Lady Erin, Annakki, Izzy, and you."

Seren snorted. *Oh, that's exactly what I want—to be seen as your mother.* Chewing intently on the cheese-and-chocolate pastry, Jathen realized he'd just been privy to a thought she hadn't meant to send directly. She glared at him, her pretty eyes squinting. "What?"

I am *getting stronger.* Burying that thought under mental wards, he swallowed, pointing. "Spinnek's stealing another gluant."

Seren squeaked, jumping away from the basket-picking human and into Jathen. He got a wave of zaps for it, and Spinnek got whacked in the chin by the basket. The boy didn't seem to mind, though, grabbing up the four pastries that'd fallen out and scuttling off with a huge grin.

"He's like a miniature drake!" Seren huffed, a hand on her chest.

"Believe it or not, he's getting better. Annakki's and Izzy's influence, for the most part. And he's downright terrified of Lady Erin. I barely see him when she's in the house." He cocked an eyebrow at Seren, suddenly curious about her visit. "Were you here to chat about something you found while researching? If so, it might be best to continue in a place less likely to attract a certain mischievous Exemplary Talent. My room has a lock. Though honestly, if he *really* wants in, he will find a way."

"No, I just happened to pass the café after visiting my father and thought of the gluants," Seren replied. "But since you've been freed for the eve, and the snow report seems to be wrong again, I have another idea."

"Snow report?"

She shrugged, rolling her eyes. "It was supposed to be a higher snowfall tonight, but it looks like the precognitives were off again. It happens. Though it means we can abscond from here without a blizzard to sway us."

"Where?"

"You'll see." She grinned, star-speckled eyes glinting. "Let's just say I've found something else I really feel you should bring up to your teacher."

Jathen groaned. He already had a mile-long list of things he needed to discuss with the Original but couldn't gather the courage to do so. "Really, Seren? You just said you understood how intimidating she is—"

"Regardless, I think you should see this."

"Fine." Jathen popped the rest of the gluant into his mouth and chewed in a frenzy, barely finishing before he added, "Let me fetch Izzy, and we'll be off."

"See if your spider wants to come too. He might learn something as well." Her grip tightened on her basket as Jathen plucked out a second gluant, but she didn't protest. "Preferably not involving pastry pickpocketing."

Interestingly, Spinnek passed on the excursion, as he was holed up in his shared room with Rhyo and forcing the Tazu to eat pastries.

"I actually think he feels safer with me around," Rhyo said softly, a book in his lap and a partially nibbled gluant in hand. His lips played at a sad smirk, as if he didn't really believe in Spinnek's confidence in him but would humor the boy anyway. "The Lady Manna truly unnerves him." He shivered. "A shared sentiment, honestly."

Spinnek snorted while gnawing on a gluant but added nothing more.

"I don't suppose you'd want to come along, Rhyo?" Jathen offered.

The Tazu hadn't been out much since the incident with the mob, which was starting to seem worrisome. Half the time, Jathen couldn't even coax him downstairs for meals, and Spirit knew he didn't have nearly as much free time to spend on the Tazu as Rhyo probably needed from him.

"No, it's all right." Rhyo's claws played once more with the little Angani pearl he wore around his neck. He'd taken to wearing it again, which Jathen hoped was a good sign despite the overwhelming sadness seeping off him. "You two don't want me following you about."

"You wouldn't be intrusive," Seren said, rolling her eyes. "Izzy's already 'following us about,' as you put it." When the Tazu shook his head again, Seren turned to Jathen, shrugging. "Let's be off, then."

Seren led Jathen and Izzy to a part of the city he'd yet to visit, well past the Aralim and Kinawa districts and on the far west side of the Temple Citadel's street circle, full of a bevy of sprawling, stately buildings.

Jathen's curiosity turned to nervousness when he read the flags flapping outside her chosen destination. "Tar'citadel Museum of Historical and Spiritual Heritage and Evolution. A museum? Seren—" He bit his lip, stopping short at the bottom of the banded marble steps.

Intricate scrolling patterns were carved into the risers, leading up to grand double doors made of heavy bronze. Boasting an intricate geometric pattern, the doors recalled the mandala that'd been underway on the Bree floor in the Temple Citadel. The setting sun caught their shiny surface, making Jathen wince.

"The last museum I was in involved the Republic earthquake," he said.

Turning toward him from her position a few steps ahead, Seren looked at him with empathy and determination. "Oh, Jathen, I'm sorry. I should have warned you. But we're here now, and what I want to show you is inside." Descending back toward him, she stopped one step above and put a gloved hand on his shoulder. "You'll never avoid every shadow of the past, Jathen, and you'll lose out on more for trying."

Closing his eyes, he nodded. "Very well," he agreed, opening his eyes to find Seren beaming at him, which lightened his mood more than he would've liked to admit. "Show me."

Admittedly, once he was inside, the exhibits beckoned to Jathen like stars pulsing in the night. They passed an entire wing dedicated to the evolution of charms into charm-devices and processor-charms, while signs proclaimed special exhibitions on master-charms featuring lesser Artifacts. Even Izzy cooed softly in awe as they passed another exhibit dedicated entirely to the strange alchemy practiced by the Solki.

"I know, I know—it's all ridiculously fascinating," Seren said, practically pulling Jathen by the cuff of his coat, away from a display on the magical-engineering steps taken to build the citadels. "But we're here late, and the place is closing soon, and I need to show you what I want you to see."

Ignoring Izzy's amused expression as she shook her head at him, Jathen protested to Seren, "What could possibly be so vital for me to—" His breath caught in his throat when he caught sight of a tall glass case standing like a pillar in the center of the room Seren had pulled him into. Suspended inside the case, a very large hand-and-a-half sword glittered under the lights. "Is... is that—"

"Yes," Seren said with a grin, hands clasped triumphantly behind her back. "The Shatari. They bring it out from the storage vault only a few times a decade."

"The Sword of the First King," Izzy whispered.

Jathen swallowed, more overcome than he'd expected to be. "Jathen's sword."

He approached it with reverent steps, almost tiptoeing up to the glass while Seren and Izzy hung back, watching. The golden hilt was a singular work of art, so much so that Jathen couldn't fathom how it would actually function in a real swordfight. Where hilt met the blade was shaped like a female human, her dress flowing down to serve as the rain guard, while a pair of dragon wings arched from her back and downward as one cross-guard. A second loop-guard was shaped like the wings of a bird—or perhaps an angel—curled upward, back toward the rest of the grip, which had tightly twisted coils mimicking a dragon's tail. That design continued up the grip to the pommel, where the edge of the little gold tail could be seen wrapping thrice around a diamond so large that Jathen would have trouble circling his index finger and thumb around it. *The* blade, *though*. It wasn't metal but some kind of gigantic stone, faceted and sparkling. Jathen inched closer, aware of D'ilinde's buzz as he circled the case. "What is it *made* of, Seren?"

"Honestly, I'm not sure. All the texts say the hilt is what was fashioned from Montage's crystallized heart and is the main Grand Artifact portion, but nowhere is it mentioned what the blade is. Researchers who've studied it think it's some sort of mage-created mineral, probably akin to diamond and probably made by Orrick Ashton, but he's never confirmed."

"I can bet Erin Manna will prove just as tight-lipped on the matter," Jathen replied with a smirk. Putting one hand up, he knew touching the case would probably set off a ward alarm—or he'd inadvertently negate it—but he couldn't resist getting as close to the sword of his ancestor as possible. He felt a deep pulling in his soul, as if he were directly connected to it, this Grand Artifact made of the blood and bone of Montage himself.

The sword buzzed.

Jathen leapt away from it, heart throbbing as D'ilinde pulsated with high trills. Seren laughed, and he turned her way, baffled.

"The ruddy hell? Were you *expecting* that?" he asked.

"I wasn't really expecting *anything*, though I did think there might be a chance *something* would happen." Still grinning at his and Izzy's startled expressions, Seren walked to the case. "I found it in my research. The Shatari, Jathen, is a Negater's sword—and I don't mean just because the First King was one. It was *specifically* made to supplement a True Negater's Abilities, though, of course, the details on that are a bit fuzzy." Stopping beside him, she shrugged. "I assumed putting you near it might be... interesting."

D'ilinde continued its high-pitched, agitated buzzing, loud enough that Seren heard it. She arched an eye ridge in its general direction, and Jathen rubbed his chest. "I think you upset it. I get the distinct sense it feels as if the sword were somehow encroaching on its territory."

"Ha. Well, I don't think the Shatari is going to go merging with your chest anytime soon." She flipped her hair, smirking. "So D'ilinde really shouldn't be so possessive. Besides, it's *your* heart, after all. You should get to choose what you want in it."

Or who.

Her thought caught him off guard again, along with the sadness in her eyes. She glanced away, and for a moment, he worried she knew he'd heard, but she sighed lightly instead. "Anyway, I think this might be worth bringing up to Erin Manna. Given your penchant for getting into trouble, it might do to know if there's any precedent for what happens when two Grand Artifacts come into contact with one owner."

Spirit, he wanted to *do* something, *say* something. It would be so easy to just catch the bottom of her chin and tilt her head up—she was only a few scales shorter—and kiss her. Such a simple act, to carry such a massive weight of tribulations, past and future. Even the setting was too similar. He was all too aware of Izzy hanging back and looking on the way Ass'shiri had done when Jathen had kissed Ishane in the Zirconia Building the day of the earthquake. *And the future...* No matter how brave a face Jathen put on for Ambassador Chertith, she was correct—Seren didn't have an easy future if she went down that path with him. *Or any future at all, if any of my visions prove true.* So he held back, putting his hands in his pockets and lamenting his cowardice.

"Yes" was all he could conjure while reinforcing his mental wards. He swallowed, his thoughts rolling beneath his imagined greenhouse. "Though I very much doubt anyone is going to unlock this case and let me have it, I'd also like to know what, exactly, a Negater's sword is supposed to *do*."

"That may also be useful," Seren replied with a certain playfully sardonic air.

"I can actually speak on what happens with more than one Grand Artifact," Izzy said, stepping up between them to view the sword.

"Really?" Jathen asked, secretly relieved she'd broken the tension. "From the Solki?"

Izzy nodded, solemn. "I do not know much, but it was inferred that it is very dangerous to wield more than one Artifact in general, let alone the Grand ones. The Solki have legends of those who'd tried. They always ended in madness and death."

"I am, sadly, not surprised," Jathen murmured. When a tone rang out through the museum then, indicating its imminent closing, his shoulders slumped slightly. "I suppose that's the end of our little trip."

They parted ways from Seren on the steps outside though Jathen desperately didn't want to. He couldn't summon the courage to act on his deeper feelings, but the tug to be near her while he was able had a strength to it that he couldn't quite bear at the moment. "You certain I can't convince you to grab something else to eat? It'll give Izzy and me an excuse to avoid eating the travesty I left back at Annakki's."

"No, not tonight," she stated. "I'd intended a short visit today, and I need to be off. I transferred into that Grand Prophecy class, and I need to catch up on some reading before the lecture tomorrow morning. That, and the snow might still show up tonight. Anyway, I filled up on gluants." Seren smiled thinly, displaying her empty basket.

Doing his best to keep his disappointment from showing in his face, empathy, or thoughts, he asked, "See you soon?"

Seren regarded him for a moment with an interesting expression Jathen couldn't quite interpret, and he wondered briefly if he'd failed in his subterfuge—and if it would really be so terrible if he had. "Our mutually odd schedules might prevent it," she finally replied, stepping off the curb. "But I'll see what I can do."

With a sinking feeling of regret, Jathen watched her go then turned back toward Izzy, ready to return to the townhouse. They walked in silence for a while until Izzy made a little noise in the back of her throat.

Jathen shot her a very long sideways glance. "Not a word."

Her brow tattoos twitched. "I said nothing. And I know you don't hear my thoughts."

"I know you well enough to estimate them." He pulled up his collar against the cold, every glare from every high-blood he'd ever passed in hallways during mating season suddenly running through his head at once. "And Orne's."

Izzy exhaled, voicing a deep sadness in the breath. "I very much doubt you'd guess Orne's thoughts on any of this, Jathen." Quiet for a few steps, she then added, "But those who've never... *felt* a certain way truly should not pass judgment or presume to advise those who do."

Jathen arched an eyebrow at the fauni. "Is that Orne speaking or you?"

"Both." So softly he barely caught it, she whispered, "I'd not have Orne's regrets be yours, Jathen."

"And what are those regrets?"

Though he waited, Izzy held her tongue. A few small snowflakes drifted down from above, and Jathen knew the conversation was over.

D'ILINDE HUMMED, PACING out its vibrations to the sounds of the Endless Opus, echoing in Jathen's ears as well as his chest.

With his eyes closed, his whole world was that sound, the intensity so strong that his teeth vibrated in time with the Artifact.

"Are you all right?"

Opening his eyes, Jathen readjusted his grip on Hatori's unsheathed sword cane as he turned toward Rhyo. The Tazu was sitting near him in the solarium, smoky-quartz eyes concerned. His claws curled around the crystal music player, his posture meek but indicating a readiness to help. Jathen had given him the charm-device to operate since the iungo plant hated him for being a Negater, and simply as something for Rhyo to do. One thing Jathen had learned about grief was that having something to occupy oneself—even as trivial as sweeping a floor—provided purpose.

"I'm fine." Jathen adjusted his position upon the slate floor tiles. Kneeling still agitated his bad leg from time to time, but he didn't want the sword polish to get on any of Annakki's lovely hardwoods, nor the solarium's wrought-iron chairs or table. Turning his attention back to the sword, he took the soft cloth Master Enillydd had provided him and began running it over the blade again.

Their morning lesson had somehow migrated from him telling her about his visit to see the Shatari to a sudden stern lecture from the Kubeshian about sword maintenance and his *horrid* neglect of his piece. Jathen had not been *completely* disrespectful—having wiped it down and done his best to keep Okten guts out of the sheath—but he'd not really taken the time to properly clean and oil the blade since acquiring it, either.

"Which would have wreaked a certain level of havoc with a *normal* blade," Enillydd had told him. "You're just lucky Clan steel is shit, and they have to magic the ruddy hell out of their sheaths to protect them."

And she's right. Whatever magic was on this to keep it from degrading is probably gone now, thanks to my negation. And it means too much to me to let it decay. He smiled at the black steel, admiring the subtle swirling pattern to the blade. Clan steel was folded many times to remove impurities. Enillydd *had* also tried to sell him on acquiring a better blade—Clan steel was not known for its strength, only its rarity—but Jathen wouldn't have it. The sound of the Endless Opus once more vibrated down his arms into the sword. *You're more valuable to me as you are. My Negater's sword, as it were.*

"You just seem so... *focused*," Rhyo commented softly, still barely speaking above a whisper.

"I *am* focusing," Jathen replied. "The music, you see... It's to create a different mental structure. I've been having too hard a time thinking about expanding my negation aura over things when I'm also trying to maintain the mental wards and keep D'ilinde from using extra energy. So I had the idea to use the music to help me focus since it doesn't distract D'ilinde. I can easily play it in my head when I want to expand the negation bubble while still also thinking about my buildings for my mental wards. All those rising notes, all the cresting melodies... It *feels* like the bubble growing and strengthening. At least, that's the goal."

After putting down the cloth, he examined the black steel for nicks and, finding none, laid it across his knees. He went to pick up the sword oil Annakki had given him but sighed instead, rotating his neck. He rubbed the spot where the base met his shoulder, feeling sore and drained after even such a simple usage. "You can stop the player for now," he told Rhyo.

The Tazu nodded, and the music ebbed out.

Finally picking up the oil, Jathen shook a few drops onto a new cloth. "I just wish it didn't drain me so much."

"I think you've done well. You didn't even know how to do anything back in Dod—" Rhyo's eyes widened in the direction of the doorway.

Turning, Jathen found Erin Manna there, clad in her simple black dress. He bit his lip, surprised, as he wasn't scheduled to see her until much later in the afternoon, and the Lady didn't tend to intrude on Annakki's household unless for a direct purpose. Indeed, she and Annakki were rarely in a room together, though Jathen gathered that had more to do with Annakki's admitted terror of the Original than any scheduling conflicts. *At least she's far subtler in her expression of it than Spinnek.* Just the previous evening, the Exemplary had had an unexpected run-in with the Lady Manna after Jathen and Izzy returned from the museum, and Spinnek had actually *teleported* away. When later questioned about it, Spinnek insisted he didn't know how he'd managed it, though it'd taken him a good twenty minutes to walk back from whatever corner of Tar'citadel he'd taken himself to.

The Original strode into the room, taking it over with her presence in the same way vaulted ceilings automatically made the eyes sweep upward—one did *not* turn away from Erin Manna. "Using music to form the negation bubble is commendable. Any insight from Raleigh?"

"Sort of." Jathen squirmed a little, debating whether to mention that he'd come up with it after seeing the Shatari. Meeting Lady Manna's mirrorlike eyes, he decided not—at least for the time. "I'm just trying to 'be creative,' as she put it. High Walker Plajă gave me the music, and it just... made sense to piece it together this way." He smirked. "I'm starting to admit all these Talents have a penchant for subtle nudges."

"It's temporary, though," Rhyo said, rising to his knees. He shrank back when Lady Erin's golden eyes fell on him. He mumbled, "Until Jathen has better memory of the song."

"Wise." Her gaze actually seemed doting as it fell back on Jathen. "You've applied your lessons well, I see."

"Thank you," Jathen replied, bowing his head slightly. Her complements were rare, so he decided then would be as good a time as any to find out a few things. "If I might venture to ask after some things that have been bothering me, Lady Manna?"

She arched an eyebrow then nodded.

Swallowing, Jathen started with the concern that seemed the least volatile for the Lady herself. "You'd mentioned at our second lesson that you were aware of the renegade Gray at the summit with me. I ask you, how much did you discern? Did you know his exact name and motivations? And have actions been taken against him back in the Clan Lands?"

"Yes."

"Yes?" Jathen risked a glance at Rhyo, who still looked too intimidated to be befuddled. "So Mikkal *has* been arrested or some such?"

Erin Manna stared at him with an expression both penetrating and completely blank. "The direct answer to that is no, Jathen."

"Well, why not? He's responsible for the deaths of *thousands* of people from the Republic, not to mention his part in the Kidwellith quake! I know it was just my word against his, and because I'm a Negater, I can't be read, so I've been under the impression I couldn't pursue it, but since *you* saw it, surely you can do something."

"I told you, Jathen, that actions have been taken."

"Well, what other actions could you possibly...?" Something dawned on him, and he closed his mouth and eyes. "You're talking about that 'group,'" he said, referring to the Shadow Court but censoring himself for Rhyo's sake. "*They're* handling Mikkal."

"In part, yes," she confirmed. "Though it is also, in part, the need to see what happens. Your Gray is marked by destiny, entangled with your own—indeed, with a greater whole of the world." She sighed very softly, well-manicured nails catching the light as she smoothed out her sleeves. "He may be needed."

"Needed?" He bit his lip, feeling slightly sick. "Does this have some connection to the vision I saw that I showed you?"

"Yes."

"I... I don't understand." He tightened his grip on the sword and the oil rag, inadvertently tearing the latter. "He caused so much death. How could he be needed to *prevent* it? I just... I need to know he will pay for the horrors he unleashed—and not in some abstract karmic 'after we die' way but in the world as he is now."

"Jathen, a foundation is just being poured, and you're demanding I tell you what kind of window treatments I want to hang to match the parquet. A dozen things—a thousand, a hundred thousand—can happen between now and what you desire to know that could change what you would want or even do. This is the same as with your vision. The very act of seeing it changed every choice you made and led you to a different end. Wait. Trust."

Jathen groaned, resisting the urge to tap the sword's pommel on his forehead. *There really is nothing worse than Clan cloak and dagger mixed with the ambiguity of a precognitive.* Rhyo shot him a terrified glance, a reminder he was still in the presence of an Original, but Jathen snorted, unmoved. *This doesn't bode well for the multitude of other questions I want to ask.*

"Imagine for a moment if your uncle kills Skaniss before allowing you to interrogate him regarding who motivated him to attack you," she put forth. As Jathen pursed his lips, those bright lips of hers curled slightly. "It is about more than you see, young Tazu. It is about threads of fate yet unwoven, of secrets which need ferreting out. Trust." Cocking her head while he tried to digest her words, she asked, "Do you know how Hatori Rheadani came to own that cane?"

Twisting it in his grip, Jathen eyed the onyx-striped amber of the hilt with new scrutiny. "I assumed he made it."

"He did not." Putting out a hand, she waited but a moment before Jathen handed over his only physical tie to the departed charm master. Running two fingers lightly over the blade's edge, she stared blankly at the black steel as she spoke. "Hatori Chann kept two items with him when he was banished from his home. The first was a mundane, albeit well-crafted, pocket watch created by the hands of Yvette Ashton. She had given it to him at the completion of his training as a private joke between them, that 'not all items of value have to be charms and thusly magical in nature.' The other was this cane. This was crafted for him by his niece, Boleyn Rhe'a, before she Awakened."

Jathen arched an eyebrow, surprised to discover Ra'vien was the artisan who'd forged the cane, yet also validated by it—the sword might not have been an Artifact, but Boleyn's connection to it meant her interest in him as a spirit made quite a bit of sense. He didn't share his revelation, however, saying instead, "I'm surprised they let him have a weapon."

"He did not request it. I took it to him, the night before his wife leapt to her fate. It was meant as a kindness, an honorable weapon of love, to end his own life rather than suffer a Clan execution. He did not use it—not even after Sacora's suicide."

"What is a Clan execution?" Rhyo asked, looking mildly terrified the moment the words left his lips.

Erin Manna explained in a deadened tone, "The condemned is released into a surrounded wood, hunted, caught, and *drained*."

"You're right." Jathen shivered deeply and noticed Rhyo flinched hard as well. "What you did was a kindness."

"You did not know Hatori Rheadani when he was young." She sighed softly, sounding almost regretful. Putting out her other hand, she waited but a moment before Jathen gave her the cane sheath. "His pride was his undoing."

"He really did give De—er, You Know Who, soul-sever blades?"

She returned the sword to its cane, snapping it together with an overly loud click. "The very ones that killed Car'son and Boleyn, yes."

Jathen's stomach rumbled. "But Hatori couldn't have possibly known what he'd been planning. And he was highly ranked, wasn't he? The right hand of Rhean or something?"

"The appointed chancellor, yes." She held the cane back out, and Jathen took it. "But Hatori did not check with his cousin the emperor, nor his wife, Hatori's own niece and ward. He did not even mention the acquisition to them. That was deemed suspicious by the Grays—by many."

"But surely you *know* it wasn't like that," Jathen said, overly aware of Rhyo, sitting there, hanging on every word. *Quite the parallel, indeed.* "He didn't want them to die. You Know Who manipulated him."

Folding her hands delicately one atop the other over her abdomen, she replied, "Jathen, while I did not agree with the death sentence the Grays leveled upon Hatori Rheadani, I did not disagree with his guilty verdict. We are responsible for our actions—well-meaning or not. Hatori could have prevented deaths and misery simply by mentioning a conversation to one of several people, but he chose not to. And why? Because he believed he knew best. He believed his judgment was superior to that of Rhean, all because A'ron De'contes used smooth words and played to his ego—a seemingly small sin at the time but one with the direst of consequences."

Jathen bit his lip, having naught else to say as he exchanged a quick glance with Rhyo, who sat silent, looking miserable. Thinking of Hatori as guilty grated on Jathen—the man was so much more than a single bad decision—and indeed, so too was Annakki, though he had no idea what had gotten her banished. *And Rhyo.* "By your logic, then, *I* got him killed, along with Jephue and Ass'shiri. My choices, my consequences, yes? Should I be set for execution as well?"

"It was not your hand wielding the blade nor lighting the fire," she replied firmly then added more gently, "As said, I did not agree with the sentence leveled, Jathen."

"So," Rhyo whispered, sounding slightly braver, "what would you have given him?"

A little smile played on her lips, almost kind. "I assume you're unaware I serve still as the High Judge in the highest court in the Clan Lands."

"Actually, that reminds me," Jathen said. "Why didn't you oversee Hatori's trial?"

"It was entrusted to the Grays."

"Oh." Jathen fiddled with the cane, uncertain what point she was trying to make. "You didn't say how you would have sentenced him."

"Indirect treason due to misappropriation of materials and criminal neglect. The minimum sentence would be the seizure of some lands and titles. Maximum would be forfeiture of all lands, fortune, and titles, and I assure you, many a Clansman would have taken his own life directly after hearing that. I'd also have made Hatori resign as Imperial Charm Master."

"That... sounds incredibly fairer than even banishment."

She nodded, then her gold eyes darted poignantly to Rhyo. "Hatori was guilty, but we can still love him despite it. The trick is knowing who will rise up and be worthy of that forgiveness."

Jathen bit his lip, glancing at Rhyo even as he wondered if she was also alluding to Annakki and her many sins. The Tazu sat fiddling with the crystal recorder in his lap, not raising his eyes toward them.

"Thank you, Lady," Rhyo whispered, voice deep with emotions—too many for Jathen to sort with his empathy Ability.

"All things in their proper time." Erin Manna nodded ever so slightly. Gazing back at Jathen, she declared, "Regardless, I came to inform you that I shall be forgoing our training for the afternoon."

"Oh?" Jathen sighed despite himself. Though he still had innumerable questions for her, talk of normal things was welcome after such intense conversation. "More High Court duties, then? Shall I expect another sparring partner in your place? I'd love to know if you have anything else you can bribe Raleigh with."

"Amusingly enough, in the end, you'll do more to further Raleigh's happiness than she would possibly be willing to fathom."

Jathen's eyebrows shot up, and his heart nearly leapt from his chest. "Please tell me I'm not really the Aspect of Rosin after all."

Erin Manna shook her head, firm. "No, you are most decidedly not."

Jathen sighed with immense relief while thoughts of his weird life ladder results and his cowardice about asking his mother died down inside his mind. *I really do need to ask Mother, though.*

"Regardless, much progress has been made the last few weeks. A day to relax seems appropriate."

"A day?" Jathen blinked repeatedly at her. "You said just the afternoon a moment ago. And we already skipped last night."

"In honesty, I've another obligation—lunch with Ophisa and one of his Masters, who teaches a course on one of my writings. I'm uncertain how long it will take me. Such discussions can lend themselves to long hours when dealing with overly intrigued academics."

Jathen stifled his suspicion that he knew exactly what 'one of her writings' was. Instead, he let an amused smirk play on his lips. "You and Hatori shared such sentiments. Though I imagine you bear them better than he did."

"Indeed. My motivations are more for Ophisa's sake. It is always good to be owed favors, even small ones, from High Mages."

"I'll remember that."

She nodded. "Regardless, I thought it best you be left to your own devices for the most part. It's been a duration since you've spent any time dedicated to your own pursuits."

"True enough. Though Izzy is off escorting Spinnek for the next few hours," Jathen said.

She'd been trekking him over to the university and the other Ways the past few weeks during Jathen's sparring time, as he was safe enough with Erin Manna, and any measures to prevent Spinnek from wreaking havoc on the city's quartz supplies were welcome. Jathen scratched the back of his neck. "I'll need to find myself an escort. Maybe I can get Annakki to summon one of those guards she always has. If they aren't ghosts or something."

Erin Manna ignored his jest. "I thought you were one to shy away from bodyguards."

"In the past, yes, but—"

"Will it mollify you if I say I see no fights or repercussions if you venture out alone today?" she asked.

"So I can go and punch a tar'ka-besh unmolested?" Admittedly, the idea of landing a blow to Burjiro's jaw was a pleasant imagining. "Sounds like an eventful day."

The nine-thousand-year-old Clanswoman actually crossed her arms, a warble of mild amusement flitting off of her for a moment. "Within reason."

"We did agree that perhaps some recreation would do you some good," Annakki added, entering the solarium with Dor'rhean on her hip. The child squealed as she bounced him, earning a slight smile from even Lady Erin.

"Might be nice," Jathen admitted, standing. Pain tweaked his bad leg slightly but faded quickly. "I know it's been ages since I spent the day leisurely with you and Dor'rhean."

"And even longer since you've been out for something aside from training for any extended period." Annakki smoothed her son's hair. "I mourn Dor'rhean's lack of experiences beyond the yard. But for his safety's sake, I cannot risk his exposure to the world. Do not condemn yourself to the confines of a place if you do not need to."

"I suppose." Walking over to them, Jathen let Dor'rhean wrap Jathen's finger in his chubby little hand, blowing bubbles and giggling. "It's been a while since I've seen Setsu or Esop. Cy'shā and Hkym might be around too. And, of course, there's everyone at the Tazu embassy."

Pallotos, too, crossed Jathen's mind. He'd not found the time to seek out the moot captain. Rhyo made a soft, sad sound, and Jathen suddenly regretted his casual talk about the embassy. Turning back his way, Jathen offered, "You could come out with me if you like. See some of the city? Meet my other friends?"

He shook his head, not looking up. "No. It's all right. I'm not ready yet. Go find Seren. She'll go with you to see everyone, I'm sure."

"Interestingly, Ophisa remarked this morning when planning lunch that the girl had missed her morning class. She'd only just transferred into it, so he found it rather unusual." Lady Erin cocked her head, unbound red hair shimmering in the light. "She is the one from last night, the Ambassador's daughter, correct?"

"Seren? Yes, you met her." Jathen frowned, pulling his hand away from Dor'rhean. "She's unwell?"

"I'm afraid I'm unenlightened beyond what I've conveyed."

"I doubt that," he replied, managing to repress a snort. Worry mulled around inside Jathen despite the Lady's knowing smile. His "see you soon" comment when they'd last spoken had warped into a restless night of worried dreams. Seren's absence both pained and relieved him, but the thought of her actually missing the class she'd been so eager to attend tipped the scales to concern. He doubted very much that Erin Manna had mentioned it based on a premonition of true danger—more likely, Seren had a cold and could use someone to bring her soup or claim some notes for her classes. And Lady Manna's clear attempt to get him to leave wasn't lost on him. Annakki had clearly come to push him out as well, and he was curious as to what the pair combined were nudging him toward.

It's been far, far too long since I've checked in on certain people, trusting that they'll understand because of their knowledge of my circumstances. Seren's done so much for me. If she needs me in some capacity, I must help.

"Right. I'd best check on her," Jathen declared. "If she's well, we'll go see a few other friends."

He pinched Dor'rhean's cheek on the way out, grinning as the child tittered in delight. He also caught a glimpse of Erin Manna's expression—something deep and powerful seemed to glint out from those molten eyes of hers for a moment. Jathen swallowed, intuition prickling with an energy unidentifiable as either good or ill.

Chapter 3

J athen knocked softly. "Seren?"

No response. He knocked again. Nothing. After knocking once more, he put his ear to the wood. Something like a low moan reached his ear. Biting his bottom lip, he debated a moment then dug into his coat for the spare key he still had. He put it into the lock and slowly opened the door.

"Seren," Jathen called again, worried as he stepped inside, "are you sick?"

A lump beneath the blankets on the bed moaned, shifting closer to the headboard. *Well, that's a point of evidence in the "sick" column.* Despite her obvious discomfort, Jathen relaxed slightly in the knowledge that Seren had only succumbed to a virus and not something direr. He closed the door behind himself with a gentle click. "Have you been down to the infirmary?"

Another little groan answered in what he could reasonably interpret as a "no."

"Do you want me to take you?"

"Go away," she rasped, her voice breathy under the sheet. A distinct slap of emotion came with it, enough to stop Jathen short in his tracks. Still, that wasn't pain—more like embarrassment.

"I'm not leaving until I know you're all right," he replied, lightly forceful.

She moaned again, kicking her legs enough that her blue toes stuck out from under the sheet. "Please, just go!" *"Oh, Spirit in Heaven, make him stay."*

Arching an eyebrow at her contradictory thought, Jathen took a hesitant step forward. Seren might chafe against her family, but she had a touch of Chertith pride on occasion, and being sick while not wanting to admit she needed help would fit that bill.

"Do you *really* want me to go?" he asked.

Another moan escaped from under the sheet, sounding more like a whimper. "No."

Sighing lightly at the pathetic sound, Jathen closed the gap and sat down on the end of the bed. Seren scuttled away, her exposed toes curling against her feet as she plastered herself up against the headboard.

"Do you really think I care how you look while sick?" Jathen asked, trying to keep the laugh out of his voice.

"No."

"Do you want me to bring a houlen up here to examine you?"

"No."

"Maybe bring some food?"

"No."

"But you don't want me to go?"

She made a little gasp. *"No."*

Running a hand across his scalp and pulling slightly at his braid, Jathen sighed in frustration. "Well, ruddy Red, Seren, what *do* you want?"

She whimpered again, rocking back and forth under the sheet.

This is getting us nowhere. Reaching out, Jathen snatched the edge of the cloth and yanked it off her head. "Spirit, Seren, you're all flushed!"

Worry crept back into his thoughts as he took in her purple-tinted scales. Glassy eyes gazed back at him, her pupils dilated so that only a thin circle of blue ringed them.

"You *have* to have a fever."

"I feel hot," she said, breathy again. She slumped forward, unfolding onto her side but raising her chin to hold his gaze despite being upside down. "Don't go."

"Obviously," Jathen murmured, feeling her forehead.

She sighed as though enjoying a cooling touch. Sweaty, her scales were only warm, not direly feverish as he'd expected. The little sparks crackled against his skin, fiery.

"Well, something is evidently wrong with you," he said, pulling his hand away.

Seren struck like Tinzy pouncing on a bug, snagging his hand with both of hers. After breathing deeply at the inside of his palm, she kissed it, the tiny fork of her pink tongue darting against the skin there. "You taste good."

"Seren, what are you—*oh*." He balked, abruptly realizing what he'd inadvertently walked into. *That's right—she's nineteen now. Tazu girls go through their first heat around then... er, now. And the first is always the most... intense.*

A child of his mother's first heat, Jathen knew it had always, *always* been an unspoken theory that Rhodonith Monortith had bypassed propriety and coupled with an "inferior" Tazu in the fervency of the moment, producing him, a moot. Jathen had consistently frowned upon the idea of his righteous mother ever doing such a thing, but upon seeing the blazing desire in the golden flecks of Seren's blue eyes, he was suddenly more apt to believe.

He also realized he was probably too close to be prudent.

Seren rolled onto her hands and knees, pinning his palm beneath. "Did you know scent is directly related to how compatible two people's life ladders are—and thusly the quality of their offspring—and Tazu are particularly sensitive to this?" She crept closer and closer, taking longer and longer breaths of the air around him. "The more pleasing the smell, the more compatible the mate."

"I am aware," he agreed tentatively, wide-eyed as he somehow managed to yank his hand away without hurting her.

"*Oh*, Jathen." She buried her nose in his neck, breathing deeply of his flesh. "Do you have any idea how *good* you smell?"

"You, um, smell very nice too," he stammered.

Seren was pumping out pheromones in heady waves, the perfumed musk making him dizzy, along with the empathic wave of longing spouting from her. He swallowed, feeling his own body temperature rising in response.

"But right now, I'm the *only* Tazu-scented male in the room, Seren," he tried to reason while struggling to get away. The bedsheet slipped as he tried to scoot back, making him tilt sideways and dangle half off the bed. "This is obviously the heat talking—"

"Oh, you *always* smelled good," she disputed, claws curling tight around his collar and nose nudging hungrily into the hollow of his throat. "Like crystallized amber and gold dipped in chocolate and cucumbers."

"Seren, that doesn't even make any sense," he rebutted.

She'd pinned his left leg with one knee, and his attempt to wiggle out from under her without landing on the floor wasn't working. If he spent too much longer in such close proximity to a Tazu female in full heat, the battle of will with his loins would be lost. He already felt overheated, and her obvious attempt to open his shirt was far, far too much temptation. She licked sporadically across his collarbone, teasing as she tasted the beads of sweat forming there.

"You aren't exactly in your right mind at the moment." He gently tried to pry her seeking hands from his shirt. Twisting, he managed to right himself, but his lower back was pinned against the footboard.

"No, I am *more* in my right mind now than ever." Her husky voice resonated somewhere between a purr and a growl.

Twisting her wrists, she used his tactic against him, twining their fingers together and leaning more into his chest. Small but perfect breasts pressed against him through thin layers of cloth, and Jathen had to literally bite down on his lips to keep from groaning outright. His self-control was slowly crumbling into Tazu mating instinct, and she knew it.

"Come on, hatched-blood," she whispered, wiggling in his lap. She squeezed his hands, those little zaps suddenly sensual in their tickling intensity as they ran up his arms. "I know you want me. I *feel* it in you. *Hear* it in your thoughts."

"Of *course* I do!" He rallied, pulling his head back as she tried to kiss him. "But not like *this*, Seren."

"Why not?" Pretty eyes darting back and forth as vulnerability seeped through the hunger of the heat, she begged, "Isn't this our way, the way of Tazu? Why wouldn't you want this?" Her fingers loosening from his, she pulled back slightly, her expression in turmoil as she whispered, "Or me?"

"Oh, Spirit in Heaven, *Seren*—" He flinched hard, miserably awash in conflicting emotions.

Of course he wanted her in heat—the primalness of it, the carnal force of a once-feral existence that permeated every Tazu's blood, even a moot's. Their entire culture was built around the instinctual drive to breed and create a generation anew. And Seren, half-blooded, sweet, intelligent, gorgeous Seren, seeping waves of pheromones meant to encourage him—Jathen could barely hold onto sanity for all the fire running through his veins. Shaking his head did little to clear it.

"It's nothing to do with that. You just... By Beleskie, Seren, would you choose *me* if you weren't so riled up?" he exclaimed.

"Do you think I'm that far gone? I'm not incapacitated. I'm in heat!" She pulled back though, trembling, her hands still entangled with his. Jathen bit his lip again, heart torn between knowing she was right and wanting to do what was right for their futures. He'd been warned about Tazu females in heat—how it amplified their emotions overall and how dangerous they could be. If one wanted a male, she'd very clearly make it known, and if she didn't, well, a few Tazu males sported some nasty muzzle scars from trying to get too familiar with a Tazu female who wasn't interested. Seren, however, very much was—despite everything they both knew would happen if they tried.

"Can you walk away now, Jathen Monortith, if you want to?" she asked.

His heart pounded, and his head heaved with unbridled want, but if he had to, he could make for the door, leaving her behind to ride out the heat on her own. "Yes."

"Then so can I." Her eyes welled up as tremors came more quickly across her body. "But I don't want to." She tightened her fingers and moved into his space once more. Nuzzling, she mouthed around the spot where his ear met his neck, light little love bites that set every hair on end across his entire body. "I have *always* wanted you," Seren confessed as he trembled. "So badly..." Her voice choked slightly. "So dearly."

"Oh, ruddy hell," Jathen moaned, head spinning.

A wave of overwhelming pleasure overtook him, and he couldn't breathe without gasping. He'd been fighting the feeling for months, but sometime between Seren going with him to Ass'shiri's funeral and him yelling at her mother for trying to keep them apart, he'd fallen in love with her. Even with her sitting on his lap, he didn't want to broach that reality, though—didn't want to face another relationship after Ishane. But Spirit, Seren smelled good too. *Like Tazu musk and sandalwood.* His neck feeling rubbery, he found his face lolling around to rest in her hair. With a single intake of breath, the pungent tincture of pheromones washed over and drowned him. Heart pounding, he trembled harder, lost in a rose-tinted sea of pure want.

"Swear to me you won't regret this," he managed to beg, his resolve shattering.

I would never, she promised in his head then whispered in his ear, "*They* don't tell me who I want, Jathen."

Turning his head, Jathen could only hope as the last of his will died and Seren's lips found his. With one long, earth-shattering kiss, Jathen folded, and he was hers.

He did nothing but kiss her for a long while until he tasted salt on her lips—from his tears or hers, he had no idea. Exquisite relief and joy flowed between them, two empathics caught in their emotions, sent and felt and returned in an intense loop. Years of frustration and months of repression had him outright punishing her lips with his own, and she drank up every bit of it, matching his intensity with her own heat-fueled fervor. Finally, with a moan that was nearly a growl, she grabbed his collar and spun him around onto the bed, where he yanked her down on top of himself.

Seren was nothing like the Lu'shun *mei* he'd had before—especially Ishane—who'd been light and mischievous in their controlled teasing, their bedroom play an art form carefully crafted and executed. No, she was Tazu—half-blood, yes, but in this, Tazu all the same. Forceful, hungry, and uninhibited, velvet-scaled and unashamed, she was everything Jathen had ever dreamed of in his heart of hearts while sitting on the sidelines during mating season. He didn't need to hold back, as with the Lu'shun. An unspoken understanding had always existed, that those smoothly delicate women clad in false scales might break if Jathen let loose the full fervor in his heart, but Seren was different. Unfettered and passionate, they reveled in each other, simply, directly, and without restraint—no pretenses, no staging, and no *stopping*. Hours passed in the wake of the first climax, when Seren actually screamed his name and tore the bedsheets, claws digging across the mattress in fitful abandon. Afterward, only the briefest of respites was taken before Jathen and Seren began anew, their veins set afire with the joy of the other.

They were Tazu—that was their way.

Finally, both depleted sometime deep in the evening, Jathen lay back on the bed, feeling profoundly tired. A moment of awkwardness passed in the uncertainty of what came next, but without a word, Seren simply rolled into him and closed her eyes, asleep within a heartbeat. Gratified, as he'd never actually slept entangled with anyone before, he discovered she fit as easily into the crook of his body as if she'd been crafted to go there. Wrapping lazy arms around her, Jathen let his eyes fall closed as well. He planted one last kiss on the crown of her head before falling asleep, content for the first time in a very, very long time.

WHEN JATHEN WOKE SOMETIME late the next morning, he lay beside Seren in awe, reveling in the fact that their evening hadn't all been some glorious dream. Watching her slumber, he found the yellow pattern running down her back also present on her stomach, a pretty starburst radiating from her navel. He'd not noticed it before in the flurry of everything, and it struck him as endearingly cute. Stroking the line of her scales with the backs of his fingers, he smiled. The motion woke Seren, and she stretched with a little squeak so adorable that Jathen couldn't contain a chuckle.

"Morning," he said.

She got a sleepy, contented look, then her eyes flew wide. A wave of panic from her made Jathen flinch as she shot up beside him. "Did we...?" She took in Jathen's startled expression then swallowed visibly before curling her claws into her disheveled blond hair. "Oh, Spirit in Heaven, we did! *I* did... Oh, my mother is going to kill me!"

Panic, shame, and fear cascaded through Jathen. He reached out, wanting to touch her, to reassure her, but then pulled back, terrified that she wouldn't want it. "Oh, Seren, I *tried* to talk you out of it—"

"I know. I remember." She shook her head. Putting a palm on her forehead, she laughed shakily. "And I know, I really do, my mother... That's absurd. I shouldn't care about Chertith nonsense—"

"No, you shouldn't—"

"And I know! And it's not really *that*... I just..." She took a breath, her expression caught somewhere between rueful and worried. "I meant what I said last night, every word... and I just, I didn't... I mean, *you* didn't actually say if..."

Oh, by the Twelve, she's actually in love with me too. Jathen blinked in surprise, the reality just so... unfathomable. Despite everything he'd heard and felt from her, he'd still somehow thought she was being motivated by the heat, at least in part. Taking her face in his hands, he leaned in and kissed her again, all but pouring a part of his soul into the intensity of it. *I am in love with you, Seren.* She returned the kiss, wrapping her claws in his loose hair. A wave of relief washed from her into him, and he sighed against her lips.

Falling back into the bed together, they were then gentler, slower, and more exploratory of each other. Jathen found Seren a little shyer in the daylight, more uncertain, but that didn't derail them. Leisurely, he coaxed her back into the eager Tazu female of the night before, and she showed her gratitude with all the delicious Tazu ardor he'd come to expect.

Spirit, he thought in a kind of bewitched awe, *she really loves me. I heard that.* Seren giggled. *And yes, I do.*

Back to cuddling again, Seren nuzzled his neck, making little contented Tazu sounds similar to a drake's thrumming purr. "Well, this is a mildly unexpected turn of events."

"Not *that* unexpected," Jathen admitted, tightening his grip on her. Spirit, he hadn't let himself feel his love for Seren, but once freed, it simultaneously shook and anchored his soul. That she returned it was humbling. "And certainly a welcome one." Gazing more quizzically at her, he asked, "You really think I smell like gold and cucumbers?"

The laugh singing out of Seren held a chime of relief to it. "No, you were right. That made no sense whatsoever." She rolled over slightly, her eyes doting. "But I have always thought you smelled good."

"That's it?" He grinned. "I won your affections by scent alone?"

"No." With the back of one hand, she stroked his cheek, almost reverent. "I touched you once, just once, nearly ten years ago when I came to stay with my grandmother in the palace."

"*That* far back?" Jathen grimaced, ashamed by his thoughtlessness back then. "I'm sorry. I don't remember."

"It's all right—I do. In one instant, I saw all that churned under the surface of your façade. So much hurt and anger, yes, but beyond were the beautiful things: your mind, so brilliant and whimsical. The way you see things, Jathen, it's like poetry, and you don't have any idea how special it is. And your heart—it's so *good* despite all the sarcasm and disappointments. And you downright... *bedazzle* me with the sheer undercurrent of courage running through you."

"Seren, why did you *never* say anything? Was it all your family? All fear of being seen with the moot?"

"No. Don't mistake me—they've made it clear what they thought of you, but I..." She frowned. "I wanted so badly to reach you, but you were always so far away, tucked in your own world of sorrow and anger. The problems you faced every day... I couldn't hold a candle to it. I said nothing because I had nothing I *could* say to make it better."

"Because even as a half-blood, you still look like them," he murmured.

"Yes."

"For what it's worth, this"—he motioned to the space between them, struggling to put words to a feeling he'd never expected—"has been the first time in my entire life I've felt as if being a moot truly, truly does *not* matter." He cupped the curve of her face. "You've given me this, Seren, and if nothing else had ever passed between us, I'd have loved you for that."

Her eyes welling up, she trembled slightly. "Well, that's flattering."

"Only half as much as you loving me," he said. Their lips met again, long and sensuous, hands and hair entwined in a daylit haze. When they finally broke apart, he rested his forehead on hers for a moment, feeling cozy.

"Can we stay here a bit longer?" Seren murmured. "I don't want to face the world just yet."

"Happily." Content with snuggling, Jathen stayed in bed with her, legs and fingers entwined as they lay on their sides, facing each other amid a tangle of tattered bedsheets and a torn, slightly unstuffed pillow.

"Did Hatori know?" he asked, working his fingers through her blond hair. He'd never realized just how badly he'd wanted to play with it, and the silky strands were everything he'd hoped—soft and beautiful and wonderful smelling despite some minor tangles.

"Yes," she confirmed, slightly sad. "I said before there were *reasons* I was putting off coming here. The truth is, I didn't want to leave *you*, not Hatori. He saw it and told me I was being a fool."

"The day at the charm shop," Jathen recalled. She'd seemed so small, so young then, even though that'd only been a little over a year before. "When I nearly collided with you and you began to cry. Jephue had said Hatori had done you a service."

"Yes."

Jathen shifted up on one elbow as something occurred to him. "Does Thee know?"

"Yes," she said with a snicker.

"Why didn't she *tell* me?"

"Would you have believed her?"

Jathen wrinkled his nose. "No."

"Well, there you go." Released somewhat from their tangle, Seren stretched. "Do you want to know what's so strange about all of this?"

Plucking a stray bit of stuffing from her shoulder, Jathen asked, "Other than destroying your bedsheets and a good portion of the mattress?"

She stuck her tongue out at him then ebbed serious. "I'd moved past you. That day at the shop, Hatori told me I was doing myself no good by trying to live my life on a 'maybe,' on a 'someday.' You left, I came here, and I tried to live, to forget. I spent time with my parents, went to classes, made some passing friends, and slowly, I let go of the idea of you. It'd been months since I'd thought about you, and then came the word of the quake. I thought you were dead. I mourned you, Jathen, all three of you—but then I began to move on, sad for you, sad for Thee, but content in my life here. And then I got Thee's letter, and I was just walking through the city, thinking about you in *that* way for the first time in a long time. Where were you, what was happening, and somehow, if I could just reach you..."

Jathen stilled, skin breaking out into goose bumps. "And then I fell on your head."

"Yup." She tapped her claws together, looking up through the skylight. "I've wondered a dozen times since learning about D'ilinde and what it can do, that it's made of Bree's and Bron's hearts, and I thought maybe—"

"You 'summoned' me."

"Yes." Her eyes returned to him. "Does that seem strange?"

"After everything I've done and seen? No, not that strange." He kissed her forehead. "Probable, even."

A knock cut short her response. "Serendibiss," Izzy said between hurried knocks on the other side of the door. "Are you in? Jathen's not been back to Annakki's townhouse all night! He was coming by here last we heard. Have you seen him? Seren?"

The pretty blue Tazu in his arms turned nearly purple in embarrassment. Leaping over him with a speed Jathen hadn't thought possible, Seren bolted into the bathroom and slammed the door. Left gaping on the bed, Jathen sighed at the increasingly insistent knocking before rising to retrieve his pants from where they'd been tossed across the room.

"I'm here, Izzy," he said, slipping the pants on before opening the door to a flustered fauni.

Taking in the whole scene of a shirtless Jathen, the tattered bed, and a missing Seren with one quick sweep, Izzy bluntly asked, "Heat?"

"Um, yes." He fought his rising blush. "Sort of... spur of the moment."

"It always is with first heats." Izzy sighed, mild vexation bubbling off her along with crinkled brow tattoos as she stepped into the room. "I don't suppose you two had enough foresight or self-control to take precautions against an egg?"

From the sudden, loud squawk emanating from the bathroom, Jathen had to assume a negative, and so did Izzy, who shook her head. "Ruddy Red, Jathen, must I lecture you on what's sensible? An unwanted egg out of the first heat can cause all kinds of complications in a high-blood family like the Chertiths—"

"*I* might have been one of those 'unwanted eggs,' Izzy," he snapped, surprised by her venom and his own. "So whatever happens, we'll handle it," he declared toward the bathroom door before turning back to Izzy. "No regrets."

A smile twitched at the edge of Izzy's mouth. "That's one thing I can say I like about you, Jathen Monortith—you don't run. Others who've been through less would balk and flee from responsibility or change, but not you. You'll not always do it gracefully, you'll grit your jaw and bear the pain in silence, but you'll never run." She sighed then flipped her hood up onto her head. "Fine, I'll call off the search and let everyone know you've not been kidnapped. I'll also make certain Ambassador Chertith doesn't know about this." Izzy nodded toward Seren's hiding spot. "She'll be good for a few hours if you two just finished, but it'll be another day or so before the heat passes fully. Have fun."

"Thanks, *Orne*," Jathen retorted with a snort.

Izzy grinned knowingly before shutting the door.

"She's gone!" Jathen yelled toward the bathroom, though he didn't move toward it, leaning against the door instead. He banged the back of his head against the wood.

An egg. Past the initial brave front he'd shown was fear, an uncertainty tossing shadows about in the recesses of his mind—not in parenting or responsibility, per se, nor in sharing such with Seren, or even the obvious dice-roll of his child looking Tazu or not. No, what filled him with dread was a thing he'd never considered.

I don't know what I am—or, rather, what my father is.

"You really think that might affect an egg?" Seren asked, creeping slowly out of the bathroom. She'd thrown on her robe, and her dark-blue claws fiddled with the white sash.

Jathen sighed. "I'm not sure if I'll ever get used to you in my head like that. But, yes, Seren. It's concerning. Despite all my answers, I still don't know why I have my Abilities or why I look different in silver mirrors. I've floundered for so much of my life. How much easier would things be if I knew?"

"It might be harder."

"True."

"And we don't even know yet," she said, still toying with the knot in the sash. "First heats don't *always* result in an egg."

"I think that might have more to do with Tazu females shifting forms to be certain about not keeping them," he replied then regretted it as she flinched. "I'm sorry, Seren, I know shifting isn't an option."

"There are other ways," she whispered, hugging herself. "Tar'citadel has methods." She bounced uncomfortably from foot to foot, gazing at him with a certain desperate expression. "Is that what you think should be done?"

Jathen took a deep breath then shook his head. "I think what I have always thought—that the realm of eggs is entirely under the control of Tazu females, specifically the one carrying the egg." He held a hand out to her. "I meant it. We'll make the best of whatever you want to do."

She sighed softly, taking his hand. The little sparks danced between their palms, tickling and warmly comforting. "I think, as you said, I don't have the heart to turn away an 'unwanted egg.' Because I do. I've always wanted my own children. Maybe not *now*, but I don't know what will happen to us back at court. If they'll let us have this chance again."

He squeezed her hand. "You know I'll fight them for this."

"I know." She squeezed back. "But just in case this is the only egg we get, I say we take the gamble." She released his hand then stepped up against him, slipping into an embrace. "Though it does sound like you need to finally ask your mother about your father."

"I keep trying to, but the words fail me." Jathen drummed his fingers across her back as he dropped his chin to rest on her bowed head.

He'd spoken to Rhodonith twice more since she'd learned he still lived, and both conversations leaned more to keeping her abreast of his training than dredging up old secrets. *And Thee still hasn't come to speak to me. Or written word one, despite my letters.* His mother could keep making excuses, but he had a sense his little sister's pouting was far more intense than Rhodonith let on. "It's not an easy thing to ask, Seren. I never have. Out of respect, yes, but also fear."

"You're afraid he's human? Or low-blood?"

"No, I know I hatched. I've always been afraid he's *high*-blood. High-blood and hiding, ashamed of the moot. I could hate him if he were that—and at least it would make sense." He shivered as she tightened her grip on him. "Now, he might be something else entirely—absent from my life for reasons completely unknown." He bit his lip. Similar to the chasms opening beneath his feet during the many times he'd felt the ground shake, the unknown of his father left him with little reason or sense to brace against. The idea of passing such fear on to a child of his own was worse.

Far worse. Still, she's my mother. Some things need to be done in person.

Hearing him, Seren nodded against his chest.

"I'd prefer that if we can. Let's wait for now, see if there *is* going to be an egg, and then, well, if I can't ask her in person, I at least have the excuse of my own child's future to press her into telling me the truth."

"A reasonable plan." She pulled back, arms draped casually around his neck as she grinned. "So what was that about a few days until the heat passes?"

"I suppose the 'damage' has been done." He chuckled before kissing her again.

Jathen and Seren spent the majority of the rest of the day up in her room, emerging only once to go to the dining level and load up plates of food before slipping back.

"Don't you have classes?" Jathen asked while sitting on their impromptu table made from the spare desk and the two chairs, which felt oddly romantic, despite the humble nature.

"I'd honestly prefer not to go about in the general populace while still pumping out pheromones, thank you."

"After all that talk about being able to control yourself and walk away if needed?" Jathen scratched absentmindedly at one of the bandages on his shoulder. One side effect of coupling with a fervent Tazu in heat was that his thinner moot skin got scraped a bit. They'd been gentler since, and at least he was healing nicely, if itchy.

"I can. You could have. But as you noticed, it's not exactly easy to concentrate on much else, and I'd rather not disrupt classes with my moaning on about where you've gone off to." She took a bite of a spicy-smelling black rice dish Jathen had been afraid to try, chewed a moment, then swallowed. "And it's not as if I'm apt to go courting any other mates."

Jathen burst out laughing. "You certain it won't hurt your academic standing?"

She shrugged. "Who cares if it does at this point? I'm not taking anything that's relevant to a Way Path. Aside from control, I have no idea what I'm even attempting to do here."

Jathen huffed a laugh. "I know the feeling." He took her hand. "We are dreadfully alike. You do realize that?"

"In the best of ways," she said, squeezing his hand.

Chapter 4

"So what now?"

Jathen let Seren's question hang between them as a few swirls of late-falling snow drifted across their path, catching the slowly rising sun and glimmering like gold in the street. Seren's heat had finally subsided enough that she felt comfortable returning to classes, but the pair had risen early so Jathen, too, could arrive in time to resume his own morning training with Annakki. Seren's class wasn't until midmorning, so she'd opted to walk him back to the townhouse, prolonging their blissful break for as long as possible. *But now it is ending. And we do need to sort our next moves.*

Truthfully, Jathen didn't want to think about the future with Seren because it was, for the most part, devastatingly uncertain. He could speak all he wanted about fighting for it—and he knew he would—but fighting a battle and winning one were two separate things. *Much like my fight for the throne. We'll need to be careful. Measure each step the best we can once we're back at court.* He glanced her way, gaze falling fondly on her lovely blue scales and silken blond hair, but Seren was more than that—hers was a soul that understood his own, a thing he'd never had until Ass'shiri and then lost again far too quickly.

But we aren't back at court. Not yet.

"Why don't we meet for dinner tonight?" he asked, slipping his hand into hers. "You can come to the townhouse or meet me at our Republic café."

"I think that can be arranged." She stared at him, a wave of bewitched awe fluttering off her for a moment before she smiled. "I'll need to see how much work I must catch up on, though," she admitted upon reaching the townhouse. "So no late nights."

"Finally sated?" Jathen teased, only to turn around and face Chūjitsun standing in the open front door. Despite himself, Jathen flushed under the dark stare of the master servant. Averting his gaze, Jathen scudded inside without a sound while Seren stifled a giggle behind her hand.

"Fine to see you return," Chūjitsun said in his condescending tone. "I shall inform Lady Annakki."

"No need, Chu," Jathen replied. When the new nickname got an indignant eyebrow rise from the master servant and another giggle from Seren, he grinned. "Is she in the solarium? I'll just head in and see her myself."

"She currently resides in the library with Mr. Rhyo and Mr. Spinnek." Chu's eye twitched ever so slightly at applying even so low a title as "mister" to Spinnek. He stepped aside, gesturing with an open palm toward the sitting room just off the foyer. "However, Her Eminence the Lady Manna awaits you both here."

Jathen swallowed visibly, catching her porcelain profile as she reclined in one of the chairs. "Thank you, Chūjitsun."

The man clicked his heels and departed, leaving Jathen to his probable admonishing.

He exchanged glances with Seren. *Any chance you want to make a run for the door?*

She smiled softly. *Nope.*

He sighed. *Damn.* Stepping down into the sunken space with Seren just behind, Jathen held his breath, trying to gauge what exactly his teacher might be feeling. *Is she angry about my missing class? Training time? Or just Seren in general, as Izzy was? Or did she engineer the whole thing? And if so, does she know what will happen? Spirit—what if she can see what horrid political ramifications this will have?* He shook his head as much to clear it as to keep such things from drifting over for Seren to hear.

Adopting a resting stance Annakki had taught him, he stood with hands clasped behind his back, waiting. Holding a cup of tea, Erin Manna blew leisurely upon it, the wisps of steam flowing away from her puckered lips with idealized elegance. She sipped once, not making a sound.

He waited until she swallowed then sipped again before saying, "You wished to see me, Lady?"

"Both of you." After placing the teacup upon a side table, she picked up a black box Jathen hadn't noticed sitting there.

"Oh?" Seren asked, peeking over Jathen's shoulder as Erin Manna opened the box.

Leaving it in her lap, she lifted the contents, a necklace.

But not a normal necklace. Jathen leaned forward slightly, squinting at the odd bauble. A single bright labradorite cabochon, it'd been wire wrapped in a manner he'd never seen. Jagged, intricate, and full of hard but aesthetically pleasing edges, the piece resembled an arrowhead. Two smaller green stones Jathen didn't recognize flanked the labradorite. *Peridot, maybe?* It glimmered, and not simply from the sheen of the gems. *Power* emanated from the charm.

"This is for you, Serendibiss Chertith." Erin Manna brandished the piece in her pale palm, the gems glinting beside her well-sculpted nails.

"Um, thank you?" Seren took it very tentatively, and her hands shook slightly, disturbing the thin platinum chain. "Might I ask what it is?"

"One of the last of Yvette Ashton's master-charms I have in my keeping."

Seren gaped, cradling it in her palms as if it might leap away. "Why...? I mean to say, to what do I owe such a gift from you?"

"'Tis no occasion for great gratitude. Your mind is allow'd free rein into Jathen's. What he knows, you can know." She shut the box with an authoritative *snap*. "That is a danger, a weak point for you both. The master-charm is to shield your thoughts from prodding minds and to cloak the connection you two share from outsiders' notice. Put it on, and do *not* remove it."

Seren did as bid, though Jathen could easily sense her conflict between being called a liability so bluntly and appreciating that the Lady Manna had gone so far as to supply a remedy.

Jathen squeezed Seren's hand. "Perhaps we'll have dinner another time. Tomorrow?" he murmured, planting a kiss on her cheek.

"I think that's in order," she agreed. *I get the sense she doesn't want me around.*

I don't think it's necessarily you, but yes. He squeezed her hand once more before letting go. "I'll see you tomorrow, after my morning training."

Seren smiled slightly, the genuine affection in her bright eyes warming him. "Until then."

Once she'd departed, he turned toward Erin Manna. "Did anyone actually tell you she was missing classes?" he asked, accusatory. "Or did you just *know* what would happen, sending me there?"

"As I said at our first lesson: I can't *make* you do anything, Jathen Monortith. I can only lead you to the path you've been denying yourself. As in this, you needed the push." She sipped her tea, the flutter of superior irony on her eyelids. "Tazu not quite a Tazu, yes?"

Jathen held his breath, surprised by his surprise as much as anything. *She's Erin Manna. Of course she knew about Neek's prophecy. Probably even knows about me screwing up and thinking it'd been about Ishane.* Recovering, he plastered a passable grin across his face. "I guess this is your play at being a Clan matchmaker, huh?"

She actually chuckled. "I don't walk the bawan path." Her tone ebbed back to seriousness. "You two need each other. There's strength there. More than you know."

"Strength?"

"I find it very odd, Jathen Monortith, that in all our time together, you've not once mentioned the fact she reads your mind. Or the sparks."

"Apparently, I didn't need to mention it." Jathen didn't hide his surprise, as he imagined Izzy wouldn't have said anything, and Spinnek certainly wasn't going to talk to Erin Manna. He sat, stilled. "You *do* know what is happening between us, hence your giving her the master-charm. Some aspect of empathy, then?"

"Some aspect of Aspects, actually." She smirked at his befuddled and probably somewhat frightened expression. "You and Seren are not Aspects or any such, Jathen. But you two do share a trait with the Child-Aspect pairing." She set her teacup back down, the saucer barely stirring. "You have heard of the concept of a twin-flame?"

"That nonsense about there being only one person you can love in a single lifetime?" The words felt false to him even as he spoke them as Neek's voice surged to the front of his mind. *"You blaze, Jathen Monortith."*

He squirmed a little in his chair. If Izzy had suspected, that would definitely have explained her reaction and going on about not mentioning anything to any Tazu.

"I thought that a bit of fancy from the Lu'shun Republic." He suddenly recalled the High Walker with a hand over her mouth, holding in her laughter. "Or Beleskie Walkers."

"It is not. Rare, yes, as one's twin-flame typically chooses to serve a soul in body as their Spirit Guide, observing and caring from across the Veil. But the Twelve have always incarnated with their Aspects more often than not—save for Montage." After uncrossing her legs, she shifted slightly in her seat then recrossed them. "The sparks are one indicator. It doesn't always manifest with every twin-flame set, but in empathics, it's usually the most obvious sign. The mind reading as well. Even as a Negater, your subconscious recognizes your other half and considers Seren an extension of yourself. And so, as your Ability grew, she was allowed in, where others were not."

"Well, that at least explains the Beleskie Walkers *giggling* at me." Jathen snorted then sobered. "So what does this *mean*? For us... now?"

"Other than the obvious?"

"I'm not certain what the obvious is to you versus me."

Her lips twitched in that repressed smile she often showed him. "If nothing is ever said again about my time with you, let it be known you are a source of amusing perceptional awareness, Jathen." Her bright golden eyes measured him, softening slightly. "You love her, do you not?"

"Yes." He was actually surprised by how easily that answer slipped off his tongue. Akin to his love of Rhodonith or Thee, what he felt for Seren was a statement, a fact, an inevitability of life. And that—well, if it *was* the twin-flame—could be concerning.

"Then that is what it means."

"But... the twin-flame... It gives the impression she's the only person I'll be capable of loving and vice versa." Jathen bit his lip, uncertain he could properly convey Tazu culture without sounding like a hypocritical moron. "Even if I put aside the massive dangers I've seen ahead for myself, and my death, so many times over, I just... Given my position in the Tazu court, and given hers, it's not an easy road to remain exclusively together—to be together at all, to be honest. I want to fight for it, but... if we're both doomed to be pulled apart and then *never* to find happiness again..." He closed his eyes, shivering slightly. "I could bear it. I know I could. I'd made peace with forever being alone many times in my past. But Seren?" Opening his eyes, he shook his head. "I don't want that for her."

"There are two fears in your question. To be pulled apart is the first. That is a possibility, Jathen. I know of Tazu politics, and I shall not lie to you. You will need to fight for it, as will she. But the second part, the doom—tied to either death or separation—well, that depends upon you and upon her. Can one love as deeply or as strongly once they know their twin-flame? Many would argue for both sides. Did Annakki love Ass'shiri less despite him not being her twin-flame? Did Hatori love Jephue less?"

"I can't imagine not."

She nodded. "It isn't the same, Jathen, but you *can* love another past a twin-flame." Softly, she added, "Granted, not everyone is up for the challenge."

The way she spoke those words was the most emotional he'd ever heard her. "You?"

She pursed her lips a moment then nodded. "Marin's soul and mine are twin-flames, yes. But that is different. Our history is different. *I* am different."

"How so?" Jathen blurted out before he had time to consider what he was asking.

She smoothed her dress, looking away, and for a moment, he thought he'd crossed a line.

Then surprisingly, she answered, "Before I *became* what I am now, I was a human prostitute on the streets, collapsing under the weight of my Ability. Remember, this was long ago, when Talents were new, and we did not know what we were."

Jathen blinked repeatedly, staggered. As far as he knew, *none* of the Originals had ever given up that much information about their lives previous to being Clan. The very concept that this incredibly composed, elegant, and *powerful* woman had ever been something so humble—it was nearly too alien a concept to grasp.

"How did you rise up from it?" he asked.

"Marin," she admitted. "He was... I'm not certain of the equivalent even now. Not a common guardsman but not a tar'ka-besh. A seeker of criminals. He found me and saw in me not a broken girl but someone of value. He *listened* when the whole world thought me mad. He brought me to Rhean before he was Rhean, and they found the truths hidden in my words—my prophecies." Finally meeting his eyes again, she shook her head. "You don't love someone else after that... after losing the world together, losing your *humanity* together. No one can ever hold a candle to Marin, not only because of the twin-flame but because there can never be another peer, as he was."

"I cannot imagine that loneliness, Lady." When a thought of A'ron De'contes coalesced in his head, he bit the inside of one cheek, remembering the vulnerability in the Clansman's voice, as well as his vision of the man sobbing. *"Erin is in the city?" Spirit, that'd be hard to fake, but I'm not the one to know, not for certain.*

"No," she said, startling Jathen by knowing where his mind had gone without reading it. "I will not go see *him.*"

Jathen held his words a moment, debating just how much liberty he could take with someone nearly nine thousand years old. Then it happened, a little thing, a pinch, a *feeling*—a sense of something beyond himself, a *knowing* he was correct. D'ilinde hummed softly, agreeing. "Even if De'contes *is* Marin?" When she didn't strike him down, he continued softly, purposefully. "Raleigh said he was. It's rumored and whispered about. I even saw it—in a brief flash of empathy—him covered in blood and crying his eyes out, presumably after the coup. But if anyone can know if that claim is true, it would be you, Lady Erin."

She pursed her lips again, looking away.

I've really rattled her, he realized, startled. *Unless...* "You already know." He leaned back in his chair, shocked he'd seen it, shocked

Seren had actually predicted it. "A'ron *is* Marin, and you know. You've *known*."

Heat was filling her golden eyes when she glanced back at him. "This cannot leave this room, Jathen."

"Obviously." He shifted in his seat, uncertain. "How long?"

"Since the last moments of the coup." She softened, seeming to relax.

Jathen wondered if she'd ever confessed such a thing to another soul. *Such a strange benefit to being a Negater, being the only one that anyone could be assured their secrets will stay with. As long as I don't outright tell them, that is.*

"The twin-flame was what Woke him. I'd met him, spoken with him hundreds of times, but I'd never touched him. Not until I put myself between a Red Mage and Ra'vien's children." She scowled. "You can love a person *so much*, and still there can be things you cannot forgive." *I suffer, Jathen, more than I can ever tell anyone.*

The idea of Seren hating him for monstrous things he'd done while being ignorant of who he truly was rattled Jathen to his core. An irrepressible sympathy for A'ron arose within him, despite the man's innumerable sins. "But what about what you said to me earlier—about Hatori? About loving someone despite their faults and guilt? Don't the things he's done since the coup point to a man full of remorse and a desire to make amends for his crimes, no matter how monstrous? If you really believed what he is doing with the Balori is evil or some trick, then you would have put a stop to it, yes?"

"By that same logic, I would have allowed the coup to occur as well, wouldn't I?"

Jathen bit his lip, startled. *Oh. Oh, Spirit in Heaven—she* did *know about that before it happened.* Regathering his thoughts, he replied, "You've said we see things simply because we are precognitive. But there're patterns to it. You've said as much about Mikkal, that changing one ripple can cause more problems or, in the case of my vision, prevent them. So you're forced to move only when you feel you must or when you *know* you can change it. Which means that you didn't *allow* the coup to happen so much as you were never provided enough reason—or enough detail—to prevent it. Now, I don't dare try to ascertain what you saw or didn't see to keep you from preventing such a disaster, other than now we have Balori when we didn't before. If the Balori are true to their claims, that is a higher cause than I can wrap my mind around. But for you to allow yourself to be *angry* at De'contes, who moved and chose to do what he did because he didn't know who he truly was—it seems too petty, too *mortal* for you. So I ask again, why anger? Why make him suffer under the burden of your displeasure when you yourself know such things probably happened *because* he needed to truly comprehend the core belief he founded the Balori on, that evolution arises from conflict?"

A flicker of satisfaction actually escaped her careful confines for him to feel, confirming for Jathen that this whole conversation had, indeed, been a test of sorts. "I believe, little Tazu, you just answered your own question."

He wrinkled his nose. "You *want* him to remain conflicted?"

"Evolution does not solely rise from conflict, dear child—otherwise, there would be only one Way, and it would be the Red. No. Evolution also rises from hope. So long as there is something to strive for, to hope for, then a soul may evolve, and a man may discover yet another integral truth required for the endgame."

Jathen held his breath a moment as he realized she wasn't just talking about De'contes anymore—she was also speaking about him. *An integral truth?* "But if you know this, why not simply hand over the answer and hurry up the evolution?"

"Because I *don't* know the answer. As you just surmised, precognition is not omniscient." She waved a hand dismissively. "I sense only the shifts, Jathen, the *feelings* coming upon us, not the details, as you said. I never *knew* A'ron De'contes was going to betray us all, but

I *felt* the betrayal coming, saw the blood, the fires, the deaths, though not *who* would die. The details, those finite details, were all written down in one fell swoop, left to be interpreted not even by myself. What are left now are shadows, sweeping brushstrokes of varying shades."

"Like the dream I had about the shop fire," Jathen whispered.

That memory still gave him shivers. He'd had so many details but no context to the events, so preventing them had been impossible. The current vision was much the same. He had a fair bit of confidence that taking on Erin Manna as his main teacher had subverted the deaths, and telling Na'vosh about the avalanche had probably circumvented that aspect, as Seren had so fervently tried to reassure him. Yet Jathen had no way of knowing if those changes would permanently evade the final fate he'd seen coming, the destruction and the watery death of the continent itself.

Staring hard at Erin Manna, he sensed they wouldn't—he'd gained only a means by which to better fight the coming storm. "How do you stand it? Both knowing yet... not?"

"You mean how should you bear it? Quietly. Thoughtfully. Treat precognition the same as you'd treat any other bit of information you come across. Individually. Weigh it. Plan for it. But don't be ruled by it because, in the end, you might be wrong."

"And that might be a better thing than being right." Jathen nodded, pondering everything.

"Remember, however," she added, voice turning dark, "the wicked are precognitive as well."

He swallowed, the enormity of that simple fact hitting him for the first time. "That's why you're so cautious, isn't it? You and Galduran and the others—as much as you see, you don't know what *evil* Talents see, do you?"

She nodded. "The more Talents that know a piece of information, the more likely it is for others to sense it as well—through precognition, empathy, or Guides."

"Like with Mikkal. If he *knows* you know about him and were going to do something to him, then he'd take actions to that end." He held his breath. *Or the dozens of other things I wanted to discuss with her—like negating Red Mages or the Shatari sword. Speaking could mean giving information to the enemy. Spirit.*

"Changing the pattern." Again, she nodded, bobbing her head slightly as she spoke. "And so we act and counteract, the same as on the battlefield. A single choice can tip the very path we are on and spell doom for us all." She picked up her teacup, an indicator the conversation was over. "For no one can *truly* know the future until the choice which crafts it has been made."

Inside his chest, D'ilinde buzzed, and Jathen was filled with a deep, undeterminable sense of foreboding. *Something is still coming. I know it. And she's seen it too.*

But neither of us knows what.

Revelator

Chapter 5

The energy redirected.

Jathen nearly whooped at the feeling of the negated energy from Lady Erin's attack seeping into him then blooming again as desired. *Speed!* He bolted away from the next volley, avoiding two energy bolts before zipping behind the Clanswoman. Another hit took him in the shoulder, and he grabbed the swirling power, holding his breath a moment. *Jump!* He laughed with joy when he sprang a good dozen heads into the air, high enough to scrape the falsely burning rafters before dropping again. He landed a little hard, having misjudged how much to slow his descent enough with Ability but not harshly enough to lose his footing.

Throwing his hands into the air, he grinned so widely that his face felt as if it might split. "I did it!"

"Yes." Erin Manna was wearing another robe-dress with draped sleeves, its skirt hemmed short in the front but long in the back, with a pair of formfitting black leggings underneath. Her boots clicked noticeably on the marble disk as she walked toward him. "In a training session, under controlled circumstances, but yes."

Jathen groaned, dropping his arms in an exaggerated pout. A few weeks of training had passed since his little "sabbatical" with Seren, and in addition to his current accomplishments, he'd finally stopped having massive headaches after training sessions. Though minor ones were still possible, as the vein pounding in his brow was quick to remind him. "Oh, can't you just let me enjoy a victory, please? This was hard won."

"When one considers the actual length of your journey to this point, yes." Folding her hands before herself, she smiled slightly. "But yes. Well done. It seems self-supplementation is your strength. As it is the first and easiest of energy manipulation studies, that makes sense."

"That complement sounded oddly like a criticism. But thank you." Jathen picked up a cloth he'd been keeping on the marble disk and dabbed his forehead and neck, the blue fibers coming away rather wet. *Still takes a lot out of me. I wonder if she's right, if I'll ever manage larger manipulations.*

He and Erin Manna also hadn't revisited their little conversation about De'contes and precognition during the past few weeks, for which Jathen was dually grateful and deeply anxious, prompting him to not bring it up in lieu of focusing on training.

"I simply acknowledge there is a long way yet to go." She arched an eyebrow. "Though perhaps you are already aware."

"I am." He wrung out the cloth, debating bringing up the feeling of doom again. It hadn't abated and indeed had been rolling in even stronger the past few days. Pursing his lips, he decided against it. If he'd learned one thing from Erin Manna, it was that she wouldn't tell him things he didn't need to know or didn't know herself, which led to the same outcome either way. "But you've made good on your promise to me when this started. I've got a foundation I can build on."

"Then it seems I leave you in an advantageous place to move forward without me." When Jathen cocked his head at her, she explained, "I need to go home."

He arched an eyebrow. "Really this time, or are you just trying to steer me to some point of my destiny again?"

"No, truly. I need to return for a duration."

Jathen frowned, tossing the towel back on the floor after dabbing his hands. "This isn't you just avoiding a certain enclave, is it?"

The High Walkers would be sequestering themselves to debate the Balori's fate in a few hours. With the vote approaching, Annakki had become more and more withdrawn despite Jathen having shared with her the assurances of just about every High Walker that it wouldn't pass. Oddly, Jathen was secretly looking forward to the event itself, for all the High Walkers being occupied would halt his training for the day at least, freeing him for some more quality time with Seren for however long the debate would carry on. *Though it might be too much to hope, with this unsettled feeling looming. But I'd love to know if it's that wretched vision coming to fruition or my sensing Annakki and every other person's nervousness about the Balori vote.*

"I'd prefer not to be in the city lest some political advantages be made by my presence," Erin Manna continued, "but no, that is not the reason."

Jathen nodded, somewhat relieved, though a part of him also wouldn't have minded the Original staying. He did trust Annakki, but he admittedly trusted her *more* whenever Erin Manna was occupying the city. *And my nerves could do with a little less fraying.* "For how long?"

"I am uncertain." She hesitated as if touching upon her precognition and deciding whether to elaborate. "Something needing my expertise has come to my attention back home."

"Nothing dire, I hope?" He'd not forgotten their talk about civil war in the Clan Lands, no matter how reassuring she'd been.

"I do not believe so. But admittedly, it is difficult." She nodded deeply. "As said, the more I come to care for someone or something, the less I tend to see precognitively."

"Is that an admittance of a flaw by the great Erin Manna?"

She smirked, not answering. "Have a good day, Jathen. I will see you when I return."

THE OFFICIAL CONSENSUS since Jathen and Seren had fallen into a relationship held that the daughter of the Tazu ambassador visited Jathen for dinner often at Annakki's townhouse, staying in a guest room if the hour got too late. Though that was slightly subtler than him staying overnight in her university room, Jathen found it a silly way of hiding the relationship from grumpy noble Tazu, as anyone with a brain and eyes could guess. However, it kept Izzy from having to go back and forth, escorting him or rising early to meet him in the mornings, so he relented without complaint for her sake. However, he wasn't particularly thrilled about Seren darting about the city alone, either.

"Izzy forces an escort on me, but you can come and go as you please," he griped to Seren that afternoon when she arrived. Upstairs in Dor'rhean's room, Jathen was sitting on the floor, once again happily occupied with playing with the little boy and his blocks.

"Stop fussing. I was strutting about this city long before you were in it, thank you," she proclaimed, plopping down beside him and earning a big raspberry from Dor'rhean.

"Yes, but that was before," he continued, grinning as Dor'rhean handed him another block. "There could be anything out there now," he said in his best Hatori impression as he helped Ass'shiri's son craft his wooden tower. "Spies! Ruffians! Bandits! *Teenagers!*"

"Oh please. If anything, the streets are fairly quiet, what with just about everyone in the city waiting on the enclave outside the Temple Citadel. Other than a detour or two, this was practically the fastest

I've ever made the trip." After rolling her eyes, she kissed him lightly on the lips above Dor'rhean's head. "And you're certainly in a mood."

"I'm looking forward to this respite." He pushed a lock of her hair behind her ear. The smell of the silky tresses made his toes curl in delight. "That, and I actually accomplished redirecting energy today, so yes, I'm in a good mood. I'm useful for once."

"If you were in a *good* mood, you'd be going on about a unique bit of architecture or another bridge or something you want to skip off and see in our free time."

Dor'rhean's tower crashed down between them, earning some high-pitched squeals of delight from the child. Shaking her head, Seren helped the two of them rebuild a foundation.

"Instead," she continued, "you're sniping on about ruffians and escorts and slipping back into your self-hating nonsense when you know very well you are *continuously* useful and that your self-worth isn't even based in usefulness." She leveled a concerned gaze at him over their growing tower. "Is something wrong?"

"Just the tension in general in the air," he admitted, adjusting his legs a bit on the carpet. He eyed the open but empty doorway then added in a whisper, "That, and Erin Manna's left the city."

"She leaves often, does she not?"

"Yes, but—" He bit his lip, seeing a shadow in the hall, then switched to telepathy. *She said this was a longer duration. I had the sense it might even be the end of my training with her for a while.*

And that concerns you? You think you still need her for your training?

Not exactly. I'd just... feel better if she were around. I've not even seen Annakki for three days. Chūjitsun says she's in the study, and the maids took Dor'rhean in there a few times, and I heard her in there with him, but otherwise, nothing. She's not been outside, even to play with him or eat with us. It's making me nervous.

Seren squeezed his hand. *Do you really think Annakki is going to gallivant off and try to murder De'contes again?*

No. Jathen fiddled with the block in his hand, absentmindedly following the wood's grain with his fingers before Dor'rhean snatched it from his grasp with a happy squeak. *But I honestly wouldn't put hatching some sort of long-flung plot meant to destroy De'contes at a later date past her capabilities.*

A long-flung date is not today, Seren reminded him as she stood up.

"I suppose," he murmured then ruffled Dor'rhean's dark hair.

The kid squeaked again, taking another block from Jathen. "Jah-jah-jah," he said.

"Almost," Jathen replied, tapping the boy on his little nose. "You'll get it eventually."

"I'll be more impressed if you get him to say 'Ass,'" Seren said as she stretched, arching her clasped hands behind her head. "That'd be the ultimate punishment on Chūjitsun, I'm sure."

"Oh yes, he couldn't stomach his young master's first real word being my nickname for his father." Jathen chuckled, grinning fondly at Dor'rhean's big lavender eyes as the boy gazed up at him. "I think I might just conspire to do that. What do you think, Dor'rhean? Ass, ass, ass!"

"Ahhsssssssppp," Dor'rhean replied, sticking his tongue out at the end and blowing spit bubbles.

Jathen and Seren shared a deep, heartfelt laugh, but then Seren gasped. Reaching out, she clutched the back of Jathen's desk chair, leaning over it with another audible sigh.

Jathen sprang up off the floor as the growing tower crashed down and Dor'rhean clapped his chubby little hands in delight at the destruction. "Are you all right?"

"Ah, yes. Err, no." She bit her lip then glanced up, a torn expression in her pretty eyes. "I'm starting to think I *am* pregnant."

"Seren, just because Izzy said—"

"No, I *feel* it." She put a hand over her abdomen and bit her lip again. "I'm an empathic, remember? I sense this presence, this *soul* hanging close to me." She sighed, brow furrowed. "I'm sorry."

Retrieving a giggling Dor'rhean from the floor, Jathen straightened and stepped up beside her. "What on the continent are you apologizing for? It's not exactly like I said no to you."

"But if I hadn't pressed—"

"Stop. Now." He grasped her shoulder with one hand, locking gazes while Dor'rhean sucked silently on his own fingers. "I meant it when I said we'd manage this. It's our egg, and we're going to raise it, either here or in the Nation or wherever we both may be. All right?"

One corner of Seren's lips lifted in a smile. "You are handling this extraordinarily well."

"Father issues." Jathen chuckled, pulling her into a one-armed embrace. "I'm not about to let any child of mine live with the kinds of questions I've had to."

Returning the embrace and gazing at Dor'rhean, she sighed softly. "I can understand that."

"Good." He kissed her forehead. "I'm also rather fond of his mother, you know."

Pulling back, she cocked an eye ridge at him. "Already certain it's a boy?"

Something inside Jathen shivered, and he bounced Dor'rhean once on his hip. "Yes, oddly. Is that strange?"

"No." Seren shook her head. "I actually felt the same."

"Well then." He grinned mischievously. "So which name do you think would annoy your Chertith grandmother more: Ass'shiri or Hatori?"

Seren let out an uproarious belly laugh, and her giggling continued so long and hard that she needed to lean on him for support.

"Asssssp. Assssssp!" Dor'rhean called, happy to be included.

One of the maids knocked then stuck her head in. "I'm sorry to interrupt, but the time has arrived for the young master to be put down for his nap, Prince Jathen."

"Right, right—here he is." Jathen handed Dor'rhean over to the human girl, with minimal grumpy noises from the child. "Sleep tight, little egg."

"Jah-Jah-Jah."

"Well," Seren said as the maid took the child out, "since you *are* in a good mood now, I thought I'd offer up a new museum to peruse, since we did so enjoy the last one."

"Another museum?" Jathen sighed. He'd begun feeling very cozy and didn't think he preferred going out over coaxing Seren over to the bed and remaining in it until dinner. "I'm not sure. The last one was a bit tough to top."

Crossing her arms, she smirked at him. "There are over *fifty* museums in Tar'citadel, Jathen. I'm certain I can find at least one to spark some kind of interest. Besides, it'll be quiet in most of them today, what with so many off at the enclave."

"I suppose." Pulling her back into a proper hug, Jathen rested his cheek against hers. The smaller face scales felt cool and smooth against his skin, and he could sense her strong desire to go. "What kind of museum?"

"Cryptography." Pulling back, she grinned at his perplexed expression. "Codes and encryptions, Jathen. Both mundane and of a magical nature. There's an entire exhibit on codes in dream-sendings between Talents and the different levels of universal conciseness. How to protect a code from being broken by Guides and all sorts of different procedures Talents and non-Talents practice to keep *other* Talents from discerning things with Ability. It's absurdly fascinating."

Admittedly, the topic did have a great deal of relevance to his training, given all he'd been discussing with Erin Manna. However,

Jathen good-humoredly retorted, "And I bet the whole place is run by Rheanics."

"The Way of Rhean sponsors the museum, yes." Narrowing her eyes, she poked his ribs playfully. "But I thought you'd do well to take a look and learn a thing or two about what the rest of us *normal* Talents have to go through to keep each other out of our heads. We don't all have the benefit of being a Negater, you know."

"You really want to go see this despite my terrible track record with museums and nervous feelings, don't you?"

"Yes." She grinned sweetly, putting her arms around his neck. "You and I might not get a lot of opportunities to be out, in public, *together* without scrutiny when we go home someday." She shrugged, and her voice tilted a bit melancholy as she said, "I want to enjoy the sunlight while we can."

"Well, when you put it that way..." Jathen sighed, scratching his chin. "Very well. But if I have so much as a precognitive twitch, we're retreating to somewhere with good seismic loading."

"Deal."

While Seren descended the stairs to inform Izzy of their outing and see if Spinnek or Rhyo wanted to join, Jathen took the time to change his shirt, as it had a few scattered droplets of Dor'rhean's drool on the collar. Gathering his coat as well, he debated bringing the sword cane but decided to leave it in lieu of putting a few of his daggers into his coat pockets. They needed more time to become negation charged, and he was of a mind to get into a better habit of rotating them out.

Downstairs, he found only Izzy and Seren waiting by the door. "No Spinnek or Rhyo again?"

"I cannot seem to lure that wounded Tazu out," Izzy said softly as she pulled her cloak on. Flipping up her hood, she smiled. "And Spinnek raided that basket of gluants Miss Chertith here left in the kitchen and has fallen asleep beneath Dor'rhean's crib. There will be no rousing him for quite a time."

"Don't tell me he ate the *entire* dozen," Jathen said as he pulled on his coat.

"Half a dozen," Seren said with a wink. "I had Chūjitsun hide the rest until after dinner."

"Now, that's a battle for the ages." Jathen chuckled as they stepped out into the cold air. "Chūjitsun, master hider, versus Spinnek, master food seeker. I almost regret leaving and missing it."

"Your mood is rather interesting this afternoon," Izzy commented.

"We've already discussed it," Seren said over Jathen's snort. "He's having empathic jitters."

"Understandable, with the city abuzz." Izzy fiddled with the upper clasp of Orne's bag again. "Where is our destined museum, Serendibiss? Perhaps a detour to see the Temple Citadel and the crowd would lessen the ache."

"It is on the way if we bypass directly around Temple Park, but I don't know... Sometimes, confronting the source of the abstract energy can solidify it and bring it from the subconscious to the conscious mind, but sometimes, being in the presence of such a large mass of people can cause an overload." She bit her lip. "But, considering Jathen is a Negater, I suppose we could err on the side of solidification instead of overload, but I think it's his choice."

"What's my choice now?"

Seren rolled her eyes. "We can go look at the crowd, and you might feel better, or you might get emotionally overwhelmed, thus ruining our outing and probably the rest of your day. Not to mention it's just a gigantic mass of bodies and terribly inconvenient to walk around. But it's your decision."

Jathen swayed from foot to foot, debating as he got nothing but silence from D'ilinde. "Perhaps it would be good to go and at least *look.* It is a historical, unprecedented event, and maybe I would feel better to see what all this buzz in the air is about."

"And take in the sheer number of tar'ka-besh mulling about?" Seren asked.

"That might be a factor to easing my nervousness," Jathen admitted.

. "Then off we shall go," Izzy said.

The trio headed south, past University Park, where despite the cold, a good number of students uninterested in the conclave were spending their afternoon. The weather precognitives had apparently missed the mark on snowfall again, or perhaps enough Talents had worked weather-clearing spells to keep the important day clear skied. While a cluster of the elated students was engaged in a snowball fight, Jathen caught a glimpse of some ice skaters on the pond farther off through the bare trees. *Strange how so many are either terrified of this vote or indifferent to it. It's like some bizarre national holiday.*

Seren squeezed his hand while kneading the edge of her scarf with her other hand. *Can you blame them? It's not as if you really understand how you personally feel about any of this.*

True.

Upon reaching the edge of the inner Temple Citadel's streets, the three were forced to stop as the crowd thickened into an immeasurable throng.

"Spirit," Jathen whispered.

Vendors buzzed and scurried around the edge of the larger mass, selling foodstuffs or trying to hawk other less useful wares. Jathen hadn't expected the noise, a dull rumble of a hundred thousand conversations all happening at once, akin to the hum of *Charmed Wind's* charm engines when he'd stood atop them.

"I told you—this crowd is ridiculous," Seren said. "We'd be better off just avoiding it altogether today."

"Serendibiss may be correct," Izzy murmured. She arched her neck, trying to see over the multitude of heads. "It's not as if we're capable of seeing much more than people's backs from this vantage."

"And everyone is just waiting around, being nervous," Seren agreed. "All the interesting goings-on are behind closed doors." She tugged at Jathen's sleeve. "If you've not passed out by now, you're not going to, so why don't we head back toward the museum?"

"Well, wait a moment. We are here, after all." Eyeing an obliging ledge, Jathen hopped up, caught it, and scurried halfway up the wall. Ignoring Izzy and Seren's protests, he leaned forward over the crowd, one hand on a windowsill and both feet on the wall. The width and breadth of the crowd truly was awe-inspiring. Thousands of people were crammed into the grand Temple Park, which stood before the entrance to the Temple Citadel, huddled together and waiting for the verdict despite the cold and indeterminable conclusion. *No wonder I'm feeling edgy. All four of the High Mages are sitting in on the enclave vote as well, and practically the entire city is focused on this one event, in this one place.* He could almost *see* the feeling—not the heaviness of fear in Dodbyen or the heatlike warble of rage he'd seen the night he'd been attacked by the acolyte Pearls. This energy sparkled and glittered, excited and afraid at the same time.

"Jathen, get down," Seren scolded him. "You're attracting tar'kabesh."

"Right. Very well," he said, hopping down. He smirked at the approaching mahogany-skinned human clad in white. "Sorry."

"Move along," the home-guard ordered, his expression stern. He and Izzy exchanged respectful nods as Jathen's group did as bid, turning away from the Temple Citadel and heading for the Cryptography Museum.

"Curiosity sated?" Seren asked.

"Yes—and my nerves a little, to be honest." He put an arm around her waist and exhaled a breath of minor relief. Putting his back to that crowd felt like relaxing a cramped muscle. "You were right. It is good to see so many guards about."

"Odd, however, to note the absence of the Balori on the streets," Izzy commented.

A worm of worry marred Jathen's contentment.

"Oh, no," Seren said, poking him in his arm and zapping him slightly. "The pair of you would do well to remember that we are trying to enjoy ourselves. Unless you've some dire vision directly related to today, I'm not going to have you fussing and worrying over what the Balori *might* be up to."

"*I* didn't bring it up. It was Izzy," Jathen said defensively, though memories of his vision prodded at the back of his mind. *It all begins at the fall. Well, it will stop at the fall, too, because I warned Na'vosh. So there, destiny and strange voices.*

Beside him, the fauni snorted, her bright forehead tattoos rising under her hood. "I merely meant to convey that it's interesting they would choose to remain cloistered in one area. So interesting, in fact, I suspect the tar'ka-besh probably insisted. Which, while I am not exactly sympathetic to the Balori cause, I do find a borderline violation of the First Law by Tar'citadel-mandated tar'ka-besh to be something worthy of an eyebrow raise at the very least."

"Oh, no politics either," Seren said with a light huff, her grip tightening slightly on Jathen's arm. "I've had enough of that from my mother when I see her."

"Agreed," Jathen said, though he grinned playfully at his human friend. "But yes, I raise my eyebrow with you on that, Izzy."

"The two of you," Seren said, a light smile playing on her lips as well. "You claim you don't know if you want your throne, Jathen, but you've got a mind for politics."

"Only half of one. I'm fairly certain Izzy here has a whole mind for it, or at least Orne does. Or did."

"Indeed," Izzy replied, her smile fading as they turned down a side street. "Though it seems I was mistaken. Apparently, some Balori *are* about."

Jathen followed the line of her gaze to three Balori across the street. He recognized them immediately, the same three that'd spoken to him the day he'd gone to see Rhyo at the hospital. The trio saw them, recognition growing in their eyes as they crossed the street to intercept Jathen's group.

"We all right?" Seren murmured to Izzy and Jathen.

"I think so," Jathen whispered just before the others reached them. He nonchalantly unbuttoned his lowest coat button, however, giving him quicker access to his knives if needed.

"Negater!" The Annarite smiled while also raising his hand in greeting. His dark ebony frame was encased in tougher leather armor than before, and his white hair had been shaved on one side of his head and braided close to the scalp on the other. It gave him an odd, lopsided look. "Good to see you about today. A sign of luck, I think."

"Humbled as I am by the praise, I do hope you don't hold your expectations too high today," Jathen replied softly. "This would need to be a unanimous agreement, and I do know for a certainty the Balori just don't have the votes." Eyeing the Annarite's companions, Jathen noted they were decked in better armor as well, but neither the scarred Clansman nor the scythe-faced human was exhibiting hostile body language or emotions. *Perhaps they are just being prepared in case things get ugly for them anyway. Can't say I blame them.*

The Annarite chuckled, his teeth very bright against his dark lips. "We do know, Negater. But today, we see where everyone stands, yes? That's going to account for something."

"Been in there a while," the Clansman added. "Means the Prophet might have flipped a few. Means they're taking him seriously, at least."

"I hope so. I'd like to believe the High Walkers are nothing else if not fair." Jathen plastered a half-hearted smile on his face. "Anyway, we need to be off."

"Oh?" The Annarite returned the slightly less-than-enthusiastic grin. "I never got to thank you proper from before—for talking some sense into me with those two sewage-spewers. I'd be of a mind to buy you a drink." He spread his hands, gesturing toward Seren and Izzy. "For the ladies as well, of course."

"Ah... thank you, but no," Jathen declined. "We have other plans for the day."

"Bah, that's a shame." He scratched his chin, his bright-red eyes holding Jathen's in such a way as to make the hairs on the back of Jathen's neck stand on end. "Because I'm of a mind to keep you out of the mess of today."

Jathen stiffened as Seren's grip on his arm tightened. "Mess?"

"Yes. Out of respect for you who saved the Prophet, I'd like to keep you from getting involved." His friends moved slowly, taking small steps to circle the trio. "And I am afraid I have to insist upon that, Negater."

Before Jathen could react, Izzy unclipped the bottom flap of Orne's bag. As the bones spilled out, Jathen pulled Seren behind him toward the nearest wall while abstractly wondering if he were somehow fated to endlessly come to blows in alleyways. Seren shrieked, and Jathen tried to throw up his negation bubble around them both. He had no idea if it worked, though, because it negated only magical attacks, and apparently, the Balori weren't stupid. The human simply drew his sword and held it up to Jathen's throat before he could do anything with the dagger he'd managed to pull out of his pocket. *Damn. I never did pick up a proper knife belt.*

Meanwhile, though Izzy had gotten Orne out and formed, she had few options with the Clansman Balori standing with drawn sword between her and Jathen and the Annarite standing between her and Orne. She wet her lips, looking at Jathen for instruction. Swallowing, he could do no more than shift Seren somewhat more behind him and glare into the human's flat, icy-blue eyes as he plucked Jathen's dagger out of his grip.

"Whatever you're planning," Jathen told them, "it will not help the Balori or your Prophet win today."

"We told you: we aren't stupid," the Balori human replied. "We were *never* going to win this farce. What we do now is about making sure the Prophet continues on once he fails in there."

The Clansman chuckled, a cruel sound, then added, "That and extracting penance from the self-righteous bitch who framed Nan and tried to murder him."

Raw terror coursed through Jathen's veins. *Annakki.* Seren's eyes grew very wide when she heard the thought.

"Now, like I said..." The Annarite kept his hands up, facing Izzy, though his eyes were on Orne. "Out of respect for you saving the Prophet, I don't want you and yours getting hurt today, Negater. So how about we just sheathe your golem back in your bag, Fauni Walker, and we'll all just go somewhere quiet to wait it out?" Those red eyes glanced back at Jathen. "Deal?"

Jathen swallowed again, debating while secretly hoping he might be able to stall them. If he rejected the offer and tried to fight, all they needed to do was make a lot of noise and attract some tar'ka-besh. But with the crowd still so near and so loud, they had no guarantee of being noticed. *And even if they don't kill me and Izzy outright with their first move, they'll try to take Seren hostage to keep us both quelled.*

Thanks for that, Seren thought sarcastically.

Jathen stiffened, biting his lip. *Well, do you think you can distract them without getting any of us stabbed?*

Jathen, this isn't the wilderness or a basement we're locked in. We are in Tar'citadel, a mere five blocks from the Temple Hospital and surrounded by tar'ka-besh. Stab wounds are actually highly difficult to die from. Unless one of these men takes off a limb or severs an artery, we'll probably survive. When he jerked his eyes in her direction, she shrugged the slightest bit. *What? I just think our odds are better if you don't think of me as a liability.*

"I'm waiting, Negater."

"I'm thinking!" Jathen held his breath as the human pushed his sword slightly harder against his neck. He locked gazes with Izzy. *Seren, stay against the wall. If you get a chance, run and yell as loud as you can for tar'ka-besh. And try* not *to get stabbed.*

Jathen—

Do it! he screamed in his head just as he turned sideways and slammed his right palm into the human's elbow until it popped. The man shrieked, dropping his sword. Saying a silent prayer that the Clansman wouldn't murder Izzy, Jathen ducked under the twitching arm and punched with everything he had into the human's solar plexus. It was sloppy, and his feet skidded a bit, bringing to mind Annakki's reprimands about footwork, but the Balori doubled over, eyes watering in pain. Seren, to her credit, screamed behind him as if the ground had split open and the Red himself had suddenly shot up from the Pit.

Jathen flinched at the sound as he grabbed the human's shirt collar and bashed him face-first into the wall. A quick glance caught Izzy clutching her shoulder while Orne held the Clansman upside down by a leg with one skeletal hand and slashed angrily in the direction of the Annarite with the other. Cursing under his breath, Jathen kneed the human in the solar plexus again then released him. He didn't rise but slid down the wall with a dazed expression.

Turning back toward Izzy, Jathen watched as the Clansman hacked uselessly at Orne's forearm bones with his sword then teleported out of the golem's grasp. Strangely, the Annarite stuck around, glaring daggers at Jathen even as Orne continued to swipe at him. The mineral-hard claws scraped across nothingness, for the An-narite's ward was powerful enough to stop Izzy's partner.

"You all right?" Jathen called to Izzy.

Rubbing her shoulder, she nodded. "Just bruised. He hilt bashed me. They were trying to incapacitate, not kill."

"I meant it, Negater," the Annarite said from inside his ward. "I just want you to stay out of it today."

"You and your friends aren't doing anything today," Seren scolded, putting her hands on her hips. "You underestimated us, and now one of your friends is probably going to be suffering head trauma, the other's fled, and *you* are going to face some charges."

Throwing back his head, the Annarite laughed, an unencumbered sound. "You think it was just us three? We are *Balori*. The Prophet might preach passivity, but we are born of the Red, silly Tazu. You have *no idea* what kind of fall is coming today."

It all begins at the fall.

A swell of fear grew from Jathen's stomach up into his throat. Almost afraid to look, he forced his neck to tilt upward, and his eyes found the side of Mt. Reverence all too easily.

"Oh, ruddy hell," Seren whispered, eyes wide as her gaze followed his own.

BOOM!

The earth-shattering sound echoed across the mountains, bouncing back and forth in a nearly musical, rhythmic stanza of destruction. Jathen couldn't see what had caused it or where it originated, but the cresting wave of snow and thunderous ice perfectly matched the brief flash he'd seen in his vision. It bubbled and flowed, cascading down toward the city like a thick, dirty cloud of dry ice spilling over the edge of a stage, but a thousand times faster. Jathen couldn't see it, but he knew the cascade was too much for the levee and the Dragon's Tongue, and he heard the second *boom* as the river of death slammed right through it all. Still, the water must have slowed it, for

Jathen at last had time to truly behold the white monster about to engulf the city. The eruption of powder and ice smashed into the side of an invisible barrier, pushing and covering the sky all the way up and across the citadels in a strange mimicry of Dodbyen's dome. A thin cloud of filtered snow fell across the city, like the strange sparking ash of a volcano, but no more.

Oh, thank Spirit. Na'vosh made sure it held. The thought was a small comfort right before the surge of panic emanating from every single empathic in the city hit Jathen full in the head. As if another wave of snow had covered him personally, Jathen's eyesight was bleached white just before he lost consciousness.

Chapter 6

Jathen nearly vomited.

Coming to, he felt the sudden rise of bile in the back of his throat but swallowed several times, pushing the caustic, bitter tincture back down. On the ground, he rolled onto his side, rough cobblestones and cold, dirty snow pressing into his cheek and temple as he sucked in deep breaths, trying to clear his head.

"Jathen?" Izzy sounded concerned but not panicked, oddly comforting through his haze. When he managed to nod, she helped him sit up slowly.

"Where'd the Balori go?" Jathen managed to ask, his voice coming out thick.

"The Annarite teleported the second the snow hit, but the human's still drooling by the wall," Izzy replied, much to Jathen's relief, as he was in no shape to jump back into a fight. "Not seen the Clansman."

A new surge of nausea punched Jathen in the stomach. He blinked, trying to look around, but his eyes weren't quite focusing, and his vision was flooding with dark spots. Orne, at least, seemed to have been disassembled, if not back in his bag. Squinting, Jathen got a bare outline of Izzy's face.

"Seren?" he asked.

"I'm here." Her voice sounded small. A hand found its way to his shoulder and squeezed gently. "Not doing so well, either. This has to have knocked out half the city."

"At least it's only empathically." Jathen shook his head, hard. *I almost wish I had a mage to throw magic at me about now.* He glanced up and found the sight of snow suspended over the city's invisible ward both comforting and terrifying. Wetting his lips, Jathen tried to get his mind working around what had happened. "This could have been much worse."

"Jathen, I am so sorry." Seren's voice croaked behind him. "I should have *listened*—"

Suddenly, Na'vosh's cool and calm voice boomed out across the city. "We would like to assure the populace that we have the situation well in hand, and you are safe to carry on as you normally would. Any mages who are fit to do so, please report to the Municipal Citadel to assist in snow removal and evacuation of the watchtowers. Your tar'ka-besh appreciate your assistance."

As the voice faded, Jathen said another silent prayer of thanks that his warning to the tar'ka-besh had been heeded. He held an arm out. "Izzy, help me up. We can't dawdle."

"Dawdle?" The fauni's blue forehead tattoos came into focus as she lifted him with some help from Seren. They furrowed as Jathen, mostly upright, leaned heavily against the Tazu. "And what are we off to do? Na'vosh said they have things well in hand, and none of us is a mage."

"Not with that. It might just be a distraction." Jathen shook his head then regretted it, stepping sideways against Seren.

She braced him, but not without effort.

"You heard them, right?" he continued. "They said there was 'going to be penance taken' from Annakki."

"And with all the tar'ka-besh dealing with the avalanche and the enclave, there'll be no home-guard response if they attack the townhouse," Izzy said, her umber-colored eyes growing wide.

"Exactly. Seren, you *weren't* wrong. They couldn't hurt the city. But they *can* distract everyone in it." His stomach rolling hard, Jathen cursed, but he steeled himself as half a plan formed. "We need to go to the townhouse and see if we're early enough in this plot to warn them. Seren"—he stepped back from her, gaining his feet—"go to the embassy and see if you can get some help from there."

"I'm not leaving you!" Her claws tightened around his sleeves, and he got a very clear image in her mind of the many possibilities of his deaths from the vision, plucked out of his own memories.

"Seren, please." He braced her elbows. "I'll be all right. Just get Marc and your mother."

"She's at the enclave. *Every*one is at the ruddy enclave," she hissed back. "And there is no *way* I'm going to get through the crowd to get to her with all this going on."

"Then go get Marc and a few others of the Tazu from Dodbyen or some of the guards or Bertran or anyone else who will *help*. Please, I need this from you!"

"Need it from me or need me out of the way?" Her eyes narrowed, shining with a sparkle of tears. "It's bad enough I didn't listen to you *and* talked us all into coming out here. Are you really going to concoct some nonsense to get the useless one off to where she can't do any more harm?"

Jathen, though unable to step out of her grip, had recovered enough to release her steadying arms. *There is no time,* he thought, his fists as clenched as his heart. *No time to get this wrong.* "Seren, you *helped* just now with besting them, and if you have another suggestion or anything else you can do that will be helpful going into a battle, I'll hear it. But otherwise, right now, the best help you can be is to go get more people to *fight.*"

Seren rolled her lips back under her teeth and bit them, her internal debate easy for Jathen to read. Guilt, fear, and shame poured from her eyes, making his stomach clench.

"We're trusting you to get across the city safely," Izzy broke in, her voice that easy calm she often put on. "I cannot go. The guards will listen only to you or Jathen, and we might need him in a fight against Talents. But we are not enough against all the Balori or even half their number, and in truth, we have no idea what we are running off toward." She put a hand on Seren's, dark chestnut over brilliant blue scales, still clutching at Jathen as if he might dissipate if she didn't hold on. "Please, Serendibiss, help us in this."

Closing her eyes, Seren shuddered once then nodded. "Fine." She opened her eyes and unclenched her fists from Jathen's arms. "But for the love of Spirit, you better not *die*, Jathen Monortith."

"Trust me, it's not in the plan," he promised then kissed her hard and quick. He released her, leaving her breathless, a sparkle of wetness in her eyes. "Be fast. Be safe."

"You too," she whispered then shot Izzy a stern glare. "Keep him breathing."

"My heart will stop before his does," Izzy replied with a steely assuredness that left Jathen feeling oddly humbled and unnerved. He took a moment to help Izzy put Orne back in her bag while Seren ran off, then the two of them headed for the townhouse as quickly as they could.

Plagued by strange shadows as they went, Jathen found that the pile of snow covering Tar'citadel left the city with a somber, overcast feel, as if a greater storm were coming. The effect of so many empathics panicking at once was widespread too. Talents all over the city were sitting in the streets and holding their heads, heedless of the drifting snow. Some had clearly been sick, and the sticky, sour smell of vomit permeated the air like a bad incense. Though he hadn't lost his stomach, Jathen found himself struggling to keep it even as they ran. He missed a step and stumbled, nearly going down. Staggering, he flopped against the nearest lamppost while Izzy skidded to a stop.

"You need to take a moment to ground yourself," she said.

"I don't have a moment. Annakki—"

"Will not be better served if you arrive on her doorstep only to faint once you cross the threshold."

Nodding, Jathen did what she'd ordered. Breathing deeply through his nose and out again, he imagined clearing out the house that was his mind, opening windows and setting new foundations until the shaking in his hands and legs ebbed.

"Good." Pursing her lips, Izzy then tipped her head. "Let us be off."

Fire greeted them when they reached the townhouse.

A ring of blazing glory over three Tazu stories high encompassed the building and courtyard, brushing up against the attached neighboring homes but not consuming them. Jathen and Izzy made for the iron gate leading into the courtyard but skidded slightly on a patch of ice on the cobblestones. Jathen wobbled, but Izzy steadied him. Looking about, Jathen saw no sign of the Balori nor anything through the gate but more fire, the metal of it having grown white from the heat.

"Can you hear anything?" Izzy called.

"No, it's just the roar of the barrier." Jathen thrashed his arms in frustration. *Annakki and the others could be trapped inside, being slaughtered by dozens of Balori as I stand here.* "We need to find a way in!"

"There." Izzy pointed at the top of the neighboring house's courtyard wall. "Can your negation bubble get us through?"

"I... I don't know." Feeling the burn of the heat more intensely in his widened eyes, Jathen swallowed hard as he realized she meant him to blindly jump through the barrier and drop into the courtyard. "I... I've never tried anything like this before. I suppose I'd need to throw it up then walk through the barrier. The bubble might cover us both, or it might only cover me, or it might take out the entire barrier or just part of it. It's honestly beyond my scope."

"Do you have a better plan?"

Jathen groaned. "No."

Using the neighbor's gate as a ladder, the pair scrambled up onto the adjoining wall, coming within a few heads of the blaze. "Wait here while I go," he told Izzy. "I'll get the bubble up then walk through. If I can maintain it and it looks like you can follow safely, do it. Otherwise, I'll come back for you."

Izzy nodded, clearly not thrilled to send him alone.

Creeping toward the fire half a scale at a time, Jathen put an arm up to shield his eyes, the heat a nearly physical barrier in its own right. Taking a deep breath, Jathen tried to focus on the music of the Endless Opus, but the harsh dryness of the hot air filling his lungs set him to coughing. The temperature was too high and his instinct to preserve his own skin too strong to walk into the blaze. Shaking his head in defeat, he scampered back to Izzy. "I don't think I can concentrate enough to hold it up *and* walk through it. I can't convince my brain I won't burn up!"

Izzy bit her lip then nodded. "I have a plan." Unclasping her bag, she let Orne spill out into the other courtyard and form, then she shifted him, transforming the bones into tyrn form. "He won't fly," she whispered, her gaze steady and slightly out of focus as she concentrated, "but he can carry and jump."

A wave of sickness and fear washed over Jathen as he realized what she was suggesting. "But won't my negation bubble negate *Orne*? He'll fall apart!"

"Yes. So you'll have to do it in midair, right as we hit the fire, and let the momentum carry us through."

"Oh, ruddy hell."

"Can you do it? The only other option is to wait for Seren to bring help."

Staring at the fire, Jathen's sole consolation was that he hadn't seen a crispy version of himself *with* Izzy among his visions. "I suppose I'm going to have to make it work."

With that, the tyrn Orne climbed up onto the wall with them, and they scrambled precariously aboard, Jathen in front with Izzy clasping him about the waist. Terribly uncomfortable as he straddled old bones poking at tender places, Jathen bit his lip, trying to concentrate.

"It must go up just before *you* reach the barrier. Orne feels no pain, so do not concern yourself for the front half of him," Izzy said. "I go on your mark!"

Feeling D'ilinde's fevered whirling in his chest, Jathen took a breath then released it in a soft gasp, having meant to call the charge but failing. *You can do this*, he whispered to himself. *For Annakki.* He closed his eyes. *For Dor'rhean.*

"Go!"

With a charge and a leap, Orne took to the air.

Opening his eyes with terrified effort, Jathen played the crescendo of the Endless Opus in his head—though a series of curses punctuated the melody. He waited as long as he could, until he was hit by the sensation of his eyebrows singeing, before he threw up the negation bubble.

The fire parted for them like water at the bow of a ship. It curled, swirling, close and hot, so unbearable that Jathen could barely breathe. Then a *snap* was followed by a *roar*, and Jathen, horrified, realized he'd negated the entire barrier. Fire itself melted all around them, turning back into wind, swirling and escaping like a tornado. Jathen let it fly, hoping it would do damage to enemies and not friends. The sound of windows shattering across the fronts of the houses rang in his ears as he and Izzy fell, Orne's bones dismantling from under them.

Be better! Be better! Be better! Jathen chanted frantically in his head, desperate to use the extra energy to keep himself conscious. He could feel the drain from negating so much, along with the boiling rise of a pounding headache. The tactic worked, though, and the negated blaze rushed through his veins like wildfire, healing and reviving.

They landed in a heap, tumbling across a clatter of bones. Jathen felt his ankle snap, but then it blazed with warmth, popping back into place again without more than a moment's pain. *Ruddy hell, that was a lot of extra energy.* When his body came to a stop on the ground, Jathen could only lie there a moment, staring up at the sky in bewildered awe. He giggled then cried out in joy, thrilled to be alive. *It worked! I can't believe it worked!* Continuing to giggle despite himself, he deduced the extra energy probably had a side effect of giddiness. Taking a breath, he found his way to his knees, looking about for Izzy and possible enemies.

Aside from himself, Izzy, a blanket of broken glass, and a rumpled-looking Chūjitsun lying amid Orne's scattered bones, the courtyard was empty. The master servant pressed a hand to his head, his dark eyes murderous. "What were you *thinking*?"

"I... The Balori!" Jathen sputtered, still taking in the empty courtyard.

The fountain shaped like jumping koi stood dry behind him, and other than a powdering of shattered glass and one of Orne's femurs resting in the shaped Clan maple tree on the other side of the path, the space seemed unmarred. Izzy found her way to her feet as well, looking unharmed aside from a few scrapes on her palms.

"I thought... you were stuck in here with them," Jathen finished.

"It was *my* barrier!" Chūjitsun scolded. Slowly making his way to his feet, he brushed his uniform free of dirt and glass, though he missed a few specks of the former on the white parts of his cuffs. "I stepped outside after the avalanche to check the perimeter and saw them swarming like ruddy locusts."

Jathen flinched hard, his stomach feeling as if Chūjitsun had just punched a flaming fist into it. "And I just negated the whole barrier."

"For which we are quite grateful, Negater!"

Jathen spun around in time to see the still red-hot iron gate crumple in upon itself then fly toward them. Diving out of the way with Izzy and Chūjitsun, Jathen tumbled across the pebbled gravel of the path. Coming to a stop against the side of the fountain, Jathen sprang up to his knees as quickly as he could. He took in the sight of the Annarite Balori striding into the courtyard, followed by the burned Clansman from before and six more Balori toting various shields and weapons. More were behind them, but Chūjitsun reacted with precision, the fire barrier around the house blazing back to life just as they were poised to rush through.

Thank Spirit for small favors, Jathen thought with a shaky breath.

The large Annarite eyed the new barrier with pursed lips then shook his head with a nasty grin. "Last chance, Negater," he called to Jathen and Izzy. He ran a hand across the shaved side of his scalp, scowling as he fingered the hilt of his drawn sword. "Eight against three, the odds are not in your favor, even with the mage. We just want our pound of flesh. We don't need to take it from you."

Straight backed, unruffled, and without a word, Chūjitsun stepped upon the front stoop, blocking the door to the house. The twisted Rheanic face of the doorknocker glared over his shoulder like an additional sentinel. Izzy, meanwhile, swept her arm up, making Orne's bones shiver and shake across the ground. As blue-white runes blazed to life across Izzy's body, her Tazu golem formed with an earsplitting roar.

"Eight against four," she said with steely resolve.

Jathen bit the inside of his cheek as the group of Balori didn't so much as flinch. Indeed, some grinned fiercely, eager for blood. *These are Talents, and this will not be easy.* Pulling one of his daggers from his pocket as he stood, Jathen prayed he could talk some sense into these angry men and women. "You'll need to kill every single one of us," he called to the line of them, "and the tar'ka-besh will still know what you've done here—word has gotten to the Tazu Embassy by now. Do you think what you've done here will not have repercussions for De'contes? For the vote today?" He swallowed. "You don't have to do this."

The Clansman chuckled. "You think she's going to stop? You think she's going to let him live after today?"

Jathen pursed his lips, knowing all too well whom he was referring to. "You think De'contes or the Balori will keep their sanctuary in Tar'citadel if you continue this?"

He smirked cruelly, tapping a temple with his fingers. "Banishment is better than death. I've seen it. And I've seen what happens to the world if we leave her to kill him."

Dear Spirit in Heaven, he's precognitive too. Jathen actually trembled, terrified of everything that *could be*, which he wasn't privy to. *But as much as I haven't seen, there also have to be possibilities he's not considered.* "I've seen darkness in precognitive visons you can't imagine, but I would never, *ever* set troops against someone who's yet to commit a horror—no matter what evils they've done in the past. There must be another way. I've spent *months* carving out other ways. You can too. If you just tell me, let me talk to her, convince her—"

"I've seen that too, Negater. And as said, I'd prefer to keep you out of today. But you *aren't* going to convince her. You and I both know that."

Remaining silent, Jathen bit lightly on his lip as his stomach flip-flopped. Dread set in, and he knew he couldn't turn their hearts. *Please just let one of them be stupid enough to cast at me.*

The Annarite glared down his dark nose at them. "Don't waste your spells on the Negater. Take out the fauni. Leave the mage mind-rapist to me."

Ruddy hell, Jathen thought just before they charged.

Cutting sideways behind Izzy, he gasped in a sharp breath, humming a measure of the Endless Opus in his head as he went. The negation bubble surged, growing around him and Izzy. With a wave of wind, a sharp obsidian spike crashed against the bubble with an angry growl. When Jathen released the breath, the energy negated, spilling back toward those who'd cast it. His redirection was sloppy, and the burst of wind and exploding dirt also slammed into Orne and smashed the golem back to bones, but not before crashing down atop the Clansman. The energy also caused havoc for the majority of the Balori, knocking most of the brutes backward and sideways—a few dangerously close to Chūjitsun's blazing barrier.

The Annarite kept his feet.

Head dipping forward like a bull about to charge, he raised his arms as Izzy had, and the neatly raked gravel of the pathways ripped up into the air and launched itself at Izzy, Jathen, and Chūjitsun. Jathen cut sideways again, back behind the fountain, cursing, because physical stone shrapnel wasn't energy to be negated and he hadn't saved enough of the previous spell to throw up a wave of his own. Close on his heels, Izzy collapsed onto the ground with him, slamming into his side. As pebbles peppered the air about them, Jathen looked for Chūjitsun. The master servant remained at his post before the door, unscathed. A second ward shimmered in the air before him, turning stones away so they didn't even scuff the brickwork on the front of the house.

"He shall not last long," Izzy whispered harshly to Jathen over the fray. "Not while maintaining the fire barrier as well." The runes on her head glowed once more, and behind them, Jathen heard a few shrieks as Orne reformed, presumably. "Stay back here and pick them off if you can."

"I've only got four daggers," he hissed as she slipped into a crouch.

"Make do," she replied, standing. "The Annarite mage won't cast our way. He wants Chūjitsun."

But the Clansman might cast your way. Jathen pursed his lips as he rolled into a crouch, peering cautiously over the edge of the fountain. He slipped a dagger out of his pocket just as the recovered Clansman shouted orders in another language, all while Chūjitsun stood stock still beneath the onslaught of force attacks from the Annarite.

Jathen took a breath and chucked the dagger at the Clansman. A good throw, on mark to pierce the armor around the sangcordis, but the Clansman snatched it out of the air. His eyes found Jathen's, the soft blue violet melting into a liquid silver-blue blaze.

"Kill the ruddy moot!" he shrieked at the rest of the Balori while hurling the dagger blade-first into the ground by his feet.

Jathen pulled out another dagger as he wondered if the Clansman wasn't lifting Jathen and tossing him about because he was a Negater or because of the stuff Raleigh had been saying about organic magic. Flicking the weapon at the closest Balori—a human woman clad in red-and-black leathers and wielding a broadsword—Jathen prayed his second dagger would have better luck. It caught her across the neck, causing a decent cut but not enough to put her down. Frantic, he pulled another dagger from his pockets while the blonde flexed her leather gloves, now bloody, on her hilt, stalking ever closer. Two more Balori began to flank Jathen on the other side of the fountain, and he cursed angrily in his head yet again. *Why didn't I bring the ruddy sword cane?*

Orne ripped the charging white-blond Balori away right before she reached Jathen. Her shriek rang almost comical as she was tossed hard into the line of her fellow fighters. After crashing into a large

Balori with chain mail and an axe, she and her comrade tumbled into the fire barrier. The sound and smell of people burning alive made Jathen retch. Luckily, it distracted the rest of the Balori, including the Clansman, who frantically tried to extinguish his companions with wind spells. The other two Balori warriors resorted to old-fashioned stomping to stem the tide, though with little effect. Stepping back toward Izzy again, Jathen gained control of his stomach as Orne snatched up the two Balori who'd been flanking him.

The Annarite leader turned his attention away from pummeling Chūjitsun and attacked with a furious spell, causing daggers of wind to slash at Orne's legs. Chips of bone splintered from the golem's femurs, but that wasn't enough to faze him as Izzy swept her arms up, tossing those two men into the fire barrier as well. More screaming and sizzling threatened to set Jathen to dry heaving again as the bodies fell like horrific meteorites into the empty fountain. *Four dead, at least.*

"Keep the damn golem off me!" the Annarite yelled at the Clansman then returned his attentions to Chūjitsun.

He's hoping to get the barrier down and the others through.

The Clansman waved an arm, and the sculpted maple tree opposite the fountain ripped free of the ground, roots and all. Izzy braced herself, but it didn't fly toward her or Orne. It crashed into the barrier, where it caught aflame *then* began to assault Orne.

"Kill the Negater!" the Clansman shrieked again to the remaining two Balori.

The larger of the two, a brute of a human with a thick neck and murderous eyes, charged around the fountain at Jathen, his small, round wooden shield positioned to bash Jathen in the chest. Pivoting to the side slightly, Jathen let him come, grabbing at the edges of the shield when the Balori reached him. With the shield pressed between them, Jathen dropped his weight and purposefully fell backward, intending to use the momentum against the Balori and flip his attacker over himself into the fire still smoking in the fountain.

He'd managed that type of flip all of once in training with An-nakki—and Spinnek had been considerably lighter. Jathen's leg slipped as he went down, and he kneed the Balori in the stomach rather than planting his foot, but at least it made the man drop his axe. Lacking the leverage to toss him fully, Jathen landed hard on his right side then more rolled than tossed the Balori to the right. Hear-ing a *crunch* then feeling an explosion of pain, Jathen knew he'd dis-located his shoulder even as he managed to slam the Balori into the ledge of the fountain. The back of the human's head bashed into the stone with a nasty-sounding *crack*, and Jathen's cry of pain was lost under the sound of the Balori's bloodcurdling scream.

D'ilinde buzzed a high-pitched warning, raising the hairs on Ja-then's neck. Dazed but riding the adrenaline, Jathen ripped the shield from the fallen Balori and spun it around, catching the other Balori's slashing sword with the edge of it. Gripping the wood for dear life with his left hand, he deflected another of her angry slashes. Kicking her hard as he could in the shin, Jathen slammed painfully against her tough leather shin guards. Unhurt, she sidestepped away from his legs, giving him a chance to grip the shield better and smash it hard into her hip. Gasping, she twisted farther backward, which allowed Jathen to pull himself up onto his knees and flip the shield around to grip it properly, by its straps.

In a feverish rage, she hacked and slashed against the little shield while Jathen desperately fumbled with his nearly useless right arm to get another dagger in hand. Realizing he had no thrusting power in his arm, he instead slipped the dagger through the splintering shield during one of her hits. On her next slash, he immediately thrust the shield sideways, deflecting the attack and twisting her body to the side. Using the shield, Jathen bashed her in the face over her arm, the dagger stuck in the wood implanting itself deep into her cheek. She shrieked and stumbled sideways. Gaining his feet, Jathen gave her no quarter, hitting her twice more in the face with the dagger-shield before it shattered. She went down and stayed there.

Dropping the ruined shield, Jathen stumbled a bit as he glanced about, looking for Izzy. The Clansman was down, Orne having beaten him to a cinder with the flaming tree. Abandoned, it sat smoldering beside the burning corpse while Orne pounded with both fists on the top of the Annarite's ward, still not making a dent.

Catching his breath, Jathen surveyed the rest of the scene with a momentary stab of despair. Bodies were splayed everywhere, the two occupying the fountain still glowing and smoking enough to make it look like a portal down to the Pit. The paths were gone, the carefully tended plants flattened, and the sculpted decorative Clan maple tree a smoking husk. Something was viciously feral about the destruction of Annakki's only corner of peace. *And it was my fault. I let them in. I wonder, was that something the other precognitive had seen and manipulated me into doing?* Jathen shook his head, bringing his focus back to the fight. He had no time to wax philosophical about the events of the day.

Chūjitsun was still standing in the entryway to the house, cutting a single terrifying figure of a master sentry holding his door. Jathen saw a ripple, a waver of Chūjitsun's ward faltering as his energy slowly ebbed. A single droplet of sweat rolled down the man's temple. *He's going to lose it soon.*

The Annarite's garnet eyes glittered, seeing only Chūjitsun.

He knows it too. Biting his lip against the pain, Jathen left-handedly slipped out his last dagger and ran at the Annarite with everything he had. As the Balori mage threw his spell once more at Chūjitsun, the manservant's ward faltered. In that moment, Jathen closed the gap, slipping past Orne and right through the Annarite's ward. He negated it into a burst of strength and speed, along with a command to heal, the power washing over him all at once in another gid-

dy wave. With a cry both angry and ecstatic, Jathen plunged the dagger deep into the Balori's jugular even as he felt his shoulder pop back
into place and his veins light aflame with energy.

Not until the moment the dagger plunged into the man's neck
had Jathen truly understood what a Negater was to a traditional Talent. A caveat, a foil, he could step right through their barriers and
into their space, almost as if their very Ability simply did not exist.
He saw the same understanding in the Annarite's eyes: pure incon-
ceivable shock that Jathen even existed, that he could just circumvent
the magic that had stayed everyone else. He'd even known what Jathen was, but he'd still not truly understood until that knife entered
his neck. *They will always underestimate me*, Jathen thought as the
Balori's legs went out and he flopped upon the ground. Still clutching the bloody dagger, Jathen stared at his hand. *That is my power...
as a Negater and as a moot.*

Now I just have to live long enough to use it.

Still moving as his blood gushed, the Annarite gasped, and the
last of his energy surged forward in one concluding strike past Jathen
toward Chūjitsun. The final attack of the dying man hit home, slashing across the master servant's entire body. Pressing his hand into his
hemorrhaging neck, Chūjitsun slid down the side of the doorframe,
his own dark eyes wide in pain and shock.

"Izzy, help me!" Jathen dashed to the master servant's side,
crouching to try to stem the flow. He didn't know where to put his
hands. The Balori had hit Chūjitsun with efficient precision on two
major arteries, the jugular and the femoral, and also in the gut—all
three eliciting excessive, immediate bleeding. The last time Jathen
had seen so much blood had been when he'd dug a knife into
Raudur's sangcordis, and the Clansman had not survived long past
it.

Chūjitsun must have seen the fear and panic in Jathen's eyes as
he dropped his dagger and pressed down on the older man's thigh. "I

feel my service is at an end, young prince," he sputtered, blood seeping out through his fingers and onto his chest.

Jathen looked at Izzy, who simply shook her head. He knew it too—Petalith had taught him enough. Even if he or Izzy had the Ability to mend him, doing so would take too much time. He would bleed out before they finished healing up the first wound. Jathen swallowed, plastering a cheerless smile upon his face. "You served your mistress well, Chūjitsun."

He coughed, the very barest of a grin flicking briefly across his blood-stained lips. "I have, haven't I?"

"Yes, you have." Jathen swallowed again, fighting the surprising arrival of tears.

They'd had their differences, and Jathen had never come to like the man, but he did respect the human and his loyalty to Annakki. His heart broke because his own recklessness had cost Chūjitsun his life. "How did you put it? You held onto the civility of nobility in everything you did—even in this. Annakki would be proud."

"Yes, her approval... I never faltered... anything she'd ask..." Those dark, sharklike eyes darted to Jathen, taking in his face. "The only thing... I wasn't prepared... was hurt you, that day... I knew Lady Annakki... wouldn't have desired it. I failed... because... I knew... your safety... mattered more."

Jathen took a breath then, knowing this would be his last chance, asked, "Then why didn't you simply wait until I was gone?"

"If De'contes.... convinced.... Akira or Utför... for the vote.... then it wouldn't have.... made sense.... for De'contes... to kill him. He needed... to die... before."

Jathen stiffened slightly, intuition prickling the hairs at the base of his neck. Chūjitsun's loss of blood and imminent death might explain his odd words, but then again... "Chu? What do you mean? De'contes didn't try to kill *himself*. You tried to kill *him*, right?" Jathen ran the memory through his mind again, of the fake Nannazen stabbing toward De'contes with a soul-sever blade. That was certainly what seemed to have happened. "Isn't that what Annakki ordered you to do?"

"Changed... plan... Couldn't... let you... get... hurt. Changed... plan... Kill De'contes... instead—" Chūjitsun took one last, choking breath before exhaling a barely audible sound. His hand fell away from his neck, and the little light left in those dark eyes snuffed out. The barrier of fire fell with it, a sputtering exhalation followed by the frigid wave of the cold air of Tar'citadel.

"Did you hear?" Izzy asked.

"Yes." Fingers sticky with blood, Jathen closed the master servant's eyes then stood. "He said, 'Mağrur.'"

Chapter 7

Jathen grimaced.

Tiredness slowed his thoughts, and he made to wipe his forehead free of sweat but stopped in time to prevent himself from smearing the mix of blood—the Annarite's and Chūjitsun's—all over his own face. Still staring down at the fallen servant, he couldn't fathom what to think. *Oh, Annakki, what did you do?*

"Master Mağrur?" Confusion and worry shone in Izzy's eyes and along her furrowed brow. "Why?"

Shaken, Jathen could only stare desperately back at her, grinding his teeth. "I don't—"

A scream pierced the air.

Izzy gasped. "Inside. The rest of them must have found a way in through the back."

"Damn it! Come on," Jathen ordered. He tried to turn the door handle but found it locked. "Ruddy hell!" Practically choking on the irony of Chūjitsun's death keeping him from opening the door, Jathen barely heard Izzy call his name.

"Jathen!" she repeated, waving him over to the nearest shattered window. "Here!"

After scooping up his still-bloody dagger and sparing one last glance at the fallen Chūjitsun, Jathen joined Izzy by the window. Orne cleared the remains of fractured glass and reduced what was left of the panes to splinters before Izzy followed. Jathen stumbled in next, nearly tripping over the chair Erin Manna had so often sat in when they'd chatted. Aside from the window, the living room seemed unscathed. The sounds of screaming servants getting closer distracted Jathen from further assessments. A cluster of five humans came running into the foyer, skittering to a stop with terrified shrieks at the sight of Orne.

"This way, this way," Jathen called, motioning toward the sitting room and the cleared window. "Get outside then to the street. Find some tar'ka-besh!" The group scurried past him in a frenzy, and a strange juxtaposition—saving people *from* the Balori when the last time he'd been herding panicked crowds through a townhouse, he'd been *saving* Balori—was not lost on Jathen.

Two new dark-robed figures appeared in the foyer, Annakki's private guards teleporting in. Jathen breathed a light sigh of relief. He did not know the men's Abilities or Way Paths, but more bodies with swords in hand were quite welcome when on their side. The two had seen a fight already, sporting a few scrapes and mussed clothes, as well as blood on their weapons. One was missing about half his cloak, the ripped side hanging off his back like a limp tyrn tail.

So much for them being ghosts. "How many?" Jathen asked, falling into step behind the humans and beside Izzy, with Orne in front, facing the hall.

"Too many" was the monotone reply from under one low black hood. A brief glimmer of honey-brown eyes peeked out from under the fabric before the guard turned forward once more. "Hold the stairs."

Jathen nodded. Annakki and the others had probably taken to the high ground when the barrier went up the first time. *We just have to buy time until Seren or the servants get here with help.* Jathen's fingers danced nervously over his final dagger, and he wiped the blood on his pant leg. A new cluster of five armed Balori pushed into the foyer, with more still behind. *Rhean, if you're listening, now would be a good time to be helpful.* D'ilinde buzzed ambiguously, either amused or indignant.

Orne dove into the center of the Balori, roaring, tossing and creating the havoc only he could. The two guards used the chaos to their advantage, picking off fallen foes with efficient sword strikes. Jathen kept his distance, creeping around behind Izzy and toward the stairs, watching the fray for any stragglers who might make a run for them. Eyeing the curling staircase and the first door off the landing, which led to his bedroom, he debated darting up quickly to grab his sword cane and check on the others.

A flicker of movement in the hallway caught Jathen's eye—a surge of eight more Balori. An additional three members lingered behind them in the hall doorway, and Jathen knew with deadly certainty the battle had only just begun.

Possibly in his late thirties, the one on the far left was of either southern Clan Lands or northern Lubreean human stock and had very pale brown eyes. Not a pretty color, it reminded Jathen of ryml dung left out to crackle in the Zo'den sun. He also had a mean-looking scar on his left cheek. Shaped like the Clan character meaning *outcast*, it looked to have been inflicted by a heated brand.

On the right stood a girl. *Spirit in Heaven.* Jathen recognized her, the twelve-year-old he'd collided with on the day he'd been ambushed by the acolyte Pearl Paladins. She'd been ranting on about the prophecy of the Red. Still skinny but now sporting neat braids in her brown hair, she showed hardness in her pale-blue eyes where once had been fear and awe. Wearing a tighter red-and-black uniform, she held her hands clenched stiffly around the handles of what looked like a pair of water buckets. Odd as that was, the arch of her neck said she'd come to destroy when once she would have cowered.

Last of those three, the man standing center looked human but had the mass of a Tazu, easily over six and a half heads tall. His chest would rival Esop's for thickness, and his arms were bigger around than Jathen's legs. He wore simple, thin leathers in red and black, and though he was olive skinned, his hair was Annarite white, cropped short and spiky. Grinning as if he'd just walked into a bar fight and reveling in the idea of knocking a few heads, he didn't wield a single weapon. Cracking his knuckles, he grinned more widely. "Let's clear this dance floor!"

The branded man nodded, then the guard standing closer to Izzy just dropped. Jathen cried out helplessly as a Balori thrust his sword into the prone man's back. The other guardsman put *his* sword through that Balori's gut but then dropped as well. Orne picked up another two Balori poised to murder him, tossing them into the wall so hard that the chandelier above their heads shook, its lights going out as it swung violently. Full of rage, Jathen felt a strange sort of tugging inside his mind, but then it stopped.

The branded man shook his head. "Can't penetrate the Negater," he said slowly from across the room. "And the fauni has on a hell of a master-charm on top of the divided consciousness."

"Right," the warrior replied, his voice echoing. He tilted his head to both sides, each movement producing an audible crack, which made Jathen shiver. "Let's dance!" Cackling, he plunged into the middle of the fight, not sparing his own Balori as he shoved them aside on his way to Orne. Locking hands with the golem, he grappled with the monstrous skeleton as if it were a favored wrestling partner. Meanwhile, the girl tossed one of her buckets, the water cascading annoyingly but harmlessly over half the floor.

Ignoring that oddity, Jathen took advantage of the scattered Balori, making a run for the still living but prone guard. Suddenly, the ground beneath his feet lost all traction, and he fell hard upon the slick, frozen floor. Yelping in surprise, he looked over to see the Balori girl glaring at him with one hand held in his direction. She swept her other arm toward Izzy, and a shard of ice emerged from her other bucket and launched toward the fauni. On the far side of the frozen floor, Izzy sidestepped it, scowling as her runes glowed brighter.

Ice mage, Jathen realized while sliding across the frigid parquet. *Damn it, Raleigh. You warned me but didn't tell me how to stop one.* He crashed into the still breathing guard atop a frozen pool of his brethren's blood. Shaking the man, Jathen yelled at him to wake up, but he did not stir. All around them, Balori were also succumbing to the ice mage's slick floor, and no one could keep their feet in the little cubby area to the right of the sweeping stairs. Jathen resorted to sliding the man behind himself and praying the guard would be forgotten by the rest of the Balori.

Using the railing of the stairs as a brace, Jathen tried to stand, but the ice was nearly impossible to keep his footing on. Luckily, Izzy had managed to maneuver Orne and the big warrior between herself and the ice mage, using the area of the floor the water hadn't reached. The girl's attempts to shoot more ice shards at her kept failing as they broke upon his bones. The lights spun widely as the Balori bruiser pushed harder at Orne, backing the golem up farther toward Izzy and the front door, casting disturbing shadows across the room. Several Balori slipped around behind Izzy but, ignoring her, made for the steps.

Jathen cursed, glad she was safe but terrified for those upstairs. Debating darting up there, he shook his head. *Annakki can handle a few Balori. Have to help Izzy. If they decide to kill her, we're all done.*

Jathen gazed up at the wavering chandelier directly above the clashing titans' heads. Grasping his last dagger, he kissed the blade once then let it fly. Amazingly, it flew true, clipping the rope holding the chandelier aloft before implanting into the tin ceiling. With a yelping cry, Jathen watched with sheer joy as the rope snapped and the great light fixture fell directly onto the crown of the horrific Balori bruiser. *Got him!*

"Jathen, *no!*"

He could only blink at Izzy, wondering if she'd lost her mind. Then the great hulk of a Balori laughed, a terrifying sound.

"He's debesh!" Izzy shrieked as she dodged ice shards.

"A what?" Jathen yelped back.

A loud clatter drew his eyes toward the massive bruiser lifting the chandelier up over his head. His bulk increased before Jathen's eyes, muscles bulging and thickening to impossible proportions.

"Kubesh path. They channel their pain to get stronger the more you hurt them!"

"Ruddy fucking Red in the Pit," Jathen muttered in disjointed disbelief. *And that was my last dagger.*

With a roar worthy of an angry Tazu, the debesh hurled the chandelier in Orne's direction. The golem deflected it with a swipe, and Izzy sent it toward the ice mage. The girl dodged it with a squeak, forced backward into the sitting room and upsetting her remaining water bucket. Jathen couldn't see where the branded man had gone—probably farther down the hall or trapped with the ice mage.

I just hope not upstairs. Jathen bit his lip, absentmindedly aware of two Balori trying to skid across the ruined icy parquet floor toward him as he tried to formulate a plan. Pondering, Jathen braced himself on the railing and kicked a fallen Balori's axe in the direction of the two headed his way. The weapon got underfoot and knocked the pair down. *Best try a simple approach. Big as that debesh brute is, he's going to have floor issues as well if I lure him over here.*

Saying a quick prayer to Angani or Turin or any other Child that might be offended, Jathen again braced himself on the banister then used both his feet to push one of the dead Balori bodies across the ice. After a good shove, it skittered into the path of the debesh, who'd started toward Orne again. He tripped on it, but only slightly. He turned, blinking in surprise, then seeing Jathen, crackled a laugh.

"Right, Negater! *Some* might have wanted your hide untanned through this, but I'm not one of them." With another wicked grin in Izzy's direction, he turned and stalked toward Jathen, stepping easily over bodies and across ice as he went.

Cleats, Jathen realized, feeling sick. *He wore spurs on his shoes to handle the ice.* Behind the debesh, Orne moved to intercept, but the chandelier burst in an icy explosion. Knocking the golem sideways, the blast also downed a few more Balori fighters that'd been lingering at the edges of the icy floor. The girl bolted out from behind it with a furious scream. Another ice spell born of what was left in the bucket caught Orne on one of his legs, tethering the golem to the ground. Jathen cursed as the debesh bore down on him.

Izzy let out an angry roar that bled through into Orne, her blue runes glowing brighter, and the great golem shifted into tyrn form amid the shattering of ice. Watching the bones with mild concern, the debesh hesitated long enough for Jathen to push off the side of the staircase and go sliding toward the hallway. He bumped hard into the back wall, cursing as more Balori swept into the room with weapons drawn. *They've got to have thrown nearly twenty at us by now.*

"The bitch is upstairs!" the ice mage yelled at her comrades. Ability-grabbing dirty falling snow from outside through the broken windows, she covered Orne in another layer of ice. The golem growled, cracking the frozen sheets into splinters with his bony tail, but the trick still slowed him. Izzy backed around to the left of the stairs to keep Orne between herself and the debesh and the ice mage, leaving a clear path to the steps.

"No!" Jathen screamed, blindly and stupidly tackling the nearest Balori fighter and dragging him back onto the icy portion of the floor. They skidded a little, but the Balori pulled away, shoving him down literally at the feet of the debesh. The bruiser loomed over Jathen like a nightmare, flexing fingers large enough to encircle Jathen's whole neck in one hand. Lifted by his shoulders with those meaty hands, Jathen let himself go limp, hoping the tainted Walker was gearing up to toss him, though that was a thin hope. Playing the Opus in his head, Jathen let the negation bubble swell on the bet he'd somehow negate the debesh's Ability to channel his pain and he'd drop or... something.

Nothing happened.

Jathen swallowed, his mouth dry as he waited to die, snapped like a twig by a Balori debesh. *Funny, I didn't see this one coming.*

"Get the ruddy hell off my nephew!"

Jathen barely registered the sound of Marcasith's booming voice before the big tyrn slammed into the side of the debesh. He hit the human so hard that the trio broke through a wall, falling amid plaster and broken wood into the study. Released, Jathen landed squarely on his ass, while Marcasith continued roaring and clawing on the mammoth Balori.

"He's debesh!" Jathen choked out, watching with dread as the Balori grappled with his uncle while cackling the way Esop did when he'd drunk too much and found everything funny. The brute kept growing to nearly Marcasith's size from the channeled pain, his body bulging and twisting in ways previously unimaginable and highly unnerving. Bookshelves went flying, tomes bursting off them like bombs as the debesh twisted Marcasith around and slammed him into the desk. The wood shattered, but Marcasith fought like a tyrn possessed, curling his neck around and clamping his massive jaws down upon the Balori's neck and shoulder. The debesh roared with hysterical laugher and, ignoring the spurts of his own blood, punched Marc repeatedly in the face. Grabbing books, Jathen tossed them ineffectually at the debesh's head, desperate to do *something* to help. The big human ignored them, only bothering to swat a few of the hardbacks away like flies.

A new tyrn swept past Jathen in a streak of silver, trumpeting a war roar.

Bertran Larsenitiss landed atop the debesh and Marcasith, clawing and snapping at the human's face like a cat going full tilt at a scratching post. *Ruddy hell.* Dragging his fingers through his hair, Jathen took a moment to look over his shoulder and survey the foyer. More Tazu Nation guards were surging in, most in Tazu form, and making short work of the Balori. Seren wasn't amid them, but Teal, the only other tyrn in the room, was playing cat and mouse with the ice mage.

"Jathen!" Izzy came up to the hole, bracing against Orne as she crossed the ice. "They can handle the debesh, but some of the Balori made it upstairs."

Sparing one last glance at his uncle and cousin clawing the debesh into raw meat, Jathen decided that if the Balori actually managed to survive that onslaught, he deserved to win. "Right, Izzy"—he grabbed onto Orne as he stepped through the wall—"give me a lift, and let's get up there."

"'Twas my plan," she replied with a fierce grin. Climbing up behind him, Izzy looked ghostly from the blue of her runes glowing under the shadow of her hood. With a single leap, the bony tyrn gained the upper landing, leaving the epic battle for the foyer behind.

Practically leaping off Orne, Jathen made his way down the hall, leaving Izzy to dismantle the too-big golem. The lights were out and the doors closed, leaving an eerie dullness that Jathen's eyes took a moment to adjust to. Once they did, he skittered to a stop, breath caught in his throat.

Jathen had encountered many frightening things in his time—earthquakes tearing the world asunder, a manic Mikkal coming for him, ghosts of enemies, visions of fire and blood, feral Okten, hallways full of shattering quartz, Raudur in his horrific burned state—but nothing had given him pause like the sight of Annakki Rheadani standing in that hallway.

Clutching Hatori's sword cane, Annakki was stained in a deep-crimson wash of blood up to her elbows. Not a single drop of red marred any other inch of her body—the crisp, silken lines of her pale-lavender dress were eerily immaculate. At both sides of her feet were two literal piles of bodies, Balori after Balori felled with the same efficiency Erin Manna used to slice her purple vegetables. A dozen bodies must have been lying there, and Annakki was standing amid the massacre as emotionless as in the moment they'd first met.

"I suppose I shouldn't have worried," he murmured.

By the slight crook of her mouth, she seemed to have heard. "The tide has been stinted?" she asked softly when he approached, delicately picking his way around bodies.

She arched her head past his shoulder, eyeing Izzy, who was still gathering bones. Beyond her, the sounds of fighting had dulled to a low shuffle, and Jathen could pick out the sound of Marcasith's voice barking orders, much to his deep relief.

"Seems to be," he replied, trying to keep his stomach, for more than a few Balori near him had not held their bowels when they died. *Spirit help me if I ever get used to all this death.* "Marcasith and some backup from the Tazu Embassy are here." Planting his feet on less slick ground directly before her, he met those tourmaline eyes. "Did any get past you?"

"No." Snapping her wrist, she whipped the blood clear off the dark blade before returning it to the casing she held in her other fist. "Spinnek and Rhyo are at the end of the hall with Dor'rhean," she replied, answering his unspoken question. Those gorgeous eyes searched his. "Chūjitsun? I felt the loss of him in my mind."

Unable to say the words, Jathen shook his head instead. "He never let them through the front. You would have been proud."

She nodded, stoic. "I am."

A loud crash echoed from down the hall, which Jathen barely registered before Annakki darted away. Moving with Clan speed toward Dor'rhean's bedroom, she was no more than a lavender blur. Though he would've bet she could handle just about anything, Jathen rushed after her, worried for Spinnek, Rhyo, and the baby. Izzy followed, shoving the last of Orne's bones into her bag as she did.

Annakki did not open the bedroom door but burst through it, shattering the heavy wood the way Marcasith and the debesh had made short work of the wall downstairs. A brief glance over the woman's shoulder showed Spinnek backed into a corner of the room with Dor'rhean in his arms as a figure in black slashed with fury at a ward before them. The teenager looked unfussed, yawning visibly while he bounced Dor'rhean on his shoulder. The figure in black cut more furiously at the ward, straining in such a way that Jathen caught sight of a few bands of red fabric stitched across the back of his uniform, reminiscent of slashes.

Another black-wearing fighter in a similar outfit dodged about, evading a tyrn Rhyo. The Tazu and the assassin, presumably Balori, shattered chairs and Dor'rhean's crib into splinters as they fought, the Balori slashing and the Tazu snapping jaws and swiping claws.

All that, Jathen glimpsed within a few heartbeats, then the assassin battling Rhyo stepped a bit too close to a lavender-and-black blur. He made not a sound as a ribbon of red arched through the air, and then he fell, throat ripped open so deeply that his head was nearly severed from his body. Rhyo *did* yelp, backing away from the body and pressing himself against the window like a cat that'd inadvertently put a paw into water. Jathen missed the other assassin's death, hearing only the thud as he fell.

"Hello, Jathen!" Spinnek called from the corner, still bouncing Dor'rhean as he waved.

Jathen absentmindedly waved back as he crossed to check on Rhyo, and Annakki did the same for Spinnek and Dor'rhean. "You all right?" he asked as the tyrn shifted back to Tazu form, still shaking.

Nodding, Rhyo braced himself against the wall, swallowing a few times before he managed to get out, "I think so." He held up his arms, which had quite a few bloody nicks. A bruise was slowly purpling on his collarbone. "Nothing worse than I've had before."

Jathen smiled grimly at the dark joke, patting the Tazu gently on the shoulder. "You did good."

"You have my eternal thanks," Annakki said. Holding a swaddled Dor'rhean, she looked a garish sight with all that blood smearing on the white cloth and the baby's violet eyes wide and confused. She nodded toward the doorway, where Izzy had paused to survey the scene. "All of you."

"How did they get past?" Izzy asked, frowning at the two fallen assassins. "I didn't see them in the foyer, and I'd assumed this whole house has wards built into the walls to prevent unwanted teleporting."

"That." Spinnek pointed at a kicked-open vent that didn't seem large enough to accommodate a human body. "Flow through like smoke. Spinnek warn check it." He huffed, glaring at Rhyo. "Not listen."

"That type of organic manipulation magic is nearly impossible. I thought only High Mages, Red Mages, or Avatars could manage it," Rhyo said defensively.

"Ruddy tasha-kama," Annakki said with a hiss, kicking the nearer body. "They are skilled."

"Tasha-kama?' Jathen asked.

"Ka'melie fallen to the Red," Izzy explained.

Jathen arched an eyebrow. Ka'melie were a Rheanic path exclusively specialized in hunting Red Followers. They were arguably some of the most powerful individual Way Walkers in existence. The idea of any of their number falling to the Red was disturbing. *And confusing.* "If they were as you say, powerful enough to manipulate their own bodies into a different form, wouldn't they have put up a *much* bigger fight? Not to belittle your skill, Annakki, but a ka'melie who could shift like that should have killed Rhyo in one stroke then found a way through Spinnek's ward within the time it took for us to get back here—let alone two of them."

"Excellent point," Izzy declared, stepping through the mess and pulling the dark cloth mask off one of the supposed tasha-kama. She scanned his face then shook her head. "Not any powerful mage I know of."

"Human," Annakki commented, staring with the others at the man's smooth, pale features and lifeless brown eyes. "Possibly Clan Lands... though perhaps northern Lubreean."

Spinnek helped himself to the other's mask, and they found a similar face underneath.

Annakki shook her head. "I recognize neither."

"Perhaps they used up all their energy on the organic manipulation to get in?" Rhyo suggested. "That would leave most Talents drained for a while after."

"Unless someone else cast it upon them," Izzy replied. "And if that's the case, we are dealing with an *absurdly* powerful Talent who can manipulate not one but two people with that type of spell for long enough to get them through the vents."

Jathen bit the inside of his cheek, the events thus far coalescing in his mind. He turned to Izzy. "Where'd the Balori with the Clan word branded on his face go?"

"I'm uncertain." Izzy's energy ebbed, replaced by a wave of exhaustion, as she sighed slightly and wiped some sweat from her brow. "He might have retreated somewhere when the others arrived."

Spinnek nodded toward the pile of bodies in the hall. "Or there."

Jathen's stomach rolled. "I'm not looking."

"Spinnek look!" The boy practically jumped past Izzy and out into the mess, flipping over bodies without even a breath's hesitation at all the gore.

"He's probably seen far worse in Dodbyen," Rhyo murmured.

"Probably," Jathen replied, noting that he could practically feel queasiness rising into his face, probably turning him a nice shade of green. *The battle fervor and negation euphoria have definitely worn off.* Swallowing, he turned his attention back to the others. "Let's get downstairs. I'm thinking it's over, but I want to check on Marc and Bertran and see if we can sort exactly why all this happened."

"It will not take much sorting," Annakki said stiffly as she walked past.

Jathen exchanged grim glances with Izzy then followed the Clanswoman into the bloody hall and past Spinnek, still poking at dead bodies. Downstairs, Marcasith looked a sight, bruises and cuts across one side of his face and clearly favoring his left leg. He stood slightly hunched in the middle of the foyer, leaning heavily on Teal's shoulder while Seren dabbed at his bleeding eye ridge with some gauze.

"Damn it, Greck," Marcasith barked at a blue-scaled Tazu guard Jathen didn't recognize. Dragging a protesting Teal along and ignoring frustrated groans from Seren, Marc continued, "Has no one ever taught you how to properly check to see if an enemy is dead or wounded? Or have you simply never been in the field before? Poking them with your foot is asking to lose it when they grab you and flip you off your ruddy feet!"

Admonished, Greck backed sheepishly away from the pile of bodies toward the side wall, where the remaining few living Balori sat in a line, hands behind their heads. Jathen noted the ice mage was not among them, and a quick glance found her body wedged against the front door, chest cleaved apart by tyrn claws and lifeless eyes unsettlingly pointed in Jathen's direction. Repressing a shiver, he made it to where Bertran was sitting at the bottom of the stairs. Citra was standing beside him and seeing to his shoulder, though the smirk on her lips said she'd much rather be dealing with him than Marcasith.

"The debesh?" Jathen asked his cousin.

"Dead," he replied, voice ragged from roaring. He went to run a hand across his scalp but winced and lowered the arm instead, the silvery scales speckled heavily with drying blood. "Had to break his neck before he went down. Not easy."

As Jathen wet his lips to say more, Seren called his name. Abandoning Marcasith, who was still lightly bleeding, she ran over and stopped just short of throwing her arms around him in front of Bertran and the rest of the room. "You're all right?" Her eyes darted to Izzy as well but fell back to meet his, full of relief.

"Everyone is," he said aloud but telepathically answered, *I'm fine. A few close calls, but you saved my life, bringing Marc when you did. Thank you. Love you.*

She smiled slightly. *Love you too.*

"I *told* you I saved him," Marcasith groused. "Now, get back here. I'm the one still bleeding, after all!" He grinned, waving slightly at Jathen, which made Teal grunt. "Well done, nephew."

"I *will* help you if you actually hold still," Seren replied, hands on her hips as she marched stiffly back to the big Tazu.

Jathen smiled slightly at the brief humor, noting Izzy finally took a moment to slide down a wall and sit. He turned back to Bertran. "Did the tar'ka-besh get informed of all this?"

"We tried to send out a telepathic communication, but just about all the telepaths are warding themselves mentally, thanks to the emotional backlash from the avalanche, so nothing got through. We sent someone to fly a message over, but Spirit knows how fast they'll be able to land and deliver out there today."

"Not to mention there aren't a lot of spare hands about," Citra added. She tied off the end of Bertran's bandage then straightened, her blood-spattered Tazu-leather armor creaking as she did. "We passed by at least half a dozen skirmishes in the streets on the way here, and there wasn't a tar'ka-besh to be seen."

Jathen nodded, half listening. Eyeing the cracked but still-ticking clock in the sitting room, he was struck by the absurdity of just how quickly the entire fight had gone down, which made his palms itch. *If we hadn't been here... But then again, what made them think I wouldn't be? Did they watch the house, waiting to see if I'd leave? Why? To divide the forces? Or because I helped De'contes, as they said?*

Needing answers, he marched over to the line of living Balori, though he regretted the loss of the trio who'd seemed to have some semblance of rank. "Why?"

"You know very well why," replied a single Annarite, his skin a red the shade of old rust. He spat at Jathen's feet. "The Prophet must live."

"Quit that," Marcasith rumbled, "or I'll make good on my promise to rip your spine out. I don't take kindly to those trying to kill my nephew."

"I wasn't the real target, though." Jathen crouched to meet the man's hard crimson eyes, so similar to their leader's. "Did De'contes know anything about this?"

The Balori pursed his lips, unmoving.

"You have to know this would only hurt your cause, *his* cause," Jathen whispered. "You didn't come here just to kill Annakki. You came to *hurt* her. Those two upstairs targeted her son, whom the world isn't supposed to know exists. I don't claim to know your Prophet, but murdering children seems to be something he's moved past. And even if your Annarite friend saw some premonition of Annakki harming De'contes, there was *no reason* to kill Dor'rhean. So again, I ask you: why?"

Though the man continued to glare, Jathen could sense he was shaken.

Seren's voice bloomed in his head: *Perhaps he just signed on to help and hadn't known the depths of why this portion of Balori had come to torture and kill.*

Perhaps. Shaking his head at the Balori's continued silence, Jathen stood. *Or perhaps I'm closer to the answer than I want to admit.* Seren arched an eye ridge, glancing sideways from where she was finishing Marc's bandage.

Surveying the decimated foyer as Marcasith and Bertran debated further interrogating the survivors or waiting on the tar'ka-besh, Jathen couldn't shake a deep, deep sense of displacement, as though he'd walked into a room whose apex symmetry was off, and his mind couldn't shake the unnerving thought: *Something's just not right here.* He stepped over to where the body of the young ice mage lay, eyes still gazing toward the staircase. "Seren, you'd said there was an ice mage helping the city with the snow on the mountains, correct?"

Seren wasn't the only one in the room to purse her lips at the question, but she alone nodded. "Yes. A young girl, if I recall."

"And they are nontraditional Talents and quite rare, yes?"

"Yes."

"Which makes it too much of a coincidence," Bertran finished the sentiment. "She had to be behind the avalanche."

"Or at least be the source of the information for doing so," Seren amended. "A single ice mage would take months upon months to weaken such a glacier. Even if she started the very day of the attack on De'contes, it would've been hard for one so young to pull off—and she'd still have needed something to allow for the precision of the timing." She sighed, meeting Jathen's eyes. *To be honest, it'd be easier to melt the bedrock beneath the glacier somehow. That'd be more in the vein of a Red Mage's powers—but she'd be able to tell him where to do it.*

Him? You mean De'contes. Jathen crossed his arms, murmuring, "It doesn't make sense. This is too neatly wrapped." He bit his lip, a low buzzing inside his chest telling him he'd better follow this path. "Where'd Annakki go off to?" he asked of no one in particular.

"I'd assume to wash up and settle her egg," Marcasith answered.

Izzy nodded in the direction of the kitchen. "I saw her slip away."

"Right." Jathen started walking. "Call me if the tar'ka-besh arrive." Halfway down the hall, he noticed Seren's presence at his shoulder and Izzy half a step behind her. Resigned to his escort, he simply told Izzy, "Keep to the hallway. I just want to have a chat with her."

The fauni nodded, while Seren followed him into the kitchen.

Annakki stood at the sink, wiping the blood from her hands and arms almost ritualistically, in long, meaningful strokes with a dishtowel. Hatori's sword cane lay on the counter beside her, the casing spattered in blood but the handle still shiny. Dor'rhean sat in his raised infant's chair, happily licking some wayward blood from his fingers. *Clan child*, Jathen reminded himself, suppressing the shiver.

"We wanted to make certain you two truly are all right," Seren said to break the silence, probably sensing Jathen's stumbling attempts to gather his thoughts. She stayed on the top step as Jathen walked closer to Dor'rhean. "I cannot imagine descending the stairs to find my home in such a state, wondering what could have happened."

"I've lost more than a few walls and chandeliers in my days," Annakki replied, her tone more heartrending than admonishing. "Today, even."

Seren bowed her head. "You have my deepest condolences for Chūjitsun. And your other guardsman. I'm sorry—I never learned his name."

"Zhan. His father served before him, a Dark Guard disgraced, and so he came to me." Annakki nodded in turn, her eyes slightly out of focus as she continued to wipe off the blood. Pausing, she turned slightly toward Jathen. "Were any of yours lost in the fray?"

"No." Jathen ran his hand across Dor'rhean's head as the toddler squeaked happily, clearly not traumatized in the least by the events of the day. "Marcasith and Bertran are a bit more hurt than they're telling me, and Izzy is far more exhausted, but everyone will live."

"Good." Annakki returned to washing in earnest. "That *monster* has claimed enough lives."

"I concur," Jathen said softly, smiling grimly at Dor'rhean. "Though I have to wonder if there's some deeper game with this."

"There often is, with him," Annakki agreed, though her tone seemed guarded.

"Possibly. But that Balori girl... The ice mage was there that day when the Pearl acolytes attacked. Do you not think that is unusual? A little too much to be a coincidence?"

When Annakki said nothing, continuing to wipe her arms of blood, Jathen pressed on. "And those tasha-kama upstairs, that's not magic that's possible without an incredibly powerful mage behind it. Maybe a Red Mage, but it's certainly sloppy, don't you think? Not the mark of a man as elegantly deadly as De'contes, right?"

Annakki's brow furrowed ever so slightly, marring her perfect profile. "Why are you asking me these things?"

Jathen exchanged quick glances with Seren, who nodded in encouragement though she was visibly holding her breath. "Because I don't think De'contes was behind this."

Annakki stiffened, not looking at him. "He is the only one with motive, Jathen."

"Is he? The Annarite outside who started this said he'd had a pre-cognitive vision that you needed to die for De'contes to live—because you'd still come for him."

"I have kept good faith on my promise," she whispered, still not turning his way. "My mother stayed your hand, and on my father's blood I swore to you I'd not touch him while you are here. Why would you even question this?"

"Because of what Chūjitsun said to me as he died," he said. "And because this doesn't make any sense. Why would De'contes order this? *During* his vote? This is more likely to get his sanctuary revoked than help him gain any legitimacy within the Ways—and his followers know that." Jathen held his arms out while shaking his head in utter bafflement. "There's no benefit. There's no elegance! Even if he's the worst Red Mage since Prothidian Altar, this *isn't like him*. Simply to strike out at you... It's too petty. This stinks of a setup, Annakki. And so, yes, I look at you, covered in Balori blood, and damn well ask if you had *anything* to do with it."

Twisting around with Clan speed, she practically hissed, "My *son* was in danger! Do you think I would risk his life for *any*thing?"

"No." Jathen pursed his lips then sighed, shaking his head. "I think you might not have brought this mob to your door, but I also know you're still hiding something from me about the day I saved him. Help me, Annakki. Help me to put to sleep this wretched insect buzzing about in my brain. De'contes did not order his Balori to do this. But I think *you* know who *would* have convinced them that doing so was in their greater interest."

She tightened her grip on the dishtowel ever so slightly, making blood drip into the sink in a sickening reminder of Ishane wiping Ass'shiri's blood from her hands in that Republic basement. "Chūjit-sun said something to you as he lay dying?"

He swallowed, nodding. "Yes."

Turning away again, she sighed very lightly, upper lip quivering a touch. "And you cannot just let it be? Let the man who murdered everyone I loved fall for this crime, even if it was not his own?"

Jathen looked at Seren again, the weight of the words seeming to drop onto his shoulders and drag them down.

She needs to hear it, Seren sent. *And she'll only listen to you.*

Steeling himself, Jathen continued, "Annakki, if it would bring some semblance of justice, I would, but it doesn't—and more than anything, it leaves someone out there that is devious enough to manipulate the Balori into trying to kill you and your son against their own master's interests, and you *didn't see it coming*. If we leave whoever this is out there, they will strike at you again, De'contes fallen or no. And unless we prove he was set up, your part in the first assassination attempt *will* come forward, and you will face another sentencing—one that may forever take you from Dor'rhean. Please, Annakki, give me a name."

Annakki lowered her head, a sound emanating from her lips, a cry or a sob—Jathen couldn't tell.

Finally, she whispered, "The assassination—Chūjitsun's target was never intended to be De'contes. His target was Maǧrur. Chūjitsun was supposed to escape and leave the girl with a note from De'contes hinting at his want to see the Pearls brought low and a memory of her desire to do the deed. He was supposed to be ruined, with Maǧrur a *willing* sacrifice to the purity of the Ways."

Seren gasped, and Jathen reeled, the blood draining from his face and leaving him lightheaded. He leaned heavily against the kitchen table, unable to speak for a moment. Seren had even said it—sending Chūjitsun against a Red Mage was a pathetic attempt. But taking out Maǧrur in order to destroy him was a possible feat. "You were going to use an innocent girl to frame De'contes for ordering the murder of the head of the Pearl Paladins?"

Turning back to him once more, Annakki's eyes were shaking, and a single tear worked its way down her cheek as she held his gaze. "He did it to me."

Jathen's vision blurred as tears filled his eyes from a sheer slap of empathic pain. He had no idea what sin De'contes had framed Annakki for, but if she lived daily with a fraction of what she'd just flung at him, her hate suddenly seemed much more rational. *At least to her,* Jathen thought, knowing Seren probably heard. *But this hate will get her killed.*

"If Maǧrur was in on it," Jathen whispered once his eyes and head cleared, "then when I stopped Chūjitsun, Maǧrur must have believed you'd betrayed him. So this, today, is most likely his handiwork—revenge on you atop destroying De'contes, all while using the Balori's vision against them. He himself probably even set his damn boys on me that day in the street." Suddenly, the strange feeling of betrayal he'd felt from Master Mağrur so long before made an eerie sense. Jathen coughed a pathetic laugh at his own ignorance before shaking his head sadly at her. "Oh, Annakki. How could you? How *could* you..."

"You have no idea of this pain." Clenching a fist, she pounded it upon her chest, ruining the silk once and for all with a smear of red. "You have no idea what it was to sit and sup with the face of evil and be discarded to live alone but then helplessly watch as he continued to destroy everything you still held dear."

"I felt it just now," he replied. When she arched an eyebrow, he continued, "And it is massive, Annakki. I will not belittle it. But this path will destroy you either from the inside or from some wickedness you bring upon yourself. What of Dor'rhean, his safety? Do you think this is what Ass'shiri would have wanted? To see you succumb to your own—"

"You did *not* know Ass'shiri as I did, to lecture me on what he would have wanted," she snapped, her voice close to being raised. "You did not hold him to yourself and know the depths of his heart!"

Jathen felt wetness on his own face as he shook his head again. "I know this would have broken his heart."

"Go," she said, the word barely legible around her sob. "I will hear no more from you."

Jathen bit his lower lip, uncertain if there was anything left to say. The idea of losing Dor'rhean made his heart want to shatter, but pressing Annakki further would do nothing to help.

Let her be for now, Seren whispered in his mind. *She'll think more clearly later. There is still an injustice that must be undone.*

Taking one last look at a pouty Dor'rhean, Jathen nodded. *You're right. Mağrur might do something more today if word gets back to him that this didn't end in death.* Turning away, he caught Seren's shoulder and exited back into the hall with her.

"I'm sorry," Izzy whispered—apparently, the argument had carried. "Jathen, truly—"

"I'll deal with her later," he replied, steeling his heart for the moment. "We need to get to the High Mages before Mağrur does something else. I don't trust De'contes, and I'm not an advocate of the Balori, but we cannot allow Mağrur to get away with this. And I certainly can't leave him in a position of power to try to do something like this to Annakki again." *No matter what she says.*

"There's no proof aside from Annakki's comments. If we are to keep her out of it, we need to come up with a better plan," Seren whispered. "Maybe going to Na'vosh and the tar'ka-besh?"

Izzy shook her head. "Na'vosh might be able to shield Annakki but wouldn't be helpful if we wish to clear De'contes. The Tar'ka-besh Order can't take Jathen's word alone since his mind can't readily be read. If we go to them and they assume the Balori's part in this was ordered or at least known to De'contes before the conclave dismisses, they'd have no choice but to arrest De'contes the moment it does. Even if we can sort the truth after the fact, the court of public opinion would set the Balori movement back decades, if not more." She furrowed her brow, turning back to Jathen. "But that does raise the question of how we are to prove De'contes *wasn't* to blame. Short of a confession from Mağrur, I do not see how we can, not with how the evidence is laid out."

"There might be other ways, other witnesses." Jathen worried his bottom lip a little. "Something happened up on the mountain today to set off the avalanche. I heard the boom. Given the interesting timing their ice mage had in bumping into me the other day, I wouldn't be surprised if those three Pearl acolytes who got booted for attacking me weren't somehow in on this as well." He sighed. "Right now, no one knows we know. If we move quickly, we might be able to gather enough witnesses to read telepathically and prove a precedence to then have Maǧrur read. If that happens, I don't care how good he is—one of the High Mages *will* find out his secrets."

"But also Annakki's," Seren pointed out softly.

Jathen sighed long then shook his head, his stomach rolling. "We must risk it. Now that I know Ra'vien didn't send me to save De'contes the first time, but to stop them from framing him, I'm fairly certain I need to continue, to keep that from happening." D'ilinde buzzed in agreement, and Seren nodded.

"But what are we going to tell the others?" Izzy asked, eyes darting toward the foyer. "We might be able to convince Marcasith to hold his tongue for Annakki, but Lord Larsenitiss wouldn't risk so much for her—no matter his support of you, Jathen."

"My mother would also have none of that, not with the political implications," Seren admitted. "So the rest of the embassy guards can't be relied on either."

"I have an idea for what to say to keep them from asking too many questions." Jathen pressed his teeth into his tongue. *Don't like it, but it'll probably work.* "Come."

They returned to the others in the ruins of the foyer, all clustered around Marcasith.

"The lady well?" Marc asked, eyeing them with concern as he scratched the gauze bandage on his chin.

"Shaken," Jathen admitted, "but she'll manage." He swallowed then put his plan into motion. "We've an issue, though."

As Marcasith arched an eye ridge, Bertran asked, "What do you mean?"

"I don't think De'contes was behind this. Someone else was whispering in these Balori's ears." Jathen exhaled softly at the barrage of dubious and shocked expressions flung at him.

"You have proof of this, nephew?" Marcasith asked.

"Not concrete." He wet his lips and drummed his fingers against his thighs, attempting to mask his lie with tics of nervousness. "But things that were said today by the Balori have me questioning—not to mention the entire execution of this attack. It's too sloppy for De'contes. And I saw... *things*."

The room nodded. As much as Jathen hated to use his reputation as a precognitive to lie, he was gratified at being believed unquestioningly. *Wonder how many precognitives skirt the truth to meet such ends.*

Bertran crossed his arms with a mild wince. "Did your vision lend itself to who might be behind this, if not De'contes? And consequently why?"

"No, aside from the obvious destruction of the Balori," Jathen replied, hopefully not too quickly. "But we three discussed it, and there may be more witnesses amid the Balori who could be probed telepathically. I say we start with the ones here, though we also need to find the other loose ends—like whoever started the avalanche. There's no way the ice mage could have set it off from the mountain then ended up back down here—especially not after the snow ward around the city kicked on."

"And we need to warn the High Mages before the tar'ka-besh get here and blame De'contes, allowing whoever to get away with this," Izzy added.

"It sounds as if splitting up is our best option," Marcasith surmised, scratching his chin again. "Some need to go wrangle witnesses, while the rest need to find a way to warn the High Mages before the true villain catches wind of our suspicions and conveniently wanders off."

"Or tries some other bit of malevolent mischief," Rhyo murmured, rubbing his collarbone.

"And some need to hold down the fort here, and not just restraining the hostages," Seren said. "At the very least, Annakki needs someone who knows what's been happening to deal with the tar'ka-besh when they do eventually show." Her eyes darted sideways to meet Jathen's. *And at worse, she might need legal counsel.*

"Can you do that?" Jathen tentatively asked.

Sparing him another comment about his wanting to keep her safe again, Seren nodded. "Yes, as long as no more Balori show up, looking for a fight."

"Even if Bertran and Marc decide to sit it out, we've got another four full shifters besides me and Teal," Citra said with a grin. "Any more Balori show up, they're going to be in for a nasty surprise."

"Right." Jathen matched her grin. "Marcasith, can you stay here with Rhyo, Spinnek, and most of the guards to wait with Seren and Annakki?"

His uncle cracked his neck and rotated his shoulders with a wince but then grinned as well. "I can." He shot the visibly sweating Balori from earlier a sharp glare. "You want me to take a crack at his mind? I'm not a certified Tar'citadel interrogator, but I've done my share of digging around in heads in my day."

The Annarite made such a terrified squeak that Jathen found himself feeling mildly sorry for him. However, he managed to not let that show. "Can you do it without hurting him?"

Marcasith shrugged with a smirk. "More or less."

"Do it, but make sure he rests first, Teal." Jathen turned to Bertran. "If Marcasith can generate a lead, can you take a few you trust to seek out some witnesses?"

The Tazu nodded. "I might not move as quickly as normal, but I've done more with worse injuries. We can start with the Balori barracks and make a few discreet inquiries, depending on what Marc finds. Even if he doesn't glean anything from these few, I know how to do a little rustling of underbrush to see what gets spooked out into the open."

"Don't push yourselves, but good." Jathen repressed a pleased smile. So far, his ploy was working better than he'd hoped. "Then Izzy and I will try to get into the conclave. Less is better with that crowd, but Orne can make room for us in a pinch."

"But I help," Spinnek suddenly begged, his voice breaking a bit. "I stay with Jathen?"

"I know you helped a great deal today, Spinnek." Staring long at the boy, Jathen knew Spinnek would want to protect Annakki and would be an invaluable Talent in a fight, but he also didn't think he could trust Spinnek's lack of social cues to understand exactly what protecting Annakki entailed in this case. Regretfully, he put a hand on Spinnek's shoulder. "But I need you to stay here and help Seren and Rhyo protect Annakki and Dor'rhean. The tar'ka-besh are still busy with the avalanche and the conclave. If more Balori come, they will need you."

Spinnek stared back with dejected eyes until Teal ruffled his hair and said, "Come on, little egg. We've missed you at the embassy. Spend some time with us for a bit."

The Exemplary Talent sighed long while trying to right his hair. "Fi-i-ine."

Jathen turned to Seren, whispering, "If you need me, try to call telepathically. All right?"

She nodded, solemn. "I will. Please be careful. I have a feeling this isn't done yet."

"I know it isn't."

Chapter 8

J athen's vision blurred.

Tiredness prodded him the way Tinzy would butt his little head against Jathen's temple when seeking food or attention—a gentle touch, but insistent. *And if it's anything like the real Tinzy, it's soon going to become impossible to ignore.* Rubbing his eyes to clear them, Jathen walked on, knowing Izzy, too, had grown weary. But if she was beside him, working her way through the throng without speaking a word of discomfort, he could do the same. *Though I really, really hope we're done fighting for the day. Otherwise, this might be my last day, despite dodging visions of death.*

"Do you have a plan?" Izzy asked softly when they got within sight of the main doors of the Temple Citadel. The crowd had lingered despite the avalanche, though the excited energy had been replaced by an agitated restlessness that tugged at Jathen's empathic sense. "As I assume we're not going to just walk in and tell the High Mages the same precognition story you just told the others."

"No. I'm debating just pulling rank and demanding to see De'contes." Jathen bit his lip as he slipped between a pair of plate-skinned Avenea, who shot him dirty looks but didn't protest his breach. "But I know that's a hell of a gamble. Thoughts?"

"Sneaking inside is impossible, so your idea of direct approach is all we have for getting in, at least. But telling De'contes directly? What is the logic behind that?"

"He already knew about Annakki," Jathen murmured lowly, "which means he might have already suspected Mağrur. And that means I might be able to get him to at least contain Mağrur for questioning, especially if I inform him his Balori went rogue without his knowledge."

"And as a Red Mage, he's one of a few aside from the High Mages who surpasses a master Pearl Paladin in power, should Mağrur try to fight. But what shall you do when De'contes asks you for a 'price' for keeping Annakki's involvement out of it, as you know he will?"

"Then I tell him he was spared that day because Ra'vien begged me to save her daughter from herself and doesn't give a ruddy damn about him, as far as I know." He steeled his jaw, considering all the lies he was telling for Annakki's sake. He could only hope that she proved worthy of it all and that De'contes didn't see through the ruse.

Izzy nodded, brows raised in approval. "That might work. Though we must still gain entrance." Hood down and braids in disarray, she pushed a few of the thin things off her face as she stared up at the great citadel. "Perhaps see if D'ilinde has any suggestions? It has not steered us wrong thus far."

"I'll see if I can ask it if we can find a break in the crowd. Barring that, perhaps I can pick a fight and get enough energy tossed at me to teleport inside the citadel." He smirked grimly, gazing up at the twisted expanse of the spire. "D'ilinde doesn't seem to be barred by things like international wards, so I don't think the citadel will be much trouble."

"Last resort," Izzy replied, eyes hard. "If you inadvertently run into Mağrur, I don't need you facing a ruddy Pearl Paladin alone. That is a death sentence for most combat Walkers. A partially trained Negater is not going to be much better, no matter your immunity to his stasis bubbles."

"Determined to die beside me, huh?" As the crowd thinned, he put a hand on his chest while remembering how poorly the two of them had fared against a mere three Pearl Paladin acolytes. "That's the outcome if you and I try to take on a Master Way Walker, you know."

Izzy smiled thinly. "I promised Seren... and Marcasith and more. Better to die beside you than return to them and face their grief."

Staring at his friend, Jathen was struck again by how gratifying and burdening such loyalty was, lying against his soul. *Especially considering where it led Ass'shiri.* Putting the tumultuous emotion aside, he closed his eyes, telling D'ilinde, *I need you. We need to get inside to help Annakki and De'contes. Please, can you help?* D'ilinde buzzed eagerly, pulsing like a second heartbeat. Upon opening his eyes, Jathen scanned the crowd along the edge of the golden citadel doors, stopping when the buzzing in his chest quickened slightly. Turning his head away from the spot, he found the buzzing slowed, and turning it back quickened it again.

"I have a direction," he said. "Let's go."

Following D'ilinde like a dowsing rod, Jathen picked through the crowd until he got a clear view of a single tar'ka-besh guarding the right side of the perimeter. He halted with a groan.

Izzy froze, hand hovering with a slight tremble over the latch on Orne's bag. "What is it?"

"Nothing dire, just annoying," he replied, gently pushing her hand from the clasp. He couldn't imagine she'd really want to unleash Orne in the middle of all those people. "Burjiro."

Izzy hissed through her teeth. "Well, if D'ilinde says he'll help..." She had a distinctly resigned line in her shoulders as she shrugged.

Jathen nodded, proceeding over toward Ass'shiri's brother with fists clenched. A temporary wooden barrier about waist high separated the crowd from the citadel. Leaning on it, Jathen called to the Clansman a few times, only to be ignored even though Burjiro definitely glanced their way.

"Ruddy hell," Jathen muttered then lifted one leg to hop over the barrier, which finally elicited a reaction.

The Tan jetted over to them with Clan speed. "No one crosses," he proclaimed, grasping Jathen's knee and firmly pushing it back over the barrier. "Move along."

Stumbling backward into Izzy, Jathen glared at Burjiro. "Something's happened," Jathen told the tar'ka-besh as he turned to go. He hesitated, not wanting to proclaim a desire to see De'contes after he'd seen Burjiro punch the Red Mage the first time they'd met. Instead, he said, "We need to get inside to see the chancellor. Or perhaps Na'vosh."

"No one gets inside during the enclave," Burjiro replied stiffly.

"Then bring Na'vosh out to me," Jathen begged, hoping Annakki's brother could get him inside since Ass'shiri's was being so inhospitable. "I have to speak to someone."

Burjiro stopped long enough to spout, "Na'vosh is on the mountain, dealing with the snow wards and the rescue efforts. I hardly think he's going to come down from there for *you*, as that was the very thing you warned him about, recall?" Lips pursed, Burjiro looked like he had an itch he couldn't reach. "Though I wouldn't put it past you to expect more special treatment."

"Special?" Jathen's mouth dropped open. "Do you mean the day I arrived? *You* helped me—or have you forgotten? Ass'shiri and I were blood brothers. How do you think I knew the words?"

Burjiro Tan's dark-amethyst eyes were incredibly hard. "I. Do. Not. Care." He slammed his hands down on the barrier, making a terrifically loud *snap* and denting the heavy wood. Looming like a dark god despite being shorter than Jathen, he practically growled, "Move along," before straightening and walking away as if the entire exchange hadn't happened.

"Damn it!" Jathen backed away from the barrier, snuffing the urge to pull his hair out. "How the ruddy hell is that slaga's ass related to Ass'shiri?"

The avalanche had done its job, and no other tar'ka-besh were in sight to try to reason with.

"You know, cursing about the home guard like an angry little cretin is more likely to get you arrested than helped."

Turning toward the familiar voice, Jathen found Raleigh leaning against a lamppost and exuding an air of ownership over all she surveyed. Her head was tilted, and she sported her usual mildly irritated expression. Her clothes were more streamlined than he'd seen before: a sleeveless gold montage robe over an orange shirt with split sleeves, exposing her outer arms despite the cold.

Shrugging, she added, "Then again, all the tar'ka-besh *are* a bit busy."

Izzy arched an eyebrow at the mage, as she'd not met Raleigh, though Jathen presumed his descriptions had been good enough. "Which begs me to inquire why you aren't assisting with the snow removal," she said. "All capable Talents were called upon."

"I don't *do* magic when it's *remedial*." Raleigh's mismatched eyes rolled hard across their sockets as she crossed arms and legs. "Besides, I am also not an idiot. I know a distraction when I see it. If something interesting were going to happen, it'd happen around here, not up on the mountain or at the ward."

Jathen exchanged a glance with Izzy as D'ilinde buzzed inside his chest. "You're right. Something has happened." He stepped forward, wanting to keep his voice from carrying to anyone else in the crowd. His exchange with Burjiro had already drawn some long looks. "We quelled it, but it isn't over. We need to get up into the citadel. We need to speak with De'contes before the conclave concludes. Can you help us?"

"Ugh, young soul, how many times must I tell you? I'm *not* apt for *helping*—"

"Then why did you just say you were waiting around here for something interesting to happen if you had no intention of being helpful?" Izzy exclaimed.

"To *watch*, silly fauni," Raleigh replied, still bored. Running her fingers through her hair, she paused to scratch absentmindedly at the shaved portion. "Though watching you two whine at a grumpy tar'ka-besh is *not* very riveting—"

"Raleigh, please. Mağrur has committed treason," Jathen said with a hiss, stanching her tirade and earning him a sour look. "His men are behind the avalanche and an attack by the Balori on An-nakki's townhome, all to frame De'contes and to revoke the man's sanctuary in Tar'citadel. Whatever your personal politics with either man, this is wrong. Please help us."

Cocking a dark eyebrow at them, she stood otherwise stoic for a moment, making Jathen brace to counter another rant. Instead, she nodded, straightening. "Right. Follow me, then."

Jathen stepped back, blinking. "What, really?"

"Yes, yes." She crooked her finger at them as she started walking. "I might huff and puff and brood on about being above a lot of the crap you young souls get caught up in, but I'm not so aloof I can't recognize when a situation warrants me taking five minutes to open a ruddy door."

"Thank you," Jathen sighed, though a part of him fantasized about telling Raleigh where she could shove her "generous" help. "But where are we going? There's no doors into the citadel on this side."

"Ugh, for someone with a ruddy Grand Artifact that hinges on spatial magic in his chest, you are an idiot." She turned to Izzy. "Fauni, how do you *deal* with him?"

"A modicum of respect helps," Izzy retorted, deadpan.

Raleigh snorted, a slip of a begrudging smile on her lips. "Anyway, I can't get you into the middle of the conclave, but I can get you where you need to go via the teleportation grid."

Though he suspected he'd regret it, Jathen asked, "Teleportation grid?"

"Yes, yes." Stopping, Raleigh held her hands out, one toward each of them. "It's a terribly complex pattern of locked teleportation points that bypass most of the wards keeping people from teleporting into and out of places around here. 'Turning the key' to access them is incredibly complex high magic, only used by the most powerful mages in the city and some of the tar'ka-besh. Most of the population doesn't even know it exists, let alone comprehend how to use it."

"Or bring others along?" Izzy asked as she took Raleigh's hand.

"Precisely."

Jathen hesitated. "Have you forgotten I don't teleport as a Negater?"

"Ugh, *I'm* not teleporting you, I'm going to give *D'ilinde* energy to teleport you and let it use my knowledge of the grid to take you where this fauni and I are going," she replied.

"My name is Izzy."

Raleigh groaned then said, "Now, *Izzy*, Jathen, are we doing this, or are you going to continue to question my every little execution of Ability?"

Biting back an exasperated moan, Jathen took her hand as well. A cool tingle ran up his arm, and D'ilinde made the happiest buzz. Jathen blinked, and they were transported, by far the smoothest teleportation he'd experienced, aside from a rather powerful popping of his ears. Releasing the woman's hand, he covered the slightly ringing organs to protect them from unexpected roaring wind and biting cold.

Glancing about, Jathen found himself standing on a salt-covered stone veranda, facing a hexagonal building topped with a large, pleated dome. Crags and rough peaks of dark stone jutted out from white snow on either side, reminding him of gray claws bared in white Tazu hide. Far above lay the sharp, dark curve of a mountain peak, while farther below, a wide swath of ice and snow extended down to the city's edge. The path of the avalanche was studded with jagged rocks and deep cracks, as deadly as frozen river rapids. At the bottom of the slope, the final crest of this icy wave made an unexpected bridge over the Dragon's Tongue River, stemming the flow of water down to a tiny trickle. Only a puff of mist drifted out from under the delicate arch of the hydroelectric plant spanning the top of the falls like a delicate bridge. *She's brought us to the Reverent Steps.* Jathen turned toward Raleigh, furious.

Before he could unleash a tirade of curses upon her, a Rosinic in a heavy dark-amethyst cloak exited the building and scurried over to them. Emotional waves of worry and surprise ebbed off her as she clutched a stack of papers to her chest. "Raleigh! Oh good, they'd been hoping you would—"

Raleigh put a hand up, halting the woman in her tracks. "We aren't here, Nell," she said, not even making eye contact.

The brunette human swallowed visibly, soft blue eyes wide. "All right then," she replied, monotone. She took a moment to smooth her robes before turning on her heel and walking back through the doorway whence she'd come.

Jathen cocked an eyebrow, uncertain if he'd just witnessed a stunning level of telepathic manipulation or simply a previously unknown level of authority from Raleigh. *Or both.* Shaking his head, he hissed at her, "Where in the ruddy hell did you bring us?"

Raleigh huffed while clapping her hands free of a few wayward snowflakes. "Obviously above the city and where the snow hit the ward. More precisely, this is the Observatory on the Reverent Steps."

"I see that, but why are we *here*? I wanted the conclave!"

"And that was an *idiotic* choice, but I didn't want you wailing about it in front of the citadel." She nodded to the left, where on the slope far below them, an indentation marked what had probably been the far side of the ice levee. The tops of some of the melting stations as well as watchtowers were peeking up above the snow—how deep or tall they were he couldn't determine, as only perhaps a story or two broke the white surface. Small flashes of what he assumed was magic from various mages twinkled about them, almost pretty in varying shades of purple, gold, silver, and even a few yellow and red.

"You said Mağrur was behind this," Raleigh continued, "but *I* saw you didn't have *proof*. If his little acolytes did have anything to do with this, they most likely slipped in with the removal and rescue crews down there, which means if you want them, that is where you must be to get them."

"Are you ruddy demented?" Jathen resisted the urge to flap his arms about and squeezed them against his chest for warmth instead. Raleigh brought out a desire to throttle things almost as badly as Burjiro. *Almost.* "I wanted to speak to De'contes—not Mağrur!"

"You leveled some pretty vicious accusations upon the standing head of the Pearl Paladin Order," Raleigh replied, her tone more logically firm than condescending for once and eerily reminiscent of Erin Manna. "If you don't mind, I'm inclined to find the men you claim had something to do with this avalanche and then see what they and Mağrur have to say for themselves *before* we go dropping into the middle of a historical conclave and giving De'contes or any of the High Walkers a reason to go calling for a mis-vote or some rot."

"Admirable," Izzy whispered, "but if Mağrur attempts to run or fight rather than refute our claims, none of us—perhaps not even the other tar'ka-besh up here—are capable of stopping him."

Jathen wagged his head enthusiastically. "I've already beaten death a few times today. I'm not in a mood to court it again if I might help it."

Raleigh closed her light eye, glaring down her nose at them with her dark-amethyst one. "First off, half the ruddy mages in the city are on this mountain, including some rather powerful Rosinic Way Path heads. Second: have you two *met* me? I'm about as scared of a Pearl Paladin as I am of a stiff breeze."

"Need I remind you that you are *not* a High Mage in this lifetime yet?" Jathen retorted, doing his best to keep his voice down. The last thing he needed was to unleash more snow upon the city. He could practically hear the rush of his blood pressure rising through his temples. "Last time I checked, a Pearl Paladin could go toe-to-toe with a Red Mage, thanks to the stasis bubble. They wouldn't win, but they'd put up a hell of a fight, and Mağrur is the best of them. I saw De'contes immobile in the bubble he threw. And unless I'm wrong about Pearls, I'm pretty certain they can throw up some *massive* bubbles that will catch a lot of mages at once."

"And you can *negate* them, idiot! Look"—Raleigh rolled her eyes again with yet another huff—"I am telling you two I can deal with a white cloak or three or *ten,* even. You either trust that and we go have a chat and get some proof of all your wailing allegations, or I take you both back down to the city." She held her hands up, her many rings glinting in the bright light. "I'm not put out either way, so... your choice."

Jathen grumbled deep in his throat, imagining telling Raleigh how much he hated her, excellent Negater trainer or not.

"Clearly, we shall seek to find proof," Izzy answered for them. Lips pressed into a thin line, she flicked the upper clasp on Orne's satchel a few times. "But recall that, should anything happen to Jathen because of this, it is to half the continent you shall be held responsible, most notably Erin Manna."

"Ugh, stow your threats and come on. We have to walk down, thanks to the teleport points on the hydrobridge being covered in snow." Raleigh turned and placed her hands on her hips before storming off down the wide slab steps carved into the mountain, muttering to herself. "Erin... really... I could just... with one hand, practically. Ruddy young souls... *really.*"

"I have a sad feeling that, were Ass'shiri here, he'd be laughing his head off at us right now," Jathen murmured to Izzy.

"She is right, however," the fauni replied with the slightest slip of a smile. "The Balori at the townhouse won't be enough if Marcasith doesn't glean anything from their minds. And going to De'contes would've been a gamble. We must get whoever caused the quake and pray they aren't Balori as well. As it is, that dead ice mage is a bigger suspect than Mağrur."

"Doesn't mean she's not a brat." Jathen pursed his lips. *But Izzy's right—this doesn't mean Mağrur's men did this directly. I could just be soldering another chain to bind De'contes with, poking about up here without warning him first.* Deeper inside Jathen's subconscious, another voice echoed softly: *Or he really was behind it all.*

Tension permeated the downhill hike, with Jathen silently cursing himself for leaving the ruddy sword cane on the counter in Annakki's kitchen. The path wasn't exactly wide, either, and soon they lost the icy steps completely, finding themselves waist deep in wet, shifting snow from what must have been the very edge of the avalanche. A strong gust of wind staggered Izzy into Jathen, and though he steadied her, the sudden glimpse downward made even his hatched blood run cold.

About halfway to the closest semiburied watchtower, they stopped when another Rosinic teleported in before them. Human, he looked about Raleigh and Izzy's age, with a shock of exceptionally white-blond hair sticking out from under his hat. The wide, roguish grin he flashed gave Jathen an irrational desire to smack him, though the reason might have simply been envy over his winter wear trimmed in heavy fur. As it was, Jathen's ears were completely numb.

Raleigh seemed to share the sentiment, halting with an angry huff and wrinkling her nose in unmasked distaste. "What?"

The man grinned more widely, undeterred. "I'm supposed to be handing out assignments to all new volunteers."

"Well, I'm not a volunteer, so piss off."

She started walking again, but he skidded to the side, blocking the path and replying far too gleefully, "Then you and your friends are not allowed up here, Ra-la."

Those mismatched eyes of hers narrowed into thin slivers, but then she smiled, matching his horrid grin with a devious one of her own. "Where's Master Mağrur, Loni?"

The grin melted, and Loni paled, swallowing the way Nell had up on the Observatory steps. "I don't know. He's part of the deep rescue crews, with the rest of the Pearls, I think. We're just doing basic melting and maintaining a fallback position for the medical teams to teleport to."

"How about Commander Na'vosh?" Jathen asked. When Raleigh arched an eyebrow, he just shrugged back. If she was going to the trouble, he might as well take advantage.

"He's on the melting-station line," Loni replied, monotone. "Pulling out engineers."

"Thank you," Raleigh said, stepping past him.

"That's mildly terrifying," Izzy murmured, arching her eyebrow as she passed the still-dazed-looking Loni.

Raleigh waved one of her ring-laden hands, dismissive. "That's an idiot with a crush who thinks he's too amazing a Rosinic to need a master-charm to keep people out of his head, which makes him terribly vulnerable to the person he's trying to impress."

"He's also a terrible crafter of nicknames," Jathen added snidely between the chattering of his teeth. "Ra-la? Even I flinched, and I don't like you."

Raleigh snorted. "Which is why I used him to harass *you*, young Negater. Some people need to be reminded there's always someone better."

"And who is better than you?" Izzy inquired while clutching her flapping cloak, sounding mildly curious, though her expression belied a strong sarcasm.

The peak bucked.

Rumbling echoed across the sides of the behemoth mountain faces, and the ground beneath them lurched like an unbroken riding dragon being mounted for the first time. With a shriek, Izzy slammed into Jathen, and he collided with a wall of ice shooting up another six scales past his head. His shoulder throbbing from the impact, Jathen locked eyes with Raleigh, who still had her hand up from crafting the barrier that'd kept them from hurtling over the side. At another flick of her wrist, a second sheet of ice sprang forth from the snow on their other side, a barrier against further avalanche.

"Loni, what the ruddy hell?" she yelled past them.

Craning his neck over Izzy's shoulder, Jathen looked back to see the other Talent had also been caught by Raleigh's ice wall and was sandwiched in their little tunnel. Blinking rapidly, he shook his head. "Hold on a moment. There are about a dozen telepathic voices in my head right now!"

"We need to get off this ruddy mountain," Jathen snapped at Raleigh. "If the snow shifts for another avalanche—"

"That wasn't a snow shift. That was reverberation from below traveling up," Raleigh snapped back. "Loni, *really*, what the hell?"

"It's the hydroelectric dam!" Loni had two fingers on his temple and looked whiter than the snow. "It's separating from the ledge. The weight's too much with all the snow pressing on it."

Raleigh's brow furrowed, her tone more irritated than concerned as she asked, "Isn't someone supporting the ruddy thing?"

"Yes, of course, but there's been some sort of shift." The other mage frowned, closing his eyes as he focused. "Some of the melting stations are still on, and water is flowing beneath the new layer of snow and ice, carrying larger chunks on the current into the thing."

"So tell them to just let the turbine line fall. It's not as if it will hurt anything at the base!"

"You tell them!" Loni whisper-hissed, opening his eyes to glare at her.

"I don't want them *to know I'm up here*, you little shit—"

"And I don't want to *be up here*," Jathen broke in.

A gust of wind whooshed a wave of snow through the little shelter, partially burying them in a thin layer of damp coldness.

Izzy held an arm up to protect her face but still got white flakes on the end of her dark lashes. "Raleigh, perhaps it *is* now best to get down off the mountain, as Jathen requested?"

"There're still people in the plant," Loni kept talking over them. "They can't get them out. Something about... barriers. Oh." Wide-eyed, he turned to Jathen. "They're suddenly asking about the Negater. That's you, right?"

"Yes," Jathen reluctantly murmured, wiping snow from his own face. "But what do they want from me?"

"I have no idea. They're just asking if anyone knows where you are."

"Ugh. Rhean toss this day down into the Pit with the Red." Raleigh stabbed a finger in Loni's direction. "You take her"—she pointed at Izzy—"and get back up to the damn Observatory. I'll take 'witless wonder' here down and see what the hell a Negater has to do with bracing the ruddy hydroelectric plant's turbine line before it collapses."

"Wait, no." Jathen's heart fluttered. "What about what we came for? You can't just drag us here only to abandon Izzy at the summit and dump me off on some mages!"

Raleigh groaned, pinching her fingers into the bridge of her nose. "You are like a Tazu with a gemstone. We've got a situation that even I recognize as dire, so what more do you want right now?"

"I want to make certain that if someone did cause this, they don't use a ruddy collapse as a distraction to flee."

"Right now, they've no reason to because they don't know their other plan failed! No one's going to come tell anyone what happened below while half the ruddy city is under the threat of a blackout, amid other things like, well, *lives*." Her eyes darted to Izzy then back to Jathen. "At this point, she is useless down there, and going might put her in danger even *with* me around. So having her fall back as far as the Observatory with the injured is a good idea, because chances are that's where your quarry will end up eventually. If not, I'll keep tabs on your suspects while I'm out there."

"You can find them, watch them, and help deal with the plant?"

"Jathen, truly, we do not have the time for this." Izzy yanked hard at his sleeve as another gust of wind assailed them. "We must go." She gave Raleigh a hard glare. "And I mean *both* of us. I do *not* leave Jathen's side."

Raleigh ground her teeth but acquiesced, creeping slowly along the ice wall toward them. "Keep your mouths shut about Mağrur until we know what's going on," she whispered commandingly. "I might be irritated by young souls, but keeping them alive is still a priority. Got it?" The pair of them nodded stoically before her hardened expression. Putting an arm around each of their waists, she jumped into the air.

Izzy squeaked in surprise, but Jathen had ridden with Mikkal before and had expected it. Eyes and lips pressed tightly closed against the frigid whipping wind, he held onto Raleigh's waist with one arm while the hem of Izzy's cloak got balled into the fist of the other. He had no concept of time, the numbing cold and rushing wind like a power wash to his senses.

They landed in a snowdrift, soaking the lower parts of Jathen's pants. His curses went unheard, however, as he saw hundreds of people darting about, running, teleporting, or literally flying off to assist with this or that. Raleigh had brought them to what appeared to be the roof of a mostly buried watchtower much lower on the Reverent Steps, where the view of the ice levee, much closer, stole the breath from his throat. The crest of it was completely covered in snow and ice rubble in most places, but the tops of a few melting stations stuck out here and there, square metal arches that looked oddly like torn-out stitches on a seam. Its vastness staggered him—the greater extent of the avalanche and the rescue effort. Dozens, perhaps hundreds, of people had to be trapped within all the buried buildings. Not a single tree or bush was visible beneath the vast blanket of muddy white. Perhaps they'd never existed in that hostile environment in the first place. Jathen swallowed, memories of Ca'june and Fauve after the quake making him more uneasy.

Meanwhile, Raleigh stepped past him and Izzy, stalking across the flat metal rooftop and through the crowd as if she owned the whole of Tar'citadel. Following, Jathen had to bob and weave to keep up, sparing only a few glances backward to make certain Izzy managed the same. He caught view of Raleigh's destination—a table that seemed to have been magically made from some spare ice—just before she sauntered right up to it and made an announcement to the cluster of tar'ka-besh encircling it.

"Right, I brought the Negater. Now what the ruddy hell are you all doing that you need one?"

The half-circle of them, seven in all, looked up with varying degrees of surprise and irritation written on their faces, and Jathen was deeply relieved to see Na'vosh among them.

"Miss Jo—Raleigh," he said, straightening as she scrunched up her nose in clear distaste at whatever he'd begun to call her. "Thank you for bringing Jathen so quickly."

"Yes, yes, I'm wonderful," she replied dryly, waving a hand dismissively as Jathen and Izzy stood by, both slightly out of breath from chasing her. "Answer the question: what do you need a Negater for so desperately?"

"There's a line of Pearl Paladins inside the hydroelectric plant, both the turbine bridge and the maintenance stations, holding it up with the stasis bubbles while we evacuate," the tar'ka-besh standing center explained. Physically older than everyone else there, she was a petite human, probably a good head shorter than Jathen. With white hair as dirtied as the snow around them worn in a braid circling her head, and her lined face smeared with thin spatters of mud, she'd clearly already been in the thick of the rescues. "But the breakage is happening faster than expected, and the range of the bubbles—"

"Aren't anchoring into the bedrock, what with the waterflow. Too many elemental movements to counteract," Raleigh finished. "So if the turbine bridge breaks off and the bubbles are anchored to the structure of the turbine line, then gravity will just pull the whole thing over the falls and take the stasis bubbles and their Pearls along for the ride." She frowned. "That explains why you must move quickly but not why you need a Negater."

"Only Pearls can move through the stasis bubbles, so they're gathering those trapped into ejection points that we will all teleport into and then mass-teleport everyone out of before it goes over," Na'vosh said, pointing at the buildings on each bank leading up to the turbine line, which stretched across the breadth of the river and waterfall. "The problem is the telepathic communication inside the main bubble isn't going through due to all the empathic interference—and we can't tell them the ruddy thing is going to fall faster than anticipated."

"How much faster?" Jathen asked.

"Nearly an hour sooner than we'd estimated."

"So you wish to use Jathen to negate one of the bubbles ahead of schedule, to warn them," Izzy surmised.

"Unfortunately, we'd have very little time to warn," explained another tar'ka-besh, this one a Ki'ra with a startlingly human face haloed by an impressive leonine mane. "We'd need to negate it and then grab whoever we could, because it *will* start to collapse nearly immediately."

Jathen pursed his lips, feeling ill. "You aren't expecting to get everyone out."

The Ki'ra held-up large catlike paws in a plaintive shrug. "It's some or none at this point."

Raleigh rubbed her chin, pondering. "What are we looking at structurally? Center collapse of the turbine line first, then the maintenance facilities get pulled off?"

"Yes. The evacuation sites are both inside those two, closest to the banks." He looked at Jathen, little flecks of snow glistening in his orange tresses. "Do you think you're capable of it?"

"He is." Raleigh nodded, meeting Jathen's eyes. "The trick is going to be converting the energy. It's too much to let it go wild. And..." She hesitated, looking back at the table. "Does anyone know if this is a group stasis spell? That'd explain the heavier damper on the telepathic communication."

As several tar'ka-besh shifted uncomfortably, Jathen asked, "What's the difference?"

"If multiple Pearls are all channeling their energy to a central caster of a gigantic single bubble, then the whole ruddy thing will fall *much* faster, and you'll have considerably more energy to negate." She twisted her lips a moment, then finished, "We need to assume it is. Pearls can only move through the bubbles they've cast, which means if they're trying to save people inside, they must move around to get to them. Which means a single bubble with a central caster holding it makes the most logical sense."

"That would also explain why no one can get through to Mağrur," the white-haired tar'ka-besh added. "If multiple consciousnesses are being focused, he's going to be too mentally taxed to speak telepathically, and the rest would be affected as well."

Jathen felt his stomach drop into his feet. "Mağrur is in there?"

Na'vosh nodded, eyeing him speculatively. "Yes. He's the only Pearl strong enough to hold such a spell."

"Time is not on our side," the Ki'ra tar'ka-besh reminded. "Can we execute this or no? The alternative is letting *everyone* in there die—the Pearls and the workers—nearly a hundred people."

"Of course I'll help," Jathen replied, though exhaustion pulled at his head, blurring his vision. *Hell, I just did something similar with Chu's fire barrier.* He rubbed his eyes. "But I'm tired, and Raleigh is correct, I don't know what to do with all the energy that'll be redirected. I've never negated a multiple-caster spell before, and I'm assuming that means energy reverting into multiple energy sources." Looking to Raleigh, he frowned. "I don't even know if I *can* redirect and manifest from multiple sources at once. Regular mages can't cast a single spell from multiples."

"Regular mages usually can't, but I am neither regular nor usual," she retorted then turned back to the tar'ka-besh. "Let him negate it. I'll draw in what energy he disperses and use it to make... *something* that'll brace the whole strip from going over. Should buy a few minutes at least."

A few of the tar'ka-besh looked startled by her declaration of being able to do something almost as rare as negation—the white-haired tar'ka-besh and Na'vosh were not among those.

"Right, let's begin coordinating," the white-haired woman announced then leveled a steady gaze at Raleigh. "If you think you can brace the turbine line, then it'll buy us enough time to teleport as many as they've gathered out and then, hopefully, the Pearls themselves."

"Jathen," Izzy whispered as the tar'ka-besh scattered to enact the plan, "if you do this, I cannot protect you—"

"I'll be careful, Izzy, but I have to do this. Aside from the obvious lives in danger..." He sighed, stomach flip-flopping. "If Mağrur dies, so does our proof."

Chapter 9

"Ruddy hell."

Sizing up the monster spanning the Dragon's Tongue River, Jathen flexed his fingers. The avalanche-damned river no longer flowed smoothly over and through the hydroelectric plant perched at the top of the Cathiny Falls. The exposed concrete-and-metal structure sported dozens upon dozens of clearly terminal fractures all across its base, with the weight of what had to be ten thousand dragons' worth of ice and rock pressing against it on the left and the open sky of a drop exceeding a distance of eleven hundred heads to the right. Though Na'vosh had acquired some gloves for him, working his hands open and closed to the squeaks of the stiff leather did not chase away the new numbness tingling in his fingertips. Standing atop the roof of the watchtower closest to the bank, Jathen could see the shimmer of the stasis bubble, a subtle pearlescent sheen glimmering high above the turbine bridge, its radius reaching well past the edge, made obvious where the water floated in tiny droplets, not falling off the cliff.

But there's still spray coming out the bottom. Like Raleigh said, the bubble itself isn't anchored fully to the bedrock. No mage can control gravity. When it goes, it all goes.

"I meant it when I said you can do it." Raleigh's voice broke him out of his nervous contemplation, though Jathen still didn't feel comforted.

He glanced at her out of the corner of his eyes. "Forgive me if I'm still dubious."

"I'll be with you. Quite literally."

Jathen nodded. She was planning to fly over while holding him, and he would negate the bubble somewhere over the roof of the south bank's maintenance building, hoping the Pearls had gathered many of the evacuees there, either just inside the roof-access stairwell or the floor just below. With him still in hand, Raleigh would do the seemingly impossible and use all the energy he negated to create some sort of additional brace under the whole of the plant. *Enough time to get some, but not all.*

Jathen shifted from foot to foot, the coldness in his stomach having naught to do with the temperature. Glancing back up at the small thumbnail that was the Observatory on the Reverent Steps, he wondered how Izzy fared, watching, waiting. He'd talked her into letting Na'vosh escort her back up there, though she'd given him hell. In the end, she'd relented simply because she couldn't do anything at the bottom but wait. In the Observatory, the fauni could at least assist with respectfully moving the dead.

At least one of us is safe. "How much longer?"

Raleigh squinted, focusing on the telepathic communication network the tar'ka-besh were using. Na'vosh had tried to explain it before this madness started, but Jathen hadn't retained the details.

"Few more minutes," she said. "They're letting their mass-teleportation mages rest and gather energy for as long as possible before moving into position."

The delicate arch of the pedestrian pathway spanning the top of the waterfall was twisted, showing the strain that the frozen river must have been inflicting on the submerged foundations of the turbine bridge as the stasis bubble was raised. A loud crack echoed through the air, and Jathen jumped. Realizing it had just been a bit of ice shifting against the left edge of the stasis bubble, he sighed, though his heart didn't slow. *It's strangely quiet.* The falls no longer flowed through the uniquely cantilevered outlets in the face of the dam, and the fine spray of muddy slush undermining the dam's foundation was clearly deadly but nearly silent.

"Tell me honestly, Raleigh. Even if you and I can do our parts, do the tar'ka-besh stand any chance of getting everyone out?"

"You mean will they get the Pearls—Mağrur—out," she retorted, still gazing over the river. For a moment, she fingered the gorgeous amulet on her choker, the one that looked like a dragon's eye. "It will depend entirely upon how many they have moved, if anyone was trapped when the first wave of the broken ice levee hit it, things of that nature. If they are coordinating through a telepathic link with Mağrur, then there's a chance we'll be able to warn them as soon as the bubble falls. If not..." She shook her head. "We're going in blind, and they have no idea we're coming in to help."

Turning toward him, she added, "For what it's worth, the Pearls technically follow Angani's Aspect, who embodies sacrifice. If anyone on the continent was willing to die in the act of saving lives, it'd be them."

"That's not a comfort."

"Perhaps not to you, but for them, this is what they signed on for. They'll go to Spirit believing they fulfilled their highest calling."

"I'm not sure Mağrur deserves that," Jathen whispered.

"If he doesn't, then it'll be known when he faces the Far-Side and Spirit." Raleigh took a sharp breath, then held out a hand. "Time to go."

Jathen measured her palm a moment then met her eyes. "You really can brace it?"

Smirking slightly, she tapped the amulet with two fingers. "You aren't the only one on the continent with Artifacts at your disposal, Negater. Mine might be a lesser one made from a Child's tear, but it *will* help me."

So that's how she converts and stores more than one elemental energy. Oddly comforted by the fact that Raleigh wasn't all bluster and had an Artifact at her disposal, Jathen nodded and wrapped his hands about her waist while she tucked her left arm around his. "Let's try this insanity, then."

She rose upward and, a short flight later, had them hovering over the roof of the south bank's maintenance building, where the curve of the stasis bubble was at its thinnest, just barely cresting past the southernmost corner of the building. "All right—glove off, hand out. Let's make some negation," Raleigh ordered.

Doing as bid, Jathen pulled his left glove off, clutching it tightly in his right as he braced his fist against her hip before letting go with his left. Bringing his hand up, he nodded for her to bring him down a little lower. Blinking the hair from his quite shaggy braid out of his eyes, Jathen reached out, fingers less than a scale away from the edge of the spell.

He hesitated. *Spirit help me.*

All he could think of was what had happened earlier in the day, leaping through Chūjitsun's fire barrier blindly, foolishly, and playing right into the renegade Balori's hands. *Going in blind... They'll never all get out.* An idea crystallized perfectly in his mind, a way, a third option, if he could just buy the time...

"What's the holdup, Negater? I might make this look easy, but you're still heavy."

Jathen pursed his lips hard and made his choice. "It's a mental block. I can't bring myself to do it. Not like this."

"We don't have *time* for a confidence crisis—"

"I know! I'm thinking!" Furrowing his brow, he twisted to look up at her, hoping his acting was good enough. "I did something similar earlier, but only while we were *moving* into the barrier. Maybe if you drop me onto it, I'll be able to negate it as I fall."

"Fair enough, but you're going to have to wait until I throw up the brace before I can grab you off the roof."

"Understood."

Floating a touch higher so that he'd land more cleanly on the roof, she adjusted her grip on him until he was dangling from his armpits over the bubble. "Just negate the thing," she said then released him.

He felt a brief rush of air as he concentrated as hard as he could. *Please, please, just let this work.*

He passed through the barrier like a ghost, negating nothing.

When he landed, Jathen rolled up onto his knees. All around him, snow and water floated as if suspended in time, but he alone moved without hindrance. *I was right, just like before—when Mağrur did it on the Balori townhouses.*

"What in the *Pit* are you *doing?*" Raleigh shrieked above him. Hands clenched so tight that they were shaking at her sides, she glared at him while her overcoat flapped madly in the wind behind her, and both her mismatched eyes seemed to suddenly darken with rage.

"I'm unaffected by the bubble," he called back, glad for the barrier's space between them as he gained his feet. "Tell the tar'ka-besh I'm going to warn the Pearls first! Give me five minutes. Ten at the most!"

"It's not *me* who needs to give you the minutes, you idiotic young soul. It's the Red-tainted ice in the river!"

"You were an ice mage last life. You'll figure it out!" Ignoring her enraged groan as she took off toward the bank, Jathen ran toward the roof-access door as quickly as the snow-and-ice-laden rooftop would allow. Shoving it open, he was thrilled to find no resistance, but his heart sank when he realized why. No one occupied the stairwell. *Damn it. Where are the survivors?*

After scampering down the steps two at a time, Jathen reached the landing and kicked open the door there, to find about ten wide-eyed humans dressed in brown-and-silver workers' clothes huddled just inside, unmoving. They were wet and breathing, registering his presence with waves of confusion and fear, but unable to move due to the stasis spell. Jathen bit his lip. He needed answers but wasn't certain what negating the hold the bubble had on them would do to the spell. *Have to risk it.*

He leaned down and grabbed the shoulder of the closest one, who immediately pulled away from him, blinking frantically. "How—"

"No time for explanations," Jathen interrupted, relieved the whole thing hadn't negated on him. "The turbine bridge is collapsing faster than expected, and we can't talk telepathically with the Pearls. What's delaying them? There should be more of you gathered here by now."

"There was an overpressure event. Several of the turbines and pipes on this side failed and flooded half of the access tunnels between here and the west bank. Their magic has kept it from flooding further, but the Pearls must physically carry each person through the static water. They've made a line of themselves across the plant and have been finding us then passing each person one by one to each Pearl."

"Like a relay. Ruddy hell." Jathen ran his fingers through his hair.

Even if they were passing people to both sides of the facility, they wouldn't have gotten very far. *Flood also explains the quicker collapse.* "All right. Change of plans." He pointed at the other humans, still frozen. "Grab someone, drag them up to the roof, then do it again. I'll be right back."

With that, Jathen bolted back upstairs to the rooftop, scanning the skies desperately for Raleigh. She swooped down quickly, coming from the river.

"I should ruddy kill you," she hissed. "I've got you maybe a few minutes by solidifying the ice flow, but it's not going to last, what with the damn bubble to work around—"

"Raleigh, shove it! There's only ten people down here so far!"

"*What*?"

"The Pearls are doing a relay because the turbine bridge is majorly flooded. They've not gotten many more out. I *have* to get down there and warn them."

"Jathen, there isn't *time*."

"I know! I think I have an idea!"

"It better be a fucking brilliant—"

"I'm going to give *D'ilinde* the energy from the bubble and have it teleport everyone out of the plant and to the banks! You won't admit it, but you know about this Artifact, Raleigh. Will it do it?"

Her mouth opened and closed a few times, then she snapped it shut, rolling her eyes. "I should have thought of that. It'll be more than enough energy to do it, and it's within D'ilinde's powers. But it's not foolproof. It'll only move people you tell it to—ones you can *visualize*. You'll need help from the Pearls to put the images of where each person is into your head—that likely means letting Mağrur in your head!"

Jathen's stomach quaked, but he nodded. "If that's what it takes. Buy me the time to get to the center."

"Right, like that's just so very easy! I make no promises, but I'll recruit a few more tar'ka-besh and try to get you ten more minutes, give or take. That's fifteen minutes if you don't do anything more stupid!"

Jathen barked a manic laugh. "What could possibly be more stupid that what I'm already doing?"

"Touching any of the floodwater! You'll negate the stasis on it, and it will become fluid again, which means it will fill the stasis bubble!" As Jathen winced, she huffed and floated upward. "Ruddy stupid young souls... This whole ruddy fucking day..."

Rushing back inside, Jathen grabbed a few more workers' shoulders, releasing them from the spell. "Get each other up and carry the others out! Quickly, does anyone know *exactly* where Mağrur is?" He was met with a multitude of shaking heads. "What about the survivors? Where will most of the workers be?"

"Over in the west-bank building, but several crews were attempting to turn off the turbine-charms with the manual switches," one female worker replied. She wiped her brow, meeting his eyes with concern. "If you're going through there, take the first door on the left to the main stairwell. It leads up to the highest tunnel and will bypass most of the water. The Pearl that carried us to this position was waiting for his handoff in the turbine hall up there."

"Good. Get to the roof and hold on. This may get bumpy."

With that, Jathen ran to the door she'd indicated. Opening it, he found a nearly pitch-black hallway, eerily similar to some of the dark places he'd gone spelunking through in Dodbyen. *No time for disturbing remembrances,* he mused, eyes adjusting as he sped forward in search of the proper door. Finding it open, Jathen darted through then up a set of metal-grate stairs. At the top, he found a long catwalk running along the left wall. The building's illumination, dimly glowing light-blue orbs, didn't reach much past the right-side railing, though he could discern some pipes and dark circles in the large gap below, where the turbines probably rested. He called out once, hoping to summon a Pearl Paladin who could telepathically speak with Mağrur, but his voice only echoed off the steel walls with a metallic coldness. Rubbing his shoulders against the true cold, Jathen set off at a breakneck speed across the catwalk.

He got a good distance before reaching a sagging portion of the bridge, broken by a fracture in the left wall. A large shard of ice and a wave of water were suspended in the air just as they had breached the interior. The wall must have broken only a second before the stasis bubble was cast. Twisted iron ribs that should have stayed hidden beneath the concrete wall were shattered and exposed. Clouds of dust and boulders were suspended in the air beside a veritable wall of water. Even if he had dared to touch it, the glassy surface of the immobile floodwaters provided few footholds in its dark ripples. As Jathen examined the mess, debating how to get past without negating the hold of the stasis on the water and thus the rest of the bridge, a Pearl Paladin with a worker slung over his shoulder crested the ice shard, his hazel eyes widening at the sight of Jathen.

"I thought I'd imagined the call I heard," he proclaimed, delicately maneuvering across the ice. Reaching the summit, he jumped down from floating boulder to floating boulder until he landed on the catwalk, blinking uncertainly at Jathen. "Who are you?"

"I'm the Negater, and the turbine bridge is separating from the bedrock faster than expected," Jathen explained in a rush. "We've only got minutes to get everyone out. I can teleport everyone with my Grand Artifact, but I need to know where everyone is to do it. That means getting to Mağrur. Can you call him telepathically?"

The Anganite went pale. "No. I... no, I can't. I'm not a telepath, only energy manipulative."

"Can you teleport to him?" Jathen asked. If they were lucky, he might get D'ilinde to follow along with a slight energy boost.

"No." He shook his head, adjusting the weight of the worker on his shoulder. "All our efforts went into the bubble. Technically, I'm still sustaining it through the link with Master Mağrur. I can't so much as draw in energy for an adrenaline supplementation. Everything just reroutes directly to the bubble."

"Ruddy hell." Jathen felt his shoulders sag as the tiredness of the day crept back into him. "How far in is he?"

"Too far to run with the rubble in the way. Um, the next man on the relay, Vas... He's telepathic and not far. He just handed off this man to me. If you can get to him, he can contact Master Mağrur and most of the others."

"Good. I released several of the workers back there from the stasis. Stay with them and make sure they get out if things go awry." Arching his neck, Jathen discerned a mostly clear route of handholds up the wall and across the ceiling to get him past the water and the gap in the bridge. "I'm going ahead."

"Angani be with you," the Pearl Paladin whispered before turning and taking off at a run back the way Jathen had come.

Grasping the nearest chunk of misshapen metal, Jathen pulled himself up. Twisting his body, he managed to get his feet onto a large chunk of concrete that'd separated from the wall. The moment he touched it, the floating scrap was released from the stasis, and the great boulder dropped. Yelping in surprise and fear, Jathen jumped instinctually, managing to snag a wrought-iron internal brace sticking out from the concrete. It groaned in protest but didn't bend. Straining, he pulled himself up until he could brace his feet against the wall, while below him, the concrete chunk smashed into the bridge before hitting the floor and breaking into a thousand pieces. *No way but up.*

The brush with death fueled his veins with enough adrenaline to chase away his tiredness. When he reached the top of the breach in the wall, Jathen began the precarious work of climbing hand over hand as quickly as he could across the ceiling. While traversing the highest point of the flood, the static mound of water was a velvet darkness under him. Tiny hairs that had come loose from his braid dangled off his forehead, barely missing the top of the liquid. Slipping a few times due to the darkness, Jathen flinched hard as more bits of concrete crashed into the abyss below, though he didn't spare the time to curse. Upon finally reaching the other side, he dropped the last few heads back onto the catwalk, the metal ringing loudly in the unnerving silence of the place. He took one deep breath then re-sumed his mad dash down the tunnel in search of Vas.

A shadow appeared down on the center of the catwalk, and Ja-then called out, his voice echoing desperately through the darkness. "Vas!"

The figure stopped then turned, facing the pale-blue lights. Rec-ognizing the man before him, Jathen skidded to a stop, heart pound-ing. It was one of the acolyte Pearls who'd attacked him—the tallest of the bunch.

"You," he practically hissed at Jathen, dark eyes narrowed in sus-picion and anger. He no longer wore his Angani tabard, but his heavy winter coat in beige and brown might still have been hiding chain mail. Leather-encased fingers wrapped tightly around the hilt of the short sword at his waist. "What are you *doing* here?"

Like Raleigh said, he might not know things went south at Annak-ki's. Steeling himself, Jathen repeated, "The plant is collapsing sooner than expected. The tar'ka-besh couldn't get to Mağrur telepathically, so they sent me in to negate the bubble, but I need to warn him first. I have to get to him before it collapses so *everyone* can get out." Purs-ing his lips, he gripped the railing, uncertain of what the disgraced Pearl might do. "Can you call him telepathically?"

Vas glared at him for what felt like eternity, nostrils flaring.

"We don't have much time—and whatever else you might think of me, I swear to you I'm trying to save lives today." He swallowed. "Isn't that what you're doing?"

The Paladin's dark eyes narrowed as Jathen tensed for a fight. Fi-nally, tentatively, Vas nodded, releasing his grip on his hilt. "He wants to know how much time we have to move the workers."

"None," Jathen answered. "I need him to telepathically send me the locations of every Pearl in here, as well as all the survivors he can locate. I'll then teleport everyone out of here using the Grand Arti-fact."

Vas arched an eyebrow but nodded, presumably relaying the message. When his face scrunched into a scowl after a moment, Jathen braced himself for bad news.

"Master Mağrur cannot pinpoint your mind, it seems." Scowling more deeply, he held out a hand. "I can serve as a telepathic bridge between you both. But no wandering. My mind is my own, Negater."

"The same to you," Jathen muttered darkly before removing his glove and grasping the disgraced acolyte by the hand. White light filled his vision, and D'ilinde whirred inside his chest, a high-pitched sound nearly a scream. Aware of Mağrur's presence, a crystalline castle of mental wards, and Vas's strange arrangement of nonsensical doors inside his mind, Jathen couldn't, however, control the burst of visions that suddenly flooded into his own mental architectural imagery.

After another flare of light, Jathen saw Mağrur speaking to Vas and the other two acolytes—low tones in some corner of the Angani floor of the citadel. *"Go to the Balori. Tell them the truth for me, of what had been planned. Make it seem like they've just overheard a bit of random information. It must not appear to have come purposefully from me, or the plan will fail."*

You did *tell them!* Jathen gasped, mentally yanking away from the two of them but somehow unable to break the connection completely. *This* is *all your fault!*

Confusion and irritation ruled Mağrur's emotions, the feelings rolling off the ice castle landscape of his mind. *What are you talking about?*

You told them—Jathen shot an accusatory mental finger at Vas's wall of doors—*to tell the Balori about what you and Annakki did!*

Shut up! Vas yelled.

You let those three cause the avalanche, all so the Balori could attack Annakki and you could frame De'contes for it!

Mağrur's castle shuddered, the opaque bluish color solidifying into solid white. *They weren't supposed to strike against Annakki. The Balori were supposed to come for* me. *It was I alone who should have borne their wrath.* Mağrur's mental attention shifted to Vas, feelings of horror slapping Jathen in the face. *What did you* do?

What we had to, Vas called, his voice echoing across all their minds. *Why should you be the one sacrificed, you whose intentions were just? Everyone knows* she *had been exiled for colluding with De'contes to murder an Original! The plan was sound, but it was* she *who deserved death, not you!*

With a sick, sinking feeling in his stomach, Jathen understood in full what Mağrur had done. *You tried to plant the seed of dissent in the Balori, hoping they'd come after you for revenge, thus framing De'contes. You still wanted to sacrifice yourself to stop the Balori from getting into the Ways!*

Mağrur's mental voice cracked, sounding similarly afflicted in the stomach as he continued to berate Vas. *I should have known you'd gone rogue after attacking the prince. You swore you were merely covering your tracks, that you feared he'd seen you talking too near the Balori girl, but I should have known.* Pain warped his voice as he projected, *You took the dishonorable discharge so well, claiming you understood the sacrifice—I should have known. You've truly fallen to the Red.*

Shock and rage reverberated across Vas's mind, tainting the light with a ruddy glow. *The Red does not sacrifice all they are for the sake of saving the world,* he called to his former master, then threw a manic wave of emotion toward Jathen. *You have not seen the fate Master Mağrur has seen—have not been willing to die as he has! If you had, you'd have done far worse than you accuse me of.*

Another vision? The memory of the Annarite tapping his temple and telling Jathen something similar just a few hours before seemed too much to be a coincidence.

These ends do not justify those means, Vas, Mağrur responded before Jathen could. *You've lost more than your Way. You've lost your mind.*

This is all the Negater's fault! Vas shrieked. *He ruined the original plan! De'contes would've been executed by now!*

Jathen, run! Mağrur called, then the mental bridge was broken.

Jathen opened his eyes to a sword swinging at his face.

Dropping his weight, he did the only rational thing in the immediacy of the moment. He pivoted into a low, crouched kick, trying to catch Vas's knee. Though sloppy, the strike managed to contact enough to stagger the disgraced acolyte backward but had little more power than that. Gathering his feet under himself, Jathen ran down the catwalk back toward the flooded breach in the wall, mentally cursing all the while.

Sounds of clanking echoed behind him. *Good.* That meant Vas was weighed down by armor of some type, though Jathen's tiredness still stole his own speed. *He can't manipulate energy because of the bubble, so it's just me versus his sword. I am an* idiot *for forgetting that damn sword cane!* Jathen ground his teeth as he came upon the breach in the wall. Even if he'd had the cane, a disgraced Pearl Paladin had far superior sword skills to his. *Lucky for me, I'm creative.*

Grabbing at the first set of handholds, Jathen darted up the broken concrete wall faster than a housefly seeking sunlight. Below, Vas made a sound akin to an angry feral Okten, and Jathen felt the sparks of a sword being scraped wildly but uselessly against the wall beneath his feet.

"You are killing us all, Vas," he yelled, still climbing.

If he could just keep him talking, maybe Mağrur would have enough sense to send another Pearl who could reestablish the link, and Jathen could still get everyone out.

"I know you don't give a shit for me, and maybe you and Mağrur and the rest of the Pearls don't mind making sacrifices, but about the workers? You're condemning innocent people!"

"Their sacrifice will be noted... and their next lives made to accommodate," he replied.

Jathen risked a glance down and saw a feral madness in Vas's eyes that made Mikkal's look sane.

"The same as mine!" With that dark declaration, the unhinged Talent pulled himself up onto the closest floating portion of rubble, which did not negate and fall.

Watching, Jathen concluded Vas would be close enough to start swinging rather effectively at Jathen's back with a naked blade more quickly than he'd be able to get to the other side. *Damn you to the Pit—you leave me no choice.* Digging his bare fingers as deeply as possible into his handholds, Jathen brought up his left foot and kicked at the nearest floating cluster of concrete. Negated, the rock fell in Vas's direction but missed the man by a good head's length.

Realizing Jathen's intentions, Vas made a guttural sound and launched himself out of Jathen's reach. "This will only end one way," he called, pulling himself up onto the ice shard that jutted from the wall alongside the immobile wave. "Come down, and it will be quicker. Otherwise, I'll just slash at your back until you fall."

Jathen sighed as he climbed a little higher, coming up just to the curve of the ceiling, where a metal bar made a secure perch despite its proximity to the breach. "For what it's worth"—he turned his head to gaze down at the man arching his sword to kill—"I'm sorry."

After ripping off his left glove with his teeth, Jathen plunged his bare hand into the water.

The following roar swallowed Vas's opened-mouthed cry, and Jathen had just one quick glimpse of him running to leap off the mess before turning his head to better brace against the wall. Water crashed and spattered, dragging large chunks of ice and rock along with it. The portion of ceiling Jathen clung to shuddered menacingly, and he scuttled sideways and down as fast as he could. He leapt away when more of the wall gave, crashing inward and down onto the groaning turbine pipes below. *Oh, I definitely made this worse.* Scuttling downward as quickly and carefully as he could, Jathen landed farther along the catwalk, only barely registering the still form of Vas lying toward the edge of it as he leaned over the railing. The limited lights brightened. Perhaps they'd been flickering and caught in a moment of darkness during the spell, but they were now giving enough illumination for Jathen to see the monstrous wreckage.

The large shard of ice Vas had been climbing on had joined a far more massive piece already wedged into the immense network of pipes below. Incredibly, the flood pushed a busted turbine through the breach, its spiral blades slicing through the catwalk, before it lodged in the tangle of pipes. As the water rose around it, changing temperature, it caused the whole conglomeration to twist and moan unnaturally. *Ruddy generator's charm is still active, even off its track,* Jathen realized with a sinking feeling, *and I've just gone and given the damn charm more water to spin.* He barely had time to get a better grip on the railing before the half-submerged charm detonated, throwing up a small cloud of ice and steam. A newer, deeper crack formed in the concrete ceiling above him while another portion of wall separated and crashed below.

The entire building groaned then tilted forward, the bubble beginning its separation from the bedrock. *I'll never get to Mağrur in time now.* Eyeing the growing hole in the wall, Jathen formed a slightly more insane plan. *Right. Fuck it. Bree, give me luck. D'ilinde, you know what to do.*

Arms breaking out in goose bumps as he placed his palms upon the wall, Jathen played the Endless Opus in his head. Swelling his negation bubble out and out, farther and farther, Jathen gasped as sweat broke on his brow, neck, and face. Stomach-wrenching dizziness encompassed him, but still he pushed mentally, visualizing his dark negation aura extending out to where he'd seen the shimmer of the stasis spell over the power plant.

The bubble negated.

A massive wave of power erupted through Jathen, and despite his plan, he didn't know what to do with it all. He couldn't think, couldn't remember anything when beset with the immensity of so many elemental energies, whirring, bubbling, crashing, and burning through him as if he were no more than a conductor. So he held it pressed behind his lips like a desperate breath before being pulled underwater. He didn't know if his eyes were open or closed, but lights danced and sparkled against a velvet indigo, the world seeming to spin for eternity inside his head. Jathen had no sense of time, no grasp of reality—only the notion, the drive to *hold*.

It's all right, a voice whispered in his mind, a light thing, almost playful in the mire. *I have it. And you. Let go.*

I... I can't! I don't—

I have it, the voice repeated with a smile in the words. *We know what to do.*

D'ilinde?

Let go.

He did.

Energy hummed all around him, deafening, then a moment of weightlessness passed before the world came rushing back with a crash. Jathen landed hard on his side atop the catwalk, only mildly aware of Vas's screams as the broken turbine that'd been lodged so precariously finally separated from the floor and smashed through the outer wall of the building. Open sky over the falls did not greet it. Instead, the heavy metal machine tumbled and whirled down the side of the Reverent Steps like a toy dropped down a stairwell by a child on the way to bed.

Spirit in Heaven, it worked! D'ilinde actually teleported the whole ruddy building! Jathen nearly yelped with joy but caught himself, as a tremendous amount of energy was still whirling within him, looking for purpose before being reverted to whatever energy Mağrur and the others had used to make the stasis spell.

"Jathen!"

Peering through the new gaping hole in the wall, he stifled another laugh at the sight of Izzy and a good two dozen Way Walkers in varying colors, all standing on the Observatory's veranda, staring wide-eyed at him from a relatively short two Tazu lengths away. He waved awkwardly, the press of the extra energy making him mildly nauseous and strangely stiff.

Shaking her head at him, Izzy coughed a laugh. "Wait there. I'll come to you," she called, hopping off the edge of the Reverent Steps and out into the snow. A touch of relief swept through Jathen, but then Izzy's eyes widened in horror. With a creak and a moan, the ground beneath him gave way. Panicking, Jathen found himself slipping off the side of the catwalk and then through the air, and he did what first came to mind—*Izzy! Put me with Izzy!*

The Grand Artifact complied, teleporting him out into the snow just past the hole and close enough to Izzy he could almost grasp her hand. The ground under them shifted, and the east side of the station cleaved down the center, breaking off from the rest of the plant. Suddenly, Jathen and Izzy were both skating across the ice, the great concrete structure sliding down the side of the glacier, right behind.

The ice burned him.

The pain of the frozen ground scraping across bare skin and a too-thin coat tore at Jathen's once-tired mind, sharpened by terror. Spinning, he slid, tumbling and scrambling across the ice. A deep fissure loomed before him, wide, dark, deadly. Fingers desperately flexing for grip, Jathen found no traction to stop his mad descent. Spinning like a top, he could barely think, registering a view of the coming turbine bridge, then endless ice, then fissure, then the distant city. Another rotation revealed a glimpse of Izzy not far behind him, then he was face-to-face with the crevasse once more. It seemed to have widened into a frozen mouth to swallow them whole, though perhaps he was just gaining ground toward it. Abandoning his efforts with numb, battered fingers, he twisted over to his back then dug his heels deep into the glistening whiteness.

Skidding, he slowed his descent, and all too soon, Izzy flew past him, leaving a trail of Orne's bones as she went. Bright blue sparked to life across her body, and the skeleton formed. Still sliding, Orne reached out and snatched Jathen by his coat collar. With a painful jerk of fabric digging into his armpits, Jathen was pulled closer to the golem. He mentally screamed Izzy's name as he helplessly watched her gain on the crevasse. A surge of power all around him made the hairs on Jathen's neck stand on end, and Orne shifted, still clutching Jathen's collar in his front claws. The great skeleton tyrn whipped its bony tail around, and Izzy snatched it with both hands. Orne's claws dug deep into the ground, managing to halt their slide across the ice.

Jathen's head swirled, his body acclimating to the sudden stop. He could make out Izzy climbing up Orne's tail toward him, her lips moving, but his mind couldn't make sense of the words.

"Jathen!" She finally reached him, placing one hand on his shoulder and giving him a good shake. "Are you well?"

Putting a hand on his forehead, he tried to nod, but he wasn't certain he managed it due to his wooziness. Swallowing, he pushed the held energy downward, using it as best he could in small bits to recover. He would've been proud of himself if he'd had any idea how he was doing it. Still, he held his tongue, making hand symbols to Izzy to hopefully convey his meaning: *Dizzy. But alive. Thank you.*

"Good. We have to move!"

Turning, Jathen realized he'd somehow missed the sound of the oncoming turbine bridge. Taking a breath through his nose to attempt yet another teleport with D'ilinde, Jathen was interrupted by a massive ice barrier shooting upward to stop the coming building, the crash and shake of it further grinding his teeth inside his head. *Raleigh*.

The force that stopped the broken bridge also sent a wave of shattering ice their way, and though Orne did his best, the three of them were bombarded by enough snow and shifting ice to send them right into the crevasse. Orne hit a lower ledge almost immediately, shattering into individual bones.

Somehow, through the struggle, falling and crashing, Jathen managed to snatch Izzy's arm and the ledge at the same time. Dangling and feeling as though his arm was being dislocated by the weight of her, he finally screamed, "Hold on! Hold on! Hold on!" while releasing the crashing, cracking energy to rush through his veins, strong enough to make his blood boil. Shaking, he glanced up at his straining arm and was greeted with a bizarre view: new, bright claws had replaced his fingernails, and gold scales covered his hand, disappearing inside his coat to Spirit knew how far up his arm.

He didn't know whence they'd come, but they were there when he needed them, flexing deeper into the ice and clicking against the thin sliver of rock beneath. An instinctual understanding told him to twist slightly, and the claws extended out farther and deeper into the stone. The cold cut into his cuticles and shot pain down his arm, but he didn't care. "Izzy, I've got you!" His breath came out in desperate puffs, arm laboring as pebble-sized hunks of broken ice pelted them from above. "Just hold on!"

The frozen ledge creaked loudly, threateningly.

"I'm too heavy, Jathen!" She shook her head, brown eyes suddenly hard even as she clutched him with both hands.

"I've got you!" He grinned, feral in his fear.

Hundreds of Way Walkers were up above them—tar'ka-besh, Rosinics, dozens of Way Paths—and many had to have seen Izzy make that insane dive after him. He just needed to hang on until someone got to them. *If someone gets to us. So many still on the bridge... It must be chaos there.*

"I had you before, remember? In Dodbyen? I have you now!"

"No, you don't." The line of tattoos on her brow softened. "We need to stop ending up like this."

Jathen wailed a laugh, trying to ignore his weakening arm's numbness. "Yeah, we do."

She sighed, looking up past him, perhaps scanning the sky for help or to take in Orne one last time. "You need to drop me, Jathen. Or we both will fall."

In direct defiance, he dug his fingers deeper into her wrist, hard enough that she winced, and he knew bruises would be left. "No."

"Yes, you do."

"Izzy—"

Faster than he could imagine, she betrayed him, releasing his wrist with her right hand then digging her fingers down under his own. He shrieked as she pried his fingers up against his will. Then she fell.

Shock and terror made him let go of the edge right after her.

He screamed for D'ilinde as he fell, but all he felt was the cold rush of air, whatever energy he'd had left was burned off in his desperate attempt to hold onto her. As he plummeted, a revelation took Jathen so deeply that it stole the breath from his lungs.

It begins at the fall. I have averted nothing. Not even my demise.

Darkness swallowed him, and the staggering comprehension that death had finally come hit him in the chest like a battering ram.

Raleigh caught him.

The pain of her arm suddenly locking around his body choked a sob out of Jathen, and he shrieked Izzy's name with the last willful breath he could muster. Raleigh laughed—she actually *laughed*—as she swooped deeper, faster. The mage snatched Izzy around the waist then shot straight upward out of the crevasse. Clutching them both, she flew farther across the mountainside and back toward the Observatory. The wind and cold were oppressive, and Jathen found himself flailing to keep his face covered, his body wracked by uncontrollable shivering. Raleigh noticed his plight or at last deemed they were far enough away from the crevasse to be safe. They landed roughly, Jathen and Izzy both rolling a bit in the snow as Raleigh staggered to a halt.

"Apologies for the timing there," she said, grinning as she brushed off some excess snow. "Since *someone* decided to use the ruddy energy to teleport a building, *I* had to grab a whole mess of the topmost snow and repurpose it to make an ice buttress to stop it all on my own."

Rubbing his sorely frozen hands together, Jathen ignored her posturing. Though he was grateful, his attention was only on Izzy. "Are you all right?"

"I'm alive," she replied with a deep sigh. Slowly gaining her feet, she addressed Raleigh. "My golem... I realize it's not a priority now, but—"

"Oh, fine, give me your bag and a moment." Raleigh waved a hand at Izzy as if she'd just asked her to run a quick errand. "No one's going to bother me to do anything after that set of theatrics, and it's doubtful anyone else could find all of your skeleton."

While Izzy handed over Orne's satchel, Jathen managed to stand, albeit on very wobbly legs. Teeth chattering, he suddenly became aware of just how very, very cold he was.

"Jathen, your lips are turning blue." Izzy removed her cloak, wrapping the far-too-short thing around his shoulders.

It lessened his shivering, but Jathen's teeth still chattered away.

"We'll need to get you warm sooner than later."

A wave of tar'ka-besh went flying over their heads, trailed by the flapping purple cloaks of more mages. The Walkers paid the two of them no heed, probably far more concerned for those still inside what was left of the power plant.

Shaking her head at them, Izzy pursed her lips then met Jathen's eyes. "Mağrur?"

"I didn't get to him, but I was in his mind. I'm right, Izzy. He did tell the Balori what Annakki had planned but also what part he'd played. His intention was for the Balori to go after him. Not her. The acolytes that attacked us... One of them was in there now. They somehow convinced the Balori to go after Annakki."

"Do you have proof beyond what you saw?"

"No, nothing tangible." Jathen shivered, shaking his head as much to warm himself as anything. "Vas attacked me, though, and if he survived, he can be read. But we might not need to. Mağrur was horrified at what they'd done. He'll speak truth. I know he will."

"Good—then it was worth it."

Jathen nodded, swallowing. "Izzy, please, promise me, *promise me* you won't ever, *ever* do anything like what you did back there again." The trembling of his lower lip had naught to do with the cold. "In fact, I *order* you: never, *ever* force me to sacrifice you!"

"No." Izzy straightened, stoic in the face of his pain, barely moving despite having just confronted death. "I cannot make such a promise or carry out such an order. My loyalty is to you, to the Nation, Jathen. You are our hope. If losing my life allows you to live, then I will give it up. Unquestioningly. Regardless of my feelings and flying in the face of *your* feelings, because you are my prince. You must understand that... and make your peace with it."

Jathen balled his fists at his sides. "I can't lose another friend." The words felt small in his own ears, and hot tears streamed down his cheeks. "I can't."

"Then I am not your friend." Wetness shone in Izzy's eyes. "Not when it comes to this. So long as you're heir and later king, this is how it must be."

"Maybe I don't want it, then."

She winced slightly, his words clearly wounding. "Then that is your choice."

Raleigh cleared her throat, as if the vibrations from her vocal cords could shake off what'd just happened. Blinking, they both turned toward her, having missed her return.

"Here. It's all in there, save maybe a toe or finger joint or two," she proclaimed, handing the satchel to Izzy.

"Thank you," Izzy said softly while fixing it back onto her waist. "We need to get Jathen inside. Quickly. And deal with a disgraced Pearl acolyte named Vas, who attacked him in there."

"All right, but do give me a moment to catch my breath, as it were," Raleigh replied. "I did just do a whole lot of energy manipulating. Flying around, crafting rescues, and the like."

"You mean your Artifact did," Jathen muttered through clattering teeth.

"*Helped,* not *did*," she retorted with a huff, crossing her arms. "Though speaking of such, I must admit you seemed to have managed a bit of transmogrification back there. Impressive."

Jathen could only blink rapidly at her. Every time he thought it impossible for her to surprise him anew with her randomness, she did.

"I did a what?"

She pointed at his hand. "Organic manipulation. You know, those really *hard* spells I mentioned?"

"I... I did?" Holding up his right hand, he saw that, aside from some redness from the cold, it had returned to normal. "I mean, that was real, wasn't it? What happened?"

She shrugged. "Far as I can tell, you still had negated energy, and you didn't want to have it revert when you released it, but you didn't give it a direct, conscious direction, either— probably more akin to 'don't drop my friend' than 'make me stronger'—so that left your primary subconscious desire."

"Subconscious desire?"

"Ugh." Her eyes practically rolled to the peak of the mountain. "Your body tried to *shift*, moot."

Jathen's jaw dropped. "That... that's *possible*?"

"Apparently." With one finger, she closed his jaw. "Oh, don't look so shocked. The capability is still in your life's ladder. That's how moots can pass on the trait to their children sometimes. It's reasonable to assume a moot would have a higher chance at organic manipulation into a tyrn than say, a typical Talent attempting to morph into anything else. But it's not impossible. Hell, several of the Children and a few High Mages set the precedent years ago."

"But I'm *not* an Incarnation, and normal moot Talents can't shift, let alone my being a Negater. Everyone knows how difficult that kind of organic magic is."

"Difficult, yes. Impossible?" She shrugged. "Apparently not. Though that *is* why I said 'impressive,' you know."

Jathen clenched and unclenched his fist, the memory of those golden scales and sharp claws like a syrupy, sustaining tincture running down his throat as he swallowed. He'd had dreams—*precognitive* dreams—since he was small about flying as a tyrn, feeling the beat and press of his wings' powerful movement against his shoulder blades. He'd given up on them as hatched-blood fever dreams, but having discovered it was possible—probable, even—he heaved a shaky sigh then leveled deadly serious eyes at both Raleigh and Izzy. "You are not to speak a word of this to *anyone*, hear me?"

"Obviously," Izzy replied with a certain sarcasm that would have sounded familiar coming from Raleigh, while the mage herself just snorted.

"Good." Jathen lowered his fist, frowning across the ice toward where he imagined Mağrur was probably waiting in the remains of the turbine bridge. "We need to tell the High Mages what's happened." His stomach flip-flopped when he thought about how he was going to explain the Pearl Paladin's treachery. *At least now I can avoid brining Annakki's confession into it—I hope. Thank Spirit for small favors, I suppose.* "I just hope they believe us."

Raleigh sighed long. "I'm fairly certain I can bend my parents' ears long enough to get a telepath to sift through our respective heads to see what happened."

Jathen snapped his head in her direction, suddenly terrified for Annakki. "Didn't I just say I want no one to know about my hand changing?"

"Ugh, telepaths aren't going to hunt in anyone's head beyond the scope of Maǧrur's confession, as I assume that's what you're speaking of, but fine." Raleigh poked the icy ground with her toe. "I can vouch for you two, I'm sure, and that will be enough to get Maǧrur read. Spirit knows my parents will comprehend the seriousness of the situation just from the fact I'm even speaking to them."

Jathen cocked his head at her. "Your parents?"

She huffed another sigh. "My surname is Jidoja. Dàshī and Jiāojīn are my parents, Jathen."

Izzy arched an eyebrow, making the runes on her forehead curve like a scythe. "The High Mage Chancellor of Tar'citadel and the High Walker of Rosin are your *parents*?"

Shaking her head, Raleigh shrugged again. "I know what you're thinking: what on the continent was he thinking getting involved with her? But he was young and foolish, and at least he got *me* out of it."

His mouth hanging open again, Jathen didn't know what to say and so just laughed, with tears of stress, exhaustion, and disjointed relief rolling down his cheeks.

"Well, I suppose that explains a good deal," Izzy said dryly, which made him laugh and cry harder.

Shooting them a squinty glare, Raleigh just shook her head again.

"I'LL MAKE SURE THE ambassador sends it out myself," Marcasith promised, slipping Jathen's letter to Erin Manna into his tunic pocket. "Though I don't understand why you didn't give it to her yourself. You've been staying within two lengths of her office this last week, and we spoke half a dozen times before coming here."

"I know." Jathen pulled the collar of his coat up against the wind as he followed Marcasith out of the embassy carriage, which rocked somewhat as Izzy and Seren stepped out the other side. "But it's important, and I'm feeling rather Rheanic about it. That, and I was still working on it on the ride over, and I intend to try to go back to Annakki's to speak with her after this. I want the letter on its way as soon as possible."

Marcasith huffed, leaning closer to Seren and murmuring, "Ruddy Rheanic influence, making this far more convoluted than needs be."

Seren smirked fondly at the old Tazu, probably suspecting that he avoided her mother in order to dodge the topic of his relationship with her daughter.

"You may find you've been too long out of the world and politics, Highness," Izzy said softly, taking her usual spot behind Jathen's shoulder. "Convolution can save lives."

"Or lose them," Marcasith replied.

Embassy guards closed ranks as they headed up the path to the Temple Citadel, and Jathen stared at the back of Teal's uniform. The ambassador had been rather insistent upon the transport and additional guards, and Jathen hadn't been in a mood to argue. Gazing at the column of smoke drifting up from the top of the citadel, he could honestly admit he wasn't in the mood for much at all as of late.

After Raleigh had deposited him and Izzy at the embassy to await the coming interrogation, Jathen had apparently fallen into a bed and slept nearly straight through two full days. Hazy memories of servants feeding him, a newly warm blanket, and Izzy and Seren talking in hushed tones were all he could recall.

High Walker Zhìliáo came to check on him when he finally woke, stating Jathen had severely overtaxed himself. "It takes years for Talents to build up the stamina to cast large spells over a short period—especially physical supplementation and teleportation. As a Negater with a Grand Artifact, you have an inadvertent shortcut, but not without consequence. Pace yourself next time, please, or you'll negate yourself into a coma."

Her orders had been strict and final: bed rest with few visitors, no exceptions.

After five more days of rest, he'd yet to shake his overall physical tiredness or the full sluggishness of his mind. Walking across the large entrance hall of the Temple Citadel, Jathen was even then feeling an extra weight that seemed to tug on his limbs. *Then again, I did manage the improbable.* Inside his coat pocket, he flexed his hand. The glimmer of hope in the memory of those bright-gold scales was welcome in the wake of so much disappointment, death, and uncertainty. *Someday.*

You certain you're up for this? Seren asked on the elevator ride up. *I can probably get Zhìliáo to say this is too taxing.*

I'll manage. He curled his pinky around hers, a subtle gesture they'd developed while he'd been living under the ambassador's scrutiny. *Moody as this will inevitably make me, I need to be here after what happened. And I'm sick of bed rest.*

Seren nodded, squeezing back once then releasing his finger. She didn't need to press. She knew he meant to see Annakki.

The doors opened onto the observation floor, the other public portion of the Temple Citadel and the site of a mass memorial for those who'd fallen during the avalanche. Cool wind zipped through the semi-outdoor space, whistling through the protective rails holding up the dome and encompassing the ledge overlooking the city. Dominating the center of the banded white marble floor stood Spirit's Flame, a gigantic brazier that supposedly never extinguished. Its dark smoke streamed steadily through the large round opening in the dome.

Marcasith coughed, rubbing his nose profusely. "Think the Turinics went heavy-handed with the oiled wood and incense. Smells like someone overturned a spice cart up here."

"Be respectful, old Tazu," Izzy scolded with a soft, palpable fondness.

"I *am* being respectful. I'm just also choking on heady fumes."

Jathen shook his head, mildly amused by Marc's attitude. After so long in Dodbyen, no one would deny he deserved to say and do as he pleased. They followed Teal and the other guards to where other nobles of the city were clustered around the brazier then waited on the High Mages to start the ceremony.

All told, only a half a dozen had fallen to the actual avalanche, but across the city, mischief had unfolded, and along with the attack on Annakki and Jathen's wild teleportation of the entire power plant, around a hundred souls had crossed to Far-Side, all told. A line of people holding urns stood closest to the waist-high ledge, a crescent of sadness looking out over the city. Though he mourned those lost, Jathen had no urn of his own to hold and held back, scanning the line as more entered and took their places.

The High Walker of Angani, Dresden, and several ranked Pearl Paladins held the urns for their fallen brethren—despite everything Jathen had done, five of the nearly twenty Pearls that'd been in the power plant had died, including Mağrur.

The news had hit Jathen hard. The man who'd framed De'contes had held the crumbling turbine bridge together for as long as he could after the teleport until the strain of so much energy manipulation apparently exploded his heart in his chest. The two sibling disgraced Pearl acolytes had been found as well, drowned when the water had become fluid again. Vas had not been found, but several Walkers claimed to have seen him go over the cliff that'd nearly claimed Jathen and Izzy.

Older, and a former Pearl Paladin himself, Dresden cut a stern but weathered figure in his whites, flanked by younger Pearls in full plate armor, their cloaks flapping in the wind like Angani flags. Still, Jathen could not muster pity for the man, knowing as he did what Maǧrur had tried to do—twice.

And Vas succeeded where he failed—though it ultimately falls on my shoulders as well. My actions killed them all... and the truth with them. The Balori didn't win their vote, and thanks to Angani machinating and my blundering, they shall probably never get the chance again—if the movement survives at all after this.

Annakki wasn't hard to spot, her pale face glowing despite the thin veil she wore. Her dark gloves wrapped around Chūjitsun's polished steel-gray urn. Beside her stood her remaining guard, his left arm in a sling and bearing an urn that must have held the ashes of his partner, Zhan. He wore no hood, revealing a human with circles under his eyes almost as dark as his black hair. Annakki hadn't returned a single missive Jathen had sent. They'd not spoken since the attacks, and fear had been living and growing in his stomach.

A dark shape caught his eye, and Jathen raised an eyebrow at the sight of Nannazen slipping into a spot far from the other two in the line of mourners, her own urn clutched to her chest. *That's surprising. I suppose the High Walkers are not without compassion for Nannazen. She, at least, was innocent in all this.*

I'd not bank on it being wholly compassion, Seren added to his thoughts. *De'contes did himself no favors in disappearing before Dàshī and the tar'ka-besh could question him about what had happened. Half the city wants his blood after finding out that ice mage was Balori. I overheard Mother talking—Dàshī is allowing only provenly uninvolved members of Balori their continued sanctuary to serve as bait, to lure De'contes in for questioning.*

How delightful.

The sideways glance she gave him had a mote of concern. *I know you blame yourself, but there were things you simply didn't know. And truly, are you certain De'contes couldn't have known what his people were plotting?*

He closed his eyes. *I saw what I saw in Vas and Mağrur's minds, Seren. They—especially Vas—had a hand in it. I told Dàshī what I could, but unless I let him into my mind...*

And that implicates Annakki. I know. Her pinky found his, and she squeezed softly. *As it stands, De'contes's sanctuary isn't officially revoked, but if he doesn't appear soon to answer their summons, he's at risk of losing it outright. He's making his choices, too, Jathen. He's still very guilty of a great many things. For what it's worth, I think your silence, to protect Annakki, is the right choice.*

Jathen sighed, trying to summon up some feeling of relief or perhaps vindication but failing. *Too tired to feel most days, it seems.*

That numbness carried on through the arrival of the High Mages and Walkers and Dàshī's short but sweet speech about the unity people could find in sorrow. Then the High Walker of Turin, whose face and race were completely concealed under dark-blue robes and hood, tossed a new packet into the fire, calling upon the Veil to thin and all lingering souls to cross. Darker smoke smelling of something sickly sweet floated upward, the odor mixed with char giving Jathen a slight headache. Following that cue, all those in the line stepped forward to the ledge and removed the urns' lids. The ashes swept out on the current of wind all at once, whooshing across the city like a stormfront. The deeply beautiful gesture had many shedding tears, though Jathen's eyes remained dry. Weariness and shock had stanched such sentiment, leaving him with a dry sense of emptiness, like a basin of seawater that'd evaporated, leaving only a white layer of salt.

"You're looking like I did after Bloody Ally," Marcasith murmured. "You holding up all right?"

Jathen opened his mouth to parrot some placation about how Marc had been through far worse and shouldn't fuss, then he thought better of it. "I know the situation as a whole wasn't my fault—the Balori made their choices, but so, too, did I." As his eyes found Annakki and her guard, standing and watching the ashes float away, Jathen felt a tight twinge in his heart. "Chūjitsun is dead directly from my miscalculations. And while I might have saved one of Annakki's guards, the other probably wouldn't have fallen if I'd not negated the fire barrier." *Not to mention I failed to clear De'contes. I actually got the ones who'd redeemed him killed.* Lowering his voice to prevent Izzy and Seren from hearing, he added aloud, "And Izzy almost died on the ice. Basically, told me she'd do it again, to save me."

"And it's sitting heavy on your shoulders."

Meeting Marc's golden Monortith eyes, Jathen found more understanding there than he'd hoped. "How did you bear it? Between this and Dodbyen and my mistakes that came before—" he cut himself off, unable to voice it.

Marcasith sighed long, ending in a bit of a draconic grumble. "Firstly, you need to understand it's unrealistic to expect to be some great general so early on in your training. Considering how short-lived your time with Master Enillydd has been, it's amazing how competent you were at the townhouse, and even more so for Dodbyen and before. Mourn your losses, Jathen, manage your expectations, and do your best to learn from the mistakes made."

Watching the mourners dispersing, he couldn't shake his prevailing sense of numbness. "But the cost of my education is lives lost."

"Nephew"—Marcasith put a hand on Jathen's shoulder—"sometimes you can do absolutely everything correctly and still lose. Believe me when I tell you I followed every last procedure when we were in Kinawa, and we *still* got captured and ended up in Dodbyen. In the dance of war and battle, the only true victory is avoiding a fight altogether through diplomacy and compromise. And even then, it's not a guaranteed thing. Lives can still be shattered."

Jathen swallowed, finishing the thought that'd been hovering about his mind since Izzy swore to die for him. *Maybe I truly don't want to rule. The few deaths I'm responsible for still keep me up at night—despite the lives I saved.*

And the better question is: will I save or lose more lives as a king?

Seren found his pinky again and squeezed it once. *Hate to interrupt your internal debate, but you might lose your chance if you don't move now.*

Following Seren's gaze, Jathen caught a glimpse of Annakki's graceful passage across the floor, the sea of mourners parting for her and her guard as if she were an arrow slicing through wind. Slipping between Marcasith and Scmit, Jathen made to overtake her, unmindful of the impropriety of nudging or bumping others on the way.

Barely reaching her before she entered the elevator, he mewed her name more like a plea than a call. "Annakki."

Turning, she measured him with phlegmatic eyes. "Prince Monortith."

Flinching somewhat at the use of his formal title and her dispassionate tone, Jathen found himself stumbling awkwardly with his words. "I know we haven't spoken since the attacks... I realize you've perhaps not been in a position to answer my letters, but... I just..." He dropped his voice to a low whisper. "Are you and Dor'rhean doing all right?"

Quiet a moment, she finally inclined her head slightly. "We've alternate accommodations for the time being. It has been comfortable."

"Oh, right." Fingers twitching under her scrutinizing gaze, Jathen fiddled with a loose thread on his coat. *Spirit, why is this so hard?* "The house probably wasn't livable."

Taking pity on him, her guard softly added, "Nevershen Supai provided a place for our lady and the remaining household while renovations are underway."

"I've met him." Jathen resisted an urge to snicker at his memory of the strange Rheanic standing in Seren's dorm room. "And Spinnek and Rhyo?"

"They have done my lady the service of remaining at the townhouse as informal guards."

"Good. I'd started to worry—hadn't heard from them either." He turned back to Annakki, trying not to let too much of his desperation seep through. "I was hoping we could speak on... everything that has transpired."

Her lips pursed ever so slightly, and for a moment, he thought she would deny him. "Clearly, words need to be said," she finally returned, tone still stiff. "But not here. I shall be in residence this afternoon to oversee certain aspects of the renovation. You may call upon me then."

She departed without further comment, leaving Jathen uncertain. While the conversation hadn't exactly gone well, it hadn't gone very badly, either. Then again, Annakki was never easy to read and tended to fall back to Clan neutrality in public. *And it's been an emotional day.* The long gaze her guard leveled on him before turning to follow his mistress, however, left Jathen with a foreboding knot in his stomach.

"You are well?"

Izzy's voice made Jathen start slightly, and he turned to find her and the rest of his entourage falling in around him, most looking concerned.

Patting down his coat to ease his nerves, Jathen nodded. "She'll see me later this afternoon."

Izzy nodded. "Do you want the rest of the guards to accompany you?"

"Just you, if we could."

"Not certain how my mother is going to take that." Seren crossed her arms, not bothering to stanch her protectiveness.

"I'm certain, between you and Marc, you'll be able to quell any arguments she might have," Jathen bantered.

Seren relented. "Just be quick." Glancing away, she narrowed her eyes. "And give us a few moments more here before you head out. I want to at least escort you part of the way, but first, I see Headmaster Ophisa over there, and I have to discuss my class standing with the man."

Jathen stifled a grumble. Seren's academic career couldn't have done well, given the massive distraction he'd been over the last semester, and the idea that he'd ruined her chances added another uneasy burden to his ever-growing list.

"Nothing dire, I hope?" he asked.

"No, I simply need to get some clarification on my personal-study electives. Won't take too long—just enough time to let this crowd thin." She darted off through the throng, Scmit following like a good embassy escort.

"His name was Or'sen."

Jathen spun around to find Nannazen standing there, her fists clenched tightly at her sides. Marcasith, Teal, and Citra stiffened, but Jathen held a hand up.

Heart pounding, he took a small step closer to the girl. "The one in your urn?"

"My friend." She nodded, fresh tears rolling down her cheeks. "The one you killed."

"I very much wished I hadn't had to do that." Jathen pursed his lips, his heart wrenching yet again at the thought of the blade he'd dug into the Annarite's neck. "Thank you for telling me his name. I shouldn't forget."

She blinked a few times as though uncertain how to respond then shook her head and turned to go.

"Wait," Jathen said. "Or'sen said he'd seen something, a vision, that made him believe what he did was for the greater good. Do you know what it was?"

Her eyes narrowed. "Why would you care?"

Jathen wet his lips, trying to put words to something he barely understood. "If a man dies for something he believes is right, I'd like to know what it was, to know if it *was* right, even if he acted upon it wrongly. If so, then I'd like to make sure that death is not in vain."

She pursed her lips then shook her head. "He didn't tell me. Anyone who knew is dead or fled."

Lowering his hand, Jathen nodded. "Thank you."

"I wonder," Izzy murmured, just enough for Jathen to hear, "if there aren't more than a few *'convenient'* deaths in all of this." When he furrowed his brow, staring at her, she continued, "It's just strange—all those who could have added to the story, told their deeper truths, are gone."

"Mostly because of my actions," he whispered back. "In this, I'm the architect of this failure."

"Perhaps." Izzy frowned, her eyes following Nannazen's retreat through the crowd. "But sometimes there are things we don't see."

Chapter 10

Annakki stared.

Jathen felt nothing but anxiety under the cold gaze of those beautiful tourmaline orbs as she sat, legs crossed formally at the ankles. In one of the few rooms untouched by the battle, Hatori's sword cane reflected well in the surface of the polished mahogany dining table, where it sat. Walking in, Jathen took the liberty of picking up the cane, while Izzy remained in the doorway.

Unsheathing the blade, he smiled softly. "You had it properly cleaned." A warble of hope flickered in his chest—perhaps this wouldn't go as badly as he feared. He secured it in its casing with a soft click. "Thank you."

"Gratitude is unnecessary. My mother crafted the weapon. I would never disrespect such a piece." Those beautifully cold eyes bore unblinkingly into his soul. "No matter who wields it."

Jathen's heart sank. "Is this how it is going to be, then? Veiled insults and acerbic Clan words?"

An eyebrow arched slightly on her delicate face. "You would have me be blunt, then?"

"I'd have honesty between us, always."

"Very well." Folding her hands, she then rested them atop her knees. "You are no longer welcome in my presence or home, Jathen Monortith. Thusly, I'd prefer it if you remove your sword from here today and make other permanent arrangements for your accommodations. I trust this will not be difficult." Her tone held its Clan neutrality, but the words still stung like a dozen wasps making a pincushion of his heart.

Still, Jathen stayed his venom, knowing it wouldn't do him much good. "I suppose you've lost your trust of me, then?" he asked softly, though he imagined his hurt and surprise were still detectable.

"You've made no secret you've taken the monster's side over those you'd supposedly call family," she replied, again, nothing but stale neutrality in her voice. "I cannot condone that. I cannot risk my son's exposure to that."

Jathen's throat tightened. She was correct—he'd gambled with her life when he'd run off after the attack, choosing to risk warning De'contes. Only sheer luck and his silence had kept her part in it all from exposure—but this level of venom was unexpected. "You'd keep Dor'rhean from me?"

Heat smoldered in Annakki's tourmaline eyes. "Choices have consequences, Jathen Monortith. You knew what yours would glean. I warned you enough times."

"I found the *truth* on the mountain—could have cleared 'the monster' as you call him—but instead held my tongue, kept my mind from being read, to hide your part in this. Does that mean so little? Protecting you, protecting Dor'rhean, doesn't that matter?"

"Whatever truth you think you found, it's wrong," she whispered harshly, the slightest bit of rage seeping into her tone. "*He* pulls strings you cannot fathom, weaves schemes a thousand years in advance. If you think for one moment you have been any more than his pawn, then your arrogance shall be your undoing. And I cannot allow it to become mine."

"Annakki, please—"

"I've heard enough of the subject." Her eyes turned cold again. "I've taken the liberty of sending your remaining things on to the embassy. You will find your companions' belongings along with them. I shall inform them of this after you depart."

"You're putting Rhyo and Spinnek on the street too? They've nothing to do with what's passed between us!" Jathen gaped, his tightly reined control slipping. "They saved Dor'rhean's life, for Spirit's sake!"

"And your visiting them in my home shall not be used as an excuse to seek out me or my son." Her lower lip trembled, just slightly, then she added, "No one should have known my child *existed*, save Erin Manna and those here. *She* did not violate that. *My people* did not violate that."

"Neither would any of mine!" Jathen squawked in protest.

"And yet the Balori came for him." When Jathen did not reply, her lips twitched in just the tiniest of sardonic smiles. "This is beyond your ken. I cannot allow someone who can be manipulated thusly anywhere near my son."

Jathen could only stare blankly, coldly, lost in the vast sea of difference she'd poured between them. "Very well." For a moment, he debated leaving Ass'shiri's crossbow bolt on the table for her, a gesture that it should be with Ass'shiri's son. In the end, he couldn't part with it, couldn't leave his last tie to his blood brother behind with a woman he wasn't certain would ever allow him so close again. Instead, he whispered, "I will never give up on you, Annakki. Speak the word, and I'll come."

"I do not foresee a scenario where that would ever happen," she replied, her voice unnervingly neutral again. "You may show yourselves out."

Turning, Jathen stalked out of the dining room with a blind emptiness, Izzy not far behind. Everything passed in a blur: the faces of the servants, the foyer reconstruction, then outside, the courtyard and fountain, which had once seemed so foreign when first he'd come. The idea he would never lay eyes on any of it again—that he'd never see Dor'rhean again—plunged a dagger into his soul as Izzy shut the front door behind them. Turning around, Jathen felt something inside himself crack, nearly breaking.

Dropping the sword cane, Jathen punched the door, once, twice, thrice, and then lost count, numbness spreading over his hand and deterring pain. Failing to bite back a sob, Jathen made a sound which rang hollow in his ears, seemingly inefficient to convey such pain. He slid down the side of the wood, smears of his blood mingling with the staining remainders of Chūjitsun's sacrifice forever blazoned upon the stoop. Heaving, he couldn't hold the emotions in anymore and so just sobbed. Great hulking, gasping cries wracked his entire body.

"Jathen..." Izzy seemed at a loss for words, just quietly repeating his name over and over as she crouched beside him.

"What was it all for?" he finally managed to hiccup out after a few moments of gasping. "I failed to save a man I can barely stand and a movement I don't believe in, and for *what*? To lose the last connection I have to Ass'shiri?" He thumped his forehead upon the door, the pain somewhat bracing. "A prophecy nags at me for months, and it didn't do me any *good* to try to prevent it. And now I know there were more things seen, but what good did seeing them do for Or'sen? For Mağrur or Vas? Was any of it real? What if none of it mattered at all?"

"You don't know that. It—"

"Damn it, Izzy, I know! I know things could be worse, Annakki could be dead or arrested or Spirit knows what. De'contes deserves banishment for all the rot he caused in the past, but ruddy hell, I know he didn't cause *this*. And these ruddy *what if*s are empty comfort when I've lost Annakki's trust and Dor'rhean in my life. What benefit is losing that to anyone?"

Izzy breathed deeply, as though preparing to say something profound, but then exhaled with a sad shake of her head. "Oh, Jathen.

Sometimes, there is no knowing. Sometimes, there is only the devastation of allowing someone their free will even when we know there's no good to come from it."

He swallowed hard, the heavy taste of salt on his lips. "I feel as if I've failed Ass'shiri. I protected her, but I also lost her to herself. And I can't help but wonder, if Ass'shiri hadn't died, would she have done such—"

"Jathen." Izzy placed a hand on his shoulder, her touch warm even through the coat. "None of us can change what we feel, but we can change how we react to those feelings. You are not responsible for her choices any more than she is responsible for yours. You cannot spend your days holding onto this—holding onto a death and wondering over and over, if it had not been, could the world have been different?" The strain in her voice made Jathen focus harder on her. Indeed, her eyes shimmered with wetness. "If those you see around you would be suffering as much, if only... if only he hadn't *died*—"

"Izzy." Jathen put his uninjured hand upon her shoulder. "Izzy, who is Orne?"

She coughed a gasp then lowered her gaze, resting her hands stiffly atop her thighs. For a moment, Jathen thought she would deny him again or change the subject.

Instead, she whispered, "Orne... is not a ghost, not a spirit."

Suspicion and confusion bloomed as he eyed her warily. "What is he, then?"

Izzy raised her eyes, a great deal more in their brown depths than Jathen could interpret. "He... he's me, Jathen. I was him. Last lifetime."

Absorbing the revelation, Jathen sucked in a small breath. "That's why Ass'shiri didn't see him in Dodbyen. And why you kept saying he was different from most fauni golems." *It also explains a few moments here and there, when she wanted to tell me something but didn't.*

"Yes."

"So when you said Orne led you to his bones..." Jathen swallowed. "You really meant you led yourself to what was once your own grave?"

Izzy nodded gently, and Jathen had a sense she was still withholding something but also debating her silence.

He ventured, "But who *was* he? Do you remember who, exactly, you were?"

Izzy opened her mouth then sighed, shaking her head and looking away. "I... can't, Jathen. Not yet." Looking back, her deep walnut eyes were soft, vulnerable. "Don't make me yet."

He nodded, suddenly feeling very weary. "As you said, I can choose how to react. I choose to trust you, Izzy." He squeezed her shoulder also. "I just hope you return it someday."

She smiled thinly, pained. "It's not trust. I *do* trust you, Jathen. I just... don't have the words yet."

He chuckled, bitterly amused. "That, I understand. Spirit knows I can't even manage to talk to my mother about my father. Or why Thee still hasn't spoken to me." He patted her shoulder once more before letting go. "Come on. We should get back to the embassy. My hand needs mending, and I have to somehow convince them to let Rhyo and Spinnek stay." He swallowed, squeezing his bloodied hand and thinking once more upon that beautiful hide of gold. "And it's finally time to talk to my mother."

"PRINCE JATHEN! A WORD, if you will?"

Nearly to the Tazu Embassy, Jathen turned to find the last of Annakki's guardsmen jogging down the street to catch him. "A day for waylays, it seems," Jathen murmured to Izzy as the man approached.

Hands in his pockets, Jathen measured the human, whose cloak hung over his sling-bound arm. "I don't suppose Lady Annakki has had a sudden change of heart?"

The human flinched, clutching his elbow in the sling under the cloak. "No. I am here for myself. And for you." Though his face was composed, his golden-brown eyes wavered with familiar sadness. "While I was unconscious, my partner, Zhan, told me you saved my life."

"You're a medium?"

"In small doses. Zhan and I were... very close. I'm unsurprised he spoke to me before crossing."

"I'm so sorry. I wish I could have—"

"I know." He put a hand up with a small shake of his head. "But I didn't come here to discuss Zhan. You saved me, and so I owe you a debt. To repay it, I defy my mistress and offer a single piece of knowledge as to why her hate is so focused on De'contes, in the hopes that you might better understand why she has acted as she has—and perhaps will still help her."

Jathen stepped closer, heart pounding. "You know why Annakki was banished?"

He chuckled in surprise. "No. I'm not certain even Chūjitsun or Ass'shiri knew that. No, I wanted you to know why she still believes so venomously that De'contes was behind the attack."

"Why?"

"Something went missing in the fray. It was hidden in a spatial vault behind the portrait of her family. And now, it is gone."

Jathen's heart pounded. "If that's true, then why hasn't she told the High Mages about the theft? It would give De'contes a motive for the attack *beyond* her and Mağrur's conspiracy." His stomach rolled. "Are you telling me I've been wrong about De'contes?"

"I do not know. I believe you when you say you found the truth: saw something in Mağrur's mind. I grew up here, in the shadow of De'contes, and in Annakki's service. Your logic concerning the Clansman is sound. I do not believe he'd be so sloppy as to send his own people to attack us."

"Which means perhaps there was a motivation behind this we didn't expect," Izzy added. "Convenient deaths, remember?"

"That would mean someone manipulated the Balori *and* Mağrur to get at what was taken," Jathen murmured, rubbing his chin. "Though it still doesn't explain why someone would go for Dor'rhean—or even how they knew he was there." He glanced back up at the guard. "Is there any way to convince her to report the theft to the High Mages?"

"She has not conveyed it to them because it is not something she should have ever had in the first place. It was given to her by her mother via the Shadow Court for safekeeping, and it is to them she has reported its theft. No one save her and Chūjitsun should have known it was there or been able to access it, as it is a *spatial* vault. I learned of this only immediately after the attack, after you'd gone, when she discovered its absence."

A cold, sick feeling squirmed in Jathen's stomach. "Does she think *I* used D'ilinde to take it?"

"I believe it may be a consideration in her mind, yes," he whispered. "For what it's worth, I believe if you were involved, it was accidental—the vault's wall was anchored dually to the drawing room's painting and the study's wall you were unceremoniously knocked through. If you happened to disrupt the spatial vault with your Artifact at that time, anyone in the fray could have taken it."

"What exactly was stolen?" Izzy asked softly.

"I know not which of them, but I do know *what*." He pursed his lips then sighed, looking immeasurably tired. "Another Grand Artifact."

A GLINT OF SLY PLAYFULNESS shone in Rhodonith Monor-
tith's eyes as she clasped her hands, dark claws clicking from beyond
the charm-viewer. "Come now, Jathen. I do believe this will do you
some good. Trust your mother."

Squirming in his chair, Jathen pinched the bridge of his nose.
This was not how I wanted this conversation to go. Not at all. He'd
been lucky, of sorts. His mother had been gnawing at the bit to speak
with him since word of the avalanche and his public exploits during
it had reached Kidwellith, so choosing to speak with her lent little to
no suspicion that he wanted to ask about his father. However, it also
gave Rhodonith no concept that he might want to speak on something of such import.

"I know you mean well, Mother, but a *birthday party*? Truly?"
Lowering his hand, he sighed, meeting her gaze with as much pa-
tience as he could muster. "I just don't think this is the time for such
things."

"Your birthday is not the time for a party?"

Running his hands through unbraided hair still moist from his
evening bath, Jathen stifled a desire to groan aloud. *Spirit, no wonder
why bringing up my father has always been so hard.* "My birthday
may be fast approaching, but throwing some highfalutin party after
so much death just seems... disrespectful." He scratched one cheek,
thinking on all the mysteries and miseries that still needed to be sort-
ed. *Another Grand Artifact in play. And I'm still trying to sort how
D'ilinde actually spoke to me this last time. And perhaps another mastermind behind it all.* "That, and my heart just isn't in it."

"Those are the reasons *to* do this, Jathen. Revelry after misery
chases away sorrow and offers distraction and hope. Especially a
birthday party for you—or did you forget that many of us thought

you lost? To celebrate another year of your life, a life we thought had ended—that is no minor thing." She softened. "Please, love, let me do this for you. I can't travel due to the egg and politics here, so this is my best chance to reach out a hand, as it were, and offer a loving balm for my son."

"Very well, I will consider it." As he rolled his eyes, the sight of the golden inlay in the carved wooden beams on the ceiling did little to dissuade Jathen's discomfort. Though he'd managed to argue against staying in the royal suites on the premise of not displacing Marcasith, the ambassador had convinced him to take one of the larger state rooms as his own. "But before we run out of time on the charm, there is a matter of far greater importance that I need to discuss with you—one that I admit I've neglected for far too long."

"You're wondering about Thee and why she's still not come to talk?"

"Yes—but no, that's not what..." Jathen swallowed, still reeling over how such a thing could be so hard after everything else he'd been through. "I had my life ladder drafted while here in Tar'citadel." He watched her stiffen slightly, her golden eyes widening, though she did her best to hide it. "It's been done in secret, so Kyanith will never see it, but I need to know, my father's half—"

"Came back unusual," she finished.

A wave of shock crashed through Jathen. Whatever he'd been imagining, her easy knowledge of it hadn't been it. "Yes." He swallowed, flexing his bruised and scabbed hand, remembering the scales and claws that'd been there. "I need to know, Mother."

A tear rolled down her cheek as she shook her head. "And I cannot tell you."

"What? *Why?*"

She held her hands up in a hopeless shrug. "Because I don't know."

"How can you *not*? How can you know it would come out un-usual and not know who the ruddy hell he is?" Jathen lowered his voice but still kept some of his ire in his tone. "Skaniss told me he knew who my father was—hinted it was Bertran. I spoke to Bertran, even. He told me what you told him, that he was never sure if you'd lied to him to protect him—"

"What? No." Rhod shook her head, looking pained. "Jathen, please, don't—"

"Mother!"

She was crying in earnest, big wet tears.

His stomach quavered, but he had to continue, though he did so in a more soothing tone. "I'm a moot and a Negater, and a Grand Ar-tifact has taken residence in my chest, and now I am doing things, magical things, that are rare and extraordinary and unusual even for my unusual circumstances. If my father might have some link or an-swer to any of this... I need to know."

Hands in her lap, she clicked her claws together, staring off to one side or perhaps back to over twenty-one years before. "I thought him a dream at first," she explained, so very softly. "But then he was there, again, the first night I lay you in the cradle—the most beauti-ful tyrn I've ever seen, then or since." She sighed, and her golden eyes came back to him. "Forgive me, love. I never wanted you to hear this, to imagine that I didn't want you."

Jathen blinked repeatedly as his heart clenched. "Mother... what are you *talking* about?"

"The spring of my first heat, I was down in Tourmaline. I'd flown off alone, wanting to find some peace away from my guards. We are alike in that, believe it or not, craving freedom from the shackles of nobility. In the ruins just outside the city, down by the water, I found an old tower and lay down to sleep. I woke to find a tyrn all in gold, sunning himself on the beach. We got to talking, and he was so beau-tiful... and well, I'll spare you. I fell asleep again, and after, I awoke in the tower. There was no sign of him, no footprints. Nothing. So I assumed it was a dream, brought on by the heat of sun and season. But to be certain, on the way back to Kidwellith, I... *shifted.*" A stronger wash of tears cascaded down her face as Jathen realized what she meant. "When I returned to Kidwellith, it *was* Bertran I was paired with, but after you hatched, I had my doubts. As I said, that night, my golden tyrn returned, and I knew. He told me he'd be watching and, one day, he may return to give you a choice—to stay with me or go with him."

Jathen put a hand on his forehead in the hopes it'd quell the spinning, but that didn't help much. "Mother, are you implying I'm the son of Montage or some nonsense?"

She laughed. "I don't know, my love. You are now as abreast of what happened as I am." Sorrow returned to her face. "Please, my love, forgive me. I have always wanted you. Please don't think—"

"I know, Mother," Jathen whispered, realizing in one dizzying revelation born of empathy and logic the depths of what she'd done. *Ass'shiri had said I was too smart not to be in Tar'citadel.* "You wanted me so much that you conspired to keep me in Kidwellith and thus never pressed for me to go to Tar'citadel. It's also why you made certain when I submitted my architecture work to the Bree Walkers that they rejected it, isn't it?"

Squirming, she closed her eyes, and more tears fell. "I never thought you'd hate yourself so much for that. I've lived my whole life terrified, Jathen, that one day he'd come back to take you, to claim you. That you'd go to Tar'citadel and find something else or that *they'd* find in you something else to keep you there. I'm so sorry. I just... From the first moment I held you, I loved you. More than myself, more than anything. I've lost so much—mother, uncle, father. I *couldn't* let you go." She gasped a sob. "I've debated, fought with myself a hundred thousand times over whether my choices were a violation of First Law or fueled by some precognitive maternal instinct of knowing what was best for you. And if I was wrong, if *my* actions were what led to so much misery in your heart." As she stared at him, her golden eyes seemed to ripple with wetness and sadness. "I only pray and hope you'll forgive me someday."

For the first time, Jathen saw Rhodonith Monortith as more mortal, more fallible. She'd always been the perfect parent, so giving and loving, overbearing but fair. With that façade stripped away, he saw truly how young she had been, a mere child of twenty when faced with the burden of not only a country but also a moot-child shrouded in mystery and complicated by unconditional love.

He watched her sniffle a moment more then whispered, "There's nothing to forgive, Mother."

"Jathen, I've hidden things from you, manipulated your life—"

"Out of love," he said, his heart twisting.

But he had to say it even if he didn't fully feel it. She wasn't wrong—this revelation had hurt him, but the wound was shallow compared to what so many others had done. Time could dress it with little trouble.

"And a bit of selfishness. Mother, you're not perfect, but neither am I. What am I going to do? Condemn you? Curse you? I'm sitting here, floundering with my own riddles and enigmas, the tool of Children and fate. I can't judge you. Not when I know all too easily how hard it is to navigate when you aren't given all the answers." He smiled softly as he was certain of one emotion in the mix. "You're my mother. I might not be particularly thrilled to hear this, but I love you. Nothing you could do—or have done in the past—could change that."

Rhodonith broke down then, laughing and crying. Jathen did his best to console her through the glass, and eventually, the tirade of years and years of pent-up emotions quelled. They spoke a little longer of the past and present, and he agreed, albeit reluctantly, to the party, which calmed her considerably. When the charm eventually wore down, Jathen stared at the black mirror, weary. His soul felt both tightly wound and terribly frayed at the same time, and the effort of simply rising from the chair seemed to take years off his life.

Rubbing his eyes, he sighed deeply. *How am I to make sense of all this?*

"DID ANNAKKI FRAME ME?"

Jathen nearly jumped out of his skin at the sound of A'ron De'contes's voice. As it was, he literally went rolling out of the Tazu high bed he'd finally lain in not a few hours before, having lost a long argument with Bertran, Marcasith, and the ambassador over Rhyo staying at the embassy. Tangled in bedsheets and hanging with one arm on the banded marble, Jathen squinted groggily up at the head of the Balori, his brain finally registering that, yes indeed, a fugitive Red Mage was in his room. Biting down hard upon the yelp that wanted to escape his lips, Jathen chose instead to pull himself upright.

"I will not ask again," De'contes whispered, his tone adding more sinister darkness to his silhouette.

"Then you'd better well wait, because I'm running on about three hours' sleep, and your sudden arrival did nothing for my nerves," Jathen retorted, core muscles straining as he sat up on his mattress.

He coughed once, covering his nervousness as he recalled exactly who and *what* he was talking to. De'contes's garnet eyes glowed despite the shadows, and considering the events since the avalanche, he wasn't a Clansman who had much else to lose.

"But for what it's worth," Jathen whispered, "no. While I do believe she revels in your banishment, I do not believe she designed this. Mainly because she's absolutely certain *you* were behind it all."

"And yet you left her home—or were ejected from it, along with your friends. Tell me, if you believe in my innocence enough to put a rift between you two, why not speak out on my behalf? Or were you merely fleeing in disgust from what she'd done to me?"

"I flee from nothing but her flagrant disapproval of my belief of your innocence—and as to speaking out, I have no solid proof." He spread his hands, genuinely sorry. "And while I do have secrets of Annakki's I must keep, I can give you my word that she was *not* the one pulling the strings behind your Balori. People she cared for were put in danger, and some died. She hates you, sir, but not enough to cross that particular line." He pursed his lips. "And I think you knew that, coming here."

"And I think *you* know who framed me," De'contes replied, voice taut.

"I suspected Mağrur, to be honest—and had he lived, I'd have insisted his mind be scanned."

"Mağrur?" De'contes's dark, threatening looming eased in the wake of genuine surprise. "Why?"

Jathen sighed, knowing some of Annakki's secrets would have to be betrayed if he were to help A'ron, but they were nothing the man hadn't already suspected. "Because *you* weren't the target that day I came to the Balori's door. At least, not the original one. The plot had been for *Mağrur* to die and for you to be framed for ordering it through Nannazen. And Mağrur was complicit in it—a sacrifice to prevent you from gaining ground into the Ways."

De'contes breathed in sharply. "Such a plot is not a mark in favor of her innocence, Jathen."

"Nor is it a mark in yours," he replied. "*Everything* lines up that you would have known about the attack. Your Balori confessed in front of people that they were there to murder Annakki to keep her from killing you according to some vision one of them had. The ice mage with them was working on the mountain, and the investigation

Chancellor Jidoja was running turned up clear gaps in her work log up there. She snuck away to do *something*, namely manipulating the structure of the glacier. There was no other motive, and only Annakki knows the truth of Mağrur—and she's not speaking."

"And if Mağrur felt betrayed from the first failed attempt, framing me for ordering her death would make a neat bit of sense." Seeming genuine, he placed a pale hand upon the buttoned-down front of his robes and inclined his head humbly. "Twice now, you've made efforts to protect what sad thing I call my life and, more importantly, my movement. While we are diminished, we are not gone—for that, I and the Balori owe you a debt I don't know if I can pay. But if opportunity arises, know that I shall."

"Lovely." Jathen adjusted his nightshirt, attempting to fix a few buttons that'd come undone when he nearly fell off the bed. "Now if you don't mind, get out. Much as it pains me to know you were innocent of this particular crime, the massive weight of your previous misdeeds still sits heavy. And I'm also not of a mind to further provoke Annakki nor anyone else politically by continuing this conversation with a wanted criminal for much longer." *That, and there's a ruddy Grand Artifact missing, and I'm not certain one of your supposedly reformed Balori didn't have a hand in it.*

"I deserve that, I believe." De'contes shook his head. "I know facing Annakki, trying to confront Mağrur, and protecting me could not have been easy—but I truly wish to assure you that none of what happened was done with my knowledge."

"And how the ruddy hell *is* that?" Jathen demanded, a hiss of heat in his tone. "Were you not the one who told me the more someone hides in their aura, the more you see? Or was that all smoke and mirrors? How did your own Balori manage to subvert you, the most infamous two-faced traitor on the continent?"

De'contes raised an eyebrow. "If you doubt my skill at circumventing wards of any type, need I remind you I'm standing in the bedroom of the crown prince of the Tazu Nation within their embassy in Tar'citadel, after fleeing from the city."

Jathen snorted. "Please, you probably never left Tar'citadel and are just hiding using the teleportation grid. If you were Marin, as you claim, you'd remember how to use it. Smoke and mirrors."

He huffed slightly, though that might have been a begrudging laugh. "I see you have been learning a great deal." He pursed his lips. "But there was no smoke and mirrors in this—at least of my crafting. But, very well, since you've been forthright with me, perhaps now it is I who owe you information. Perhaps it will eventually fall on the correct ears." Crossing his arms, De'contes said, "While I am proficient at reading—how can I describe it?—*along* wards, as in I do not evade them or break them, I would rather use them to determine the power of the crafter, similar to a man who, instead of trying to cross a river or build a bridge, will swim through it, within it, go with its flow, and thus understand its strengths."

"And understanding that gives you the insight into the crafter."

"Precisely. However, if one does *not* put up a ward, I'm less inclined to see what is within them—what they are capable of."

"You're telling me none of the Balori complicit in the attack and avalanche kept wards up around you at all?"

De'contes's expression turned mildly sheepish. "Trust is hardwon. To allow them to relax, I promised no obvious poking about into minds should they choose to leave wards down—or up, for that matter. But, no, you are correct, I should have seen it. But someone found a way to subvert even my skill, to craft wards that were too strong for those who had them, and *without* the obvious use of a master-charm."

Thoughts of the tasha-kama and their strong manipulations dashed through Jathen's mind. "So you *were* poking about."

"Of course." He smirked. "I am who I am—and what happened to Nannazen gave me reason to respectively 'prod' now and again without consequence. But I did not know details. Only that something was working amid my people. My decision was to gently nudge them, speak with them, try to get them to reveal what they were hiding. But all I ever managed to divulge with my lighter touch was a deep protectiveness of myself—not a thing to warrant ripping asunder a mind for answers, as I would have done had I sensed any mental manipulation akin to what had happened to Nannazen."

"And her friend, Or'sen? He seemed to be the major player on the Balori's side at least. And Nannazen claimed he saw something—a vision of Annakki trying to kill you. Did he ever speak of that to you? There must have been some hint."

"No, at least not one that would have led me to this particular conclusion. Strangely," De'contes murmured, a nearly wistful undercurrent to his tone, "he and Mağrur were very similar in ideology. Mağrur wanted to martyr himself for the cause of keeping the Balori out, and Or'sen was willing to die to ensure my life and the continuation of the Balori. But what happened did not make him a martyr, and he would have been smart enough, even if delusional, to see that. But still, he did not, and things happened as they did. No, something or someone manipulated him into believing what he did had meaning even though a part of him screamed up until the end for me to save him." Brow furrowed, he sighed lightly, the most regret Jathen had ever seen out of him. "I should have seen it."

"What could have done something like that? And for how long?" Jathen asked. "A demonic?"

"No," De'contes replied. "Or'sen might not have been as powerful as some, but he could keep a demonic out. I train my people heavily to do so, as most are already struggling with attachments. And I certainly didn't sense one. No, this wasn't an incorporeal. This was something else. *Someone* else. Someone alive." He shifted on his feet, crossing his arms. "As I said, what he did wasn't self-sacrifice, and if you are correct, *someone* was cleaning up their loose ends."

Jathen bit his lip. *Izzy was right.* He asked almost hopefully, "Do you think it was Mağrur?"

"I very much doubt that. He might have been complicit in a conspiracy, but he himself was unlikely to construct these types of mental subversions because of skill, raw power, and philosophy," he replied firmly, causing Jathen to feel a warble of deeper concern wiggling about in his stomach. "Whoever this is, they are subtle. Master trained or self-taught over a *long* time to run in the undercurrents of the subconscious, to the point their impact is completely unrecognizable to the victim as an outside influence. And they had to do this quickly too. Granted, Or'sen already had some framework to work with to get him to pursue Annakki, but to make him *betray me*, to go against his very core sense of self at a proverbial snap of fingers..." He frowned, grim. "We're talking a nearly unprecedented Talent."

Jathen closed his eyes, his insides tumultuous. *So there is another player in all this—but who and why? To destroy Annakki or frame De'contes? Or was it all just to get the Grand Artifact? And if so, how did they know it was there? How did they know about Dor'rhean?*

De'contes sighed a sad laugh, breaking Jathen out of his internal debate. "For once, I am the victim of subversion, and I can't imagine a more bitter lesson the Children would heap upon me so I might better understand the impact of my past on those who suffered from it."

"Victim? Lessons?" The tottering stress of everything came boiling to the surface for Jathen, manifesting as something between fury and disgust as he scowled at the Clansman. "You think for *one second* that you didn't bring a great deal of this down upon yourself? That you suddenly feel *anything* like those you murdered and the lives you left broken? They didn't *do* anything, De'contes. This was born of your crimes, yes, but also your neglect. What have you ever done, truly, to make amends with Annakki? Or anyone you destroyed?"

Eyelids wide around those garnet irises, De'contes held silent a moment before softly replying, "I tried several times in the past to approach Annakki, to talk to her, to express some fraction of my sorrow and remorse—"

"Words!" Jathen found himself hissing, the tight knot of his control loosening. "Words mean nothing, De'contes. You spin them more than anyone I've ever known, and I can imagine they get you far, but they are hollow. What have you *done* to make up for what you did to her? You save lives, yes—you bring Red followers back, yes—and perhaps on some karmic level, that's making Rhean and Ra'vien and the rest of the Twelve happy on Far-Side. I don't know, and I don't ruddy care. And neither does Annakki!"

Jathen bit his lip slightly, tempering his tone to prevent his voice from carrying to the hall and the ears of the guards or to the adjacent room where Izzy slept. "You used Annakki, framed her, and manipulated her into distracting everyone by doing something so terrible she won't even talk about it, which allowed you to murder Yvette. It got Annakki banished for life from her home, and then you *murdered her parents*. What have you done to make *that* right for her, De'contes? What have you even tried, aside from proclaiming she can have your head?" Jathen shook his head at De'contes's red eyes staring soulfully back. "I thought not."

"I am no fool, Jathen. There is nothing I can do," De'contes whispered, "to make that right."

"How about you start by telling the Clan Lands and the rest of the world she's innocent? I checked—you never did admit to it. People have assumed, but never once did you tell anyone you *used* her." Jathen pursed his lips, body shaking even as his fists balled tightly around bedsheets. "Why is that? Did you just never get around to it, or did you simply not think of it?"

Cocking his head, the Red Mage asked, "Did Annakki ever tell you, Jathen, what it was, exactly, that she did?"

Losing his grip on the sheets somewhat, Jathen shook his head. "Only that she tried to open what should never be opened. And that you manipulated her into doing it."

"But I didn't," De'contes said with a sigh. "I took advantage. I will not now deny I murdered Yvette during that time, but I was warned, informed of that unique timing by another. I never touched the mind of Annakki Rheadani. And if I had, I would never have made her do what she did. There are some lines not even I would have crossed, not even then."

Despite himself, Jathen felt his eyebrow arch in curiosity. "What did she do?"

He shook his head. "I cannot say."

"Then who was it in her head? Who made her do... whatever it was?"

De'contes's lips twitched in a mirthless smile. "Let us just say I am not the only powerful Talent to fall to the Red. Despite all my crimes, there are those far worse than I had been who are still out in the world." He closed his eyes, huffing a sad laugh. "And still imprisoned elsewhere."

Jathen pursed his lips, unwilling to mention to De'contes the similarities between what he'd just said and the swath of strange telepathy and power that'd made its mark since Jathen entered Tar'citadel. *Maybe ever further back than that,* he realized, thinking about the shadow in the fire from the summit. *It's Erin Manna I must tell,* he decided when the Clansman finally teleported away. *She's the one who'll put it all together.*

"Quite often, the price of revelation is the blossoming of deeper questions."

The sound of Erin Manna's voice jolted him out of his malaise and onto his feet, wobbling precariously upon the mattress. Waiting in the little sitting area closer to the door of the suite, the Original lounged on a Tazu chaise as if she'd always been there.

"Were you in here the *entire time*?"

"Invisibility does have its uses."

Jathen coughed a shaky laugh as he slid down the headboard and fell back upon the mattress with a huff. "Is everyone able to just slip in and out of my room?"

"The ambassador let me in some time ago. I chose to allow you to sleep, as we have many things to discuss. Even more now, it seems. Would you be of the mind to discuss them?"

Past the surprise, a wave of relief strong enough to stagger him swept through Jathen. "You got my letter."

"Indeed. Before you sent it, actually." She gestured at the chair across from her. "Come. Sit."

Chuckling lightly at the impeccable timing of the master precognitive, Jathen did as bid, though the turmoil of what direction this conversation might take stole any deeper comfort. Her clothes were styled more in a Tazu cut for this visit, and little pearls of gold shimmered against the gathered folds of the rouge-colored silk. She let him sit in silence a moment while he straightened his nightshirt.

Finally, he conjured the best question he could muster: "How much of what's happened did you know would happen?"

"You're asking did I knowingly leave you to possibly die." She nodded. "I foresaw this outcome, yes."

Jathen dug his fingers into the soft purple velvet of the chair. "Then why did you not prevent it? Why did so many have to die when you could have just warned us? Or just stayed and helped or... I don't know, stopped Mağrur from even doing any of it or..." He trailed off, realizing himself just how insane trying to prevent everything she could possibly see with precognition would be.

"Tonight, I came and sat silently in your room and watched a man I both revile and care for beyond measure have a conversation with a student I am fond of—a man who could have swatted you like a fly should the argument have turned heated. And yet I did nothing. Why do you think that is?"

He sighed. "Logically, I can assume it's because the conversation needed to happen. And if you'd interfered, too late or too soon, then some aspect of it would have been voided."

"Precisely. While there was some possibility things would have gone badly—a very small one, I promise—the act of interference would have tipped the scale toward even more negative outcomes, not only for this meeting but in longer-reaching events as well." Without the slightest bit of hesitation, she held out a hand. "Would you like to see what would have occurred if I had interfered in the events leading up to and around the avalanche?"

Jathen tensed as if that gorgeous pale hand were a ral. "Is it bad?" His own visions were hard enough on him—the risk of seeing what Erin Manna could see staggered him to his core. *I honestly don't know if I could handle inviting that kind of madness into my head.*

"Do you trust me when I say this outcome we are currently living in was the best I could hope for?"

The light-blue veins in her wrist pulsed under the skin like a reptile breathing. Biting his lip and leaning back, Jathen nodded.

Tucking her hand back onto her lap, Erin Manna sighed softly. "I left you to your own devices here, Jathen, because I knew I could. I knew the choices you would make well enough to know you would most likely come out on this end of it. I also knew what would happen if I stayed or if I'd warned you more, as well as dozens of other variants. I deemed this was the best path."

He grimaced. "If this is the best, I hate to imagine how much worse it all could have been."

A thin smile that could almost be called kind flitted across her lips. "Do remember that simply because we can *imagine* a better outcome to a situation, it doesn't mean that outcome is *possible* in reality, even with our preknowledge. We imagine the best of people, the fastest of reflexes, and the simplest of solutions. But life, and people, are far more complex." Folding her hands, she clicked her pinky nails together. "We can only lead them. And then hope. I cannot condemn someone for crimes they have not yet committed."

"And what of crimes they *have* committed?" He straightened, staring hard at her. "Can you not do something to bring whoever manipulated everyone to justice, or is it just going to be like Mikkal, and you tell me destiny isn't done with them and we have to let evil people live to meet some other, supposedly better end? Isn't that more than a little hypocritical?"

"Yes. But in this case, I would rather fall on the humane, hopeful side of that hypocrisy."

Jathen sighed. Her easy agreements were always surprising, and he never knew how to react to them. "Do you know who was behind all of this? Who stole Annakki's Grand Artifact and who might have been in Or'sen's, maybe even Mağrur's and Vas's, heads?"

"You are assuming there was only one person poking around inside heads."

Jathen leaned back in his chair again, stunned. *Spirit, I really am just a minor player in all of this, aren't I?* "Do you truly know all of what is going on, Lady?"

"I have my suspicions. But I am not certain, no. I have shared my thoughts with those who need to know."

"And I'm not one of them."

A glimmer of fondness showed for a moment in her deep bullion eyes. "I am here, am I not? I may not answer the way you want, but I am telling you what you need, Jathen. Believe that."

He laughed, the sound ringing tired in his own ears. *I have a feeling there are some much older and wiser than I who would be far more grateful for this conversation.* He nodded toward where A'ron had been standing. "Did I at least make the right choice, trying to save De'contes at the cost of Annakki?"

"That depends entirely upon your definition of what a 'right choice' is—"

"Damn it, Lady Erin," Jathen said with a small huff. He ran a hand up across his forehead and pressed the palm into his hairline, where a wetness lingered that had naught to do with his bath from hours before. "I'm not asking for some deep, long-construed debate about moral quandaries. I just want to know if I have any right to sleep at night or not—unceremonious visits from Clan notwithstanding."

A small smile spread across her lips. "You made the right choice for yourself, Jathen. For your soul, for your morals, for your evolution in this life. In other words, you made the choice that would allow you to sleep at night—though you and I both know that is hardly a comfort and hardly a guarantee of sleep."

"Thank you." He wet his lips then dared, "I'm no fool, to think your timing today wasn't purposeful on a multitude of levels, but I'll also address the personal one. Do you happen to know anything about my father?"

"Yes."

Jathen swallowed. Simple answers were never very helpful from her. "Such as who and what he is?"

"Yes."

Squirming in his seat, Jathen swore his heart thudded a few hundred extra beats. "Are you able to tell me?"

"I could. And it would not harm you. Though it would raise more questions that, in truth, would not be my place to answer. And the lack of *those* answers *would* cause harm."

"So... no." He swallowed again, disappointed but not surprised. "I suppose it was too much to hope you'd tell me anything about him."

"Jathen, I'm telling you *he* will be the one to tell you who and what he is." A detectable sense of certainty accompanied her lips quirking again in that small smile of hers. "In his own time—but that time *is* approaching. Be patient."

He held his breath, stomach full of butterflies. "Are you able to tell me any kind of when?"

"When you get home."

He laughed again. "I don't suppose you'll let me know the best time to do that, then?"

"No. But he knows the movements you make. He always has. He'll move when you do."

Jathen found himself surprised by a little burst of desperation welling up inside himself, a vulnerable sort of nervousness. After so very, very long, even he had underestimated how badly he wanted to know to whom he owed the other half of his existence. *And even more now, having heard Mother's story.* "You're certain?"

"You and I both know nothing is ever certain until it has happened and the choice has been made," she said kindly. "But mostly, yes. The decision hasn't been finalized yet, but the majority of factors lean toward such a conclusion. And there isn't much that will change that outcome as things are currently progressing."

"But something *could* derail it?"

"Yes, but it's an infinitesimal chance, considering what has happened." Unfolding her hands, she held a palm out toward his. "You did something recently, Jathen, that was extraordinary. That action is what has tipped this scale."

"The shifting." Flexing the fingers on his healing hand, he wet his lips. "Mother said he would come and give me a choice—to stay or go. If he'd come to see me any time before this year, I probably would have gone with just about anyone to get away from home and forge something, *anything* different. Now..." He measured her neutral face. "Has he just been waiting all this time for me to have as much reason to stay as to go?"

"You shall have to ask him that," she replied, though he sensed that his question impressed her. She stood amid the sparkle of her beaded robes. "I believe it is time for us to part ways for now. You need rest, and I do have things at home that need attending to. But before I leave you, I wish to give you something."

"A birthday present?" Jathen joked as he stood as well. Admittedly, he felt disappointed Erin Manna would likely not be returning to attend his forced birthday party. *Would love to see Ambassador Chertith's face while trying to make small talk with an Original.* "I confess I was jealous Seren got a present before and not me."

Ignoring his teasing, she placed two fingers on his neck, just above the collarbone. "This shall involve a touch of high magic, but relax and accept the spell, and you shouldn't negate it."

Jathen nodded. He did as instructed, feeling a high, excited buzz of wind energy pressing against him. Breathing rhythmically, he allowed it to congeal then felt a painful jabbing as if with a needle as Erin stroked her fingers down across his collarbone. Hissing in pain, he rubbed the wound after she pulled away but found no blood, only heated, irritated skin.

"Some gift. That really hurt."

"Worth the discomfort, I assure you." Taking him by one shoulder, she turned him toward the wall, where a large mirror hung above a dresser carved of light oak. There, he saw her gift reflected despite the dim light—an odd little marking, an arc of symbols about two scales long down the left side of his neck and collarbone. Artful, the pink-and-gold squiggles were reminiscent of the Clan language yet beyond Jathen's understanding.

"So your gift is a strange tattoo? Not certain what my mother will think of this."

Erin Manna's reflection smirked. "In the long-ago past, in a time we Clan don't discuss, humans were marked in this manner to show ownership. A great lord would not allow his servants to be Fed upon by more common Clan, as it were."

"Now I'm *really* not sure what my mother will think."

"The practice has evolved over the years, and now these marks show stewardship, protection, and are a sign of family. Humans with such tattoos are considered 'untouchable', protected by the Clansperson who marked them." She stroked the line on his collarbone. "This is my personal insignia. I have not put it on anyone in over a thousand years. Any Clansperson who sees this—and fears me—will not *dare* touch you."

Jathen exhaled slowly as a shiver carrying the immensity of those words ran from his neck down to his toes. "Thank you."

"A smaller deterrent than I'd prefer. It will not make you indestructible, Jathen." She turned away from the mirror. "There shall always be those who do not fear me. But it will offer some pull, should you need it."

Jathen sighed, admiring the reflection once more before buttoning up his shirt. "Why do I have a feeling you think I'm going to need it?"

"Because you are a smart boy and a fine precognitive."

He swallowed hard as the reality of all he'd been feeling became quite clear. "There's more coming for me, isn't there? That's why you're leaving again."

"Yes. And the longer I stay, the closer I become—"

"The less you see. You leave as often as you do to protect me." He nodded then chuckled lightly, suddenly struck by a bout of morbid humor. "I'm surprised you don't try to live out your life isolated in some tower, watching to safeguard the world."

"Something similar has been attempted in the past," she admitted. "It is not... *good* for me."

"I can't imagine it would be." Adopting a stance he'd often seen from Chūjitsun, Jathen bowed with Clan-style formality. "Thank you, Lady Erin. For everything."

"We shall see each other again, Jathen. Of that, I am reasonably certain."

"I should hope so. I still have a lot of training to accomplish between now and... whatever it is you've seen. And I don't think we can convince Raleigh to do any more of it. I think her distaste of me trumps her desire to find and train Aspects."

Her eyes hardened into the deep, penetrating gaze that portended she spoke of hard prophecy. "You will do far more for Raleigh to help her meet her aims than you can possibly imagine, Jathen. That stands for De'contes as well."

"You mentioned such about Raleigh before—but now De'contes too?" He raised an eyebrow. "I'm not going to even bother asking after that."

She smiled fully. "Wise."

Epilogue: Mastermind

Tar'ka-besh scurried about.

Matamir watched them running back and forth around Tar'citadel's Great Gate with muted pleasure while being sure to keep his emotion tightly "under his lid," or so he'd always imagined such things. The outer trappings of his personal "box" he'd decorated in concern and mild irritation, as would befit a Casfeildian trader attempting to get back to Torfeild on the last teleport and being held up by some unknown cause. Pulling his wide-brimmed hat lower to keep snow and suspicion from landing on his face, he huffed, his breath coming out as an angry puff. Of course, Matamir was part and parcel to the cause of the tar'ka-besh distress. Indeed, he'd orchestrated much of it—though they were unlikely to discern that.

They wouldn't be expecting the culprit to have arrived months in advance then hang about, watching the final true act of his handiwork unfold, the last great "surprise" for Jathen after all his plotting. No, they wouldn't even spare a glance for a human waiting about with the rest of the stranded hoping to get on to their respective destinations, worried more about the delay than what would be a most fitting birthday gift from Sister to a certain Tazu prince. The only thing that might give the tar'ka-besh reason to even pause by him would be his scar, but as Matamir didn't have it, thanks to some good old-fashioned clay makeup, he didn't have any concern to bury in one

263

of his many nesting containers, which served as his personal mental wards.

Instead, he stood and watched, stepping from foot to foot and fiddling with the straps on his pack in a perfect mimicry of what an anxious traveler should be doing. Internally, he mused over just how wonderfully it'd all gone and how very, *very* pleased Sister would be once he got home. *Though not as pleased as she should be, given what she assigned and what I'd had to work with.*

Matamir pulled his collar closer as a cold wind bit into his side. Tar'citadel was a cruel climate for someone raised in the southern Clan Lands and then the foothills of Aralim. Still, he'd never been one to complain, and Sister had been good to him—far better than Mikkal ever had been, at least. *How long has it been? I left with her when she split from the Court, oh... nearly thirty-five years ago.* Biting his lip in what looked like an expression of indecision on whether to ask a passing tar'ka-besh about the trouble, he held in his grin. *Barely an adult when we started this glorious madness, and after thirty-five years, this was far and away my finest hour.*

Distracting competent precognitives was always a challenge, and in Tar'citadel, he at least had the advantage of the future possibilities already being muddled by the sheer number of them canceling themselves out—but a precognitive Negater? When Sister told him about the moot, he'd nearly refused her. For the first time in all their years, Matamir hadn't thought it possible. Jathen wasn't susceptible to implantations of faux visions like normal Talents, and though he was empathic, Jathen wasn't as tapped into the blanket consciousness the way normal Talents were, making him *less* affected by the gnosis of mortal decisions, which meant *his* precognition came directly from Spirit, and Matamir couldn't replicate or distort that.

That meant if they were to distract him from Sister's real move against Jathen, Matamir had to make his own true distraction for everyone to precognitively sense—a genuine threat to those Jathen cared for and much, much closer to the moot—and carry it out without all of Tar'citadel, including the four ruddy High Mages, finding out or figuring out the two were connected. He had almost thrown his hands up into the air in her office. He smirked, making sure the action happened under the shadow of his hat. *But I didn't.*

Thank the Red he'd had enough to work with once he reached the city. He knew the secret: the more Talents or masses of people knew something, the more other Talents could become aware of it—but if one man kept his secrets to himself and only to himself, well then, that man could move mountains. A single human could accomplish *so much* by manipulating more powerful Talents, who lived their lives with their heads in the clouds, sucking on higher vibrations or some nonsense and never tilting their gazes down toward the dregs. It hadn't been hard to fan the flames of Mağrur's fear of De'contes and to place a few well-seeded "visions" into his mind, followed by whispering a mistrust of Annakki Rheadani into the ears of his men. The Balori were an amber mine worth of treasured manipulations as well. No matter how far removed so many of them were from the true Red, they were still his creatures and trusted only in certain ways. If a person knew which strings to pull, what thoughts to implant, they would do just about anything. *Like a sad, secondary orchestra, supplementing the songs of the true followers. Pathetic things.*

The moot's obsession with finding a trainer had thrown Matamir a little bit. But that was the problem with creating real distractions and not implanting his own false visions into someone's mind. He never knew how, exactly, the precognition of the distraction event would unfold or if it would unfold at all.

And the little moot had enough sense to keep his visions close to the chest, so I couldn't read what he'd been seeing from other Talents. Lucky little Negater shit. I still don't know what he saw, exactly, aside from the ruddy avalanche. Matamir spat in the snow, feeling damn lucky that the moot had never caught on and was stupid enough to warn the tar'ka-besh about the danger. That had inspired Matamir's brilliant idea to have the Balori's ice mage set it up and use it as his distraction. *Then again, don't suppose the moot could have survived Mikkal's company intact without learning a thing or two about keeping secrets.*

The only true frustration had been Erin Manna suddenly showing up, but her presence distracted De'contes and shoved him into his work for his precious vote, and *that* gave Matamir what he needed to finish off the plan to get Mağrur and Or'sen to slide unknowingly into their own destruction. Mağrur pushing himself till his heart gave out had been a bit of a surprise as well. Perhaps Matamir's little pushes had touched some underlying mental issues he'd been unable to detect, and the man's common sense had snapped. *He had, after all, been intent to die a couple of times by that point. Perhaps the thought had finally become too much, and he subconsciously took himself down.* Still, that had been a bit of luck, not having the man's mind open to inspection. Matamir's skill was such that he'd left little behind, but leaving Mağrur, his boys, and most of the Balori dead was better.

Matamir breathed deeply of the crisp night air, the cold breeze carrying the scent of glacial ice and wood-burning fireplaces. He'd completed the impossible, a win to end all wins, the ultimate feather in his cap.

Not to mention what he'd managed to liberate from Annakki's little library.

It'd been a rumor, a whisper, one small trickle of information Sister had left over from the Shadow Court, a far-flung possibility unlikely to glean any fruit but worth checking if he could. *And I had, lo and behold, a prize of prizes, and silly little Annakki can't even report it missing because she was never supposed to have it!* He resisted the urge to pat the spatial bag his prize was stashed in. His disguise as a trader did not exempt him from someone attempting to rob him on the road—an unwelcome complication. *If foolhardy. I pity any poor bandit who crosses me while I have this to use.*

Forget about Bree and Bron. Sister had wanted a Child–Aspect pairing of Grand Artifacts, and thanks to Matamir, she would finally have the other half of her current Grand Artifact. *And she wasn't even expecting me to bring it home. Maps are one thing, but to walk through the door with* this? *Oh, she will be over the moon and nigh unstoppable. If I can manage a few organic manipulations with my limited energy skills, she will be all-powerful. And Jathen, for all his growing skill and helpful allies, will be in for one ruddy hell of a surprise when he gets to her—and he will go, now, once he discovers what we've done.*

Confident no one was looking, Matamir allowed his grin to bloom, giddy at the prospect that Sister would soon have everything they needed for the true plan to finally get underway after so many, many long years. *After all this time...*

A telepathic force slammed into Matamir, paralyzing him on the spot.

Making short work of his extensive mental defenses, it tore off lids, upturned boxes, and shredded them, dumping their contents onto the landscape of Matamir's mind. Nothing of Matamir was unseen, unknown. It laid him bare, and he could do nothing. Frozen in rigid terror, he couldn't even scream. Finally, *the thing* found it—the final secret, the one Sister herself had buried within Matamir, a truth only he knew about her long-reaching plans.

Ah, the darkness whispered, puffing up inside Matamir's mind like a contented vapor, warming and comforting after such terror. That *is what Sister is after. How interesting. How... fortuitous. Perhaps I shall let this little drama play out after all.*

Matamir wanted to sigh in relief as the thing retreated from his mind, but it still held his body, his muscles not his own.

Though I can't have her mucking up my continent again. The data won't weather another seismic shift. How fortunate she's left me you, though. And you're headed right back to her. Matamir's throat constricted as the thing slithered across his mind, righting and mending boxes, straightening up what it had ruined.

But it left something behind.

Eventually, Matamir shivered, a mote of dizziness shooting through him. Letting out a light gasp, he touched his own forehead, his thoughts suddenly fuzzy. He had a sense of... *something*, but then it was gone, forgotten as he waited with the crowd hoping to head to Casfeild.

"Sir, are you well?" a passing tar'ka-besh asked.

Matamir blinked a few times then shook his head to clear it before donning his best Torfeild industrial-district accent. "Ruddy no. I'm freezing my digits off out here! What's the holdup? Did a Red Mage fart too close to the Middle Lands border or something?"

Around him, a few of the others waiting stifled snickers, but the tar'ka-besh curled his lip in barely hidden annoyance.

"There is an issue, but we are resolving it," he replied stiffly.

"Good. I don't want to miss my teleport window," Matamir huffed. Then he inhaled a little herbal tincture he kept smeared inside part of his collar for such occasions. His nose twitched, and he sneezed violently then rubbed the dribbling aftermath on his sleeve. "Gonna catch my death out here, and none of your ruddy Talents give a shit."

The tar'ka-besh's frown deepened, but then he moved on, just as Matamir knew he would. *Resolving it, ha. Poor bastards must be pissing themselves, thinking about who's going to have to report my orchestrated calamity to the Tazu Nation.* After fetching a handkerchief out of a pocket, he muttered an irritated comment to a fellow traveler about the disrespect of Talents for the common folk while dabbing at his profusely running nose.

HE WATCHED AS MATAMIR moved onward, unaware that he was still lurking in the shadows behind the Clan half-breed. For nine millennia, he'd slept in Dodbyen, and not since awakening—not since he'd warned Jathen not once but *twice*—had he felt such a sweet delight in a plan coming together. In the darkness, he smiled, reveling in having made Matamir his own, much as he'd shattered Mağrur's heart in the end. After all, the fun couldn't end before he accomplished his task.

This shall be an interesting little adventure.

Authors' Notes:

S o I'm sure everyone reading this has noticed the official inclusion of Mac J. Rea on the cover, and yes, that is the same Mac whom *Broken City* was dedicated to and who has just had a slew of *thank yous* throughout previous author's notes, as well as co-authoring *Way Walkers: University's Halloween* expansion. The simple truth is Mac has been adding and helping with Way Walkers for so many, many years that the time has finally come for them/her to be on the cover with me. She deserves it for creating the languages; refining the Okten, the Red, and the Muilan; and helping work out literally hundreds to thousands of details too numerous to list. She raised this continent with me, and I'm glad she's finally, truly my co-author. It's the way it always should have been, and I'm beyond excited for the future writing with her. Be on the lookout for the next Tazu Saga installment, *Implied Permissions,* which will be coming to you via Amazon's Vella in serial format, as well as the interactive novel *Way Walkers: University 3*. Mac and I are already doing great things, and you will see them soon.

I still do have those I must thank: my readers, our Patreon members who have allowed us to stick to a schedule, whose feedback is invaluable, thank you. Your curiosity helps round out the world, and your support helps us keep the lights on.

For all the fans and readers, you are amazing, and I'm humbled every day by your kind words and support. We wouldn't be here without you.

Thank you to the RAP family, but especially to Lynn, who took a chance on me and still takes chances on me. Thank you especially for supporting Mac so seamlessly into RAP. Tazu Saga and Way Walkers will be all the better for it, and that wouldn't have been possible without you, your professionalism, and your general awesomeness. Also, special thanks to Erica Lucke Dean, for letting me read your books when my mind needed a break, for working so hard on the cover art, and for just being a friend when I was losing my mind at times. Thank you!

My Dad always, for holding my hand in the hard times, and for fighting, always, to be here for me.

Mom, thank you so much for watching The Toddler so I could write. You're amazing for dealing with yet another strong-willed child of my blood. All the respect and awe I can conjure goes to you—I'd have neither a writing career nor a functional family without your endless help.

Adrian, love of my life, thank you for everything.

~J. Leigh, April 2021

J, thank you for saying, "I want you to be my co-author"—and then saying it countless more times over almost two decades until I stopped being an idiot and realized I already was. To the readers, especially y'all on the Discord server, thank you. Our Patrons keep the lights on in more than one way. Your questions, kitten pictures, and bug reports fire up my creativity and always make my day. Thank you to everyone at Red Adept, who made my participation in the Tazu Saga possible and corralled my verbs into their proper tense.

Mama, words like "thank you" and "I love you" are too small to capture all that I feel, but I know it was you who taught me to never hide my light under a bushel. Sabrina and Michael, thank you for always giving me sunflowers, safety, and home, the room to recover and try again. To all the Reas and those unfortunate enough to be related to one of us—I love you. Also, good luck. To the Podstawskis, thank you for making me part of the family. Thank you, Alex, more than I can say, for the steady supply of hot tea. Marrying me was a nice thing to do, too, I suppose, and very brave.

Thank you, Daddy, for reading me a bedtime story every day when I was a child—even when you had to work late, even when you were already exhausted. Thank you for telling me both the good truths and the hard truths and for saying both "You have a gift" and "This is very technical. Do you really think there is any audience for this?" Sometimes, the truths that hurt will also make me laugh for years to come, and thank you for teaching me that too.

My dad died this past year, and he would be very surprised to see this book dedicated to him. As a tease and a ham who cherished making others laugh, he didn't know how deeply he affected those who loved him. But if you, Dear Reader, have read the end of *Negating Destiny* and have made it *this* far into the notes, I can at least someday tell him with confidence, "Yes, Dad, it turns out there is an audience for stories about engineering failures, even if it gets kinda technical!" I feel like he is laughing on the Other Side—so thank you, Dear Reader, for that!

~Mac J. Rea, April 2021

Terms, Races, People, Children, and Ways

A

Ability: term referring to magical or supernatural aptitude, classified formally into five major categories: empathy (emotional or energy), medium (emotional or visual), telepathy, precognition, and energy manipulative.

Ahalteke: half-Tazu, half-Msāfryan trader.

Akira, Master: Way Walker of Rosin, head of matter deconstruction.

Alodie: owner of a boarding house in Ca'june.

Altaiss: a Tazu of Dodbyen.

Amtmann: leader of the *sanbarna* of Dodbyen.

Angani: the Child that represents the Way of Purity. Also see **Pearl Dragon**.

Angel Guide: a Guide attached to a mortal soul that has never been born to a physical body itself; they watch their Charge and offer advice and spiritual guidance.

Annakki Rheadani: Clanswoman, second child of the last living Avatar Rhean and his Aspect Ra'vien; mother of Dor'rhean and a friend of Jathen.

Annarite: the race of the Red and natural inhabitants of the Middle Lands. Known also as "the Tainted."

Anorna: High Walker of Feator.

Antqāl Mdynh: "moving city." The native Msāfryan name for the city of Zo'den.

A'ron De'contes: former Red follower/Red Mage and head of the Balori order of the Red. He is also responsible for the murder of Yvette Ashton; the last Avatar of Rhean, Car'son des Rheadani de la Rhean; and the Aspect of Rhean, Bolynne des Rheadani de la Ra'vien.

Aralim: the Nation founded by Angani followers. Shares a border with the Tazu Nation.

Ascended: term referring to an Incarnation of one of the Children that has Awakened and come into their full power.

Aspect: term referring to the "other side" of each of the Twelve Children. They are the Incarnations of the Children's twin-flames.

Ass'shiri Tan: Way Walker, Path of the Kasior, part of Setsu's crew.

Avatar: term referring to the Awakened and Ascended Incarnation of one of the Children; the mortal body of the Child Awakened.

Avenea: the chosen race of Feator and residents of the country Casfeild, they are characterized by an almost turtle-like appearance, with bone-like plates covering their arms and legs and a shell-like plate covering a large portion of their backs.

Awakened: term referring to souls, usually Avatars, who remember more than one lifetime's worth of experiences. An Awakened Avatar usually indicates full memory of all their previous past lives.

B

Balori: the Balori movement is a divergent Path amid the Red that believes the Red went mad and must be brought back to Spirit.

Basimess: High Montage Walker before Hausmannith.

Bawan: a Beleskie Way Path that specializes in matchmaking.

Beleskie: Rose Quartz Dragon, Child of Love and Relationships.

Bertrandith Larsenitiss: Royal advisor to the King's Office, heir to the Larsenitiss House, and Kyanith Monortith's youngest son.

Bolynne des Rheadani de la Ra'vien: historical figure of the Clan Lands, the last Awakened Aspect of Rhean. Murdered by A'ron De'contes.

Born, Born Clan: referring to Clan that were born vampiric Clan, versus a human that was Changed into Clan.

Bree: Child of Creativity, the Amber Dragon.

Bron: Aspect of Bree, he embodies application, while Bree embodies inspiration.

C

Car'son des Rheadani de la Rhean: historical figure, the last Avatar of Rhean to Walk and be emperor of the Clan Lands. Murdered by A'ron De'contes.

Casfeild: a country on the southern border of Tar'citadel and home to the Avenea race. Founded by the Avatar of Feator.

Cathiny Falls: the waterfall to the east of Tar'citadel, emptying the Dragon Tongue River into the Cathiny River Gorge. Famous near-final stop on the Pilgrim's Road before arriving at Tar'citadel and home to the city's hydroelectric generators.

Cathiny Mountains: the highest, longest mountain range on the Continent.

Cathiny River: river running beside the Cathiny Mountains. It forms a deep gorge between the Three Sentinels, dividing two Sentinel mountains and Tar'citadel's alpine plateau from the northern Sentinel mountain.

Chaotic: an evil soul meant for the Pit that did not get there but instead "hijacked" the body of a stillborn child and proceeded to live a life in the new living body.

Citra: Tazu female born in Dodbyen, peach scaled with pale-yellow hair and pale-green eyes.

Clan: the vampiric race of the Clan Lands.

Clan Lands: one of the largest countries on the continent and home of both human and Clan. Founded by Rhean.

Changed: to be changed/having been changed into Clan. (Humans are the only race able to be Changed.)

Charge: term referring to the soul that Spirit Guides are assigned to watch and look after.

charm: a magical item, usually a crystal or metal, created to "hold" a certain spell within itself. Usually very small and meant for singular personal use. See also processor-charm, master-charm, or charm-device.

charm-device: a more complex version of a master-charm, a charm-device refers to an object that uses a charm spell or multiple charm spells in order to activate a third-party device. It is usually small to medium in size and meant for personal use. See also: charm, processor-charm, or master-charm.

Charm Master: a maker of master-charms.

Children, the: see also The Twelve. They represent twelve facets of Spirit and incarnate again and again to teach their different Ways to evolve the souls of mortals to become one with Spirit once again.

Chūjitsun: a manservant in Annakki's household.

cor'mon: Tar'cil greeting meaning "good day."

crystal-recorder: a charm-device usually including a recorder crystal, used to record information. See also: recorder crystal.

Cy'shā: empathic and precognitive Talent for Setsu's crew, wife to Hkym.

Cyaone D. Ja'han: historical figure, author of *Lost in the Landscape*.

D

D'ilinde: Msāfryan name for the Grand Artifact of Bree and Bron.

Daughter of Desmoulein: a Way Path of Desmoulein, they are healers and doctors.

Dàshī Jidoja: High Mage merged with the element of air. Elected High Chancellor of Tar'citadel.

death marker: also just called a "marker," it indicates in a life contract one of the seven times a person might "exit a lifetime" or die.

debesh: Way Path of Kubesh; they channel their pain to gain strength as they are injured. More powerful ones will actually gain height and mass as a result.

demon: an incorporeal spirit that feeds off negative emotions. Hundreds of different types of demons of varying strengths and powers exist, as well as dozens of different classifications of intelligence.

Desmoulein: the Child whose Way is the Way of the Healer; the Emerald Dragon.

Dicinith Attieth: Thee's father.

Dodbyen: one of the Kinawan "floating cities," it was lost during one of the last battles of the War of Truth.

Dolomith Monortith: Son of Rhodonith Monortith and Clevelandith Freibergith Grandidieriss. Prince of the blood and possible heir to the King of the Tazu Nation's throne. Baby half-brother of Thee and Jathen.

Dragon's Teeth: massive waterfall to the west of Tar'citadel, where Drayu's Mouth empties into the Cathiny River Gorge, forming the Red's Whirlpools.

Drannic: a very mysterious race, rarely seen and said to harbor the secrets of the Children. They resemble Tazu but have wings and tails and do not shift into dragons.

Drayu's Mouth: large, high alpine river, tributary of the Cathiny River, which divides Tar'citadel's alpine plateau from the base of West Sentinel mountain. At Tar'citadel, the main branch of Drayu's Mouth meets the Cathiny River at a waterfall known as the Dragon's Teeth. The smaller southern branch of Drayu's Mouth, known as the

Dragon Tongue River, demarcates the southeastern border of the Tar'citadel plateau. This smaller branch terminates in a second waterfall, known as the Cathiny Falls.

Dresden, High Walker: High Walker of Angani in Tar'citadel.

E

Elemental empathy: not to be confused with Empathic, elemental empathy falls under the Ability category of "energy manipulative" and refers to an above-average ability to draw in the vibrational energy of a particular element.

empathy, empathic: Empathy refers to a person's sensitivity to the constantly moving energy fields around them, also known as the near side of the Veil. Two types exist: emotional empathy, with which one can sense the emotions of things; and energy empathy, with which one can only feel the shift in the energies. Having both makes one a True empathic. An empathic is someone who has one or both types of empathy.

Enillydd, Master: Walker of Kubesh, head of the tesagree Way Path.

Erin Manna: historical figure, one of the eight Originals of the Clan race. She and her husband Marin Manna were the founders of the Mannachi clan.

Esop: a Ki'ra, Walker of Kubesh; part of Setsu's crew.

F

fauni: a Way Path of Turin, specializing in the usage of a golem.

Feator: Child whose Way is the Way of History, the Bronze Dragon. He covers not only written history but also past lives.

Feed: Clan term referring to the drinking of blood for sustenance.

Fersmannith Chertith: current head of the Chertith house, son of Halith Chertith, and uncle to Serendibiss Chertith.

Furōrin-Iki: from "furora" for "flora," "shinrin" for "forest," and "iki" for "breathers." Name of the country/region where the Nijū-Iki live.

G

Galduran, High Walker: High Mage merged with the element of air. Serves as High Walker of Montage in Tar'citadel.

Galena Torberniss: Lady of the Torberniss bloodline, sister of Arsenopyrith Torberniss.

Genthelvith Proustith Attieth: Thee's paternal grandmother and namesake; Dicinith's mother.

Guide(s): referring to Angel or Spirit Guides that are attached to mortal souls. They are usually in pairs and are spiritual "assistants" to mortal souls while they are in body.

Great Fall, the: also the "Fall of the Red" and "War between the Veils." Refers to when the Red whispered in the ear of Prothidian Altar and together destroyed the Old World. It was Rhean who finally threw the Red back into the Pit, and for a thousand years, the survivors hid underground before resettling the new Continent.

Great Gate: One built in each of the twelve countries' capitols, the Great Gates allow small groups to teleport from their respective capitols into Tar'citadel.

Grays: a group of Clansmen who hunt Red followers in the Clan Lands outside the Way orders.

ground drake: Native to parts of southern and eastern Casfeild as well as parts of the Clan Lands, ground drakes are large, wingless dragons of moderate intelligence. They are quite territorial and rather dangerous.

Gwydion Trahern: Serendibiss Chertith's father.

H

Halfling: Clan term referring to a child whose parentage is half Born-Clan and half human.

Hatori Chann: Clansman charm master for the Monortith family.

Hausmannith: High Montage Walker of the Montage Temple in Kidwellith.

Hauyne: a light-blue-scaled, silver-blue-eyed Tazu from Dodbyen. A relative of Spinelith, he took issue with the leniency given to Rhyo.

head: Tazu unit of measurement, equal to six scales or one foot.

High Mage: a powerful elemental empathic Talent that has undergone a ritual to fuse themselves forever with their element. This process makes them physically immortal and incapable of becoming "drained" of energy with which to cast.

high magic: magic that is far more complex than typical energy manipulative work; it usually involves multiple elements of ritual and artifacts to supplement the work.

Hkym: medium for Setsu's crew; husband to Cy'shā.

I

Iki: a shortened term for the word Nijū-Iki.

Incarnation: a Child reborn into a body that has not Awakened or Ascended.

iungo plant: meaning "connector" or "bridge," it is an empathic, energy-manipulative plant created by Prothidian Altar to bridge the gap between non-Talents and Ability-driven devices. Variations of it also carry power, sound, and a variety of other currents in a manner similar to electrical wire.

Ishane: Way Walker, Path of the Mei at Véridique Meison.

Ishim: meaning "incarnated souls" or "angels of the material world," it is a general term referring to any spiritual soul incarnated into a body as a person.

Izzy: a fauni from the Tazu Nation.

J

Ja'heir Mountains: the V-shaped mountain range of the Clan Lands.

Jathen Cornetith Iridosmine Monortith: Prince of the blood and heir to the king of the Tazu Nation.

Jephue: Romantic and business partner to Hatori Chann.

Jiãojĭn, High Walker: The head of the Way of Rosin.

Jörŏ: historical figure, one of the supposed Incarnations of Ulic, Child of Truth during the War of Truth.

K

kasior: Way Path of Rhean, crossbow snipers.

ka'moya: Way Path, Rheanic messengers.

Kidwellith: Capital city of the Tazu Nation.

Ki'ra: a race resembling humans mixed with a menagerie of bears, large canines, and large felines. Native to the nation of Nor'wah.

Kubesh: the Citrine Dragon of the Children, Way of the Warrior.

Kriger, High Walker: High Walker of Kubesh in Tar'citadel.

Kyanith Monortith: King of the Tazu Nation.

L

Laws of Heaven: the five laws of Spirit: Do not impede upon the free will of another. Do no harm. Do not deny Spirit. Respect all the Ways and find your place amongst them. Respect all physical forms of Spirit.

length: Tazu unit of measurement, equal to twelve heads or twelve feet.

life('s) contract: refers to the "terms" that each soul agrees to before being born into the world as a person. It supposedly covers everything from birthplace and parents to major life lessons and contains all the possible paths and choices a soul can have presented to them while they are alive.

life ladder: the actual genetic code that maps certain aspects of the life's contract.

Lu'shun: Beleskie's chosen race. All of them have bright-blue eyes and hair, but the rest of what they appear to be is dependent on who is looking at them. Whoever looks upon a Lu'shun will see a person of their own race reflected back.

Lubreean: country to the southwest of the Clan Lands; home of the Muilan; founded by Rosin.

M

mage: more common term referring to an energy-manipulative Talent, it often indicates one not trained as a Way Walker.

Mağrur, Master: Way Walker of Angani, head of the Pearl Paladin order.

Marin Manna: historical figure, one of the Original eight Clan. He and his wife Erin Manna founded the Mannachi clan.

master-charm: an object created when multiple charm-spells are infused into a singular charm. They are usually more complex and involve more magical and energy work to be created. See also: charm, charm-device, or processor-charm.

Matamir: in Sister's employment, one of several agents of the Shadow Court she brought over to her side.

Mei, Mei Path: a Way Path of Beleskie that focuses on the physical aspect of interpersonal relationships.

Middle Lands: the Land of the Red, it is a province sitting in the middle of the Continent and is not quite an official country.

Mikkal Lan'chi: A member of the Grays in the Clan Lands; powerful Energy Manipulative Talent.

Monortith: the royal family of the Tazu Nation.

Montage: the Gold Dragon of the Children, whose Way tries to merge the teachings of all the Ways in order to create an Ultimate Way.

moot: Tazu children born looking human and lacking the ability to shift into dragon form.

Muilan: Rosin's chosen race, they are a semi-incorporeal people, capable of "phasing" in and out of the physical plane for brief periods.

Msāfryan: meaning "travelers," this is the proper name for the people that live in the Zo'den territory (human and shifter).

N

Neek: shaman for the Iki settlement.

Nevershen Supai: Clansman and Rheanic Walker in Tar'citadel.

Nhr: native name of the Zo River in Zo'den.

Nijū-Iki: meaning "double breath" or "dual breathers," this refers to the plant hybrid race that live in the Furōrin-Iki. See also Iki.

Nor'wah: the country north of the Clan Lands, home to the Ki'ra race and founded by Kubesh.

Nosalia, Lady: Clanswoman resident of Fauve in the Lu'shun Republic, patron of the arts and historical excavation.

O

Obsidian Dragon: see Rhean.

old soul: a soul that has incarnated a massive amount of times and had a vast amount of experiences, though not necessarily going the furthest back in history.

Ophisa, High Mage: merged with element of earth. Headmaster of Tar'citadel University.

Originals, the: the first eight vampires who gave rise to the race known as Clan; four couples who founded the four Great Clans.

Orrick Ashton: a Clan Original, he and his wife Yvette founded the Ashoni Clan and the Ashton bloodline.

Or'sen: an Annarite amid the Balori; friend of Nannazen.

P

Pallotos Nuummith: Moot captain of the dirigible *Charmed Wind*.

Path: also "Way Path," referring to the different orders and classes under each Way.

Pearl Dragon: Angani, one of the Twelve Children; she represents purity.

Petalith: personal Daughter of Desmoulein for the Monortith family.

Phine, Phine Path: Way Path of Beleskie focusing on psychological study and counseling services.

Pit, the: banishment place of the Red, a dimension even deeper than Hell. Also the birthplace of all demons.

Plajă, High Walker: Head of the Way of Bree in Tar'citadel.

processor-charm: the most complex of the charmed objects, processor-charms are charm-devices used to absorb one type of energy and then put out another type of energy, spell, or information. See also: charm, master-charm, or charm-device.

Prothidian Altar: historical figure, supposedly imprisoned beneath one of the capitals. The first Red Mage, he is responsible for both destroying the world and reseeding it with his own creations, including many of the current races.

R

Ra'vien: formal name of the Aspect of Rhean, known also as "the Punisher" or "Shadow Bird," represented by a dark-feathered phoenix. Hers is the task of dispensing spiritual justice.

ral: Old Clan word for "bad or nasty." Ral snakes are black and green and are the deadliest animal on the continent in terms of venom.

Raudur: historical figure relating to the sky-city Dodbyen; responsible for the deaths of Marc's family, as well as countless others in the city. Ultimately killed by Jathen.

recorder crystal: a single charm usually made from a quartz crystal, used to record information. see also: crystal recorder.

Red, the: the Red Dragon, the Fallen One, the disgraced Child. His Way turns from Spirit's laws and is commonly known as the Way of Evil.

Red Mage: a powerful Talent that has given the Red a piece of their soul; the effect of this actually fuses them with both the elements of fire and air, unlike High Mages, who are fused with only one. Immortal of body and very, very dangerous.

Red Tide: historical event during which a hundred Red Mages attacked half of the Continent during a search for Prothidian Altar.

Red Star: the prophesied signal that time is "up" and the Red shall be freed from the Pit if the world is too evil.

Rhe'don: another formal title for the High Walker of Rhean.

Rhean: the Obsidian Dragon of the Children, Way of the Protector.

Rhodonith Monortith: Queen of the Tazu Nation and mother of Jathen and Thee.

rmlkoka: meaning "sand cat," this is a large feline capable of shifting into sand for short periods.

Rosin: the Amethyst Dragon, whose Way is the Way of Magic. Also called the Mistress of Mages.

Ryml: a large, flightless bird that serves as a primary pack animal and is prized among the Msāfryan for meat, oil, and leather.

S

Sacora Rheadani: Hatori's deceased wife.

Sanbarna: the "true children" of Dodbyen.

sangcordis: the organ in Clan bodies that regulates blood intake; it is located in the chest between the lungs and heart, with an attachment to the esophagus.

sangui mandat: meaning "blood command," this is a powerful Ability of the Originals and Rhean to forcibly compel any Clansperson to follow their orders.

scale: Tazu unit of measurement equal to two inches.

Scmit: half-blood Tazu female born in Dodbyen, gray scaled and white haired with dark-blue eyes.

second sight: another term for medium Ability, which allows one to see spirits and spiritual beings.

Serendibiss Iolith Chertith, Ambassador: Seren's mother and the Tazu Nation ambassador to Tar'citadel. Nicknamed Seri.

Serendibiss Spheniss Chertith: Thee's best friend, nicknamed Seren.

Setsuken Daten: Way Walker, Tesgree Path. Leader of a mercenary group in Zo'den.

Si'hir, High Mage: merged with the element of air, served as High Walker of Rosin previous to Jiāojīn. Retired, he does his best to do as little as possible.

Simpsoniss Chertith: cousin to Marcasith and Kyanith Monortith; uncle of Fersmannith Chertith.

Skaniss Malachith: Captain of the Monortith Royal Guard.

slaga: pack beast in the Tazu Nation, similar to large salamanders.

slikan: Path of Ulic, trained to delve into minds and find the truth for the various justice systems of the Continent.

Solki: Turin's chosen race, they are sexless and inhumanly strange, feeding only on the emotional energy of fear and pain.

soul-mate: a term used for souls that choose to incarnate together often, sometimes as friends, sometimes as lovers, sometimes as family, and often changing roles with each other.

soul-circle: term referring to a group of soul-mates that incarnate together often.

Spirit: the recognized God of the Way Walkers, the eternal consciousness that all souls return to once evolved enough.

Spirit Guide: a Guide attached to a mortal soul that has been born to a physical body itself; they watch their Charge and offer advice and spiritual guidance.

T

Ta'ekni: Aspect of Kubesh, she is the embodiment of strategy.

Talent: term referring to a person with more than one measurable classification of the five Abilities. General Talent describes most empathics or low-level mediums, Classic Talent describes the empathic-telepathic combination, True Talent is reserved for people who have at least three combined Abilities, and Exemplary Talent refers to a Talent with measurable levels of all five Abilities. There is also the term Nontraditional Talent, which refers to those Abilities and combinations that don't readily fit into the typical categories.

Taint: term referring to the evil influence of the Red that interferes with the soul's evolution, often manifested in large amounts of anger, fear, sorrow, arrogance, or even full-blown psychotic behaviors. To be Tainted is to be under the influence of Taint; also "the Tainted" describes the race of the Annarite. Can also manifest in the environment; places where extreme violence has occurred are often Tainted.

Tar'cil: the scholar's tongue and written language of Tar'citadel.

Tar'citadel: the holy city of ice and light, where lies the Great Temple of Spirit, the Tar'citadel University, and the formal meeting place of the twelve nations.

tar'ka-besh: the home guard of Tar'citadel, they learn all the fighting Paths.

Tazu: Montage's race, they are shapeshifters who can appear humanoid (Tazu) or as a full dragon (tyrn).

Tazu Nation: the country founded by Montage and home of the Tazu.

Tealanithiss: a black-scaled Tazu born in Dodbyen.

telekinetic: also known as Energy Manipulative, it is an Ability to move/channel energy either about oneself or into oneself to fuel other magical works.

teleportation: the spell to transport one's physical body through time and space; powerful Talents can also move multiple people with it. A physical destination must be in one's head to do it, though, so a user would have to have been in the destination once before.

Tesgree: Kubesh Way Path, masters of the bastard sword.

Tghyyr'sāqyn: meaning "changing legs," this is a native term for the native race of Zo'den, whose legs shapeshift. Tg'sāqyn is also used commonly as a shortened version of the term.

The Three Sentinels: the three mountains surrounding Tar'citadel to the north, east, and west, known by multiple names in other languages/cultures on the continent.

The Twelve: another name for the Children of Spirit. See Children.

The Twelve Ways: the twelve individual Ways taught by the Children; each Way is an aspect of Spirit and aids the soul in evolving to become one with Spirit once more. They are: Ultimate Way, Truth, Protection, Magic, Healing, Warrior, Death, Creativity, Love, Purity, History, and "the Way of Evil," which diverts from the rest and goes against evolution.

Thee (Genthelvith) Monortith: Jathen's half-sister, daughter of Rhodonith Monortith and Dicinith Attieth; princess of the blood, heir to the Queen of the Tazu Nation.

Tourmalith Larsenitiss: Bertran Larsenitiss's uncle and the head of the Larsenitiss line.

tru'suli: a Path under Ulic's Way of Truth; known as "truth seekers," they are academics and lecturers.

tyrn: a Tazu in their dragon form.

Turin: Sapphire Dragon of the Children, Way of Death.

twin-flame: term referring to the soul-pairing of each mortal soul, the masculine and feminine aspects. Each twin-flame pairing is romantically linked to each other for eternity.

Tyr'sat: Tar'cil word for the shifter race of the Zo'den region. From "Tghyyr'sāqyn" and "shifter."

U

Ulic: silver dragon of the Children, Way of Truth.

Utför, Master: Way Walker, head of the Shandi Path.

V

Vas: an acolyte Pearl Paladin.

Veil: term referring to the invisible spiritual barrier that divides the physical world from the spiritual world. There is the distinction between the near and far side of the Veil; the near side refers to spiritual beings that can be sensed and interacted with by physical beings while in physical form. The far side of the Veil refers to the higher planes and the whole of Spirit, also known as Heaven.

veil-sliding: term referring to when one raises the vibration of their body high enough to slide along the barrier between time and space. Unlike teleportation, it is easier to take people along for the ride, and no distinct destination is needed, but it does take longer than teleportation.

Volaille, High Walker: Way Walker, High Walker of Beleskie.

W

ward: a magical protective barrier.

Way: one of the individual twelve Ways.

Way Walker: a trained disciple of a Way, usually a member of one of the many Paths; essentially an ordained priest or priestess of an individual Way, as opposed to a "follower," who is not ordained. They are almost always Talents of measurable Ability.

Whydā Shrā: meaning "lonely desert," the native name for Zo'den Desert.

Y

Yvette Ashton: Historical figure, deceased; Mistress of Metals, the greatest charm master to ever live; one of the eight Original Clan who founded the Clan race; wife of Orrick Ashton; founder of the Ashoni Clan of the Clan Lands. Murdered by A'ron De'contes.

Z

Zhìliáo, High Walker: High Walker of the Way of Desmoulein.

Zo'den: refers to the country as well as two "city sites" of the nomadic Msāfryan and Tghyyr'sāqyn peoples. The country borders the Tazu Nation.

About the Author

J. Leigh wrote her first novel at the tender age of eleven, delving deep into the extensive fantasy world she entitled Way Walkers . Since then, she has never really left, though occasionally does emerge to enjoy the company of friends, family, horror movies and the ever-popular sushi dinner. She currently lives in southern New Jersey with a chow-chow, several cats and fictional cast of hundreds. Leigh's published works include a "choose your own" interactive novel, Way Walkers: University, with Choice of Games.

Mac J Rea has been writing stories and sharing them on the internet since GeoCities was the hot new thing. Fortunately, most were never read. Despite earning a M.A. in English Literature and the ability to cheerfully bore people with heartfelt opinions on semiotics, Mac credits fanfiction communities that share writing online as their primary influence.

Therefore, it should be no surprise that Mac has spent years of friendship with J. Leigh, collaborating over the world of Way Walkers. Mac currently lives in northern New Jersey with their spouse, mother, piebald cat, and a fleet of airplanes in almost every scale.

Read more at https://waywalkersguide.com/.

About the Publisher

Dear Reader,

We hope you enjoyed this book. Please consider leaving a review on your favorite book site.

Visit https://RedAdeptPublishing.com to see our entire catalogue.

Don't forget to subscribe to our monthly newsletter to be notified of future releases and special sales.

www.ingramcontent.com/pod-product-compliance
Lightning Source LLC
Chambersburg PA
CBHW071850220626
47052CB00002B/45